A SAINT AT THE HIGHLAND COURT

THE HIGHLAND LADIES BOOK SIX

CELESTE BARCLAY

OLIVER
HEBER
BOOKS

GNARLY WOOL PUBLISHING

0 9 8 7 6 5 4 3 2 1

Published by Oliver Heber Books

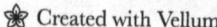 Created with Vellum

In education, we say FAIL means "first attempt in learning."
To those who have failed but not given up.

Happy reading, y'all,
Celeste

SUBSCRIBE TO CELESTE'S NEWSLETTER

Subscribe to Celeste's bimonthly newsletter to receive exclusive insider perks.

Have you read *Their Highland Beginning, The Clan Sinclair Prequel*? Learn how the saga begins! This FREE novella is available to all new subscribers to Celeste's monthly newsletter. Subscribe on her website.

Subscribe Now

THE HIGHLAND LADIES

A Spinster at the Highland Court
A Spy at the Highland Court
A Wallflower at the Highland Court
A Rogue at the Highland Court
A Rake at the Highland Court
An Enemy at the Highland Court
A Saint at the Highland Court
A Beauty at the Highland Court
A Sinner at the Highland Court
A Hellion at the Highland Court
An Angel at the Highland Court
A Harlot at the Highland Court

PREFACE

The Highland Ladies series is a spin-off to my first
series, *The Clan Sinclair,* and follows the lives of ladies-
in-waiting at King Robert the Bruce's court. If you
are a fan of Highlander romances, then you have
surely encountered the time period that spans the
Wars of Scottish Independence, along with the rise
and reign of Robert the Bruce.

While I was intentionally vague about the time
period and royal couple in *The Clan Sinclair,* there is
little way to avoid the history of Robert the Bruce
when this series takes place predominantly at Stirling
Castle after he was crowned king. I have taken creative license in a number of areas, especially the cre-
ation of characters, but the events and clan dynamics
are true to history.

A Saint at the Highland Court follows the love story
of the fictitious Hardwin "Hardi" Cameron and the
fictitious Blair Sutherland. While neither were people
from history, there are elements to the story that are
factual. I have taken some liberty in changing the
dates but not the events themselves. Clan Cameron
land was in the Western Highlands, and the neigh-
boring clans in this story are true to history. Histo-

rians say that Clan Cameron and Clan Chattan shared ancestors, but they were not allies.

Clan Chattan was an individual clan with traditional clan leadership and membership. But in the 14th century, they and several other clans banded together to create the Clan Chattan Confederation. Included in this alliance were the Mackintoshes, Macphersons, MacBeans, and Davidsons. Some clans were linked through common ancestry while others were not originally connected by blood. The Camerons at one time or another feuded with individual members: the Mackintoshes, Macphersons, and the Davidsons along with the Chattan Confederation and the Grants. Their sporadic feuds with the Clan Mackintosh and Clan Chattan lasted nearly 300 years.

The Battle of the North Inch occurred in 1396, which is well past the end of the King Robert's reign, but this event inspired a turning point in our hero's life. The Camerons faced off against the Mackintoshes in a trial by combat where thirty warriors from each side were chosen to represent their clans. It was a crushing defeat for the Camerons. The Mackintoshes lost only nineteen men, but the Camerons had only one survivor. That attack that takes place in this story between the Camerons and the Mackintoshes is purely a work of my imagination but is based upon their known feud.

Clan Cameron was loyal to King Robert the Bruce and was awarded land to their north, which lay between two septs of Clan MacDonald. Tor Castle was a Cameron stronghold, but it was a source of strife for the clan. Clan Cameron claimed that Clan Mackintosh abandoned the castle after a marriage allied them with Clan Chattan. The Camerons sought refuge at Tor Castle during a conflict with Clan MacDonald of Keppoch (to the Camerons' east). The Camerons built a larger castle on the site and claimed it as their own.

To remedy the conflict between the Camerons and the MacDonalds, I opted to have the MacDonalds become the guardians of Inverlochy Castle as, in reality, it lies within an hour's drive from Tor Castle. Inverlochy Castle was originally built by John "the Black" Comyn, but after the clan's defeat and harrying during Robert the Bruce's rise to power, Inverlochy came under the control of Clan Cameron. This is another instance where I took creative license with the date and the details. The Lord of the Isles fought a battle against King James I in 1431, a century after King Robert's reign, that became known as the first Battle of Inverlochy.

This allowed me to have reason to include John of Islay, Lord of the Isles. The details describing him in this story are true to fact as best as historians know. He was a highly ambitious man who married for political gain. He held influence throughout the Hebrides, but he also had dominion over land within the Lochaber region, where Clan Cameron territory laid. He did marry Amie Mac Ruari (after the events of this story) because her brother controlled several Hebridean islands. When his brother-in-law, Raghnall Mac Ruaidhrí died, John of Islay consolidated his power, and his dominion included all the Hebrides except for Skye, and a substantial part of the western seaboard. This position of influence allowed me to make John of Islay the overlord of the MacDonald guardian at Inverlochy. In reality, John of Islay's influence in Lochaber and three other regions made the MacDonalds of the Hebrides, formerly considered a lesser sept, into one of the most powerful kindreds along the north-western seaboard. Historians say that had he not been loyal to Robert the Bruce, he would have styled himself as the King of the Isles rather than *only* the Lord of the Isles.

Blair's sister Maude married Laird Kieran Mac-Leod of Lewis in *A Wallflower at the Highland Court*. Kieran is mentioned as one of the Lord of the Isles' four "greatest of nobles, called lords." This included the MacLeods of Lewis, the MacLeods of Dunvegan (Skye), the Macleans of Lochbuie, and the Macleans of Duart. The use of this factoid allowed Blair to remind other characters of her familial connections and influence.

The Camerons were allied with Clan MacMillan and Clan Donald. The latter clan was the antecedent for several similarly named clans, which are easy to confuse. Clan MacDonald and Clan MacDonnell, with their septs and branches, descended from Clan Donald. In modern day, Clan Donald is also recognized as Clan MacDonald, and the current chief is a MacDonald. There is no historical record of the Camerons and Sutherlands being allied.

The familial bond between the Sutherlands and Sinclairs is also fictitious, but it is a main feature in both *The Clan Sinclair* and *The Highland Ladies* series. Since all the siblings in the Sinclairs and Sutherlands are fictitious, none were the godchildren of King Robert the Bruce and Queen Elizabeth de Burgh. It's just a handy connection when you write about ladies-in-waiting and alliances with the king.

I hope you enjoy *A Saint at the Highland Court* and come to love Blair Sutherland and Hardwin Cameron as much as I have.

Happy reading,

Celeste

CHARACTER NAME PRONUNCIATION

There are several names used in this story that because of their Gaelic etymology are not phonetic for English speakers. To make it easier for the reader, I thought to include this note on pronunciation.

Artair—AR-ter

Cathal—KAH-hul

Ceana—KAH-na

Drostan—DROST an

Faolán—FOO-lan (Scottish), FWAY-lawn (Irish), FAY-lawn (Irish), FOO-lawn (Irish),

or FEE-lawn (Irish) The first is more typically Scottish, but I prefer the second.

Fionn—FYOON

Hamish—HA-mish

Niall—NEE-ul

Osgar—OS-kar

Mungan—MOON-gun

ONE

Blair Sutherland swept her eyes over the throng of dancers who milled and twirled around Stirling Castle's Great Hall. Blair immediately recognized Arabella Johnstone and Laurel Ross, the only two ladies-in-waiting who had been at court as long as she. Ever since Blair left her home on the northwest Highland coast, she had served as a lady-in-waiting to Queen Elizabeth de Burgh. She'd been bright-eyed and naïve when she arrived, mesmerized by the glamour and excitement of life at the royal court. But after several years of service, the luster had worn off. As her anniversary at court loomed, Blair discovered she was growing more introspective as she wondered about her future. She felt lonelier, and became more reflective. She thought of when her older sister Maude used to stand beside her in the crush of people, but Maude married more than two years ago and already had her first two children—twins, a boy and a girl. Blair didn't begrudge Maude the love she had with her husband, Kieran MacLeod; it was hard won. Other friends she'd made at court were also married.

The first of the ladies she knew well, Elizabeth Fraser, had married Robert the Bruce's adopted

1

brother, Edward. No one imagined that the spinster with four broken betrothals would capture the eye of the king's roguish brother. Isabella Dunbar, unassuming and bookish, married a man who arrived at court to spy for the English king, Edward Longshanks. Blair recalled how the man, the son of an English father and Scottish mother, had been torn between two heritages. She'd never envied the position he found himself in. Her sister Maude was the third of the "originals," as Blair thought of her friends at court to marry. Maude had battled nasty comments about her appearance the entire time she served the queen. But Kieran MacLeod, one of the most eligible bachelors in Scotland, took one look at Maude and fell hopelessly in love with her. Blair had never been so happy as she was when she saw the joy her sister and husband shared on the day they were married.

Blair couldn't help but smile to herself as she pictured how the Gordon twins found their brides. Allyson Elliot was furious the day she learned she was to marry Ewan, the older twin. In fact, she was so irate at the notion of marrying the former rogue that she ran away from court. It amazed everyone when the couple returned to court in love and blissfully happy. Eoin pretended to be the shrewish Cairstine Grant's betrothed, but much like his twin, he found love with a woman who was far more than she seemed. The most recent bride was Cairren Kennedy, whose Arab heritage showed in her complexion. This made it nearly unbearable to join her new clan when King Robert ordered her to marry Padraig Munro. Blair's heart broke when she learned of the prejudice Cairren faced and for how long it took Padraig to realize he loved his wife.

As she swept her eyes across the crowd, Blair noticed Cairren's younger sister Caitlyn once again danced with Alexander Armstrong, the heir to his clan's lairdship. The warrior had made several trips to court of late to discuss border conflicts with the king. Caitlyn and Alex were childhood friends, but Blair wondered if there might be more to their relationship than they realized. Laurel Ross danced by with a man Blair didn't recognize. She squinted as she thought about Laurel. She developed a sharp and vicious tongue after she befriended Kieran MacLeod's younger sister Madeline, the unofficial ringleader of the ladies-in-waiting. But after Kieran sent Madeline to a convent, both Laurel and Cairstine smoothed their rougher edges and were less spiteful. She wasn't sure what lay beneath Laurel's facade, but Blair was certain Laurel wasn't entirely as she appeared.

"Sister," Lachlan Sutherland approached Blair with Arabella Johnstone on his arm. Arabella had been Maude's only other close friend while she was at court. The women had been roommates, and Arabella took Maude—and by extension Blair—under her wing when she arrived. "Every mon in this gathering hall keeps looking at you, and yet you seem to be in a world of your own, uninterested in them. Well done. I approve."

Lachlan grinned at his youngest sibling as Arabella released his arm. He swiped three mugs of ale from a passing servant, handing one to each lady. The three Sutherland siblings were very close, and Blair was ecstatic any time Lachlan appeared at court. The only family she knew that shared this kind of closeness were the Sutherlands' cousins, the Sinclairs. Lachlan wrapped his arm around Blair's shoulders and dropped a kiss on the crown of her head. They hadn't seen one another since Lachlan's unexpected arrival in late autumn, when he accompanied Cairren and Padraig to Stirling, but he had returned to settle the annual taxes their clan owed the crown. The brother and sister enjoyed a fortnight of each other's company. With Maude no longer beside her, Blair was starved for time with her family. Lachlan never shied away from showing his affection for his sisters, and Blair welcomed it.

"Shall I take you for a lap around the floor?" Lachlan inquired as he grinned at Blair. "Or will you prop up this wall a little longer? I may be your brother, but I shall be the envy of every mon with a heartbeat."

Blair attempted to suppress her smile. It was well established that Arabella Johnstone was the most beautiful woman among the ladies-in-waiting. She possessed an effortless grace that accentuated her perfect features and figure. She glanced at Arabella, who smiled at the siblings. Blair suspected the pair held a tendre for one another, but Blair sensed neither felt comfortable acknowledging it.

"I suppose I can spare you a dance, dear brother," Blair returned her brother's grin as they eased their way among the dancers and picked up the rhythm of the music.

"Blair, why were you standing alone? Even if Arabella and I were dancing, you have other friends. Why aren't you socializing like usual?" Lachlan whispered in an attempt to keep their conversation private.

"I'm simply not in the mood. I enjoy watching the others." Blair assured her brother, but his skeptical expression told her he wasn't satisfied. "I'm not a wallflower like Maude became. I was just thinking about my friends who have left court to marry. Only Arabella and Laurel remain as part of the original group of ladies I joined."

"Are you wondering when it will be your turn?" Blair heard the concern in Lachlan's voice, and she wasn't sure if she wanted to wince or fall against his chest for a brotherly hug.

"A little. I will never take for granted that Mama and Da are allowing each of us to find our own mate, but I wonder if I shall find a love match like the ones our parents and sister have." Blair stopped herself before she asked Lachlan if he thought the same thing. She intuited that he didn't, as she thought about how natural he and Arabella appeared when they spoke and danced.

"You aren't thinking of settling, are you?" Lachlan broke into Blair's thoughts.

She shook her head. "I don't want to marry just for the sake of marrying. I don't think my expectations are unreasonable, but I haven't met a mon who meets them."

"And what are those expectations?" Lachlan's serious gaze told Blair he wasn't mocking her; he was honestly interested in what Blair believed would make her happy.

"I want a mon with a strong character, but not someone who is domineering. There needs to be compassion along with his determination. I want a mon who is protective but not possessive. Even Kieran tends to be rather possessive of Maude, though I think he believes he's only protecting her. Someone who will make me smile, but also listens to me and takes me seriously. I want a mon who will prioritize me and our marriage over his friends. If he's a laird or will be one, I want to be sure that he balances his duty to his clan with his duty to his family." Blair paused and shrugged. "I suppose I want a lot of things."

"It sounds like you described me. Or Da," Lachlan chuckled.

Blair pursed her lips in a mock scowl, but she knew her brother was right. She'd listed characteris-

5

tics that she'd always seen in her father and that Lachlan emulated. She wanted a husband who had the honor that the men in her family had.

"It also sounds like you described Callum, Alex, Tavish, and Magnus." Lachlan listed the names of their Sinclair cousins.

"They're among the best men I ken. After you and Da, of course." Blair smirked as Lachlan pinched her waist. "Do you think I'm being unreasonable? Am I expecting too much? I know we and our cousins have unique families compared to most. Mama and Da love each other as much as Uncle Liam loved Aunt Kyla. Even after all these years after her passing, he's still devoted to her."

"I think they have set the standard to be very high, but they're also proof that it's possible. It must be if..." Lachlan paused for a moment to count. "Eight couples have found what you desire. Mairghread would probably cut off her brothers' cods—and her husband's too—if they didn't live up to our parents and their parents. She and Tristan are deeply in love."

"Aye, but part of the reason I came to court was to find a husband. You ken others have made offers, but I just couldn't bring myself to accept any. Maybe I've turned away all the ones that will come." Blair sighed.

"It's your future, one that should be very long, so don't settle, Blair. It's not as though you're long in the tooth. There is someone bound to make you happy. He just hasn't shown up yet."

"I know you're right," Blair tried to smile. "I just find it hard to be patient when I look around, and none of the men in sight are appealing. Marriage may be aboot alliances, but not all of them must include manipulation and ulterior motives. That's what

I shall find here. Think aboot it. None of my friends have married men from court."

"That is true," Lachlan agreed. "I ken it doesn't help for me to say your turn will come, but it will. You don't see me in a rush."

Blair opened her mouth to say that was because he'd already found someone, but she chose another perspective. "You're a mon. You're supposed to take your time and be older." Blair's grin split her face. "It takes men a long time to pull their heads out of their arses."

Lachlan pinched her again, and Blair giggled. "It's a good thing I love you, Sister." Lachlan spun them in an exaggerated twirl that left Blair dizzy, but she knew before Lachlan turned that she would reap what she sowed.

After her conversation with her brother, Blair felt more amicable. She spent the rest of the night dancing with one partner after another. She allowed herself to enjoy the music, and she even enjoyed some of her partners' conversation. She was exhausted by the time she fell into bed.

TWO

Blair raced through the gardens toward the lists with a missive flapping in her hands. She knew Lachlan would finish training soon, and she wanted to catch her brother before he disappeared into the bachelor wing. Her brother wasn't difficult to spot since he stood nearly a head and shoulders taller than several of the male courtiers. She often wondered what it was about their Highland air and food that made the men appear more like mountains, while most Lowlanders looked like hills.

"Lach!" Blair called out as Lachlan returned his dulled practice sword to the armorer and gathered his belongs. "Lach!"

Lachlan put out his hands to capture Blair's upper arms as she barreled toward him, breathless and giddy. Wisps of hair had come loose from the ribbon that tied it back, and her cheeks were rosy from her mad dash from the castle. She drew in a wheezing breath and placed her hand over her heart.

"Maude's had her bairn!" Blair practically squealed as Lachlan drew her in for a tight embrace, lifting her off her feet. Maude suffered a terrible accident while she carried her twins and had nearly died from the wildcat attack. Lachlan and Blair, along with their parents, had rushed to the Isle of Lewis when Kieran's missive arrived. There had been fear throughout Maude's first pregnancy that she would lose the babes. Even though there hadn't been a reason to be fearful during this second one, all the Sutherlands silently worried. "It's a lass."

"Does she have a name?" Lachlan tried to pull the missive from his sister's hand. Blair glanced down; she'd forgotten that she brought the parchment with her. She handed it over to Lachlan, who scanned its contents. "Mairi, after our cousin. Apparently, the lass has been tiny but determined since the moment she arrived, just like Mairghread." Lachlan looked up at Blair. "I like it."

"Me, too," Blair chirped as Lachlan pulled her in for another embrace. This time Blair pulled away and turned her head to the side. "Ugh. You stink."

"Thank you." Lachlan prepared to lift his arm since Blair stood even with his armpit, but she thrust a playful fist into his stomach. "You wound me, Blair."

"Nay more than you trying to poison me."

Lachlan donned his leine before he accompanied Blair back to the castle. They parted ways as Lachlan wound through the passageways to his chamber to bathe, and Blair reported to the queen's solar. Blair had raced from the queen's solar when the page delivered the missive. She'd barely looked to the queen for permission to leave, her mind singularly on reaching her brother. As the guard opened the door to the queen's solar, she slipped into the room quietly.

"I take it the missive was wonderful news, Lady Blair," Queen Elizabeth cocked an eyebrow.

"The very best, Your Majesty. My sister had her

bairn." Blair smiled as she curtseyed before the queen.

"That is delightful news. I know how you worried. Your mind must be at ease now. What is it now? Three babes?"

"Yes, Your Majesty. The twins and now another lass. Both my sister and her bairn are doing well."

"One of these days, it shall be your turn." The queen offered a benevolent smile as her hand skimmed over her own rounded belly. The queen was expecting her first child. The royal couple had been married for several years, but the queen's capture and house arrest by King Edward of England had made it impossible for the queen to bear the king an heir. King Robert already had a daughter, Marjorie, by his first wife Isabella. It was no secret that King Robert was in a hurry to sire a legitimate heir. He already had at least three sons, but none could inherit the throne.

Blair nodded, but some of her excitement waned as she returned to her seat and resumed her embroidery. It had been one thing when it was her sister who was pregnant and lived far from court, but the queen's reminder that she was expecting a child made Blair once more consider that marriage and children were nowhere on her horizon. She bowed her head over her work and listened to those who chattered around her. It was the distraction she needed.

———

Blair found herself in a better mood that evening. She was uncertain if it was the ongoing happiness of Maude's news or perhaps the extra chalice or two of wine, but she was more amenable to dancing. She partnered with Lachlan at least five times, but she ac-

11

cepted the offer of nearly every other man. Alexander Armstrong intrigued her, but she knew his interest lay elsewhere, and she would never agree to live along the border. The climate might have been milder than the Highlanders, but the strife certainly was not. She wished none of her clansmen to ride off into battle, but she would take clan skirmishes over a war with England.

Alasdair Dunbar was another man, with his sandy blond hair and deep dimple, who caught her attention. He was her friend and former lady-in-waiting Isabella's cousin, but that meant he and the Armstrongs were neighbors. Along with that strike against him, she found him a touch too arrogant at times. He knew his dimple and wolfish grin drew women like flies to honey, and Blair refused to be one of them. He was an enjoyable partner though, both light on his feet and an interesting conversationalist. He was one of her favorite partners during reels, as he was like Lachlan and would twirl her until she giggled from dizziness.

There were delegates from Highland clans, who, like Lachlan, were at court to pay their clan's annual taxes. Many were married men or friends of her father. She recognized plaids belonging to Mackenzies, Gunns, MacLeods, and Frasers. None were family or close alliances, but it pleased her when the Highlanders asked her to dance. She felt more comfortable with them than she did the Lowlanders, even allowing her burr to return to her voice.

As the night progressed, the dazzling clothing and laughter distracted her from her earlier ruminations. She was tired but smiling when she retired to the chamber she now shared with Arabella. It seemed like a silent agreement that they spoke about Blair's family but avoided talking about Lachlan and his bachelor status. Blair considered playing matchmaker, but she opted to let the burgeoning romance —if there even was one—take its own course. She and Arabella were both soon fast asleep, having dismissed their maids and helping one another out of their gowns. Blair dreamed of herself as a doting aunt with babies surrounding her as she played and cooed at them. When she woke, she felt lighter and happier than she had in months.

THREE

"I'll race you to the crest of the hill, and when I win, you shall give me the flask of Da's whisky that I ken you brought," Blair goaded Lachlan.

"And just what will you be doing with that?" Lachlan arched an eyebrow with an authority his sibling knew he didn't possess.

"Keeping warm," Blair said slyly. She didn't really want the whisky, but she knew Lachlan was far less eager to part with it than she was excited to win it.

"And when I win, you shall have to kiss a toad. I'd like to see how long it takes for the warts to appear."

"You are wretched!" Blair giggled. She squeezed her thighs against her horse's flanks, and the animal shot forward. She didn't wait for Lachlan to turn his horse around.

"You cheat!" Lachlan called. While he rode a stallion, her gelding was an equal match to his mount. Her father tried to insist that she ride a more sedate mare, but Blair had always had a wild streak about her. She'd gained her horse's loyalty by sneaking it apples, carrots, and sugar when it was a colt. It had followed her like a lamb, and Hamish Sutherland relented when the horse wouldn't allow anyone but Blair to mount him.

Blair was nearly to the submit of the hill when she noticed movement on the other side. She pulled her horse to an abrupt stop and looked back at Lachlan. "Riders approach." Blair wouldn't put herself in full view of strangers without Lachlan and their guards at her side. Of the half a dozen Sutherlands riding with them, two were Blair's permanent guard while she was at court, and four had traveled with Lachlan. She shaded her eyes as she watched the mounted party approach. She could tell they wore plaids, but they weren't yet close enough for her to make out the pattern. Until she could, she couldn't tell if they were friend or foe.

Lachlan maneuvered his horse alongside hers, but the approaching group of men veered toward the castle rather than encounter the Sutherlands. Blair assumed they couldn't recognize the Sutherland plaid from a distance either, and opted for a different path to the castle lest there be a conflict. Lachlan looked over at Blair before asking, "Could you tell who they are?"

"Nay. They were too far away." Blair shook her head, but she was less eager to linger outside the castle walls knowing a group of strangers was nearby. It was obvious they were Highlanders from the plaids, but that didn't mean they were allied with the Sutherlands. Brother and sister exchanged a look before the Sutherland horses turned back toward the castle. Blair sensed Lachlan and their guards were even more alert than they had been when they rode away from the keep. Rather than charging ahead, Blair rode in the center of the riders. She didn't expect a problem, but she knew the men would never take lightly their duty to protect her. As they clattered into the bailey, Blair gasped from a joyful surprise. "They're Camerons."

"Aye, there's Hardwin," Lachlan pointed. He called out, "Hardi!"

A man with short, shaggy tawny hair turned toward them as his feet touched the ground. His face beamed as he recognized the Sutherlands. "Lach. Blair."

Hardi reached up to Blair when her mount stopped before him. His warm hands grasped her waist, and Blair realized the callow man who'd left Sutherland years ago was now a muscle-hewn warrior. Her fingers felt the ripple of muscle beneath his shoulders as he eased her to the ground. She playfully kicked his shin, crossed her arms, and pouted much as she had as a child when Hardi wouldn't agree to let her join the boys when they went hunting. Lachlan had always refused immediately, but Blair nearly always wore Hardwin down until he acquiesced. "You never visit."

"If this is the welcome I can expect, then I've been wise to stay away," Hardi's deep chuckle rumbled against Blair as they embraced. She stepped aside as he and Lachlan exchanged a more manly embrace that involved thumping one another's backs before quickly shoving at one another's shoulders. "Now that is a welcome I can enjoy."

Blair stuck the tip of her tongue out at Hardi as he smirked at her. "Hardi, what brings you to court? Ta—" Blair stopped short when the genial smile dropped from her friend's face. She glanced at Lachlan, whose eyes had gone wide as he tried to warn her to remain quiet. Blair glanced back at Hardi and saw a sadness she never imagined her easy-natured childhood friend would possess.

"I suppose ye havenae heard," Hardi's voice was laced with grief as he peered down at Blair. She could only shake her head.

"Let's have this conversation somewhere else," Lachlan interrupted. His gaze swept around the bailey, and while it didn't appear as though they drew anyone's attention, he already knew the tale of woe Hardi would share, and he wouldn't have his friend do it where anyone could watch and listen.

Blair nodded as she gazed into Hardi's eyes. It was as if she couldn't look away, and an icy fear crept out of her belly and into her chest as she imagined what he might share. She led her brother and friend to a music chamber she knew wouldn't be in use. Without her brother at her side, she never would have slipped into the empty chamber alone, and certainly not with a man outside her family. But she knew it would afford them the privacy they needed. Lachlan turned the lock to ensure no one would interrupt them. Hardi went to the fireplace and soon had a cheery blaze flickering in the hearth, but no one's mood seemed to match the warmth the fire emanated. Blair settled in a chair across from the two the men occupied. She glanced between the two and held her breath.

"Blair, I'm now Laird Cameron," Hardi began, but he felt compelled to reach out and take Blair's hand when her eyes widened, her mouth dropped open, and she shook her head. "Aye, lass. As of a moon ago, I've become the clan's leader."

"How can that be? There's so many people ahead of you," Blair blurted. She looked at Lachlan, who wore his own expression of grief. She glared at her brother before she whispered. "Whatever's happened, how could you not have told me?"

"Blair, it's nae his fault. Much of what's transpired has happened in a brief period. There wouldnae have been a way to tell ye." Hardi gave her hands a squeeze before leaning back in his chair. "I think ye ken how Dougal died."

Blair nodded her head as tears sprang to her eyes. Dougal had been Hardwin's older brother. Both brothers had arrived at Dunrobin Castle when they were barely more than boys. They'd been sent to foster with the Sutherlands because both had shown an aptitude for strategy and sword fighting. They were the Cameron laird's nephews, so it was unusual for them to be fostered, but Hardi's uncle had seen the wisdom in having several men prepared to lead the Cameron warriors once he was gone. The clan had a lengthy list of rivals and seemed to always be at odds with someone. Their warriors were often split, fighting in more than one skirmish at a time. Dougal and Hardi had been more like brothers to Blair and Maude than just friends.

Dougal and Hardi had been on patrol four years earlier when an unexpected blizzard caught them unprepared. The whiteout made it impossible to see even their hands in front of their faces. Dougal became separated from the other men and froze to death. It was Hardi who found him several days later. He'd believed his life would end the moment that he pushed the last of the snow away and found his brother's body. The news of Dougal's death had wrapped the Sutherlands in a shroud of grief until it was time for Maude and Blair to move to Stirling. Blair swallowed several times as she nodded for Hardi to continue.

"Ye ken Angus led a raid on the Grants nae long after ye and Maude came here. As ma uncle's heir and tánaiste, Angus refused to remain at the keep while we planned our response to the last raid. He rode out with far too few men. The others returned with cattle and Angus's body thrown over a saddle. I was there and watched ma foolish cousin try to attack Laird Grant. He never saw Fingal coming until he looked down to see the blade through his gut. After Angus died, David became Uncle Farlane's heir. I ken Lachlan heard aboot the next battle. Did ye?"

Blair shook her head. Tears streamed down her cheeks as she witnessed a haunting grief overtake Hardi's eyes. She felt his sorrow as though it had taken residence in her own soul. It was her turn to reach out and take his hands. Hardi swallowed several times before he was ready to recount the bloodiest battle he'd ever fought. He still had nightmares as he watched one Cameron after another perish.

"Once the Clan Chattan Confederation unified, each clan believed themselves unstoppable. Try as ma uncle might to avoid more fights with the Mackintoshes, they challenged us, and we couldnae refuse. Uncle Farlane sent thirty men to fight trial by combat against thirty Mackintoshes." Hardi swallowed the gorge that rose in his throat, closing his eyes against the images that danced before them. Blair couldn't bear the pain she saw her friend suffer. She moved to sit on the arm of Hardi's chair. She leaned against him as she lifted his hands into her lap, encouraging him to continue. "David, Peter, and Seamus died that day."

Blair gasped when she heard Hardi name his three cousins, the last men standing between him and his clan's lairdship. In the space of one battle, he'd become tánaiste when he hadn't even been anyone's second or captain of any guard.

"When?" Blair croaked.

"Two moons ago," Hardi whispered. He feared he would break down and cry if he spoke any louder. Blair's compassion nearly overwhelmed him, urging him to lay his heart bare rather than bolstering his courage.

"You said you became laird a moon ago. What happened to your uncle?" Blair glanced at Lachlan to see if she'd erred in asking. Her brother's face was etched with his own grief, but he shrugged, unknowing how Hardi would respond.

"A sickness swept through the clan, and I believe grief had already weakened him. Ma father died years ago, then his nephew, then his sons. He didna have the strength to carry on after losing nearly everyone. He lived long enough to instruct me on some basics of being laird, but nae nearly enough." Hardi shrugged. "I dealt with the most urgent of clan matters as best I could, but the king ordered me to appear before him rather than send a delegate to pay our taxes. I dinna think this is the best time to leave ma clan, but what could I do? The king summons, ye come."

Blair and Lachlan exchanged a look that expressed thoughts they couldn't speak aloud. Lachlan shook his head, but Blair understood how hard it was for Lachlan to admit he couldn't stay in Stirling to help Hardi. Blair knew Lachlan wanted to, but he had his own duties to their clan. She thought it best that they steer away from discussing the source of their grief when Hardi took a rasping breath, and she knew he was on the verge of breaking down.

"You must be starving. The nooning will be soon. I'm sure Lachlan can help you find a chamber, then you both can join me in the Great Hall," Blair suggested.

Hardi's grateful expression tore once more at Blair's heart. They both knew she was trying to distract him, and while she wasn't successful, he appreciated her attempt. The men walked Blair to the passageway that contained the ladies-in-waiting chambers. As she scrubbed her face and neck, she considered what aid she could offer her friend, since she knew Lachlan was set to depart in two days. That wouldn't be nearly enough time for Lachlan to impart all the wisdom it had taken their father a lifetime to teach him.

FOUR

"I wish I could remain here longer now that you've just arrived," Lachlan looked over his shoulder at Hardi as both men prepared to don fresh leines. There was a second bed in Lachlan's chamber that was unoccupied, so he decided Hardi could share his chamber, and they would deal with any grumbling about his presumptuousness later. "I ken Mama and Da will leave soon to visit Maude and her family on the Isle of Lewis, but they won't go until I return. They will chomp at the bit to get there. Maude's just had a third bairn, and I ken Mama would have preferred to be with Maude but couldn't leave."

"I understand. How is Maude?" Hardi was glad to discuss someone else's family rather than his own, even if he knew he would never be an uncle. That opportunity perished alongside his brother. "Is she happy with Kieran? I dinna ken much aboot him."

"Blissfully. It's disgusting," Lachlan grimaced.

"Come now. If I recall, ye dinna think kissing—and all that comes after—is as horrible as ye once did," Hardi teased.

"It is when it's my wee sister."

Hardi chuckled at Lachlan's disgusted face. He

23

and Lachlan used to sneak out to the village tavern together as they entered their manhood. They'd been in the same chamber when they each tupped their first wench. As Hardi reflected upon that, it was his turn to grimace. He chalked it up to youth, but he would never share a chamber with another couple while being intimate with a woman.

"Remembering, aren't you? I don't care for an audience anymore either." Lachlan grinned. "I wouldn't want to be a distraction to another mon's woman."

"Aye, all that fumbling is distracting," Hardi snorted.

"Don't confuse the two of us. I ken very well where all the parts go." Lachlan smirked.

"I'll believe you, thousands wouldnae." Hardi broke out into a deep laugh as Lachlan flung the wet washing linen at his friend. "Shall we go? Ma stomach is ready to eat the rest of me alive. Will Blair really be able to join us? Doesnae she have duties?"

"Aye, she does, but she's able to share the nooning with me, even if she has to sit with the other ladies for the evening meal," Lachlan explained. He was grateful for the time he spent with Blair. He didn't look forward to leaving her behind; he dreaded knowing his younger sister would be alone at court. It had been hard enough for Lachlan and his father to leave both sisters at court, but knowing Blair was without Maude made his stomach churn. He'd made her swear countless times that she would never enter any passageway or chamber alone. He knew inevitably she walked places without a companion, but he also knew she wasn't foolish enough to enter a room without another woman or a guard to accompany her.

"When do you leave?" Hardi brought them back to their original conversation.

"In two days' time. I hate leaving Blair behind, but I detest being at court," Lachlan grumbled.

"Blair seems happy here," Hardi observed.

"Nay. She's happy to see us, and she can manage here, but she isn't happy per se."

"Per se?" Hardi asked softly.

Lachlan darted a look at Hardi and wanted to kick himself. He'd forgotten that Hardi hadn't had Latin drilled into him like most laird's heirs. He hadn't been an heir until two months ago. While they fostered with the Sutherlands, Hardwin and Dougal's father refused to allow the boys to join Lachlan in his studies. Hamish and Amelia Sutherland insisted that Lachlan sit still and listen, while his sisters were model pupils. Maude and Blair had run circles around him while their tutor—a priest, no less—struggled to maintain his patience with Lachlan. But despite Lachlan's disinterest, he'd learned to read and write Latin and to read, write, and speak French. He'd grown up speaking Gaelic and Scots, though he disliked having to speak the latter. He prided himself on being a Highlander. He opted for French when he could at court. He'd also learned sums and figures, which were among the most necessary skills for a laird.

"It means 'in itself,' but it can be used to mean per—. Well, it means 'not exactly'." Lachlan stumbled to explain. He watched Hardi nod, and his reflective expression told Lachlan he tucked away the new phrase to recall or even use at another time. He switched back to discussing Blair, hoping he wouldn't remind his friend again of the skills he lacked. "She makes do here. She and Arabella Johnstone are close. Arabella was Maude's friend before she left court, and Blair moved into Arabella's chamber once Maude left. She's friendly with the other ladies, but she mentioned to me the other eve that there aren't many ladies left that were here when she arrived."

"They've all married?" Hardi opened their chamber door.

"Aye. She feels a bit left behind, and she doesn't care for all the politics that goes along with life here. She'd rather be back in the Highlands, but when your godmother invites you to serve her, you can't refuse." It was a little-known fact, but King Robert and Queen Elizabeth were the Sutherland siblings' godparents; they were also godparents to their Sinclair cousins. Hardi knew from the royal visits to Dunrobin while he lived there for six years.

"Does she want to be at Dunrobin in particular? She's of an age to marry. I'm surprised she isn't already." Hardi considered the beautiful young woman who greeted him in the bailey. It surprised him to think that Blair hadn't married years ago. She was attractive, friendly, and well-trained to be the chatelaine of a large keep.

"She would happily return home, but nay, not Dunrobin in particular. She just won't consider a Lowlander."

"Would ye?" Hardi pretended to shiver. "I wouldnae want a little mon climbing into ma bed if I were her."

"That's my sister." Lachlan playfully punched his friend in the shoulder, but he put a little strength into it to remind Hardi there was no humor in hearing someone discuss a man bedding Blair. Hardi threw his hands up in defeat.

"So why hasnae she married?" Hardi continued to wonder how Blair had remained at court for several years without a proposal.

"She's turned down the offers made. They were Lowlanders—and it's because she doesn't want a life near the border, not that they're weak—or she doesn't like the mon who asks. She has expectations that only a Sutherland or Sinclair could meet, and none of us can marry her."

"Still think the sun shines out of yer arse, I see," Hardi smirked. "There must be someone she'd be willing to marry."

"There's bound to be. She just hasn't met him yet." Lachlan shot Hardi a warning glance as they entered the Great Hall, and Blair approached. Lachlan noticed she'd been standing with Arabella and Laurel, but excused herself when she spotted her brother and friend entering.

"Where are your men?" Blair asked Hardi, and he pointed to a table where the Sutherland and Cameron guards already sat together. Without any thought, he offered Blair his arm and escorted her to the table. Neither saw the speculative expression on Lachlan's face as he watched one of his closest friends whisper something to his younger sister.

FIVE

Blair swallowed her tears as she watched Lachlan ride through the castle gates. She'd enjoyed the past two days more than any she could remember since Maude married. While the men were in the lists in the morning, Blair joined the queen on her morning constitutional and in her solar. After the noon meal, she, Lachlan, and Hardi went for rides and practiced their archery both afternoons. The queen had granted her permission to sit with Lachlan and Hardi for both evening meals, since she knew Lachlan would leave soon. While not openly expressive, Queen Elizabeth was a kind godmother, and Blair suspected she still felt guilty about not intervening on Maude's behalf when some of the other ladies taunted and bullied her.

Now that Lachlan departed, Blair wouldn't be able to spend much time with Hardi since she was a maiden. She understood Hardi would have several meetings with the king before he left, as well. She was prepared to say goodbye to Hardi and return to the queen's solar when he silently looped her arm around his and guided her toward the gardens. They walked into the topiary maze where they were hidden from sight before Hardi pulled Blair against his chest and rubbed her back as she sobbed.

Blair didn't know how Hardi understood this was what she needed, but she appreciated that he did. Loneliness that had abated while Lachlan visited threatened to drown her, and Hardi felt like the only buoy in a rough sea. His height and broad shoulders made him feel colossal compared to her, but she drew comfort from the difference in size. As his arms remained around her, it was as though a wall encased her, protecting her from the world around her. If given the opportunity, she might have stayed that way forever rather than returning to the reality of courtly life.

When her sobs subsided, she drew away and reached into her sleeve for a handkerchief, but Hardi offered a corner of the swath of plaid draped over his shoulder. The softly worn wool was the comfort she needed, reminding her that her home was in the Highlands, and life at court was but a temporary detour. She dabbed at the tears that continued to trickle down her cheeks even though her breathing was back under control. Hardi tucked hair behind Blair's ears before tilting her chin up.

"Do ye recall what I would tell ye when ye were too wee to join Lachlan and me when we left the keep?"

"Of course. Ye'd say that I wasna being left behind. I made ye look forward to returning. But Lachlan doesnae look forward to coming to court. He dislikes being here."

"Aye. But he always looks forward to seeing ye. He doesnae like leaving ye here any more than ye like watching him ride away. If he werenae riding with his men, he'd be sobbing too." Hardi's smile was so warm that it reassured Blair, and she nodded. "It's nae that men dinna want to cry. It's that we arenae allowed to."

Blair gazed into tired blue-hazel eyes, and she felt guilty for her display of emotions when she considered that her parting from Lachlan was temporary. The men who'd left Hardi's life would never return. She was embarrassed to have made such a scene and didn't know where to look.

"Wheest," Hardi whispered. "Dinna feel guilty for being sad that yer brother isnae here. Ye can be upset for yer loss, and it doesnae mean yer arenae sympathetic to mine. I canna imagine what life is like for ye here. At least at home, I have ma clan. I've kenned them ma entire life."

"Thank ye," Blair whispered, not noticing she'd slipped back into her own brogue as she listened to Hardi comfort her. "It is hard to be here without Maude. And watching Lachlan leave reminds me how much I dinna want to be here anymore. It was exciting at first. So much to see, so many people to meet. But life here is nae what I hoped."

Hardi guided them to a bench and sat beside Blair. He'd intended to keep an appropriate distance between them, but she looked so deflated and tiny that his heart ached. He wrapped his arm around her shoulders and pulled her against him. She leaned her head on his shoulder just as she had when they were younger. "What did ye hope for?"

"To have genuine friendships with the other ladies. I'm friendly with them all, but Arabella is the only one here who I trust. The others have left and married. I'd hoped I would find someone to marry since Mama and Da promise none of us will have an arranged marriage. Ma time here has dragged on, but I havenae met a single mon I would want to marry. The men who come here from the Highlands are never here long enough for me to get to ken

31

them, and I dinna blame them for nae wanting to dillydally here."

They sat in silence for a moment while Blair once again struggled to stem her tears.

"There are foreign delegates, but I dinna want to leave Scotland," Blair continued. "That leaves those who choose to be lifelong courtiers. I refuse to imagine spending the rest of ma life here. I dinna want a mon who is always grasping for the next pouch of coin or the next position to get closer to the king. Every eve when a courtier asks me to dance, I'm glad that nay one here kens I'm the king and queen's goddaughter. I wouldnae be able to keep the leeches off me if people learned of that connection."

Blair sighed, once again embarrassed, but this time it was because she felt as though she'd spoken for too long. It didn't feel right to unburden her feelings to Hardi when her troubles were so insignificant compared to his.

"Dinna do that, Blair," Hardi murmured against her hair. She pulled away; her brow furrowed as she looked at him. "I ken ye have more to say. But I can also ken ye're feeling guilty again for telling me what upsets ye. Ye think yer problems arenae important compared to mine."

"How do ye ken?"

"Because I've kenned ye since I was ten summers, and ye were seven summers." Hardi shrugged as though that explained everything. But at Blair's confused expression, he continued to explain. "After ye sighed, I felt ye tense. It was only slightly, but it was there. Then ye tucked yer chin as if to hide from me. Ye still havenae relaxed."

Blair realized he was right. Her body was taut, and her eyebrows pinched together. It shocked her that Hardi could read such slight mannerisms and understand what they meant. But she and Hardi had spent a great deal of time together when they were children. Lachlan and their cousin Michael were practically inseparable until Michael left to become a priest. When they became adolescents, Lachlan and Michael had been among the group of boys who teased Maude about her weight. When their sister collapsed on the stairs from not eating, it was Lachlan who'd caught her. After that, Lachlan and Michael had been fiercely protective of Maude, getting into more than one fight when the other boys didn't cease their taunting.

Hardi and Dougal had stayed away from the fracas, knowing they weren't members of the clan and Laird Sutherland could send them home if they displeased him. When trouble began in the lists or bailey, Dougal and Hardi would slip into the keep and keep out of sight. They weren't afraid to fight, and they were drawn in more than once to stand shoulder-to-shoulder with Lachlan and Michael, but they preferred not to draw attention to themselves.

Blair preferred to be indoors more than Maude, so Hardi often found her sewing or reading before the fire in the Great Hall. They would talk about their day and what they'd done, and sometimes Blair read to Hardi. She'd once heard some lads a few years older than her snickering that she and Hardi looked like an old married couple, and that Hardi was sniffing at her quim. At only thirteen, she hadn't understood what they meant, but Hardi had heard them. He'd glanced at Blair and calmly walked over to the boys his age and jerked his head toward the doors of the keep. Blair hadn't been able to see his face, but when they returned, the boy who'd made the comment had a torn leine, and his eye was already bruising. Hardi had resumed his seat and asked Blair to continue reading. She hadn't thought of that event in years, but it had signaled an end to how much time they spent together, and he and Dougal left a year later. Before that, she realized, Hardi had been her best friend after Maude. She supposed he knew her well.

"Thank ye for listening to me." Blair whispered.

"Always, Blair," Hardi kissed her temple. "Ye need never fear sharing yer thoughts or feelings with me, Blair. I willna think less of ye for it."

"I ken. Since Maude left, I've had to keep much to maself. I didna realize it was bothering me so much." Blair heard the deep tones from the bell tower and pulled away from Hardi. "Bluidy hell, I'm late!"

Blair hadn't realized at least an hour had slipped by since she'd entered the bailey to bid Lachlan goodbye. The queen had granted her permission to say her farewells, not to while away the morning. She rose from the bench and shook out her skirts.

"I'm sorry, but I must go before the queen notices just how tardy I am. I will find ye later today, and we shall talk. But nae aboot me. I want to hear more from ye." Blair squeezed Hardi's hands before dashing out of the garden.

SIX

Once Blair left the gardens, there was no reason for Hardi to linger. He made his way to the lists where he found his guardsmen already in the midst of training. He selected a dulled sword from the armorer and found a partner. He didn't recognize the man, but he could tell from the plaid that he was a representative from the MacLeods of Lewis. Blair and Lachlan mentioned Maude gave birth to a bairn recently, so he inquired about his friend's health and her new babe. It pleased him to see the smile that spread across the man's face as he described how besotted Kieran was with his wife and children. Hardi was far too aware of how Maude suffered constant teasing for her weight while he was still at Dunrobin. To know that she had a husband who adored her made him happy. He wouldn't admit it to the man swinging a sword at his head, but he loved babies, and he was overjoyed that Maude's family had grown by one more.

Hardi moved from one partner to another as he recognized men from various clans. Four guards accompanied him to court, which made it easy for them to partner with one another, but it left him as the odd man out. He refused to interrupt their rotation just because he was their laird. He didn't mind training alongside members of other clans. He watched their strategy and maneuvers, attempting to imitate those he thought useful, and tucking away weaknesses in case he should need to remember them on the battlefield.

By the time the nooning approached, he was famished. Rather than winding his way through the castle to his chamber, he opted to follow his men to the barracks. He'd stripped off his leine when he felt himself growing sweaty, so it was still fresh. After borrowing a bar of soap and washing linen, he scrubbed himself over a bucket of water set aside for the men's hurried ablutions before entering the Great Hall.

The Cameron laird and his men found an unclaimed table. They kept their heads and voices down throughout the meal as they compared what they'd observed in the lists. Hardi shared what he'd noticed from the men he sparred with before suggesting that his men find members of other clans to practice against the next day. They understood the importance of remaining familiar with both their potential allies and their potential enemies. When the meal concluded, Hardi wondered what he should do next. He considered going for a ride, but his men had earned an afternoon off. He parted ways with them as they headed to the barracks, and he made his way to his chamber to retrieve his bow and quiver.

It had been several years since he practiced archery at Stirling Castle, and he hadn't paid enough attention when Lachlan and Blair took him to the range, so he had to ask more than one person to point him in the range's direction. By the time he reached his destination, he was hot and irritated. There wasn't an empty target in sight, and there was no shade to speak of. As the sun beat down on him, twin rivulets of sweat rolled down between his shoulder blades and the planes of his chest. Hardi shaded his eyes as he swept them over the archery field, once more hoping someone was readying to leave. After half an hour, he wondered if he should give up and find another way to pass the afternoon. He'd laid his bow and quiver at his feet and prepared to gather them when the target in front of him became available. He hurried to stake his claim before a pair of men just arriving could make their way to it.

Hardi pulled the string of his bow several times, testing its tautness, happy he'd restrung it just before leaving Tor Castle. He retrieved an arrow from his quiver and nocked it against his bow. He inhaled deeply, lifting the bow to shoulder height. He closed one eye as he set his sight on the target. He released the arrow as he exhaled. A sudden gust of wind caught the arrow in its crosshairs and made it tremble midair before pushing it off course. His arrow landed far to the left of the target. Hardi shook his head and grumbled, "Where was that bluidy breeze while I was melting ma cods?"

He drew another arrow and repeated the steps to prepare to fire. He was releasing his fingers when the range master called a halt to firing. Hardi jerked his bow away from the target, but it was too late. His fingers had let go, but rather than fly toward the target, his sudden movement caused the arrow to launch upward a few feet before falling to the ground between his position and the target. Several snickers reached his ear as he pursed his lips. He stepped away from the shooting line and reclaimed his two arrows just as the other archers retrieved theirs. He stepped back in line as the range master gave the signal that they could recommence shooting.

Hardi attempted a third shot, but with no forewarning a pigeon flew between him and his target, his arrow nipping its wing. Startled, the bird christened his arrow before flapping away. The laughter from the targets on either side seemed deafening.

"*Sard!*" Hardi hissed. "Ye canna be fucking serious? Fucking bird."

A feminine gasp behind him made him spin around. Staring at him with appalled expressions, Arabella and Laurel stood behind him. Between the two shocked ladies was Blair, clutching her sides and laughing.

"I dinna find it funny," Hardi growled.

"Tis a shame because I find it hilarious," Blair gasped. "Ruddy bird shat on yer arrow." Blair forced the words out between gales of laughter. Her burr once more returned as she eyed the seething Highlander. "Its aim is better than yers."

With her last comment, Blair could no longer speak as the hilarity of the situation and her assessment made her snort more than once. Arabella and Laurel turned stunned faces toward Blair, but their fearful eyes darted to Hardi.

"He willna hurt me," Blair whispered, quietening her laughter until she once more looked at Hardi's infuriated visage. She failed to smother her chortle. "He'd have to hit his target to do that."

"Blair," Arabella warned. "I don't think Laird Cameron finds the humor like you do. And you're drawing attention. Stop."

Blair turned her attention to the men watching her mock Hardi, and she sobered immediately. She stepped before him and turned her face up to his. "I'm sorry," she spoke clearly, ensuring her voice carried. "I shouldn't have been so rude, Laird Cameron. I beg your forgiveness for my atrocious manners."

"I accept yer apology, Lady Blair," Hardi's graciousness didn't fool Blair. Her heart sank, knowing what would come next. "On the condition that ye agree to take yer turn at the target."

Blair nodded before looking for the artillator. Spotting the man, she made her way toward him, but before she was within speaking distance, she could already see that the only bows available were far too large for her to maneuver. The man hadn't planned for any ladies to be present, so none of the smaller bows were there. Compared to her size, the weapons all looked more like Welsh longbows than the notably smaller Scottish ones. She knew Hardi was behind her when she spoke over her shoulder, "Ye knew."

"Aye." It was Hardi's turn to laugh. He reached out to accept the bow and quiver. He could have offered his own, but having restrung it recently, it would have been virtually impossible for Blair to draw the string even an inch. He checked the elasticity of the bow the artillator handed him. Satisfied that she had a passable chance, he turned toward his target. Blair marched beside him, knowing she had earned her comeuppance.

Blair took her place and accepted the bow from Hardi. The weight of the weapon pulled on her arm before she even attempted to position it. She tested the string herself, relieved to feel some give in the tension. However, while she could pull back the string and nock an arrow, she feared the bow wouldn't fire straight.

"*Crétin*," Blair muttered the French insult.

"Nae need to call names, Blair. I amnae an oaf." Hardi recognized the insult even though he didn't speak French. "I will enjoy this though. Shall we make it interesting? I wager ye a meat pie if ye win. And if I win," Hardi paused for effect. "Four meat pies."

"Four!" Blair lowered the bow as she spun around.

"Aye, four. One is reasonable for ye, but I willna be full with aught less than four."

Blair rattled off several other oaths under her breath, which elicited a deep rumble of laughter from Hardi. Her cheeks pinked as Hardi gave fair turnaround. She'd already noticed quite a few of the nearby archers had ceased their practice as Hardi and Blair returned to their target. Now it seemed as if every eye was on her. Blair lifted the bow, struggling to keep her arm from shaking from its weight and cumbersome size. She felt the arrow wobble, but she clenched her core and backside before drawing in a deep breath. It wasn't the first time she'd fired a bow that was too large for her; it wasn't the first time Hardi had posed such a challenge. She loosed the arrow and sighed when it hit the target just right of the center of bullseye but still within it. She turned her head and smirked, but it dropped when Hardi nudged her out of the way. In a flash, he'd drawn another arrow and set it whizzing toward the target. It hit the bullseye only seconds before another arrow split hers.

Blair huffed and elbowed Hardi before squinting at the target. Once more she tightened every muscle between her ribs and her knees and fired again. This one hit the bullseye and made Hardi's arrow wobble.

"Best out of three," Hardi announced. He set his sights before releasing his arrow. He exaggerated his movements as he lowered his bow, smug satisfaction from not only hitting the bullseye but doing it with such force that Blair's shallowly embedded arrow fell from the target. Blair's face went from pink to red as Hardi gloated. "Ye have a face like a skelped arse."

Blair didn't appreciate Hardi pointing out what she felt. Her flushed cheeks felt on fire, and she knew she was scowling. "I laughed," she hissed.

"At ma expense." Hardi reminded her.

"This is far worse, and ye ken it."

"How? I dinna ken another woman who shoots with the precision ye do. Ye've hit the target nigh on perfectly both times with a bow far too large for ye. Ye may nae appreciate the challenge in front of everyone, but it'll be me who willna hear the end of how a wee lass nearly bested me." Hardi pointed out. He lowered his voice, so it wouldn't carry. "I would never challenge ye if I didna already ken ye might beat me. I amnae trying to humiliate ye. Just make ye sweat a wee bit."

Blair's shoulders slumped, knowing Hardi spoke the truth. This competition wasn't really retribution. She had embarrassed him in front of the other men and likely still was. He'd taken advantage of her competitive nature to rile her temper, but she knew her prowess surprised everyone watching. She raised the bow again.

"Dinna do it, Blair," Hardi warned. She glanced at him and nodded. He knew she intended to throw the competition and miss the center of the target on purpose. "Dinna ever pretend to be less than ye are to make me look better."

Blair focused her attention on the target, blocking out the surrounding sounds, even Hardi, who stood close enough for her to smell the fresh air and pine scent that clung to him. She briefly wondered how he still smelled so clean when she was certain she smelled like she'd been rolling around inside a stable. She launched her third arrow toward the center and struck the target perfectly. She lowered the bow without a word. They'd both shot a perfect round.

"I owe ye a meat pie, and ye owe me four," Hardi gloated.

"What? Nay!" Blair shook her head.

"It was a tie. We both won."

41

"Or we both lost, and I dinna need to feed a behemoth," Blair retorted.

"I'd rather look at the positive." Hardi's expression mirrored the merriment in his voice.

"I dinna ken if I can lift ma arms to eat the bluidy thing," Blair bemoaned.

"And if I added penydes to sweeten the deal?" Hardi goaded.

"Penydes? Ye remembered that I like them?" Hardi's memory of her favorite sugary treat stunned her. They were a rarity at Dunrobin, her mother not believing in sweets. She had learned her lesson after watching her three children run wild when the king and queen brought the penydes as gifts when Lachlan, Maude, and Blair were very young.

"Aye. The few times we had them while I fostered, ye hoarded them. I thought ye'd take ma fingers off with yer teeth or a blade when I tried to filch a few," Hardi laughed.

"If you'll forgive us," Arabella interrupted. "The sun is a tad much for us. We shall return to the castle."

Blair turned to Arabella and Laurel, having forgotten they were observing the challenge between childhood friends. She felt guilty for ignoring them and causing them to stand for so long in the sun.

"I'm sorry to have kept you waiting," Blair's voice signaled her contrition, her courtly speech returned. She handed the bow back to Hardi and stepped toward the women.

"Stay," Laurel assured her. "You still haven't beaten him."

"Besides," Arabella pointed to one of her Sutherland guards approaching. "Your guard has just fetched a bow that's the proper size."

The ladies grinned at Hardi before Arabella winked at Blair, who knew her friend had arranged for the bow. The ladies turned away, but Blair and Hardi watched them put their heads together as their shoulders shook with mirth on their way to the castle.

With both her guards as chaperones, Blair and Hardi spent the afternoon at the archery range, but they were no longer competing. As the sun slipped lower into the sky and dusk approached, the Sutherland guards accompanied the pair into town where Blair and Hardi enjoyed their spoils.

SEVEN

Five days after their standoff at the archery range, Hardi and Blair ambled through the gardens as the queen and the other ladies-in-waiting walked ahead. There had been ceaseless chatter about the challenge, and Blair had grown tired of the false praise and the constant inquiries about the handsome Highlander. She understood the women's interest in the unattached warrior, but she was tired of repeating herself. No, he wasn't married. No, he wasn't betrothed. No, he wasn't looking for a wife. And no, she didn't have her sights set on him. She reassured each woman that theirs was an almost sibling-like relationship, but something rankled as she watched the women fawn over him. They attempted to lure him into conversation, tittering over his brogue. They tried to seduce him into dancing each night, but more often than not, Hardi partnered with Blair for a few sets, then leaned against a wall, sipping his ale. More than one lady mused about what might be beneath his plaid while the women sat together for meals.

While they enjoyed one another's company, Blair was aware Hardi grew restless waiting for an audience with the king. She sensed his apprehension and wondered if a substantial part came from knowing he wouldn't be able to read any documents placed before him. She didn't dare ask if he knew how to sign his name, but she feared where King Robert might force him to pen his X. She wished she were a fae, able to sit on his shoulder and whisper in his ear as she read the documents from her invisible perch. As his impatience and nervousness grew, so did hers.

"Has anyone given you a sign of when the king might summon you?" Blair kept her voice low, but she knew it would carry. They may have walked behind the group, but the wind carried her words toward the always eagerly eavesdropping gossips.

"Nay. I canna linger here forever, but I havenae a choice but to wait." Hardi glanced down at Blair's upturned face. "Eager to be rid of me?"

"Not at all," Blair murmured. Her eyes shifted toward the cluster of women before returning to gaze at Hardi. "I enjoy your company. I feel less homesick with you here."

"Do ye feel that way often? Homesick, that is."

"Aye. It wasn't so difficult when Maude was here. The Mistress of the Bedchamber refused to consider us being roommates, but I spent all day with her until Kieran began courting her. The only time we were apart was when she tended the sick or went to the abbey to see Michael. It was useful having our cousin at the abbey that supplies the castle with medicinals. Sometimes I accompanied her." Blair shrugged as she stared into the distance, almost as if she could see her sister all the way northwest on the Isle of Lewis. "I'm busy though, so that helps. I've impressed Queen Elizabeth with my embroidery, so she has asked me to stitch the christening gown for her bairn."

"The lad or lass isnae due for several more moons," Hardi pointed out.

"I ken, but I don't begrudge her any eagerness. She's waited a long time to get with child, so the anticipation must be difficult to ignore. If sewing the gown pleases my godmother, then I'm happy to do it." Blair was careful not to admit her connection to the queen too loudly. It was a secret few knew, and she preferred to keep it that way.

"Ye are a lass of many talents. I remember ye practiced yer stitching on ma leines. Dougal and I had the bonniest clothes of all the men in the lists," Hardi chuckled.

"Maude was sewing her own clothes, so what else did I have to work on?" Blair countered.

"Lachlan and Michael's clothes." Hardi bit his tongue when several heads turned back at his rumbling laughter. "Though I'm certain yer skills with a needle and thread have only improved. I have some mending ye can do if ye tire of yer fancy stitching."

Blair shot him a withering glare as they stopped to allow an approaching couple to pass. It offered an excuse for them to fall back further from the group. Blair clasped her hands before her as she summoned the courage to return to talking about Hardi's impending meeting with the king.

"Do you have any idea what the king may ask of you, other than your oath of fealty?"

"Nay. There's bound to be matters regarding our neighbors and ongoing strife with the Mackintoshes and Macphersons, but I dinna ken what he might ask of me."

"Did your uncle give you any hint of what pledges he made to the Bruce that the king will expect you to uphold?" Blair asked.

Hardi shook his head. "I ken the king can order

ma clan to provide warriors, and we proudly support him. We will lend any aid asked of us. There are the taxes I'm here to pay. King Robert granted us extra land nae long after the war ended, so he may inquire aboot its use. I have several missives ma uncle left me, and some concern potential clan alliances. It may interest King Robert to learn of the negotiations ma uncle began."

"Alliances?" Blair's stomach tightened as she thought about what usually bound clans together. She feared that Hardi would mention an impending betrothal. She didn't understand why the thought suddenly bothered her so much.

"Aye. Trading grain and wool mostly," Hardi's tone reassured Blair that there wasn't anything of grave concern, but it only bothered her more not knowing if a betrothal might be on Hardi's horizon.

Hardi considered whether to tell Blair about the graver matters in the missives his uncle left him. He didn't want to worry her or bore her with the reality of how precarious his position was with two rival clans breathing down his neck. But he also knew Blair was the only person at court who he could trust with the information, and the only person he could ask to read the missives to him to refresh his memory before meeting with Robert the Bruce. He drew Blair off the path, his hand lightly grasping her elbow.

"There are several missives that ma uncle left me. Some of them contain troubling information. I didna want to trouble ye with ma woes, but I need to ask for yer help. It would serve me well to have those details fresh in mind to prepare for King Robert's inevitable questioning. Will ye read them to me?" Hardi tried to keep his voice even despite his embarrassment at having to ask Blair to complete such a simple task. A task a laird should have been able to do on his own.

"Of course. Hardi, please don't hide things from me if I can help you. I won't pretend to understand your position as laird, but I can still aid you by reading anything that benefits—or might harm—you." Hardi looked into Blair's beseeching eyes, finding himself lured into their deep whisky hue. He would have promised her anything if it meant he didn't have to look away. Intelligence, kindness, and worry drew him in.

"I will accept yer offer. I trust ye, Blair." Hardi realized he'd never spoken truer words as he continued to lock eyes with the petite woman standing before him. He'd looked into those eyes countless times in the six years he lived among the Sutherlands, but they'd never before felt so magnetic.

Blair bit her lower lip as she considered the offer she wanted to make. She didn't want to insult Hardi, but she knew she could help him by doing more than just reading the missives. Before she could speak, he pulled her lip loose from where her teeth were creating divots.

"Ye shall bite yer way through it," Hardi warned.

"Hardi, will you let me teach you to read?" Blair blurted. She felt her cheeks go up in flames. "I mean, since I still remember how, mayhap I could teach you what I ken."

"Dinna do that, Blair. That really will anger me. Dinna pretend to nae be intelligent or educated just because I amnae. Dinna make it sound like ye dinna read anymore and that it's some far stretch for ye to do so. I'm certain ye read most days." A hard edge crept into Hardi's voice, and Blair regretted sounding foolish after agreeing to read the missives, but she'd feared offending him. Once more, Hardi seemed to read her mind. "I amnae too proud to ask and accept yer help. I asked if Lachlan could teach me, but he couldnae stay. Just because ye're a lass doesnae mean

49

ye arenae able to teach me what I need to ken. I dinna pretend to be more than I am, so dinna pretend to be less than ye are."

Hardi's steely gaze and iron tone didn't intimidate Blair; still, she could see the resolve within Hardi that would make him a powerful laird. She prayed that she could teach him the mundane tasks that would be as much of a necessity as swinging a sword. She searched his face, but she wasn't certain what she was looking for. She couldn't name what she needed to see, but a sense of reassurance and calm swept over her. Perhaps it was a hint of the boy she'd once known that still lurked within Hardi. The familiarity that had developed over six years of growing up together was once again in place.

"I'm sorry," Blair murmured.

"Blair, who is this meek creature? This isnae the lass I kenned growing up, or even the young woman I kenned when I left. Dinna be anyone ye arenae when ye are with me. Dinna simper and coddle me. It willna do either of us any good, and I havenae long to stay here and play games. If this is who ye must be at court, then do what ye must. But I hope ye can be yerself with me. We've kenned each other too long to be aught else."

Blair lifted her chin and set back her shoulders, her eyes narrowed as her mouth set in a firm line. Hardi wanted to laugh as he recognized the stubborn expression he'd seen all too often. He waited with bated breath to hear what Blair would order him to do. He admitted to himself that he had followed her about like a puppy when they were younger. While not spoiled or arrogant, Blair had an inherent sense of command that made people comply with minor effort on her part.

"Meet me in the music room we were in a few days ago and bring any missives you have," Blair's burr fell from her voice, and she once more sounded like a lady-in-waiting rather than a Highland lass. "Do not keep me waiting, and for the sake of all the saints, be discreet."

"Aye, my lady." Hardi stood from the bench they'd found and offered his hand, bowing over hers. "As you wish."

Blair nodded, but she looked down her nose at Hardi despite his superior height. "You told me not to pretend to be someone I'm not. Get rid of that hideous Scots accent and sound like a proper Highlander." She didn't wait for a response, spinning on her heel before sweeping through the garden. If Hardi didn't understand Blair's need to appear from the gardens as though she hadn't just arranged a secret rendezvous with a man—even if they would only be talking—he would have found her haughtiness obnoxious. Instead, it seemed somehow endearing. He knew she was protecting him just as much as herself. If anyone learned they'd been together without a chaperone, they'd be forced to marry. Blair was attempting to keep him from being trapped.

———

Hardi returned to the chamber he'd shared with Lachlan, the chamberlain having given him permission to remain until he, too, departed Stirling Castle. He unlocked the small chest he'd brought with him that carried various documents his uncle left in his possession before his death. His uncle read most of them to Hardi, but now he had no way of knowing which was which. He also couldn't remember everything they contained. He'd been swallowed whole by his grief and overwhelmed at the prospect of becoming laird when he'd sat beside his uncle's bed. The man's rasping voice had often been difficult to hear and understand. Coupled with Hardi's inability to remain focused, most of what Hardi heard had gone in one ear and out the other. What he recalled was his uncle's warning that he shouldn't share at least three of the missives with the clan council until the king officially recognized Hardi as laird to Clan Cameron. Hardi wished he'd marked those. He dropped the folded pieces of parchment into his sporran and slipped from his chamber.

Hardi was nearly to the music room when he recognized three MacMillan men approaching him. Their clans were allies, so Hardi knew there was little chance he could avoid being detained. He was certain Blair would already be waiting, but he would only appear suspicious and rude if he didn't stop.

"Hardwin," Henry MacMillan greeted him, thrusting out his arm before clasping Hardi's forearm in a warrior handshake. "My mother and father would have me pass along their condolences. You have mine as well."

Hardi listened to the man's insincere tone. He was certain that Laird and Lady MacMillan would mean well, but Henry was arrogant and self-centered. The man had adopted a Scots accent when they were younger, much like many members of a laird's family, but he wielded it as though it were a weapon to make others feel inferior.

"Ma thanks to ye and yer kin." In contrast, Hardi allowed the words to roll across his tongue, his burr more pronounced than ever. "Are ye here to pay yer taxes as I am?"

"Pay taxes, pay whores. A little of both, I suppose." Henry's comment drew laughter from the men beside him, but it died when Hardi failed to smile. Henry shifted uncomfortably before continuing. "Aye. We arrived recently. Just in time to see you strolling among the ladies-in-waiting. Imagine my surprise to see you and little Blair Sutherland slipping away together as the queen and her ladies continued their walk. I waited for you for as long as I could, but alas you never appeared."

Hardi refused to take the bait. "Aye. We spoke of ma new position as laird. *Lady* Blair asked how things are among the Camerons. We parted ways while in the garden. I returned to my chamber, and I believe the queen expected her." None of what he said was a lie. He merely left out the part about needing Blair to read the missives to him. And he didn't intend to confess that the queen might have expected Blair, but she'd been offering to teach him to read instead. He wished to change the subject, and he was certain he knew how. "MacMillan, perhaps we can share a table at the evening meal."

"It's MacGillemhaoil," Henry snarled. His branch of the MacMillan clan preferred the alternative address. Hardi had never understood why being known as "son of a tonsured servant" was so imperative. To his mind, they were the same MacMillans as those known as "son of one who bore the tonsure of St. John" or Mhaoil-Iain. Either way, he knew it drew Henry's attention away from discussing Blair. "Aye. We shall join you, but you will pay for the first round of whisky when we go to the tavern later."

Hardi hid his grimace. He had no intention of going anywhere with Henry or the other MacMillans. He wasn't interested in finding himself in a tavern fight, nor was he interested in bedding a whore. He nodded and stepped out of the MacMillans' way, silently encouraging Henry to continue to wherever he headed. Hardi breathed a sigh of relief when he recalled there were two more turns down different passageways before he would reach Blair's hiding place, so Henry wasn't likely to see where he went. As he made his way, he kept his ears open for even the softest footsteps following him. At each turn, he glanced back to see if he'd gained an extra shadow or three. He strained to see into the distance in each direction before slipping into what appeared to be an empty room.

EIGHT

"Ye can come out, Blair. Tis only me." Hardi looked toward the window embrasures and watched as Blair materialized from behind an enormous tapestry that hung to the floor. She'd once been the best at playing hide-and-seek, but Hardi had learned where to look for her first. He'd caught a whiff of her lemongrass scent as he entered, so he knew she'd arrived before him. He turned back to the door and locked the portal before offering an unrepentant smile. She watched as Hardi approached. His broad shoulders looked as if they could bear the weight of the world, and Blair feared that was how he felt.

"Before ye chew ma leg off for keeping ye waiting, I ran into Henry MacMillan." Hardi held his hands up in surrender, but Blair was happy to hear the humor in his voice.

Blair arched an eyebrow as she smirked. "And which tavern will you be going to first? The Wolf and Sheep, The Merry Widow, or The Picked Over Plum."

Hardi's eyebrows shot to his hairline, shocked that Blair knew the unofficial names of the three bawdiest taverns in Stirling. The Wolf and Sheep was known for a tavern owner and whores who fleeced their customers after getting them drunk with cheap whisky. The Merry Widow was where matrons from court slipped away to their illicit assignations. And the whores from The Picked Over Plum couldn't remember the blush of youth.

"Don't look so shocked and don't you dare reprimand me for knowing. I've been here for three years. How could I not ken aboot such places?" Blair didn't contain her merriment as Hardi grew redder in the face. "You needn't fear that I've been to any of those places. At least not after dark."

"Blair," Hardi warned.

"I've walked past them enough times to know one from another, and neither of us needs to pretend I don't know what happens there. I might not be a guest at any of those establishments, but I know both men and women who are. I won't judge if you're among them."

Hardi stalked across the chamber before stopping with his hands on his hips. He leaned over to bring himself at eye level with Blair. "I dinna go whoring. I have nay wish for the pox, and I'm nae interested in aught a woman can offer that she finished doing five minutes ago with someone else."

Blair cocked her head to the side and cast Hardi a look that said she didn't believe him, but she chose not to argue. "Very well. Keep yourself to your leman. But I ken where you, Dougal, Lachlan, and Michael used to go."

Hardi's face grew so red, Blair feared a vein would rupture. "What I got up to back then was nae yer concern. And to be clear, Michael didna do aught but drink. And as for a leman, who the bluidy hell said I keep one?"

Blair shrugged. "You're not married, and you're very braw. I just assumed." She shrugged once again.

"I dinna keep a mistress, and I dinna go wenching."

"But ye're a mon with needs," Blair persisted, attempting to swallow her laugh as Hardi grew more uncomfortable.

"I'm a mon who needs to learn how to lead his bluidy clan," Hardi snapped, and Blair was immediately contrite.

"I didn't mean to imply you shirk your duties. It's none of my business who you do or don't visit. I'm sorry." Blair's apology eased Hardi's frustration, and he reminded himself that it had been a long time since they'd seen one another. They may have fallen back into their jovial relationship, but Blair had no way to know what life had been like for him over the past few years. He'd been too grief stricken to think of bedding a woman often. He'd sought release but never found comfort. Eventually, he opted to forgo visiting the village women he'd once preferred. They asked too many questions about how he felt, and he didn't have the strength or trust to explain his emotions. He'd been a veritable recluse the past several months, training in the lists and meeting with his uncle, then the clan council. He took meals in his Great Hall only because he couldn't ignore his clan's expectations.

"I dinna mean to be short-tempered, lass. I ken ye were teasing. There hasnae been much time for merriment of late, and there isnae a woman I dally with." Hardi watched Blair nod, but she opted to remain quiet as she led them toward a table with chairs on each side. She gestured to a seat before gathering and lighting several candles. The light in the chamber was dim and would make it difficult to read whatever the documents contained without the candles. Hardi drew the folded vellum from his sporran and laid them out on the table. He opened each one,

57

stacking them by the handwriting since he had no other way of categorizing them. Blair slipped into the chair beside him, waiting for him to offer her the first one to read. When he didn't move, she glanced at him. "Lass, I dinna ken what any of them say. I mean Uncle Farlane read them to me, but I dinna ken one from another now."

Blair turned her head to look sideways at Hardi, sensing his embarrassment now that they sat together, and the proof of his lack of education sat before them. She placed her smaller hand over his fist that lay on the table. She tunneled her fingers into his palm before brushing her thumb over his knuckles. She drew her hand away just before Hardi opened his to accept her touch. Her sympathetic gesture surprised him, but he felt bereft once it ended. For a heartbeat, he hadn't felt alone. The aching isolation had disappeared while he held Blair in the garden the morning Lachlan left, but it had returned as soon as they parted. And for a moment, just now, he'd had another respite.

It took Blair quite some time to make her way through the missives. Several were written so poorly that she had to guess what certain lines meant. There were more that she expected, so time slipped away quickly. As though she sensed his ever-churning emotions, Blair laid down the final missive she'd picked up but hadn't read. She turned to face Hardi.

"Ye can talk to me aboot aught, Hardi. I willna think less of ye for aught ye tell me. I willna push ye, but ken that I am here if ye should want an ear to listen to ye." In the privacy and intimacy of the music room, Blair didn't notice that she abandoned her refined speech. She turned back to the missive before Hardi could respond, and he appreciated that she had. He was grateful not to be put on the spot to answer, and she didn't see the tears that misted his eyes. He nodded, knowing she would see the movement in her peripheral vision, but the lump in his throat kept him from speaking. He watched as Blair reread one document after another before sitting back. Her grave expression matched how he'd felt each time his uncle shared one with him.

"I ken some are aboot the Mackintoshes, and some are aboot the Macphersons. There are two from Henry's father aboot trading sheep. One is from the king. I recognize his seal, so I ken which one that is. Laird Donald sent several aboot our alliance, both hinting at a marriage between David and his daughter and how to weaken the Clan Chattan Confederation. I just dinna ken which is which. I separated them by handwriting, but I dinna ken what script belongs to which writer. Mayhap they should be separated by topic, but I canna do that maself."

Blair ignored Hardi and asked, "Have all the members of yer clan council seen these? How many of them can read? Who can? Do ye trust those who can?" She rattled off one question after another, a sense of urgency forcing her to speak. She was so disturbed by what she'd read, she still didn't notice that she'd reverted to her burr once again. She feared Hardi's uncle hadn't read the entirety of some if Hardi so calmly handed them over to her.

"Ma uncle said there were three or four that I shouldnae share with the council until after I met with King Robert, but I dinna ken which ones those are. I hadnae seen the handwriting when Uncle Farlane read them to me. So nay, nae all the council has seen them. At least I havenae shown them to anyone, and I ken who ma uncle shared them with. If the men have talked amongst themselves, nay one has hinted at it to me. Only two of the men can read. They're ma father and uncle's cousins. And nay, I dinna trust them." Hardi disliked knowing there were members of his clan who he didn't trust, and it was uncomfortable to admit they were members of his own family and council.

"Hardi, who read the missive to ye summoning ye to court? It arrived after ye became laird."

"Aye. Ma father's cousin, Faolán," Hardi answered.

Blair blinked several times. "He came with yer father when it was time for ye and Dougal to return home. He made me uncomfortable with the way he looked at Maude and me. I remember thinking his name suited him. He was a small wolf. Shorter than ye, yer brother, or yer father, and he had an air aboot him that made me nae trust him. Made ma skin crawl, and Maude's too. We didna go anywhere without Lachlan or Michael until ye and yer kin rode out of the bailey."

"I remember that. He's always been a lecher. I asked Lachlan and Michael to guard ye both until we left."

"Ye asked them?" Blair was surprised. "I thought they agreed because Maude and I asked."

Hardi shrugged. "Either way, I wanted to be sure ye were both safe. I didna have any sisters, but ye and Maude were as close as I have ever had."

"Do ye recall what Faolán told ye the king wrote?"

"Aye, he said the king offered his condolences but expected me to appear within a moon to swear ma fealty as a laird and to settle the clan's taxes."

"And?" Blair pressed.

"And naught. That's it." Hardi shook his head.

"Och, Hardi. Look at the length of this missive. Did ye nae wonder why it would be so long if that was all the king had to say?"

"Faolán claimed it was just the king's flowery language when I asked him aboot that. I didna believe him, but the only other person I could ask was his brother. While I think Drostan would tell me the truth, I never had an opportunity to ask. Faolán was glued to ma side or Drostan's until I departed. It felt as though he was keeping us apart, but he didna do aught that I could call out. I would have insulted him and appeared inept before the clan if I did. I couldnae risk it that soon after being sworn in as the laird." Hardi watched as anger and apprehension flickered back and forth in Blair's eyes. "What didna he tell me?"

Blair's shoulders sank, dreading having to tell Hardi what the missive contained. "How much did Faolán tell ye yer clan owes the crown?"

"He said the *cáin* was six shillings, eight doyt for each sack of wool we traded. Ma uncle grew our herd over the last few years, so we produced five score and ten sacks." Hardi paused, his expression blank as he looked at Blair. He didn't know how much that came to. "We also owe the crown taxes for the land itself which Faolán said came to six pounds, thirteen shillings, four doyt."

"That's all he said the land tax was?" Blair was incredulous. The amount Faolán told Hardi was a pittance compared to what Blair expected him to say. "What about the grain ye milled? The whisky ye distilled? How many head of cattle do ye have?" Blair's heart sank as she suspected Faolán hadn't sent Hardi with nearly enough funds. The missive warned that failure to pay the taxes in full would mean forfeiting the strip of land the Camerons received as a gift honoring their loyalty to the crown.

"We didna trade any of our grain this year," Hardi rasped. He sensed Blair feared the same thing that he did. He would have to stand before the king and be made a fool for not having the correct amount of coins for the levied taxes.

"Hardi, ye pay for what ye produce, nae just what ye sell or trade. Do ye ken the amounts? There's a thirlage charged on the grain."

"Aye. We have five score cows, twenty barrels of whisky, and nearly fifteen score bushels of grain."

"Fifteen score bushels? That's nearly five score bolls, which is how it's measured to calculate its value." Blair had placed a piece of parchment, a quill, and a pot of ink on the table before lighting the candles. She pulled the writing utensils toward her. She wrote out a row of numbers, pausing after each one to show which number each figure represented. Once Hardi committed the figures to memory, she moved on to work out the amount of taxes the Camerons owed. Hardi watched in silence as Blair tallied one column of figures after another. When she finished, she rubbed her forehead before forcing a smile.

"Do ye see these numbers?" Blair asked as she pointed to the first row. "These are the amounts ye told me. Five score and ten is one hundred and ten sacks of wool. That means we must add together six shillings, eight doyts for each sack. That comes to six hundred and sixty shillings, and eight hundred and eighty doyts. But we can group the shillings and doyts to make merks and pounds. Ye ken there are twenty shillings in a pound. If I had the coins before us, I would take the six hundred and sixty shillings and put them in groups of twenty. I'd have thirty-three pounds. Since there are twelve doyts in a shilling, we would have seventy-three shillings."

Blair stopped to look at Hardi, surprised that he didn't look confused. She feared she went too fast for him, but he seemed to follow her explanation. She raised her quill to make the next set of calculations, but Hardi brushed his hand on her forearm, stopping her.

"If we have seventy-three shillings, then we should put those in groups of twenty again. Aye?"

"Aye. That would give us three pounds and thirteen shillings. If we add that to the thirty-three pounds we already calculated, the Camerons must pay forty-six pounds, thirteen shillings."

"Isnae thirteen shillings a merk?" Hardi asked quietly. He knew what each coin looked like and what they were worth. He could count and do much of the math Blair showed him, but only if he had the money in front of him and could physically move them into the groups Blair described.

"Aye, so ye can say it's forty-six pounds, one merk." Blair drew her lips in on one side of her mouth as she waited to hear whether Faolán told Hardi the correct amount.

"That's what I brought for the wool. At least that amount of tax is covered. But I didna bring aught to cover the grain, whisky, or cattle." Hardi's palms were clammy, and he felt a trickle of sweat roll between his shoulder blades despite the coolness of the chamber.

"Did ye bring aught for the land tax? Ye said he told ye it was six pounds, thirteen shillings, four doyt." Blair cringed as she asked about yet another levy.

"Aye. I asked Faolán aboot that. He pretended as if he'd forgotten to mention it, but even without Uncle Farlane telling me before he died, I kenned every laird pays for the land. I brought the amount he told me, but now I believe it is far too little."

"It's far, *far* too little, Hardi. The levy is two shillings per hide." Blair's stomach clenched. The Camerons didn't possess the largest clan territory, but it was sizable. A hide was roughly equivalent to a hundred and twenty acres. The amount Hardi brought would barely scratch the surface of what the king expected.

"We have five hundred hides of land," Hardi explained.

"That's a thousand shillings. Give me a moment," Blair murmured as she began writing numbers as she tried to determine the geld the king expected the Camerons to pay. "That's fifty pounds when I take a thousand shillings and put them in groups of twenty again."

"That's an outrageous amount!" Hardi straightened. "That isnae even close to what Faolán told me."

"Ye have the right amount for the *cáin* but only a small portion of what's required for the geld. Did ye bring any of the grain or wool with ye that ye could give for the thirlage?"

"Nay. I suggested we use our excess to pay the fees, but the council refused. They feared we'd nae have enough for winter if we gave it away."

"It isnae giving it away. It's keeping the king from taking it and yer land from ye." Blair seethed at how men Hardi should have been able to trust and rely upon had played him for a fool. "Hardi, does Faolán want to be laird? Is that why he's done this to ye?"

"He does."

"Nay wonder yer uncle told ye nae to trust everyone on the council. He's done this to anger the king and put yer head in the noose. Can yer clan afford the amounts owed and Faolán is keeping it from the king? Or are the amounts too steep?"

"Ma uncle said we were prospering. He never hinted that we couldnae afford to pay what's expected. I just didna ken there were so many kinds of taxes. How do ye ken?" Hardi felt like he was being carried out to sea, and solid land grew further from view with each breath.

"A chatelaine must keep an inventory of how much grain and wool the clan produces and uses. She keeps track of the number of cows and sheep butchered nae only to ensure the clan has enough food to last the winter, but to give that information to the laird when he keeps track of the clan's accounts. It's something ma mother trained me to do."

Hardi ran the pad of his thumb between her brows, smoothing the deep crevices. "Dinna frown. It'll give ye wrinkles."

"Explains why ye look so auld," Blair smirked, but Hardi's gentle touch eased some tension from her forehead. "Who is yer chatelaine? Is yer aunt still alive?"

"I dinna have one. Ma aunt died just after Angus. Uncle Farlane didna replace ma aunt with a seneschal. He kept the ledgers until he died," Hardi explained ruefully.

"Ye need to meet with the king as soon as he will grant ye an audience. If he thinks ye've been here, enjoying his hospitality when ye canna afford yer levies, he'll be furious. Hardi, ye must tell him the truth aboot Faolán. Dinna try to save face or protect yer clan's image. That pride will get ye nay where, and yer people will be the ones to suffer."

"Would ye go with me?" Hardi's voice was barely above a whisper, and Blair understood what it cost him to admit he needed her help and that he feared appearing before King Robert.

"Would ye be angry if I told ye I already planned to?"

"Neither angry nor surprised," Hardi's lips twitched before he smiled. "Thank ye, Blair. I thought I would only ask ye to teach me ma letters and numbers. I dinna plan to embroil ye in ma financial woes."

"If I can help, why wouldnae I?" Blair asked as if Hardi were a simpleton.

"Because it's nae yer problem nor yer duty."

"It is since we're friends. I wouldnae leave ye out in a blizzard if I could offer ye a warm hearth. I wouldnae leave ye to face a pack of wolves if I had a sword. So why would I leave ye alone to survive this?" Blair's piercing gaze drilled into Hardi's, and her matter-of-fact tone made him realize she couldn't fathom not helping him.

"Thank ye, lass."

Blair glanced at the window embrasure, and the slight shadow the sun cast upon the floor. It was far later than she realized. "We've missed the nooning, and it must be only an hour or two before the evening meal. We should attempt an audience with the king before it grows too late."

"It is too late. I must get in line in the morn."

"It's nae too late if I'm going with ye." Blair shot him a pointed look as she rose from her seat and collected the writing utensils. Hardi opened his sporran and offered to carry them before they quit the chamber. She pulled aside four folded sheets of vellum and tucked them inside her arisaid. It was chilly that morning, so she'd worn her plaid when she walked in the gardens. She hadn't bothered to take it off when she stopped in her chamber for the parchment, quill, and ink. Now she was grateful she could tuck the missives into the folds of her plaid. "These dinna need sharing unless we must."

NINE

Blair and Hardi stood before the Chamberlain of the Privy Council as the smug man looked down his hawkish nose at Blair. "The king is no longer accepting petitioners."

"Wonderful," Blair's grin was as patronizing as the man's tone, but she kept her voice low. "Then he shall have time for family. Tell the king his god-daughter wishes to speak with him."

The chamberlain drew in a deep breath, his chest puffing out as he prepared to refuse Blair. She inched closer until only the chamberlain, Hardi, and the guards at the door could hear her whisper. "Who will he believe? His lady-goddaughter, who he used to bounce on his knee, or a puffed-up popinjay drunk on his dreams of grandeur?"

The man scowled but nodded to the guards. The three men stepped out of Blair and Hardi's way, and Blair entered without waiting to be announced. She'd never been so brazen in her life, nor had she ever taken advantage of her royal connection, but she was too afraid of what might happen to Hardi if she allowed the chamberlain to turn them away.

"Lady Blair," King Robert intoned. "I did not expect a visit from you."

Blair could tell the king was less than enthused to see her, but she dipped into a low curtsy, balancing until he signaled for her to rise. She sensed more than saw Hardi bend into a low bow. When she rose, she caught the king's speculative gaze pass over her and Hardi. King Robert's eyes narrowed slightly before he raised his chin and an imperious eyebrow. Blair bit her tongue to keep from speaking before she was asked to. She wanted to run to her godfather's side and lay bare all that she'd learned and ask his advice much as she had as a child when he and Queen Elizabeth visited. She would tell him how her older siblings never waited for her shorter legs to keep up when they went swimming, or how she wasn't tall enough to snag apple tarts from the tables in the kitchens and Lachlan would eat all of his and then half of hers before she enjoyed one. He would lift her high in the air to sit on his shoulder and tell her to survey the land as if it were her own kingdom. Then he would offer her sneaky solutions he swore he used against his own brothers when he was a lad.

She was too old to giggle and climb into the king's lap, but she trusted him to hear her out and to be fair. She held her breath and waited for him to invite her to speak. She glanced around the Council chamber and wished it weren't full. She didn't want the Camerons' clan finances to become fodder for court gossip. King Robert noticed how her eyes darted from one person to another and ordered all but his personal guard and scribe to leave. Blair pressed her lips together to keep from laughing when the order forced the chamberlain to exit along with everyone else.

"Blair, why have you dragged Laird Cameron here?" King Robert asked. It was the first time Blair heard Hardi addressed by his title in such a formal setting, and it was incongruous with the humble man who'd sat beside her and listened as she explained matters most women knew nothing about. She realized she hadn't noticed when others called him his new title.

"Your Majesty, may we approach?" Blair asked softly. When the king nodded, Blair and Hardi walked to the table where King Robert sat with maps and parchments strewn before him. Hardi pulled out a chair for Blair and waited until she sat before he took his own. Blair offered him a slight smile before looking at King Robert. "Your Majesty, I've come to speak to you as my sovereign about a matter that concerns Clan Cameron." Blair swallowed as she glanced once more at Hardi. "But I've also come to ask your advice as my Uncle Robert."

"Blair," King Robert warned.

"I know, Your Majesty. But I don't know what else to do," Blair admitted. "I don't like putting you in such a position, but neither is it an easy position for me. I would seek your council as a mon I respect and trust, but it's aboot a matter that concerns you as king."

King Robert sat back in his chair and steepled his fingers. He gazed at Blair, the young lady-in-waiting who sat before him, but he saw the little girl who had once trailed after him with a never-ending stream of questions. He doted on all of his godchildren, but Blair was the youngest and held a special place in his heart. He'd struggled not to insist that Queen Elizabeth intervene when they noticed the ladies bullying Maude, but he'd reassured himself that Maude and Blair had one another. Now Blair was alone at court and had never asked a single favor in the time since she arrived. He understood the situation must be dire if she were sitting before him. He shifted his gaze to Hardi. The inexperienced man's bearing impressed him, but he knew Hardi must have been struggling with all that had been thrust upon him. He suspected he knew what brought the pair to see him, and he admitted to himself that he felt sympathetic to Hardi.

"What brings you here, Lady Blair, Laird Cameron?" King Robert finally asked.

Blair looked at Hardi and dipped her chin in a tiny nod of encouragement. She wished she could take his hand in hers and offer him the little courage she had to spare. Hardi darted his eyes to her before addressing the king.

"I am here to answer yer call to appear at court, Yer Majesty, and to pay ma clan's taxes. I ken I should have waited for yer summons to appear in this chamber, but Lady Blair has brought several pressing matters to ma attention. It seemed prudent to request an audience sooner rather than later." Hardi met King Robert's eye and refused to look away. He knew he faced certain humiliation in only a matter of moments, but he would do so without cowering.

"And what are these matters, Laird Cameron?"

Hardi inhaled deeply. "I canna read nor write, Yer Majesty, so I relied upon ma uncle, and then other council members, to share the contents of various missives, including the one ye sent. This reliance has nae served me well. With Lady Blair's help, she has made me aware that the amounts I arrived with to pay ma clan's taxes are woefully insufficient."

"Does your clan not have the funds with which to pay what it owes the crown?" King Robert watched the pair before him, but waited for Hardi to answer.

"We have the funds, Yer Majesty. However, I dinna have the skills to read the ledgers nor the skills to do the sums to ken what we owed. I didna ken there were more types of taxes than ma council told me."

"And now you do?"

"Aye, now I do. Lady Blair explained the levies on production, nae just on trade, and she computed what I owe. It's far more than what I brought with me."

"Why did your clan council not provide you with the correct information? Why did they not prepare you?" King Robert drilled Hardi.

"Because nay one expected me to become laird, Yer Majesty. And there are several older members of the council who believe they are better suited to the position. I'd have agreed with them until now. Nay mon who's willing to jeopardize his entire clan to make a fool of one member should ever hold such responsibility or power."

"Let me guess, Laird Cameron. Faolán lied." King Robert detested the man and had often questioned Farlane Cameron about why he allowed his own duplicitous cousin to remain on the clan council. But he'd understood and accepted that Farlane kept his enemy close, so the man was never out of laird's sight. Robert was furious to learn that Farlane died without warning Hardi.

"He did, Yer Majesty. Ma uncle said there were a few members of the council I shouldnae trust, but he didna tell me who before he died. His cousins, Faolán and Drostan, are the only members of the council who can read. I had to rely upon them to tell me what yer missive said and to prepare our payment."

"Is Drostan as bad as Faolán, or is he just weak?" King Robert demanded.

"I believe that he's weak, and that makes him just as bad as his brother. Based on Faolán's instructions, I arrived with enough coin to pay our *cáin* and a small portion of the geld. Lady Blair explained that I must pay a thirlage on our grain, whisky, and cattle, and she tallied how much I owe on the land. She did the sums for the other taxes but didna discuss them when she realized I canna pay the ones I kenned aboot. She suggested I seek yer council, Yer Majesty."

"You brought only coin? Did you not bring any sacks of grain or barrels of whisky? Clans may pay in kind," the Bruce pointed out.

"I kenned that and suggested it to the clan council. They sided with Faolán and insisted we shouldnae risk giving up our grain in case we need it over the winter. They assured me I had what I needed."

"And if Lady Blair hadn't helped you?" King Robert kept his eyes on Blair, wondering how she'd been drawn into this mess. He'd seen her seated with her brother and Lachlan for several meals and watched the pair dance each evening, but it surprised him to see Hardi seeking a woman's help.

"I'd be in debtors' prison before the end of the sennight. I'd hoped Lachlan might teach me ma letters and numbers before he returned home, but there wasna time. Lady Blair agreed to assist me, so I asked her to read the missives I brought," Hardi explained.

"Lady Blair, what are the tallies?" King Robert shifted his focus back to Blair, who was prepared to answer. She glanced at Hardi's sporran, so he retrieved the parchment on which she'd done her computations.

"Your Majesty, Laird Cameron has what he owes for the wool, which is forty-six pounds, one merk. He has just over a fifth of what he owes for the geld. Faolán told him it was six pounds, thirteen shillings, four doyt. The Camerons' geld is actually fifty pounds. I calculated the thirlage on the grain to be thirty-five pounds, four shillings. The levy on whisky comes to twenty-seven pounds even." Blair looked at King Robert, then Hardi. "I would pay that in barrels, not in coin, Laird. The same for the grain. If the king will allow it."

King Robert observed the youthful woman advise the inexperienced laird, and he saw not only kindness toward a friend but also the wisdom that passed from a tutor to tutee. He nodded his agreement that he would accept payment in kind for the whisky and grain.

"The Camerons' cattle are worth more to them than to the crown," Blair asserted. "They owe sixty pounds, two shillings, five doyt for the heads they own. With a geld balance of forty-three pounds, six shillings, eight doyt and the cattle levy, the final sum they need in coin is one hundred and three pounds, nine shillings." Blair cringed as she said the final amount. That was more than some clans earned in a decade, let alone what they owed in a year. She prayed the Camerons really had the funds to pay for the levy. She didn't doubt that Hardi's uncle spoke the truth about the clan prospering; however, she feared Faolán and the clan council might have squandered the revenue.

"Yer Majesty, I ken ma clan has those funds. Or at least they did before ma uncle passed away," Hardi spoke up. His caveat echoed Blair's thoughts.

"Very well. Since Lady Blair has taken up your banner, I shall extend the time in which you may pay. You will need to return home before you appear before me again." King Robert nodded, and both Blair and Hardwin prepared to leave. They froze at the king's next comment. "Since you haven't brought it up, I take it no one read to you the part of my missive that informed you that since David can no longer fulfill the role of groom, there is your betrothal to settle."

Blair couldn't catch her breath. She didn't understand why the news came a shock, or why she reacted

73

so strongly when she'd skipped that part of the king's missive. But the thought of Hardi leaving court to marry a faceless bride suddenly made her chest ache. She gripped her skirts in her lap as she waited for the king to speak. She slid her eyes to Hardi to see if he welcomed the news of an impending marriage, but he appeared to be a light shade of green. She caught herself as she lifted her hand to comfort him, knotting her fingers together instead.

"Marriage, Yer Majesty?" Hardi croaked before clearing his throat. "I'm nae certain this is the time to bring a bride to a clan with unresolved matters."

"It's the perfect time to use a dowry to pay what you owe," King Robert countered.

"Nay. Clan Cameron can pay its taxes, and I willna buy a wife to pay off a debt. I amnae opposed to marrying, but I willna use a woman like that. Ma wife will lead Clan Cameron at ma side. I dinna want to take a bride for her money only to realize that she canna be a proper Lady Cameron. I'm sorry, Yer Majesty, but I willna be pushed into wedding a woman I dinna ken and who may nae be what's best for ma people."

Blair held her breath at the brittle tone in Hardi's voice. She wasn't certain she could protect him if the king lashed out for his impertinence. She looked back and forth between the two men, her anxiety growing as they stared one another down. She knew Hardi wouldn't capitulate, and she feared he'd spend at least one night in the dungeon for it.

"Very well. You may remain here a fortnight, though a moon would likely suit you better, during which Lady Blair shall tutor you. Then you will return to Tor Castle, where you will get your clan council under control before bringing back what you owe. We will discuss your wedding then. Lady Blair, the queen will be made aware of your absence."

"Yes, Your Majesty."

"Aye, Yer Majesty."

"You may go," King Robert dismissed them. Blair and Hardi hurried to gather the documents the king never reviewed and pushed back their chairs. When they had nearly reached the Council chamber's doors, King Robert called out, "Lady Blair, a moment, if you will."

Blair's eyes flicked toward Hardi, and she saw his worry as she turned toward the king. She walked back to the table at which the monarch still sat. He motioned for her to step around the table and come to his side. When she approached, the king reached into a sack that sat on the table near his left hand. He withdrew a honeyed penyde from it and held it out to Blair. They were the same ones he and Queen Elizabeth would give to the Sutherland and Sinclair siblings when they were children. Blair's soft chuckle made King Robert's lips twitch as she held out her hand. He dropped the candy in her palm, wrapping his larger hand over hers when she enclosed it in her fist.

"He needs you more than either of you realize, Blair. I admire that he isn't too proud to ask, but he isn't aware of just how much he must learn. And you haven't much time to teach him. He must return to Tor Castle, and there is a betrothal looming. He won't be able to put that off forever. I tell you this not as your king, but as a concerned uncle who sees that the little girl he once knew is now a loyal and resolute friend to a young mon very much out of his depth. Do what you can, Blair."

"I will, Uncle Robert," Blair whispered, and without thought, she bent down and wrapped her arms around the king's neck. "Thank you. For everything." She dropped a quick kiss on his bristly cheek before stepping away.

"You're a good lass. Your parents are proud of you, just as the queen and I are." The king patted her arm. Blair dipped a curtsy and hurried back to Hardi's side as he pushed open the door to the Privy Council chamber.

TEN

Hardi wanted to be ill. He'd struggled throughout the meeting with the Bruce, anxiously sitting before a sovereign who could sentence him to death and strip away all of his clan's wealth and land. The weight of his duty had never felt so heavy. He'd been in the king's presence many times as a delegate for Clan Cameron, but he'd never been the representative who spoke before the sovereign. He'd been trying to hide his nervousness, but his temper flared when the king suggested he become betrothed soon. He knew the woman David had been set to marry, Una Macquarie, and while he wasn't fond of her, he'd already expected having to take on the betrothal. However, he'd wanted to run for the hills when the king mentioned it. For some reason, it was the most unpalatable thing he could imagine. He wasn't prepared to marry anyone while amid his grief and his transition into leading his clan. He refused to even think about Laird Donald's inquiry about David marrying his daughter and what that would mean for him.

As he sat beside Blair and listened to her advocate on his behalf, he couldn't keep himself from thinking about how much better suited Blair would be as Lady Cameron than Una. The two women were close in age, but Blair carried an innate ability to command respect while Una demanded it by being a harridan. The latter had a reputation for demanding her father bedeck her in lavish clothing, despite being part of a clan branch that possessed only the small island of Ulva. It had surprised him to learn that his uncle considered a Macquarie--and not one from the senior branch on the Isle of Mull--rather than the Donald lass. David had appeared more excited to have the blacksmith pull a tooth than accept Una. Hardi had been more philosophical in his acceptance, knowing there was little he could do, but he wasn't willing to rush into the arrangement either.

Now, as he and Blair entered the passageway, he was keenly aware of the grace with which she handled what was an embarrassing situation for him. She'd silently reassured him when he worried he would have tripped over his tongue several times. He wished he could whisk Blair home with him, hand over all the ledgers, and run away to the lists. As his mind continued to wander, Blair caught him off-guard when she clasped his hand and pulled him into an alcove, a tapestry providing them privacy. He looked down into Blair's beaming eyes and was struck by the umber hue that seemed to shimmer in the scant light that filtered past the tapestry. They shone brighter than the whisky color they'd been in the music room.

"We survived!" Blair bubbled as she squeezed Hardi's hand and bounced onto her toes to kiss his cheek. His arms came around her, but they froze as they stared at one another. As if each grain of sand in an hourglass took twice its normal time to drop, their mouths drifted together. They watched one another until their lips pressed, and their eyes slipped closed. The kiss was unhurried as Blair's hands slid along Hardi's chest, his muscles twitching beneath her touch, until her arms wrapped around his neck. His tongue pressed against the seal of her lips. She gasped with surprise, but even without personal experience, she knew what he wanted. She opened to him tentatively until she felt his tongue swipe across the satiny recesses of her mouth. She moaned softly as she melted against him.

Hardi was certain his heart would explode from its rapid staccato. His ears rung as the kiss continued, his breathing echoing within them. He didn't dare move anything but his mouth, lest he break the spell. Before returning home from fostering, he'd wondered more than once what it would have been like to steal a kiss from Blair Sutherland, but he'd never acted upon it, and the curiosity had slipped away after he returned to Tor Castle. Ever since reuniting, he'd been aware of her attractiveness, but he hadn't thought—no, hadn't considered—acting upon it. Her beauty, inside and out, was too great to ignore, and she was even more appealing to him than she had been when he was six-and-ten. But he hadn't dared imagine doing more than appreciating it from a distance. Now she was wrapped in his arms, and he wasn't certain he could ever let go. It was only when they were both breathless that they pulled apart.

With their arms still around one another, Blair and Hardi gazed into one another's eyes. Passion glazed, the sparks of attraction remained, but neither acted upon it. They eased apart, unwilling to address what had happened but not in a hurry for it to end. Once they were no longer touching, they both remembered to breathe again.

"Thank—" Hardi began.

"That wen—" Blair spoke at the same time. Their laughter eased any awkwardness before it could develop. Blair tucked hair behind her ear before trying again. "That went well."

"Better than I imagined. Thank ye." Hardi dropped into a bow, and Blair used the opportunity to tousle his hair.

"None of that. We need to figure out when and where we can meet for your lessons. When will ye finish in the lists? Midday?"

"I willna be going. Aye, a fortnight or even a moon is too long to be away from training, but it isnae nearly long enough for ye to teach me what took ye years to learn."

"Willna people ask where ye are? Ye said the MacMillans are here. Surely, Henry will notice if ye're nae in the lists. He'll want to ken why."

"Henry MacMillan can bluidy well keep his neb out of ma business," Hardi grumbled.

"But he willna," Blair countered. "Wouldnae it be better if ye made an appearance each day, even if it's only a brief one?"

"Nay. That'll just make people ask where I'm going," Hardi replied. "It's best if I remain out of sight, out of mind."

"Then we'll meet at least in the morning, and if we can, in the afternoon, too. That leaves where. Voices carry in that music room if ye're nae careful, and it's too easy for someone to notice one or both of us slipping in and out."

"Must we stay here? I mean in the castle."

"I canna go to a tavern with ye!" Blair screeched.

"I didna mean that." Hardi chortled.

"Where else in town can we sit with books and parchment before us?"

"We dinna go into town. Yer guards can accompany us, and we'll ride out somewhere. The weather is warm enough during the day, and if nae, I'll either pack an extra plaid, or we'll make do with missing a day."

Blair considered what Hardi suggested and recognized it was the best option. She didn't want to imagine what the other ladies-in-waiting would conjure as an explanation for her absence, but she trusted Queen Elizabeth to devise an excuse. She wondered if the queen would say she was ill. It would excuse her from the noise and heat of the evening meal. It would also make it possible for Blair to avoid unwanted questions, but she suspected she wouldn't be so lucky.

"We can begin tomorrow morn after we break our fast. I must return to ma chamber now to prepare for the evening meal, or I will be late. I pray King Robert explains the situation soon to Queen Elizabeth, so she might have a story in place. As curious as Henry might be, he will be naught compared to the other ladies."

Hardi nodded and drew back the corner of the tapestry. He looked in both directions, slowly counting to twenty each time before he stepped into the passageway. He blocked Blair's way until he counted to twenty once more. Without looking back, he moved in the bachelor quarters' direction, and Blair slipped out soon after, winding her way to her chamber.

ELEVEN

"Little Blair Sutherland has grown into a lush berry waiting to be picked," Henry MacMillan sniggered. "Perhaps I'll steal a taste and learn how sweet her juices are."

The MacMillans seated with the Camerons roared, but the Camerons glared at them. Hardi struggled to keep his expression neutral when he wanted to bash Henry's face in. His guards knew how he felt about disrespectful comments made about women, and they were all aware that Hardi and Blair grew up together. Even if Hardi hadn't tasted Blair's kisses that afternoon, he wouldn't have appreciated Henry's ribald comments. In the space of a breath, Blair went from still seeming much like a younger sister to a woman Hardi wanted. But neither of them had addressed the kiss, pretending as though it hadn't happened. He would follow Blair's lead. He wouldn't make any advances, and he prayed it wouldn't be uncomfortable when they were once again in each other's company. He caught glimpses of her from the corner of his eye, but his back was to her.

"I wouldnae speak that way again unless ye care to lose yer tongue," Hardi warned.

"Staking a claim? I thought she was but your wee little sister," Henry countered.

"And ye would say such things aboot a lady in front of her brother?" Hardi put down his mug of ale and straightened. They were of a similar height, but Hardi outweighed Henry by at least two stones of muscle. "Did ye notice the MacLeods at yon table? They're from Lewis. I dinna think ye want Kieran MacLeod to hear how ye speak aboot his sister-by-marriage. It would upset Lady MacLeod to hear someone speak so crassly aboot her sister, and there isnae aught Kieran wouldnae do to keep Lady Maude happy."

"Aye. We saw how he chased her like she was a bitch in heat," Henry's younger brother Daniel said as he made an obscene gesture. "He'd do aught to keep dipping his wick in that wax."

Hardi struggled to hide his disgust, but he could tell his guards were just as angered by the MacMillans as he was. As the servants cleared away the remnants of the meal, Hardi tried to devise an excuse for his men and him to retire. As the musicians began tuning their instruments, Hardi watched Henry adjust his groin while he stared over Hardi's shoulder. Hardi knew exactly on whom Henry set his sights. Without a word, Hardi rose and walked to Blair's table.

"Lady Blair, may I request the first dance with ye?" Hardi asked softly, but all the women froze when he approached, making his voice the only sound at the table.

"I would enjoy that, Laird Cameron," Blair grinned. She glanced at the other ladies, her grin widening. "It's like having my brother back at court." To Blair's mind, after the kiss they shared, it was the extreme opposite of having Lachlan at court, but she'd sworn over and over that she and Hardi were nothing more than friends.

"Dinna let Henry partner with ye, lass," Hardi whispered in her ear as they moved into the line of dancers. They stepped into their spots and waited for the music to begin. As they came together, Blair's fingers rested in Hardi's palm. She was certain the heat scorched her fingertips, and his hand tingled where her fingers grazed his skin. "I dinna care for the comments he made. I dinna trust him nay to do something ye dinna agree to."

"Thank you for the warning," Blair nodded. They separated and turned to their other partner, moving through several steps before returning to one another. "He makes my skin crawl."

"Mine, too," Hardi chortled.

"But it's not your skin he's trying to crawl into," Blair reminded him.

"Aye." Hardi glanced around the Great Hall and noticed more than one set of male eyes on Blair. "Do ye still carry a blade on ye? Nae yer eating knife but a proper dirk?"

"Always. Papa insists upon it."

"And ye remember what Lachlan and I taught ye?" Hardi persisted.

"Aye. Maude and I practiced while she was still here." Blair blushed as she glanced toward Arabella, who danced three couples down from them. "I taught Arabella when we became roommates, so I would have someone to practice against. And there may or may not be a hundred or so nicks in the walls of the two chambers I've occupied from where I practiced throwing them." Her lips twitched, her unrepentance obvious.

"Good, lass," Hardi smiled. He let the matter drop, and they remained quiet for the last strains of music. Another man asked Blair to partner with him before Hardi let go of her hands. She accepted without looking back, and she left Hardi wondering if he'd imagined the kiss they shared. Blair appeared utterly unchanged by it, whereas he'd felt the world shift when she stepped into his arms for the dance.

"Lachlan asked me before he left to be sure you weren't left without a partner too often." Hardi looked down to find Arabella Johnstone's perfectly sculpted face staring up at him. He agreed that she was the most beautiful woman in the Great Hall, but her features were a little too perfect for Hardi's taste. He glanced over her head to where Blair's partner was already moving her through the steps of the country reel. He found he much preferred Blair's deep chestnut hair and eyes to Arabella's auburn hair and green eyes. He glanced down and nodded. As they moved into the dancers swirling about the floor, he chatted with Arabella, but after the dance ended, he couldn't recall what they discussed. He found it was that way with each of the ladies he partnered with.

Several widows and matrons made their appreciation of his physique apparent by the looks they cast him and how they attempted to press their bodies against his, but he wasn't interested in a tumble with any of them. Once upon a time, before his life fell apart, he would have gladly accepted one or all of their offers, but now none appealed. He knew it wasn't just the kiss with Blair that left him unenthusiastic. In fact, kissing Blair was the first time in months his body had stirred at the chance to be intimate. He hadn't been able to drum up an interest in bed sport when he couldn't set aside the misery of losing so many family members he'd cared deeply for. He hadn't always agreed with his cousins or his brother, but the six young men had grown close since he and Dougal returned to Tor Castle just after Angus returned from his fostering.

"Hardi?" Blair's voice broke through his haze. He straightened against the wall he leaned against and accepted the mug of ale she offered. "You seemed very far away."

"I was," Hardi conceded.

"I canna imagine how ye must miss them," Blair abandoned her courtly speech, disliking its pretentious sound when speaking to Hardi about his grief.

"I didna ken a heart could ache so much without actually breaking," Hardi admitted. "One moment I'm fine, and the next, the weight of sadness on ma chest makes it feel as though I canna draw another breath."

"Ye dinna have to stay in here," Blair shifted closer. "Nay one will notice if ye retire for the night. Ye dinna look comfortable here."

"I'm nae. I keep thinking the music and dancing will distract me. But each eve it's the same. I feel as though I'm watching through a window rather than being a part of what's happening around me."

"Go to bed, Hardi. Ye look exhausted." Blair squeezed his forearm, the wall and her body blocking anyone from seeing the sympathetic gesture. "Meet me in the bailey after ye break yer fast."

"I think I will." Hardi handed his empty mug to Blair, offering her a smile that didn't reach his eyes before turning toward the door. Blair watched him go before handing over the mugs to a passing servant. She spent the rest of the night dancing, but her mind kept straying. She wished she knew how to bring back some of the light and happiness she'd once seen in Hardi's hazel eyes.

TWELVE

H ardi and his guards were already in the bailey with their horses when the Sutherland guards entered with Blair between them. She introduced them as Donald and Tomas. He noticed both guards carried large baskets, while she had a satchel over her shoulder. He cocked an eyebrow as she drew near, but he smelled the scent of freshly baked loaves and understood she'd had a picnic packed for them. By the size of the baskets and how the two men hefted them, he suspected she'd ordered enough food to feed a small army rather than the eight people present. As she came to stand before him, stable boys led the horses to the Sutherland guards.

"Good morn," Blair offered as she turned to hook her satchel onto her saddle. "I wasn't sure how long you could be gone, but I didn't want hunger to be what brought us back early."

"And so ye packed enough food should we decide to ride all the way back to Dunrobin," Hardi teased.

"I've seen ye eat. Dinna pretend like ye plan to share." Blair squealed as Hardi wrapped his hands around her waist and hoisted her into the saddle. She was unprepared, and felt like she was soaring through the air even though it was only a few feet.

"What's to share when all ye leave me are scraps?" Hardi smirked.

"If ye're so feeble from hunger, ye had best pray ye can keep up." Blair spurred her horse and led the party toward the postern gate. Once she cleared the portal, she urged her horse into a gallop, taking a low wall without a second thought. She pushed her gelding to stay in the lead despite sensing the stallions trying to draw even. Her horse was as competitive as she and disliked having to ride anywhere but the front of the pack. He'd received more than one angry hoof toward his barrel chest when he was a colt when he nipped and tried to push his way forward. Blair's father, Hamish, had threatened to take the horse from her if she couldn't control him. Hamish had feared she'd be injured because of her horse's bad temper, even though he was more like a lamb when she handled him. Blair led them to the ridge where she and Lachlan had first spotted the Cameron party arriving. When she reached the crest, the other horses were neck-and-neck with her mount's rump.

"I'm fairly certain yer da doesnae approve of ye taking jumps like that," Hardi mused.

"Dinna be a sore loser because ma horse is braver than yers," Blair quipped. It was a ridiculous statement since it was clear Hardi's horse was a battled-tested warhorse. But Blair leaned over and patted her horse's neck, playfully whispering, "We canna win next time, *Buannaiche*. It makes them feel bad."

Hardi growled, and several of the men, both Camerons and Sutherlands, grumbled as Blair hooted with laughter. "I didna name ma horse Winner for naught." Blair swung down from the saddle and led her animal to a patch of tall grass. She pulled a handful loose and rubbed it over the horse's neck and flanks before hobbling him. She left him to nibble after lifting the satchel from the saddle. She wasn't sure what to say to the guards since she didn't think about how they would entertain themselves, but they'd already broken into pairs and were drawing their swords to practice. A Cameron and a Sutherland stood facing away from the group on either side, on watch.

Hardi lifted the satchel, which was heavier than he expected, from Blair's shoulder. He walked beside Blair to a clearing where she spread out a plaid. Once they settled, she opened the bag and withdrew three books. Hardi already felt intimidated by their size. He trusted Blair, but he had no wish to make a fool of himself. He hadn't had to do much besides listen the day before. Now she would expect him to read.

"Hardi?" Blair kept her voice low. "Do ye ken any of the letters?"

Hardi wasn't sure if it was the situation itself or Blair's soothing tone that put him on edge. He'd never been ashamed of not knowing how to read or write because he'd never been in a situation where the skills were needed; there was always someone of consequence who possessed them. He'd never felt so lacking in his life.

"Some," Hardi answered, but he couldn't bring himself to look Blair in the eye.

Blair set aside the book she held and inched closer to Hardi. "We willna get anywhere if ye're embarrassed around me. I dinna think less of ye because ye dinna ken. I think less of yer father for refusing to accept ma father's offer for ye and Dougal to learn. It was shortsighted and filled with useless pride. I doubt anyone gave ye another opportunity, so I dinna think ye canna read or write because ye squandered the chance."

Blair looked across the meadow as she collected her thoughts. She attempted to bury her frustration because it wasn't directed at Hardi. It was simmering anger toward the people in Hardi's life who let him down over the years.

"I think ye've spent yer life serving yer clan on the battlefield and on patrol," Blair went on. "I'm guessing ye have plowed and reaped acres of fields and built leagues of walls, thatched countless roofs, and ensured the welfare of yer people well before ye became laird. Ye arenae lazy or useless. Ye just dinna ken how to do something that I do. I dinna ken how to build a wall or thatch a roof. Do ye think less of me for it?"

"Nay. Ye ken I dinna."

"Will ye teach me if I teach ye?" Blair asked.

"I dinna follow."

"Will ye teach me aboot building walls and thatching roofs? What aboot kenning what to plant and which fields to leave fallow? What if I marry a useless mon who doesnae ken these things? What if he's a laird who dies before our son can lead? I would need to ken at least a little aboot these things. I will teach ye to read and write, and ye can teach me aboot how to care for the clan outside of a keep."

"I never thought aboot those being skills anyone would think to ask to learn. Either ye're taught them or ye arenae," Hardi admitted.

"That's the point, Hardi. Either ye're taught to read and write or ye arenae. Did ye think to have Angus teach ye? Mayhap, but it's clear it didna happen. But those other skills are ones a laird uses all the time. Ye already ken them. I dinna think ye realize how prepared ye already are to be laird."

"Ye really think that?" Hardi hated the uncertainty and neediness he heard in his voice. It sounded pathetic to his own ears, as if he was begging for validation.

"Hardi, there's more to being a good laird than any of those things I mentioned. A good laird is patient, forgiving, compassionate, fair, focused, driven, compromising, and more than aught, devoted to his clan. Ye are all of those. Ma da wasna meant to be a laird. He was the third son and never imagined his father and two older brothers would die in battle right before his eyes. He didna ken what he was doing. He was so lost and overwhelmed, that he rode to the Sinclairs as soon as the battle was over to ask ma Aunt Kyla for help. He arrived on her wedding day of all times. Aunt Kyla and Uncle Liam agreed to come back to Dunrobin with him for nearly a moon while he sorted out the mess his father and brothers left behind. Aunt Kyla got the keep back in order, but it was Uncle Liam who taught Da how to carry out the duties of a laird. I mean, Da kenned them, but he'd never had them placed on his shoulder and he wasna trained for them. Uncle Liam had been. Lachlan isnae here to help ye the way Uncle Liam helped Da, but I can do a wee bit."

Hardi took in the earnestness in Blair's eyes and her tone. She was pleading with him to let her help, and he would be a fool not to accept what she offered. He'd never considered himself a prideful man, having seen where that got the other men in his family. He wouldn't become one because it was a woman and a friend offering him help. He couldn't ignore the beautiful face staring up at him, waiting for his answer.

But he didn't understand how his emotions suddenly vacillated between seeing her as the spindly young girl who would race him up apple trees and lob the fruit at him when he wasn't fast enough to seeing her as one of the most desirable women he'd ever laid eyes on. One moment she was still much like a younger sister, and the next he wanted to steal more kisses. Hardi forced himself to stop thinking about what he wanted—especially since he didn't even know what that was—and start thinking about what was best for his clan.

She's what's best for the clan. A nagging voice kept echoing in his head. *She's who's best for ye. Nae that horrid Una Macquarie. Nae any other woman. But I amnae what's best for her. She deserves to marry a mon, a laird, who isnae little more than an ignorant warrior.*

Hardi nodded his head, and Blair picked up the book she'd put down. She opened it to the middle and rested a cover on each of their thighs, making it easy for them both to see. Hardi looked at the jumble of shapes and marks, not understanding any of it.

"I dinna expect ye to read this by the nooning, Hardi," Blair reassured. "I just want to ken if there are any letters ye recognize."

Hardi stared at the pages, certain he knew nothing and that he was bound to fail, but as he swept his eyes over the letters before him, he remembered some of them. "I can find the ones that spell ma name." He pointed to an "h", an "a," an "n," a "d," an "r," and an "i," but he didn't recognize a "w." He lowered his eyes, his excitement fizzling.

"There isnae one, Hardi. There's nae a "w" on this page. Ye did vera well."

"Ye were the one who insisted I at least learn to read and write ma own name." Hardi looked back at the page and pointed to each letter in his surname. He was proud of himself, and much of the dread slipped away.

"Do ye recall what order the letters go in?" Blair tilted her head to see his face since he'd lowered it to look at the book.

"Aye," Hardi nodded. He pointed to each letter, but he forced himself to find ones that weren't the original ones he'd picked out.

"Excellent. Do ye ken the sounds they make? I mean if ye think aboot how yer name sounds, do ye ken which one is which?"

"Aye. 'H' is the *h-h* at the beginning." Hardi repeated the sound twice. "'A' is the *arr* sound." Hardi stopped when Blair shook her head.

"Nae quite. In yer Christian name, the 'a' doesnae follow the regular rules. It does in yer clan name. C-ahh-meron." Blair sounded out. "Because there is an 'r' next to the 'a', the 'r' sound is stronger. H-arr-dwin. Besides that sneaky 'a,' what other sounds do ye hear?"

Hardi appreciated that Blair attempted to downplay what he didn't know and acknowledge what he did. He continued. "The 'd' is *d-d* in the middle, then the 'w' is the *w-w*. The 'i' is *ih*, and the 'n' is *n-n*."

"Vera good. Are there any others ye can find?" Blair waited as Hardi scanned the rows of letters before him and slowly pointed out one letter after another until he had half of the alphabet identified. He recalled all the sounds of the letters he found. Once he could find no more, Blair asked him to recite as many in order as he could. He stumbled over a few in the middle, but they were both surprised that he only left out three.

"I didna believe I kenned any of that." Hardi's voice reflected his shock.

"Ye havenae needed to ken it in a long time, and ye werenae given the encouragement ye needed to learn. I can understand why ye thought ye dinna ken them," Blair smiled.

"It's nae just that. I didna believe I was smart enough to ken them," Hardi confessed. Blair's heart broke to see the giant of a man sitting beside her appear so unsure of himself. She'd believed as a child that he was among the bravest lads she knew. That belief had solidified as they grew older, and she hadn't questioned it since seeing him again at court. It took her aback to realize even this rugged warrior could feel self-conscious.

"Will ye walk with me for a while? We dinna need to go far. Mayhap just back and forth," Blair asked. She remained quiet until they walked out of earshot of the guards but remained within their sight. She didn't want to whisper what she had to say, as though it were some secret or source of shame she intended to keep hidden. "Hardi, I will say this once, then I willna speak it again because I dinna believe in speaking ill of the dead. But yer father was a bluidy selfish bastard who should have let his betters decide what was right for ye and Dougal, cause he clearly didna ken. I dinna ken what he said to ye aboot nae allowing ma father to have ye tutored. I only ken what I heard aboot. But he was wrong to refuse to let ye learn. Nae because now ye need it. But because he made ye doubt yerself, made ye think ye werenae smart. I would beat him to a pulp if I could. Then I would kick him."

Blair turned away, but then spun back to face Hardi. Her movement was so abrupt that her skirts twisted around her ankles. Hardi watched the anger in her eyes burst into flames where they had been sparks only minutes ago.

"Learning to read and write doesnae mean someone is smart. It means they're willing to work hard enough to learn. What makes ye smart is kenning ye canna do everything by yerself and that ye arenae a lesser mon for asking for help. What makes ye smart is being willing to learn now that ye're a mon. What makes ye smart is accepting that a woman is teaching ye and nae pretending to ken more than her or acting as though she's an eejit. Reading and writing isnae a measure of intelligence. What ye do with it is what makes ye intelligent." Blair was out of breath by the time she finished.

Hardi reached out a hand and cupped Blair's face. Her eyes drifted close as she leaned into the warmth of his palm, the callouses were rough against her skin. She covered Hardi's hand with hers, and they stood together for a long moment before she opened her eyes again. Neither moved to bring their bodies closer together, but neither moved away.

"Thank ye, Blair," Hardi whispered. He cleared his throat when his voice broke. "Ye canna ken how much yer faith in me means."

"Ye wouldnae do aught less for me. And I didna lie. I meant all of it."

"I ken ye did, and that's what makes it—ye—so special. I felt timid and uncertain when we started. Now I feel invincible. I dinna ken anyone else who's ever made me feel this way."

"That's what friends—" Blair trailed off. Whatever passed between them in the alcove was the same electrifying connection they had now, and calling it friendship seemed wholly inadequate. "That's why I want to help."

Hardi reached out his other hand and rested it on Blair's waist. When she didn't resist, he drew her closer. She fisted his leine at his waist as though clinging to his shirt would anchor her in the growing storm between them.

"Blair, there is naught I want to do more right now than kiss ye, but I canna. There are too many people watching. Standing here like this is enough to ruin yer reputation, but I canna seem to let ye go."

"I understand. I shouldnae have kissed ye yesterday. Ye're practically betrothed."

"I dinna ken who kissed who first, and I dinna

97

care. I amnae practically betrothed. I wouldnae have kissed ye if I were. There's been talk of it. I assumed I would have to take on that duty too, but I havenae negotiated any contract or signed any documents. I dinna want to think aboot another woman when I'm standing here with ye. I canna think of anyone after that kiss."

"King Robert didna sound like he would give ye much choice. It sounded like, in his mind, ye're already betrothed to the woman."

"Mayhap that's how he looks at it, but it isnae how I ever have," Hardi insisted. "The woman is nae one I wish to marry. She isnae right for ma clan, and she isnae right for me."

"Ye canna ken that unless ye ken her well," Blair whispered. She wasn't sure she wanted to hear how well acquainted Hardi was with another a woman while she stood in his embrace.

"I've met her a handful of times when her family visited ma clan and when I accompanied David to meet hers. She's spoiled and frivolous. Ye read the missives. Ma clan is in turmoil. There are threats on every side, and there's unrest within, if nae a traitor. I canna bring a woman like that into ma clan, into ma home, into ma life." Hardi gazed over Blair's head for a long moment before peering into her chocolate-colored eyes. He released his hold on Blair. "I'm nae trying to dally with ye or lead ye astray. This is nae the right time for me to consider marriage."

Blair let go of his leine, offering a soft smile before stepping back. He watched her chin notch up as she firmed her resolve. "I didna come out here to seduce ye, and I amnae looking to snare ye into marriage. We are friends and have been most of our lives. I willna give that up, so we neednae discuss this again. We had a moment—or two—and now we have cleared the air."

"Blair—" Hardi understood what she was doing, but it felt wrong to pretend as though there wasn't something between them. But he had nothing to offer. What was he supposed to do? Ask her to wait indefinitely for him to decide he was ready to play house? He couldn't do that.

"Come back to the blanket. It must be near the nooning. Ye and yer men must be hungry. After we eat, we shall work on yer numbers." Blair made to step around him, but he caught her forearm.

"I like it when ye sound like the lass I kenned." Hardi murmured. But when it was clear Blair didn't understand what he meant, he clarified. "I like it when ye dinna sound like a bluidy Scot. God intended ye to be a Highlander, and I like it better when ye sound like one."

Blair blinked several times as she considered how she'd been speaking since they left the castle. She hadn't once realized that she'd slipped back into her brogue. It felt natural to be near Hardi, and so her regular accent had taken over her speech. She smiled and nodded before leading them back to the blanket.

THIRTEEN

Blair watched as the seven men devoured the picnic she'd ordered from the castle's kitchens. She'd heard the teasing about the amount of food she'd packed, but she'd been right in her estimation. She turned to Hardi, "And ye said this looked like I was packing to ride back to Dunrobin. It's barely gotten us outside Stirling's gates."

She munched on her apple as the men finished the last of the meal and tidied up after themselves. She wondered how the men would occupy themselves during the afternoon, having finished sparring before the noon meal. She watched as they moved away from the blanket and sat together, laughing and telling stories. A Sutherland and a Cameron once again took turns on watch. As Hardi wiped crumbs from his leine, Blair watched as the shirt tugged across his arms with each movement, hinting at the defined muscles that lay beneath the fabric. She forced her mind back to planning how to introduce Hardi's first lesson on numbers.

"How high can ye count?" Blair jumped straight in.

"To at least a hundred," Hardi answered as he looked up.

"Can ye count by skipping numbers?" Blair held up her hand and pinched her first two fingers together. "Two." She pinched her last two fingers. "Four." She alternated grasping pairs of fingers as she continued to count. "Six, eight, ten, and so forth? What about by fives?" She held up one hand then the other until she'd counted to twenty, then held up both hands, raising and lowering them as she counted by tens.

"Aye, I've done that before," Hardi nodded as he picked up where she left off, counting by each increment until he reached one hundred. "I ken that a score is twenty, so when I count things like barrels of whisky and sacks of grain or wool, I keep a tally on a stick."

Hardi looked around the blanket until he found one that would work before pulling out his dirk. He cut twenty small notches, then cut a horizontal line through them. "I ken that one set of notches is twenty, two sets is forty, three sets is sixty, four sets is eighty, and five sets is one hundred. I repeat that until I've finished whatever I'm counting."

"That's excellent. Did someone teach ye that?" Blair asked quietly.

"Yer da taught me that twenty is a score, but I figured out that I couldnae remember how many times I counted to twenty unless I had a way to make marks to keep track. I found a twig one day and cut the notches to help. I've done it ever since." Hardi shrugged as he watched Blair.

"If ye ken how many notches are on yer stick, can ye figure out how many are there without recounting each one?" At Hardi's blank expression, she clarified. "Say ye have one set of twenty and then eight more ticks, do ye ken that's twenty-eight or do ye have to count the notches again, maybe starting with the score and adding the others?

"I dinna need to count them. I ken what it sums by kenning the two parts."

"Can ye do that in yer head with more than two numbers?"

"I can if they arenae too large between one and twenty. I struggle around thirteen or fourteen. I can do it from one hundred and two hundred up and so forth."

"Then ye already ken the hard part. Ye just need to learn what the numbers look like when ye need to read or write them. I can show ye how to add a column of figures, but ye understand the idea behind it. If ye already ken how much different sets of twenty are, then ye can learn that for other numbers. Three sets of four is twelve, just like four sets of three is twelve. That takes a while to memorize, but it can be done."

Blair gazed up at the sky filled with dozens of puffy white clouds. She laid back and patted the spot beside her. She pointed above her and began counting, changing her method now and then before asking Hardi to do the same. They passed an hour counting and grouping the clouds before counting those. When they were certain they'd counted each cloud at least ten unique ways, they fell silent as they both became lost in their own thoughts. The changing of the guard brought them back to the present.

"I canna thank ye enough for helping me, Blair. It's nae just the letters and numbers. It's embarrassed me for years that I'm part of the laird's family but couldnae read and write. Ma father and all the other men assured me that I would never need such skills. I wanted to better understand what was happening around me when I traveled with Uncle Farlane or Angus or David, but I'm just a warrior and a sometimes farmer."

Blair rolled onto her side to look at Hardi, who turned his head. "Ye arenae 'just' aught. Ye're a good mon who's served his clan in every way ye've been asked. Who could have predicted ye would one day become laird? I already told ye how I feel aboot yer father refusing to allow mine to help ye. But we canna change the past. Ye are, however, changing yer future. I admire that ye're willing to take help from a woman."

"Why wouldnae I? I ken plenty who think women arenae capable of such learning, but it's obviously nae true. Ye and Maude can read and write. I would imagine most of the ladies-in-waiting can too. Or at least those who had a convent near their homes. Ye benefited from yer brother's tutor. Now ye're willing to help. I'd be an eejit nae to accept."

"Even if people learn of this? Of me tutoring ye?" Blair shifted her eyes down. Hardi used his forefinger and thumb to lift her chin.

"I'd be proud if people heard of how learned ye are and that ye are teaching me because I amnae. Ye're ma friend—" Hardi broke off as he swallowed. He grasped Blair's hand as he rose, practically dragging her away from the blanket. He whistled once as they entered a copse of trees. Blair looked over her shoulder to see two Cameron guards and both Sutherland guards spread out along the tree line, facing away from them. The other two Cameron guards entered the stand of trees but soon melted into them. Hardi spotted a gigantic oak tree, and once they rounded it, he eased Blair against the bark.

They came together in a heated kiss, their lips fused together as Blair opened her mouth to Hardi's questing tongue. Hardi drew her tight against his body, as she went onto her toes to press her chest to his. With a frustrated growl, Hardi pushed his sporran out of the way, his pulsing length relieved to be free of the weight pressing against it, preferring the feel of Blair's mons instead. Hardi's hands cupped her backside as she shifted with curiosity and growing need.

Everything fell away—time, people, duty—as they explored passion that had been simmering just below the surface since Hardi's arrival. His hand slid along her ribs until he cupped her breast, relishing the soft moan he elicited. His fingers slid along the neckline of Blair's gown until he could feel her nipple. The tight nub poked against his fingers as he passed his calloused palm over it. Blair's fingers tunneled into Hardi's tawny locks as her other hand slid under the open neckline of his leine. Her fingers warmed as she absorbed the heat from his smooth skin.

An abrupt whistle had them jerking apart. "Mac-Millans," a guard called. Blair hurried to flatten her hair, grateful it was down. It would pass for wind-blown. Hardi pushed his sporran back into place as he offered Blair his arm. They both recognized Henry and Daniel galloping toward them as they exited the woods.

"Thank you for guarding me while I needed a moment of privacy," Blair said, certain she'd spoken loud enough for the MacMillans to hear. It was the only thing she could think of to justify them coming out of the trees together. She let go of Hardi's arm and walked toward the horses, then around them before returning to the blanket. She gathered her books and slid them back into the satchel before the Mac-Millan brothers could spy them. Once she folded the blanket and placed it on top of a basket, she carried her satchel to her horse and fastened it to her saddle.

"A quaint little picnic between friends," Henry droned.

"Aye. I've been at court for some time, but Lady

Blair and I havenae had an opportunity to catch up on news from our families. I learned that Lady Maude recently had a bairn, and I was curious to hear of the lady's other children."

"How cozy," Daniel chimed in.

"And without chaperones," Henry mused.

"We have six guards," Hardi gestured.

"Aye, to protect you from someone else attacking. Who's to protect Lady Blair from you?" Henry wondered aloud, the accusations clear to one and all.

Blair mounted her horse and turned it back toward the castle. With little choice once their lady mounted, Donald and Tomas mounted too. Hardi didn't look back before he swung into his saddle. Blair spurred her horse into a gallop before they could exchange another word, leaving Henry's question hanging in the air. They remained quiet until they reined in as a group of stable boys rushed out to gather their horses. In silence, Blair led Hardi under several archways before pushing open the door to an empty storeroom. It was one Blair knew; the room was used to store medicinals that Maude used to fetch from the nearby abbey. Hardi kicked the door closed and reached back to turn the key in the lock.

Their arms wrapped around each other as Hardi steered them toward a table in the center of the room until the back of Blair's legs brushed against the side. Hardi lifted her onto the table as his lips trailed a scorching line of kisses along her jaw until he reached her ear. His teeth tugged her earlobe before sucking, his warm breath in her ear eliciting a purely carnal moan from Blair.

"Do ye understand what I want to do with ye, Blair? The ideas floating within ma mind as I kiss ye?" Hardi's voice was hoarse as he whispered into Blair's ear.

"Aye. I ken. I canna stop wanting to feel ye

against me. Ma body aches in a way that only happens when ye are touching me."

"I want to taste every inch of ye," Hardi murmured as he tugged the laces loose at the top of Blair's back until her sleeve sagged. She arched her back toward his questing hand as it slipped beneath the material. This time her kirtle was slack enough for him to palm the bare flesh. He kneaded the mound, her nipple caught between his forefinger and middle finger before brushing his thumb over it. When it puckered into a tight dart, he rolled it between his thumb and forefinger. As Blair's breathy moans filled his ears, he pinched her nipple with just enough pressure to make her legs quiver.

His hand squeezed her covered breast while the other hand pulled her skirts high enough to allow Blair to wrap her calves around his. He stepped into the space as she leaned back onto the table. Hardi's body followed hers. As his rod pressed against her mound, Hardi brought his mouth to her breast, suckling.

"I willna ever look at ye like ma little sister. Ye are the woman I crave, Blair. I want to be inside of ye, bringing ye hours of pleasure night after night," Hardi pledged.

"The space between ma thighs aches and feels so empty. I ken it's because ma body is begging for ye to fill it. I want to touch ye, Hardi. Without clothes in the way. I want to learn what every part of ye feels like." Blair's eyes met Hardi's in the dim light. "Does it shock ye to hear I ken what I want, that I ken how a mon and woman join?"

"Mayhap a little, but I'm glad ye understand. I dinna ever want to scare ye, Blair," Hardi reassured her.

"And I am grateful for what Maude explained, or this would have been terrifying." Blair smiled, but

Hardi's eyes widened. "I mean nae understanding why ma body reacts so strongly to ye, why it aches for ye. I've never felt aught like it."

"There's a great deal more that I would like to make ye feel, but I willna do it in some storeroom atop a table." Hardi pulled away from Blair, the passion still sizzling between them, but the moment of intimacy passed. He eased Blair's sleeve back onto her shoulder before she reached behind her to tie the ribbons. She once again smoothed her hair as Hardi tugged at the front of his leine and brushed out his plaid.

"I must go to prepare for the evening meal." Blair made to step around Hardi but paused. She went onto her toes and strained her neck to kiss the corner of his mouth. Hardi's arms longed to wrap around her, but he knew if he did, they would never leave the storeroom. He settled for giving her waist a squeeze. Blair slipped away, and Hardi waited several minutes before he left.

FOURTEEN

"**M**eet me in the scriptorium when ye're done," Blair whispered as she passed Hardi on the way out of Mass the following morning. As soon as the last hymn ended and the priests retired to the sacristy, Blair followed them. She rapidly explained her request that she and Hardi be allowed to work there since they needed somewhere properly chaperoned—after all, who better to keep people from kissing than an observing monk— but would afford them privacy as Laird Cameron learned to read and write.

Blair already sat at an enormous table as a monk worked in a corner, barely glancing at Hardi as he entered. Hardi eased onto the bench beside Blair and looked at the books set out before them. He felt just as intimidated by the sight as he had the day before, when she pulled the three tomes from her satchel.

"We'll start with a primer today. I'm sorry that the stories are for a child just beginning his education, but the lessons will serve our purpose." Blair opened the book, and before Hardi could consider whether the book embarrassed him, Blair began reading. She sounded out each letter as she moved from word to word, then she instructed Hardi to read along with her as she once again sounded out each word. They continued the process until they were halfway through the primer. When Blair felt confident that Hardi could piece together the words, she asked him to read a page on his own. Hardi's rapid progress impressed them both, and he pointed out that he was recognizing certain words, making it easier to read. However, there was an impediment to Hardi's continued reading.

"I am learning to read these words, but I dinna ken what any of them mean," Hardi rubbed his temple.

"I ken. I dinna have time to teach ye Latin in a moon, but I can get ye started," Blair assured him, even though her stomach churned knowing it had taken her years to understand Latin. "If most contracts and documents werenae written in Latin, I would teach ye Scots first. I want ye to read missives like the one from the king, so nay one can fool ye again."

"I want the same thing, but it seems impossible nae only in a moon but in time to keep ma clan safe. I dinna want to sign something I dinna understand, trusting that the clan council isnae leading me astray."

"Like the tax levies and yer betrothal contract," Blair said.

"I amnae reading aught that looks like a betrothal contract if it involves Una or the Donald's daughter. I canna marry them. Nae when I ken they arenae aught like ye. They arenae who's right for me or ma clan. They arenae ye." Hardi's words spilled forth, but each one was heartfelt. Blair turned wide eyes toward him. Hardi's broad shoulder had brushed hers throughout the time they sat together on the narrow bench, but when she shifted to look at him, his shoulder grazed her breast. They froze. Blair and Hardi glanced back at the priest, both relieved that the old man was stooped over his work, his back toward them. "Blair, I amnae asking ye to marry me. Nae yet because I canna. I ken the king believes I will go forward with an alliance to the Macquaries, but I willna, nae matter happens between us. I dinna want to force ye or rush ye either. I still have a wee longer here, and we will continue to work together. I want ye to have time to decide if ye think we suit."

Blair nodded, still too dumbfounded by Hardi's declaration. It was what she wanted, she just hadn't imagined it would ever come, or at least not so soon. When he took hold of her icy hands and rubbed them between his, a brief thought of how he always radiated heat skidded across her mind before she returned her focus to their conversation.

"If ye decide ye would like to move forward with a betrothal and marriage, I will speak to the king." Hardi glanced away as Blair watched his cheeks turn pink, then red. "But I canna court ye in earnest without asking yer da's permission to marry ye. I canna ask him without sending a missive—one I must ask ye to write."

Blair reached out her hand to cup his cheek, her thumb brushing over his cheekbone. She lowered her voice, so only Hardi could hear. "I will gladly help ye. Dinna ever be embarrassed aboot aught in front of me, Hardi. If we marry, I will stand by yer side through everything, good and bad. I admire ye more than I think ye understand."

Hardi turned his face into Blair's palm and kissed it before leaning forward to brush a kiss against her lips. The clearing of a throat made them smile, ending the kiss before it began. They spent the rest of the morning reading as Hardi attempted more complex words. Before they began his mathematics lesson, Blair drafted the missive Hardi dictated asking Laird Hamish Sutherland for permission to court and marry his younger daughter. He explained his interest in Blair, making it her turn to blush, and what he could offer her in return for her hand.

The next fortnight passed in a cozy routine that brought Hardi and Blair a happiness they hadn't expected. Tucked away for most of the day in the scriptorium, they poured over books. Hardi absorbed his lessons with a single-minded focus that convinced Blair that Hardi would be an indomitable leader. Duty forced Blair to spend an hour or two in the queen's solar each afternoon, but she ensconced herself in a window embrasure with her embroidery, her face turned toward the light and away from the other ladies. She made it obvious that she wasn't interested in socializing unless it was with Arabella and Laurel. It surprised her to see how magnanimous and even kind Laurel could be, but she still had a wickedly sharp tongue that she pointed at anyone who tried to pry into Blair's whereabouts. While neither Arabella nor Laurel were privy to what kept Blair away from the other courtiers, they both suspected it had something to do with Hardi. Neither asked.

As for Hardi, he spent the time in the lists or meeting with delegates from other clans as he negotiated potential trade agreements. Before the end of the first week, Blair introduced Hardi to the rudimentary rules of Latin, and he began memorizing how to conjugate basic verbs. He asked Blair to assist him with several contracts, and it created an opportunity for him to use the Latin he was gradually absorbing.

Hardi enjoyed their routine, looking forward to the hours tucked away with Blair. She told him children's riddles in Latin that became easier as the fortnight progressed. He realized she still had the wickedly dry sense of humor that she'd had when they were younger. But he discovered she'd developed a fear of heights after a particularly treacherous journey through the Cairngorms the second spring after she'd arrived at court. He also learned that she loved to swim; her cousin Mairghread had encouraged her try deeper water while she visited Castle Dunbeath. Both the Sinclairs and Sutherlands lived along the North Sea, so only the hardiest of swimmers dared enter the water even during the warmest summer day. She reminded him of her most prized possession: a figurine Hamish carved for each of his children and his wife. It depicted their family standing arm-in-arm. He'd given the wood carvings to his family the day before Lachlan rode into his first battle.

Blair enjoyed telling Hardi stories about the years since he'd finished his fostering, and she was reminded of what an attentive listener he was when anyone spoke of something that held importance to them. She asked what felt like myriad questions about the time between his return to Tor Castle and when his brother died. She never brought up the brief years between losing Dougal and becoming laird. A great melancholy entered his eyes when he mentioned losing his brother, and it was clear to Blair that the grief of losing Dougal was still fresh. Coupled with losing his uncle and cousins, Blair wondered how Hardi hadn't crumpled under the weight of sadness. She commented on his fortitude, and he offered self-deprecating humor in return. They returned to the ease they'd shared when they were younger and Hardi joined her before the fire in the Great Hall. They often sat together, their little fingers linked as they read and talked.

In the evenings, Blair sat with the other ladies-in-waiting, listening to their chatter as they shared gossip and speculation about which widow or matron was carrying on an affair with various courtiers and visitors. Blair joined in only to keep from turning attention toward her, but she looked forward to when the music began and she could partner with Hardi. Neither enjoyed watching the other dance with different partners, but they trusted one another. Blair had seen the possessive glares her brother-by-marriage had given men who approached Maude, but she understood his reasoning. Maude's endowments meant men often made inappropriate advances, and Kieran strove to protect her. But Hardi encouraged her to continue partnering with those who approached, assuring her that he understood she enjoyed dancing and didn't want to keep her from participating just because they were courting. They hadn't shared that information with anyone, so Blair agreed only to keep up appearances. Hardi danced with a handful of women each evening to keep his interest in Blair from becoming too obvious, but more often than not, he found a spot along the wall to observe or returned to his table to sit among his men.

The Cameron guards arrived at the evening meal early each night to secure seats that wouldn't force them to socialize with courtiers. They chose tables with fellow Highlanders, who were happy to share mugs of ale and a dram or two of whisky but knew how to mind their own business. More than once, this meant they shared a table with the MacMillans, but Hardi kept the conversation flowing by asking questions rather than answering them. When he was able, he discussed with his guards what they observed in the lists or heard among the guards. Every man knew, even if they never admitted it, that men gossiped just as much as women.

It was gossip that eventually put an end to Blair and Hardi's idyllic arrangement. Blair watched as a group of newer ladies-in-waiting tittered as they glanced at her during the evening meal. Blair sat between Arabella and Laurel, listening to them complain about the extra two hours of prayer they'd been forced to endure because Queen Elizabeth felt compelled to both thank and implore God to watch over her unborn child. When it was impossible for the three women to ignore the attention from the other group, Laurel explained. "Blair, there's been talk aboot you and Laird Cameron slipping away together. When we went on our morning walk today, those ladies," she flashed a glance at the younger ladies, "overheard two priests walking ahead of them."

Blair's stomach sank. She was certain where this story led, and she felt embarrassed on Hardi's behalf. She didn't consider what the rumors meant for her reputation. She worried what disparaging remarks were being made about Hardi needing tutoring—from a woman.

Arabella picked up the story. "Apparently, the monks were discussing how kind and patient you are to be teaching a mon as old as Laird Cameron to read and write. I don't know if it was the monks who said it or the ladies exaggerating, but they implied Laird Cameron was slow to learn, and that's why he hadn't been able to as a child. They suggested he isn't very smart."

Blair squinted at the ladies who chose that moment to approach. The word "smart" reminded her of how self-conscious Hardi had been in the beginning. Her temper rose; she feared the rumors would make Hardi unwilling to continue his studies. Every protective instinct she had rose to the surface, prepared to the gut the women if they said the wrong thing.

"We've seen you watching Laird Cameron each night, and now we ken why," the lady in the middle gushed. Blair could tell she had a vindictive streak much like Madeline MacLeod had. It had made Madeline the de facto leader of the attendants, and no one wanted to be caught in her sights. Blair was not about to let an upstart, this newly arrived woman, make her the brunt of any jokes.

"I'm surprised you can see anything so far below the salt," Blair mused before taking a bite of lamb, reminding the women of their low rank. The three women lifted their chins in unison, but before any of them spoke, Blair continued. "If you last long enough, one day you might earn a place at our table. You can see far more in the Great Hall when you can see the salt."

"Your warm breath on my food is making it taste foul," Laurel quipped. "You may go now." The disdain in her tone only added to the insult of being dismissed. Laurel, Blair, and Arabella picked up their conversation as if they'd never noticed the other ladies. Forced to retreat, the younger ladies-in-waiting slinked back to their seats, but Blair didn't miss their venomous glares.

FIFTEEN

H ardi sat on the same side of the table as Henry, which gave them a clear view of Blair's table even if she had her back to them. Henry elbowed Daniel on his right and his guard on his left before laughing raucously. The MacMillans and Camerons watched as the trio of smirking women approached Blair. They witnessed their smug miens evaporate at whatever Blair and her friends said.

"It appears little Blair is having a rather heated tête-a-tête with those women." Daniel observed. He leaned past Henry and the guard to see Hardi. "That's French for a head-to-head."

The only head-to-head Hardi was interested in was bashing the MacMillan brothers' together. He'd been informed of the rumors when Henry and Daniel arrived at the table, crowing about how Hardi sang nursery rhymes all day. He'd shrugged and turned back to his men, refusing to engage. However, Hardi was forced to leave the table when Henry and Daniel stood. He was certain they were headed to Blair, and he wouldn't leave her to handle the situation on her own. Henry and Daniel rounded Blair's table and took the spots that had been vacated by the three ladies-in-waiting only moments ago. She sensed Hardi was behind her, but she commanded herself not to look over her shoulder.

"Hiding behind a woman's skirt, Cameron," Henry directed his first jab at Hardi.

"Ye might fit behind them, but I'm a wee too big," Hardi smirked, pointing out the obvious differences in their physiques. The people further down each side of the table turned to stare and listen.

Not able to goad Hardi, Henry turned his attention to Blair. "Now we know where you've been hiding away in your love nest."

"With monks surrounding us? I can't think of anyone less likely to create an atmosphere for kissing than a priest," Blair sighed with boredom.

"Perhaps there hasn't been time since Cameron is still learning to count. Do you even ken how many days you've been here, Cameron? Has Lady Blair taught you that many numbers?" Daniel crossed his arms.

"I'm certain he can count how many times you've been turned away from The Picked Over Plum," Blair muttered, but she ensured her voice carried. She'd taken on the mantle to defend Hardi, and she was prepared to go into battle. "Unfortunate you haven't learned not to have your pockets picked at the Wolf and Sheep so many times that you can't even afford a withered plum."

Daniel blinked rapidly, uncertain what to say as people chuckled and elbowed one another. Blair tossed back her hair and cocked an eyebrow at Henry, daring him to say something. He refused to look at her, keeping his eyes on Hardi.

"I never took you for a dimwit, but you need Lady Blair to fight your battles now," Henry goaded.

"I'm proud to have Lady Blair defend me. She's

more intelligent than either ye or me," Hardi shrugged.

"I can understand a woman being more intelligent than you, but none of them will be smarter than me," Henry argued.

"That's not how it seemed last year with Lady Bevan," Blair stated, her eyes locked with Henry's. "It seems she left you cowering in a corner after the tongue lashing you received. Seemed that was the only thing she wanted to use her tongue for by the time she was through with you. As I recall, she laid bare *all* your shortcomings." More laughter ensued from those who crowded closer to hear. Diners from the tables around them leaning.

Lady Bevan had been a notorious widow at court who'd had brief encounters with Kieran and both Gordon twins. The queen ordered her married off to an old man when Lady Bevan erred and tried to seduce the king where the queen could overhear. Early the previous spring, Lady Bevan and Henry were caught in a spat that echoed through the passageways outside the matrons' chamber.

"Bitch," Henry grumbled.

"Bastard," Blair smiled. It was a poorly kept secret that Lady MacMillan had been handfasted, against her father's wishes to a warrior who died in battle; she was then hurriedly married off to Laird MacMillan. When Henry arrived as a healthy, squalling bairn, there was no claiming he was premature. Laird MacMillan claimed Henry as his son, but it was Daniel who was the laird's true firstborn son.

"It's a pathetic mon who needs a woman to speak for him," Henry returned to taunting Hardi.

"And it's a fool who can't remember no mon lives forever, and no alliance is written in stone," Hardi raised both eyebrows. The Camerons were a larger and more prosperous clan than the MacMillans. The latter needed the alliance far more than the Camerons, depending on them to buy the MacMillans' grain.

"Pride goeth before the fall. That explains why you're missing so many teeth. That or you keep your mouth in foul places that rot your teeth," Blair observed as she peered under her lashes at Henry.

"I can only imagine what your mouth has been around lately," Daniel hissed. There was a collective gasp. It was one thing for Blair to point out commonly known gossip about a man, but it was entirely different for a man to besmirch a lady's reputation. Hardi looked down at Blair, giving her the opportunity to defend herself even though he wanted to run Daniel through. He knew Blair could hold her own, and he wouldn't belittle her by making it appear she couldn't.

"It is a wee mon," Blair held up her thumb and forefinger a small distance apart. "Who must insult a lady to win an argument. Have I said aught that is a lie? But you must make up stories aboot me to make you feel bigger. You would ridicule a mon brave enough to recognize he needs help and is willing to seek and accept it, kenning what others might say. You look down your nose at a mon with the strength to weather the insults and taunts because he's dedicated to being the best leader he can for his clan. You belittle a mon never groomed to be laird because he didn't have everything handed to him like some. He has worked for everything, including learning after that opportunity was taken from him. You two are the weak ones. You have naught to offer anyone, so you try to make yourself look better by bringing others down to your level. The problem with that is cream will always rise to the top while shite sinks to the bottom."

A collective silence fell over those who'd been listening to the exchange. The sudden hush made people from other tables turn to see what happened. Lady Blair stood from the table, her chin held high, her back straight, and her shoulders back. She dared the MacMillans to say anything more. Neither brother opened his mouth, but the vindictive gleam was clear.

"Touch Lady Blair, and I will chop ye up and send ye back to yer parents like haggis," Hardi warned. He wrapped Blair's arm around his, and the onlookers parted for them as they walked to where couples gathered waiting for the music to begin. When they found a spot where they could speak quietly, Hardi released Blair's arm, both knowing it was for decorum. "Are ye angry that I didna step in to defend ye?"

"Nay. Ye were there when I needed ye. Are ye insulted that I fought yer battle?" Blair bit her lip.

Hardi leaned forward. "I would vera much like to be the one biting that lip, so unless ye want a scene of another sort, I wouldnae keep tempting me." He straightened with a wink. "And I amnae insulted. I told the truth when I said I'm proud of ye, and ye are more intelligent than any of us men. This was as much aboot yer reputation as it was mine. I kenned ye'd run circles around those two eejits. I would've stepped in if ye wanted me to, but I wasna going to let anyone think ye arenae strong enough to stand on yer own two feet. Ye arenae a weak woman, Blair, so I willna treat ye as one. I will protect ye with ma dying breath, but I respect ye and yer ability to speak for yerself."

"How did ye become so sage at such a young age?" Blair asked.

"Yer da. I watched how he treats yer mama," Hardi smiled. "I told ye, I have spent every day since I met Laird Hamish Sutherland trying to be the mon he is. I dinna always get it right, but I try ma damnedest."

Blair nodded as she blinked back tears. When the lump in her throat dissolved enough for her to speak, she whispered. "I dinna want to dance, Hardi. I want to be far away with just ye. But if we leave, then the rumors will only be worse."

"I ken, *fear glic*."

"I dinna think I'm the wise one," Blair offered a watery smile. "I meant every word I said aboot ye, Hardi."

The music began. Blair and Hardi were both relieved that it was a set that would keep them together rather than forcing them to switch partners. Hardi held Blair closer than was appropriate, but Blair longed for the contact as much as he did. She locked stares with Hardi as he led them around the floor. They could tell when something shifted between them, something shifted within each of them.

"I love ye, Blair," Hardi kept his tone hushed, but his words were clear.

"I love ye, Hardi. I dinna need any more time to decide if I want to marry ye. I ken I do." Blair didn't blink as she confessed her feelings, wanting Hardi to know that she didn't waver or hesitate. Blair looked over at King Robert and Queen Elizabeth as they watched their subjects from their elevated seats on the dais. "What do ye think the king will say?"

"I pray he finds me worthy of his goddaughter," Hardi said sheepishly.

"If he doesnae, I will remind him of just how obstinate I was as a child. I havenae changed. I've just found better ways to get what I want." The stubborn tilt to Blair's chin and the defiant gleam in her eyes reminded Hardi of what King Robert also knew.

"I'm grateful ye're on ma side, lass." Hardi pulled her closer. "*Tha mi a 'gealltainn a bhith nad dhuine math dhut, a ghràidh."* Blair's breath hitched as Hardi said "I promise to be a good husband to you, my love."

Blair once again swallowed down the lump in her throat before responding. *"Tha mi a 'mionnachadh gur e am bean as fheàrr as urrainn dhomh a bhith, mo chridhe."* Blair meant it with every fiber of her being when she told Hardi "I swear to be the best wife I can be, my heart." They continued dancing until one song blended into the next.

"Hardi, I dinna want to keep hiding. I dinna want how I feel to be a secret like I'm ashamed of what we're doing, of who ye are."

"Do ye think King Robert would grant me an audience tomorrow?" Hardi shifted his gaze to the dais.

"I dinna ken, but I dinna plan to wait. I'll risk abusing ma privilege of being their goddaughter if it means I ken we can marry," Blair answered. Hardi slid her hand into his as they squeezed their way between the dancers until they reached the dais, the royal couple noticing their joined hands at first glance.

SIXTEEN

"Lady Blair, you have the same look aboot you that you did when you were a wee lass and put out by Lachlan, Michael, Dougal and, I believe, the mon standing beside you. Somehow, I don't think another piece of candied honey will solve this," King Robert spoke from the dais. "Does this have to do with the stir you caused with the Mac-Millans?"

Blair dipped into an elegant curtsy as Hardi bowed. She looked at King Robert then Queen Elizabeth before returning her gaze to King Robert. "I didn't begin the disagreement with Henry and Daniel MacMillan, but I did end it. I'm not put out by Laird Cameron at all, and while I will never turn down candied honey, no, it won't solve what I've come to you aboot." Blair gave King Robert a pointed look as her lips tightened into a thin line before turning down.

"You may approach, Lady Blair," Queen Elizabeth intoned. "You may as well come along, Laird Cameron." When Blair and Hardi stood across the table from the royal couple, Queen Elizabeth's smile was benevolent, while King Robert's was skeptical.

"I assume you're here to tell me you refuse to

move forward with the Macquarie betrothal and that you intend to turn down the Donald too," the king guessed.

"Yer Majesty, Lady Una wouldnae be an appropriate choice to become Lady Cameron. Ye are aware of the position in which ma clan finds itself. The Camerons need—deserve—a selfless, judicious, and thoughtful lady," Hardi explained.

"And will you tell Laird Macquarie that his daughter is not those things?" King Robert pressed.

"Nay. There's nae reason to be hurtful. Ma uncle considered Lady Una for Angus, but it wasna until David became his heir that he inquired. David and I were of the same opinion of Lady Una. She may make a mon a suitable wife one day, but it wouldnae have been either of us. I dinna think I need to haver on aboot it when ye can see for yerself who I wish to marry. I dinna doubt ye are aware of everything Lady Blair and I have discussed and what she's taught me since we began using the scriptorium. Ye also ken we've been well suited to one another since we were adolescents."

"Laird Cameron, we've known you and Lady Blair would have made an excellent match since the first time we visited Dunbeath a month after you arrived to foster," Queen Elizabeth interjected. "It doesn't come as a surprise that you stand before us. But it was my understanding that you believed this was not the right time for you to take a wife."

"It wasna before I realized Blair—Lady Blair is the woman I need," Hardi replied.

"Need to be Lady Cameron," King Robert clarified.

"Nay. The woman I need to be ma wife, ma partner. With that comes being Lady Cameron, but I believe Lady Blair would marry me even if I was still seventh in line to inherit. And I ken I would still ask to marry her even if I was just a laird's guard, and she was meant to marry a laird."

"Do you share his sentiments, Lady Blair?" King Robert asked.

"Aye, Your Majesty. Laird Cameron sent a missive to my father to request permission to court me and, in time, marry me. I believe my parents will support this union, and I believe you know that." Blair's expression challenged the king to disagree.

"So, you are here to demand my approval," King Robert stated.

"Nae demand, Yer Majesty. I would ask yer permission, just as I did Laird Sutherland's," Hardi spoke up.

"And if I say no?" King Robert retorted.

"I'll marry him anyway," Blair blurted. She knew what the king was doing, and she'd engaged in his game for as long as she was willing. Her encounter with the MacMillans shredded her patience and goodwill. She took a step forward, scowling at the guards who moved toward the royal couple. "Uncle Robert, I have asked one thing of you since I arrived here, and it wasn't for my sake. The only other requests I've ever made were not those one asks a king, but what a wee lass asks her uncle. Rides upon your shoulders, candies and treats, and—well, I suppose I asked you to banish Lachlan and Michael—but you ken none of your godchildren have ever tried to abuse their position. I'm not asking you as my king. I'm asking you as my Uncle Robert, who can grant this in my father's stead."

"You ken it's not as simple as that, Blair," King Robert shook his head.

"And you ken it is in my family. We marry for love. Even Callum and Siùsan, and Tavish and Ceit. Both couples fell in love before they married, even if you and Uncle Liam arranged their marriages. I love

Hardi, Uncle Robert. Please. You ken me as well as you do Marjorie. You know I'm telling the truth." Blair took a leap, mentioning the king's daughter. "Aunt Elizabeth just said Hardi and I have been an obvious match since we were children."

"I did say that," Queen Elizabeth interjected. "But it has also been several years since you've spent a prolonged amount of time around one another. Less than a moon is not very long. How can you be sure?"

Blair was growing frustrated. She knew her godfather was being awkward for the sake of it, and she knew her godmother was trying to protect her. But she was emotionally spent, and she didn't want to play the game of courtly manipulation. She'd hoped she might talk to her extended family rather than her monarchs. Her shoulders slumped until she felt Hardi step beside her. He wrapped Blair's arm around his, so anyone standing behind them would think little of how they stood, but Hardi's hand covered Blair's smaller one. It was comforting and protective in the way she'd once described to Lachlan that she wanted.

"Blair has attempted to ask ye as her family to help. Now I am asking ye as a laird of a clan that pledged its support to ye, King Robert, and yer cause from the vera beginning. We have been naught but loyal. We havenae asked for aught, even when ye have seen fit to reward us. If an alliance wasna being considered, then I wouldnae have fostered at Dunrobin. Whether Laird Sutherland considered Dougal or me, I dinna ken, but he and ma uncle meant it to ally our clans. Marriage will make that permanent." Hardi squeezed Blair's hand. He glanced down at her the same time Queen Elizabeth leaned forward. "Blair?"

"I'm all right. I'm just tired. Your Majesty, may I

be excused?" Blair attempted to dip into a curtsy, but when she wobbled, Hardi's hand gripped her elbow to steady her.

"Lady Blair, I haven't said no. I will consider your request." King Robert leaned his arms on the table as he stretched toward her. "Lass, your Uncle Robert is satisfied that Hardi will make an exemplary husband for you. It's obvious he cares for you and will be a loving husband. If it were Uncle Robert who ruled this land, I would have you married by morn. But King Robert must consider what is best for Scotland. The Macquaries are not an influential clan, but they are located along a coast I need their help to defend. I must consider whether a Sutherland daughter would create a better alliance elsewhere."

Blair blinked several times before she nodded. She couldn't explain what happened, but it was as though the last dregs of energy leeched from her. She was too tired to continue to fight that night, but she hadn't given up. She was as stubborn as she'd warned Hardi, and the king's evasiveness wouldn't dissuade her. She needed time to rest and clear her mind before she planned her next approach.

"Lass," King Robert drew her attention. "I did the same before Maude and Kieran married. If I hadn't thought it was a match than not only made Maude happy but was good for the Highlands, I would have said no."

Blair nodded. She turned her exhausted face to Hardi and nodded to him before turning away from the dais. Hardi shot a glare at the king that he wouldn't have dared if the change that came over Blair didn't worry him so much. Hardi registered the shock on King Robert's face before the king called out to Blair.

"Blair?" She turned back to the king, and he waved her closer. "Your evening hasn't gone well, and I suspect you need a good night's sleep. But I shouldn't take this sudden quietness as resignation, should I? You still intend to have your way, don't you?"

Blair lifted her chin but didn't answer. A spark of defiance took hold, and she was certain the king read it in her face when he continued. "Bluidy hell. I may as well say yes. Everyone in your family seems to solve their problems with a handfast. If I don't relent now, for all I ken you'll be wed by morning." Robert gestured for Blair to step up to the table. "Blair, I ken you like my Marjorie, and I love you like a niece. I'm not trying to hurt you. I'm conceding now because sometimes being a father and an uncle need to come first."

Blair smiled as she reached her hands across the table. King Robert took one while Queen Elizabeth took the other. "Thank you," Blair rasped. "I love you both, too."

SEVENTEEN

Blair felt much improved in the morning. After leaving the Great Hall, Hardi had walked her to her chamber, but she could hear Arabella and her maid moving around within, so they said an all-too-brief goodnight. Hardi pressed a kiss to Blair's lips as they embraced. Neither wanted to let go, but approaching voices forced Hardi to dash from the ladies-in-waiting passageway. She broke her fast after Mass, Queen Elizabeth granting her permission to sit beside Hardi in the kirk and in the Great Hall. It declared to all and sundry that not only were Hardi and Blair courting, but the royal couple approved. Blair wasn't certain how to describe the limbo in which they found themselves. Without Hamish present or contracts sent to him, there was no way to set the betrothal. The king could order them to marry, but Hamish and Hardi still needed to agree to the dowry and bride price, then sign the documents.

Blair and Hardi drafted another missive to her parents explaining that the king granted his blessing for them to marry, and they wished to move forward. Blair wondered if the messenger carrying the newest missive would encounter the one returning with Hamish and Amelia's first response. She knew her father would never respond without first listening to her mother's opinion. Hamish might have the official say, but Blair and Hardi addressed both missives to Hamish and Amelia. As Hardi sat beside Blair while they drafted the letter together, he was stuck by how natural it felt to work alongside one another.

"Blair, would ye consider sharing ma solar once we return to Tor Castle?" Hardi asked unexpectedly.

Blair lowered the quill and looked at him. "Share yer solar?"

"Aye. When ye are working on the accounts and such, would ye work on them in our shared solar?"

Blair laid the quill down and leaned forward to kiss Hardi before the priests in the scriptorium could censor them. "I would like that vera much, ma laird." Blair grinned. Hardi dropped a kiss on her nose.

"I'm nae yer laird, Blair. I want to be yer husband, and that makes us equal. Ye dinna serve me or belong to me." Hardi took Blair's left hand in his, running his thumb over where he prayed a ring would soon sit. "I ken I will need yer help for quite some time in the beginning, but I dinna want ye to think that's why I'd like to share the chamber with ye. I want to be near ye because I enjoy yer company, because it feels right to sit beside ye."

"I understood that, but I appreciate ye saying it. I feel the same way," Blair squeezed his hand before turning back to finish the missive. When they felt they had included sufficient details, she passed the quill to Hardi. They'd been practicing every day so that Hardi could affix his signature with confidence and clear penmanship. Hardi folded the parchment and sealed it with wax that he imprinted with his signet ring. They opted for a day away from the books and lessons. After Hardi handed the missive to a page with specific instructions that a messenger was to leave immediately, Blair and Hardi went to the kitchens to gather the picnic baskets she requested. Hardi grinned when he discovered she'd ordered three instead of two.

"Is one of these just for ye, or will ye share the scraps with me again?" Hardi teased.

"Ye can see if yer guards will share. The meat pies and apple tarts are mine, *mo chridhe*," Blair teased. Heat passed between them at the simple term of affection. With their hands full and a kitchen filled with servants, there was little they could do. Hardi carried two baskets while Blair maneuvered the third until Tomas caught sight and rushed to help her. She looked for Buannaiche, but her horse wasn't in the bailey.

"Ye ride with me today, lass," Hardi whispered behind her. "I amnae missing an opportunity to feel ye pressed against me with ma arms around ye."

"And if I should want to ride pillion, so I can wrap ma arms around ye?" Blair giggled.

"Mayhap I'll consider it on the way back." Hardi lifted her into the saddle and pulled himself onto the horse behind her, giving her no chance to argue or move. As Hardi nudged his horse forward, Blair fell back against Hardi's chest. She realized that she was much happier in the cocoon of his arms than she would be trying to reach her arms around his broad back. Hardi chuckled as Blair nestled closer. "Nae so bad?"

"Nae bad at all," Blair agreed. Hardi's wrapped his arm tighter around her waist as his other hand held the reins. Blair clutched a hank of the horse's mane until she realized that Hardi's brawny arm and muscular thighs pinning her to the horse would keep her from slipping, even at a gallop. She rested her hands on Hardi's thighs and felt him shudder. Realizing he enjoyed the feel of her hands on him, she slowly stroked her hand up and down his legs, careful to keep her movements small and unnoticeable. In return, Hardi nuzzled Blair's neck. His warm breath beneath her ear made her shiver.

"The only thing I wish to dine upon this nooning is ye," Hardi murmured against her throat.

Blair glanced at the guards surrounding her, hoping she and Hardi could slip away again. "I think we should plan to enjoy dessert, just the two of us." A growl vibrated from deep in Hardi's chest as he pressed a series of scorching kisses along her throat as they rode. They approached a ridge with a steep downhill slope on the other side. Blair knew there was a denser set of woods than the copse they'd picnicked near a fortnight earlier. There was a clearing within the forest, but it wasn't visible from the path. She sighed as she realized Hardi intended to take her there where prying eyes wouldn't intrude or create gossip.

"Ye ken where we're headed?" Hardi asked as he focused on maneuvering his horse along the steep grade, no longer tempting Blair with his kisses.

"Aye. The clearing to the right. It's a ways into the trees to find it, but it's large enough for us to picnic. Maude, Lachlan, and I used to go there when Lachlan visited. Mama and Da took us there the first time and said that should we ever need a place to speak as a family where there wouldnae be walls with ears, we were to go to the clearing. Maude, Lachlan, and I went there just so Maude and I could escape the castle from time to time."

"Did ye and Lachlan go there the last time he visited?" Hardi inquired.

"Aye. Lach and I wanted time away from the castle. Nae to discuss aught specific. He understood I needed a change of scenery."

"Are ye unhappy at court, Blair?" Hardi's voice was little more than a whisper.

"Nae unhappy per se," Blair paused, realizing the Latin phrase wasn't one she'd taught Hardi.

"Dinna fash. Lachlan explained it to me," Hardi reassured.

"I've just been growing restless, I suppose." Blair turned her head to look at the expanse of trees that met them as they left the hill behind them. The trees to the left of the path were just as dense as to the right, but there was nowhere to picnic.

"Restless?" Hardi was puzzled.

"Maude married nearly two years ago. Ma other friends have left too. There's only Arabella and Laurel still here from when I arrived. I suspect Arabella won't remain much longer."

"Lachlan?"

"Mayhap. But Arabella suspects her father has begun a search for a husband for her. There are few ladies-in-waiting who enjoy life at court. I think there are few women who enjoy it at all. Matrons join the court on their husband's arm or as the queen's attendant. Widows remain when there is nowhere else for them to go. The queen is happy to be anywhere that she can move freely, coming and going as she wishes. The king loathes being at court. I think he'd rather still live in a tent as long as he didna have to go to battle," Blair explained with a sigh. "It's all fake. The laughter, the merriment. While in the moment, people may enjoy themselves. But few enjoy the lifestyle. Or rather, most dinna. There are courtiers who canna imagine living anywhere else. They thrive on the political maneuvering and living a luxurious lifestyle on someone else's bill."

"So ye are eager to escape?" Hardi's stomach tightened, a sudden fear that Blair was more excited about the prospect of leaving court than the prospect of marrying him.

Blair tried to twist enough to look Hardi in the eye, but it was impossible. Frustrated, she clenched his plaid. "I freely admit that I wondered when I would marry. I felt left behind and told Lachlan that before he left too. But I am nae marrying ye just to leave. If I were that desperate, I would beg ma parents to fetch me. Yer arrival made me forget that I wanted to leave. It made me forget ma loneliness, and even ma jealousy that the others left because they married for love. At least most of them did." Blair's mind flashed to Cairren Kennedy's departure. The arranged marriage had been an unmitigated disaster at the beginning, but it grew into a loving one where Cairren was happy and building a family. "I didna ken I would fall in love with ye, Hardi. I kenned I was attracted to ye, but ye were ma friend first."

Hardi relaxed with Blair's reassurance, and the arm he hadn't realized was squeezing Blair far too tightly eased its punishing grip.

136

EIGHTEEN

When they arrived in the clearing, Blair's immediate dismount made Hardi worry that he'd insulted her by doubting her motivation to marry. Once he was on the ground, she grabbed his hand and tugged him to the far side of the clearing and into the trees. He whistled to the guards just as he had the last time they slipped away. It was Blair's turn to push Hardi against an enormous tree trunk. She grasped two handfuls of his leine and rose onto her toes. Her kiss was punishing, giving no quarter. She swiped her tongue across the seam of Hardi's mouth, plunging it into the smooth recesses as soon as he gave way. Annoyed at his sporran once again being in the way, she pushed it aside.

Blair's attack caught Hardi unprepared, but he eagerly met Blair's passion with his own. Once the full length of his straining cock pressed against Blair, he lifted her high off the ground; her legs wrapping around his waist. He turned them so Blair's back was against the tree. He thrust his hips against her, imitating how he longed to be inside her. Grumbling at the yards of fabric he was forced to gather, both sighed when Hardi's hands finally gripped Blair's buttocks. She rocked her hips against him as one hand fisted the back of his leine while the other cupped his jaw and nape.

She ripped her mouth away, panting. "Could I kiss ye like this if I wanted to marry ye for convenience?" she demanded before swooping in for another kiss. They devoured one another, days of frustrated chastity finally giving way. Hardi's fingers slid along her slick seam until Blair mumbled "yes" against his lips. He dipped his middle finger into her entrance, and Blair squeezed her legs around Hardi's waist as though she could press their bodies closer together. Encouraged, Hardi's forefinger joined the other as he explored what he could reach.

"Blair, I will put ye down on yer feet, but only so I can touch ye more," Hardi gasped, breathless and impatient. He steadied Blair on her feet before thrusting his fingers into her core. Her head rested against his shoulder as she struggled to stifle her moan. As Hardi's thumb rubbed small circles on her pearl, Blair's teeth bit into his shoulder. Not enough to hurt, but more than enough to excite Hardi beyond restraint. He felt his cock pulse as his seed coated his leg and the inner folds of his plaid. He'd never been more thankful for the layers of wool as he was then, knowing they would hide the evidence of his overly eager cock.

"I want to touch ye too, Hardi," Blair begged. When he said nothing, she pulled back to find him blushing, but focused on pleasuring her. She wanted to know why he said nothing, but her mind went blank as the ache low in her belly coiled into a knot before a wave of pleasure surged from her core and washed over her. Her hands cupped Hardi's face as she poured every bit of astonishment and need and pleasure into this kiss. "Hardi, please. I want to touch ye."

"Blair, ye canna. It's too late, at least for a minute or two," Hardi smiled ruefully.

"Ye mean—Did ye—like me?" Blair wasn't sure what words to use to describe what just happened to her. It felt like far more than just a release. It consumed her. And climax felt too detached.

"Aye, Blair. I couldnae help it. That's never happened to me before," Hardi laughed, but his cheeks were bright red. At Blair's furrowed brow, he closed his eyes. "I've never lost control like that and finished without being touched. I would vera much like for ye to touch me. Vera much."

Blair pulled her lips in, trying to keep from laughing, but she knew she appeared smug when Hardi shook his head and grinned. "Mayhap after we eat?" Blair offered.

Hardi growled before his teeth grazed her neck, his tongue adding to the erotic sensation. His hand cradled Blair's head as he kissed behind her ear. His other hand squeezed her breast almost painfully. Blair's hands grasped his backside and drew his hips against her. She could feel his cock lengthening as it hardened.

"When we are alone, I will show ye just what I fancy eating," Hardi growled. At Blair's gasp, he realized she might not understand what he meant. He pulled away, but her cunning grin made him wonder if she knew more than he expected.

"Maude told me," Blair explained. She slid her hand over his hip and cupped his rod. "And I ken how a woman can enjoy a feast of her own. I dinna ken that I'll be any good, but I shall be an apt student if ye will be ma teacher."

"*Mo ghaol.*" My love. "I dinna think ye ken how hard it is for me to keep from mauling ye right now."

"I think I ken exactly how hard it is." Blair

139

wrapped her hand around Hardi's length, the plaid pulling tight around his rod.

"Ye'll be glad to ken how hard ye make me when I'm buried inside ye," Hardi promised. He watched Blair's eyes squeeze shut, and he wasn't sure how to interpret her expression. "I shouldnae say such things."

Blair's eyes flew open. "I like hearing it." She blinked several times, and it was her turn to flush red.

"Do ye, lass? Ye like it when I tell ye what I want to do to ye?" Hardi's voice deepened.

"Aye," Blair whispered.

"I want to strip ye bare and kiss yer throat before making ma way to yer perfect breasts. I want to suckle them like a starving bairn, but I promise ye, ye will ken I want ye like a mon." Hardi watched Blair's reaction as her body swayed toward him. When her eyes reopened, he understood the need he recognized.

"Hardi, is it wrong to tell ye that I want to ken what it feels like for us to join? That I canna stop wondering what it will feel like to have ye inside me. I —I dinna mean I'm wondering that just now. I've been thinking aboot it. I canna stop thinking aboot it since we kissed in the alcove."

"Nay, *mo ghaol*. It isnae wrong. I'm glad to ken ye want me as much as I want ye, that ye want to make love to me like I do with ye."

"Make love?" Blair swallowed. "Mama told me years ago that many married people couple. It's what's expected. People who join just for pleasure have other names for it. I ken I shouldnae ken them, but Mama wanted me to understand before I arrived at court. She didna want me to be naïve and vulnerable. She also said it was a rare thing when couples truly make love. That people say it, but dinna really mean it. They use it too loosely."

140

Blair looked away as she licked her lips. She gathered her courage before looking back at Hardi. "If what we will have is just coupling or rutting, then dinna feel ye have to say we're making love. I'd rather ye didna." Blair couldn't meet his eyes. When she stepped back and her shoulders brushed the bark, she realized they'd both let go of each other's clothing. She was unprepared for the intensity in Hardi's eyes or how close he brought his face as he pressed his hand onto the trunk beside her head.

"I dinna use that phrase loosely either, Blair. I have rutted. I have tupped. I have even fucked. I'm fairly certain ye learned that one at court. But I have never made love to a woman. I have never, ever felt before what I do for ye. I willna promise there willna be times when I want ye with a fierceness that borders on being rough. I felt that today. But I want to take ye to our bed, lay ye down, and worship ye until ye ken that what our bodies do is the most intimate way to show how we feel. I dinna ken the words to use, but I can show ye I love ye, Blair."

Blair nodded as she tried to blink away tears. "I love ye, too. And it scares me just how strongly I feel. I dinna want to feel this way if ye—"

"If I dinna feel the same and will take a leman. Is that what ye're trying to say?" Hardi asked. Blair nodded her head as she closed her eyes. Hardi pressed a soft kiss to her mouth before pulling back, taking both of Blair's hands in his. "Look at me, Blair. It's nae secret many lairds keep mistresses. They marry who they are told to. Ladies are made to believe there is nay pleasure in the marriage bed, that seeking it is a sin. But that isnae us. Yer da wouldnae stray from yer mama. I dinna think his mind could even conjure such an idea. They were the first noble couple I ever heard of sharing a chamber. I've told ye before, I respect yer father more than

141

I've ever respected any mon. I didna lie when I said I have tried to live ma life with the honor yer father does." Hardi squeezed Blair's hands before pulling her into his embrace. "If I didna believe I could be faithful to ye until the end of our lives, I wouldnae marry ye. I shouldnae have assumed ye would ken there willna be a bedchamber for each of us. I willna visit ye as though I am some guest staying at Tor Castle. It will be our bedchamber. It is where I shall fall asleep with ye in ma arms every night that I'm home. It's where we will conceive our children, and ye'll bring them into this world. And if I'm lucky, it's beside ye in that bed where I shall breathe ma last."

Blair squeezed her arms around Hardi's waist. His much larger body provided a haven she didn't know she needed. "I dinna ken what to say. I love ye."

"That's all I need to hear. I love ye, too, *mo chridhe*."

They stood together until they both knew they'd been hiding far too long. Hardi kissed Blair's forehead, and they walked out of the trees with their arms wrapped around one another. Blair was grateful all the guards, especially her two Sutherland ones, didn't look as though anything was out of the ordinary. She laid out the picnic, and by the end, they'd consumed all the food. Blair wondered if she could ever pack enough.

Full and happy, Blair laid back to watch the sun shine through the leaves at the edges of the clearing. Hardi laid beside her, their hands clasped. But rather than counting clouds, they enjoyed the companionable silence. The guards moved away, and their quiet chatter was the only background sound. Blair felt herself dozing off as her eyelids grew heavy.

Hardi gently shook Blair awake, pressing a kiss to her temple as her eyes fluttered open. Her eyes registered the position of the sun and how the light had softened. She hadn't realized that she'd fallen into a deeper sleep than she intended. She turned her head toward Hardi, and his soft smile and gaze warmed her to her toes.

"Did ye ken yer nose twitches when ye sleep?" Hardi asked.

"Ma nose? Nay, I didna ken. Were ye watching me sleep? How long did I sleep?"

"I couldnae help it. Ye looked so peaceful, but I didna watch the entire time. I spoke with ma guards for part of it. I'd say ye rested for aboot two hours."

"Two hours?" Blair jerked up before running her fingers through her hair. She sat watching her guards attach the picnic baskets to the saddles. She quickly rose, allowing Hardi to fold the blanket. It stunned her to realize how tired she was. She hadn't thought she would fall asleep, but she remembered how soothing it was to feel Hardi's thumb brushing back and forth over her knuckles. His pine scent mingled with those in the forest, and she'd felt like she was back on Sutherland.

Hardi led her to his horse before lifting her onto its back. He mounted behind her, guiding his horse through the trees. They opted to take a longer route back to the castle to avoid the steep incline, giving the horses a reprieve. Neither Hardi nor Blair minded the extra time with Blair curled against Hardi's chest. She rode with both legs over one side rather than astride like she had when they left the keep. She found her eyes growing heavy once again, and she deduced that it was Hardi's protective presence that allowed her to lower her guard even more than she did in her own chamber. They parted inside the castle, each preparing for the evening meal. Duty obligated Blair to sit with the other ladies-in-waiting. She dreaded another confrontation like the evening before, but the younger ladies appeared to be on their best behavior. Arabella and Laurel explained that the women had received a dressing down from the Mistress of the Bedchamber, who oversaw the ladies-in-waiting. The MacMillans departed earlier that day, and the Camerons sat with the MacLeods. Blair enjoyed a perfect evening after a perfect day.

NINETEEN

With their courtship no longer a secret, Blair and Hardi openly spent their mornings in the scriptorium, choosing to work on sums and figures before going for long afternoon walks where Blair drilled Latin subjects and predicates into Hardi. When they were away from the castle, they held hands during their walks, but while still on the castle grounds and in town, decorum forced them to hide their familiarity. Both were content to have Blair's arm wound around Hardi's, but neither found it satisfying after their interlude in the woods.

They took a lengthy walk on the fourth afternoon, both losing track of the distance as Hardi recited what he'd learned the previous days. Blair praised him, amazed at his determination to excel as a pupil. She hadn't expected him to learn as much as he had in the brief time they'd worked together, but she understood his motivation, and they both felt the time constraints closing in on them.

"Cameron approaching," a guard called out. Hardi spun around as two horse galloped toward him. He recognized the Cameron plaid first, then his own horse, *Uaill.* Anxiety spread through Hardi, knowing something dire had happened if the messenger brought his horse to speed their return to the keep.

"Laird Cameron!" As the approaching rider called out, Blair could see the strain on the man's face and his obvious exhaustion. Deep shadows sat beneath his eyes, and mud caked his leine and plaid. "I bring an urgent message from Faolán."

"Hand me Uaill's reins. Lady Blair rides back with me," Hardi stated. Blair didn't hesitate to follow Hardi's command. She pulled herself into the saddle and moved as far forward as she could while Hardi issued instructions for the other guards to follow. Only one Sutherland and one Cameron accompanied them on horseback. Hardi insisted on the protocol anytime they walked beyond sight of the castle in case of attack, and they needed to rush Blair to safety.

Once the four horses were on their way, Blair asked, "Ye named yer horse Pride?"

"Aye. I received him as a gift from Uncle Farlane when I returned from fostering. He said I was a mon and needed a mon's horse." Hardi explained. "He was my pride and joy, so I named him for it."

The powerful stallion ate up the miles as his hooves churned up the ground beneath them. Blair felt the muscles bunch and release with each stride. "We should find a mare and name her Joy. Then Pride should be her stud."

Hardi chuckled but tucked the thought away for another day. He liked the idea of giving Blair the mare as a wedding gift, even though she already had Buannaiche. Chickens scattered as they raced through town, angry fists raised at them, curses flung at them about hens never laying eggs again. Once in the castle's bailey, the guard handed the missive to Hardi. He ordered the man to eat and retire to the barracks. Hardi glanced around before taking Blair's hand and leading her to the gardens. They walked in silence until they reached the center, and he handed the parchment to her. Blair tore open the wax seal and unfolded the vellum. She scanned the missive and gasped before starting at the beginning and reading it aloud.

Hardwin,

The Mackintoshes and Macphersons raided our borders a week apart. They razed the fields and burned the crofts before executing the villagers. The attacks were too similar not to have been organized. They've made camp on our side of the border from the Macphersons. The council believes they intend to lay siege while you dally at court. If you do not decide to lead soon, you may have no clan left to lead at all. I will make decisions in your stead to protect your people.

Loyal servant to Clan Cameron,

Faolán Cameron.

The tone and contents stunned Blair. She never imagined a clan member writing with such disrespect to their laird. Even the salutation wasn't befitting a laird, regardless if they were family. She ground her teeth as she looked up at Hardi. The anger she anticipated wasn't there. She saw shame instead. She glanced down at the missive Hardi now held but still couldn't read. She placed her hand on his arm, and Hardi jumped as though he'd forgotten she stood beside him even though her voice still filled his head.

"Hardi?" Blair murmured.

"I must leave. Today," Hardi looked back at the castle, his mind already a blur of things he needed to do to depart before sundown.

"Hardi, wait. Listen to me," Blair clung to his sleeve as he turned away. "This doesnae make sense."

"It makes plenty of sense to me. While I spent ma days courting ye and pretending to be more than I am, ma clan suffered because I dinna have any business being their laird." Hardi's voice bit into Blair's heart as she recoiled from his veiled insinuation. She gritted her teeth to keep from lashing out, knowing Hardi was a drowning man who didn't need water pouring over his head.

"Listen to me, Hardi." Blair grabbed his upper arm, her fingers barely wrapping around the sides, and shook it. "Just stop for a moment. Riding out without a plan and without reasoning through what this missive *doesnae* say is likely to get ye killed."

Hardi looked down at Blair's face. She wasn't pleading with him. She wasn't even trying to reason with him. Hardi realized that she was thinking more like a clan leader than he was. He nodded for her to continue.

"When did this happen? Faolán says the attacks happened a week apart. Why didna he send a missive after the first one? Why wait? It took yer mon at least five days to get here. That means the first one happened at least a fortnight ago, if nae longer." Blair pulled the missive from Hardi's hand and shook it. "Ye could've already been back if ye'd been told. Mayhap even prevented the second attack. This isnae something Faolán and the council should have kept from ye. Where were yer patrols to keep the Mackintoshes and Macphersons from setting up camp? Why werenae more patrols set after the first attack? Faolán doesnae say whether either Laird Mackintosh or Laird Macpherson led the raids. Who's in charge, and did they send any demands? There's nay mention of what they want. It isnae yer land. There are too many hills in the area to do more than keep goats. The Macphersons have enough land for that. What do they want?"

Blair pointed at the castle and tapped her temple. She crossed her arms and raised her eyebrows at Hardi. "Both lairds ken ye're away. That's why they timed it when they did. But they must also ken ye're here, at court, with the king. They wouldnae massacre yer people for naught kenning ye can tell the king. Hardi, ye need to find yer messenger and find out what really happened. I dinna think this even scratches the surface of the truth." Blair was breathless by the time she finished.

Hardi nodded as he considered the questions Blair asked. They were ones his brain should have thought of, but guilt and shame took hold, slowing his mind until it stalled. He was embarrassed that he'd failed to wonder the same things as Blair, which only made him feel like a greater failure. He feared Faolán was the better choice for leading the Camerons.

"Dinna do that, Hardi," Blair's icy voice warned. "Dinna think Faolán should be laird. He wrote that missive hoping this is how ye would react. He wants to make ye feel guilty and ashamed. He's manipulating ye, and I'll be damned if I watch him succeed. Hardi, how much time did ye spend with yer uncle when he had to decide these matters? How much time did ye spend following orders that ye didna questions the reasons for?"

"Until I became ma uncle's heir, I rarely was a part of discussing clan business. I patrolled and stood watch. Otherwise, I trained or helped where I was sent."

"Exactly. Do ye ken why these questions came to me? Because I was trained to be a chatelaine. That doesnae just mean counting vegetables and bedlinens. Who do ye think protects the keep and the clan when the laird rides out? If ye think it's guardsmen, then ye are as blind as every other mon. The lady of the clan must ensure everyone eats, everyone has a roof over their heads, and ensures the wounded and sick are cared for. Under a siege, who rations the

149

food and supplies? It isnae the laird, that's for bluidy sure." Blair took Hardi's hands in hers and squeezed until he looked her in the eye. "And who do ye think ensures enough food is available when patrols ride out all of a sudden? Who decides what supplies are sent along with warriors to give to survivors?"

"I didna ken a clan's lady did all of that," Hardi admitted. He felt just as overwhelmed as he did a moment ago, and even more foolish for not knowing what was obvious to Blair.

"Stop, Hardi," Blair's frustration echoed in her voice. "What do ye think I was doing when I wasna sitting and embroidering? Mama was teaching me these things. What do ye think I was doing during the years between ye returning home and me coming to court? I was practicing these skills. I've kenned ma entire life that I would likely be the lady of a clan. Ye've kenned all of two moons that ye would be laird. Faolán is taking advantage of that. Ye need to decide now, Hardi. Are ye going to let Faolán take the lairdship from ye, or are ye going to take help when it's offered and stand yer ground?"

Hardi took in the determined face before him. Blair's resilience radiated from her. He'd been self-conscious when he asked her to teach him to read and write, but not too prideful to accept her help. Not only had he fallen in love with Blair, he'd gained confidence as a laird. He wouldn't let Faolán or anyone else strip away Blair's hard work. He knew the moral support she'd given him was worth even more than the academics she taught him.

"I dinna trust Faolán to lead a fly out of a chamber pot. Ye're right that I wasna trained to be laird, but that's what fate and the Lord dealt me. Blair, I dinna ken what I would do without ye." Hardi pulled her into his embrace, pressing a tender kiss against her lips. She opened for him on a sigh, her arms wrapping around his neck. They heard the shocked gasps not far from them, but neither pulled away. After a handful of small kisses, Hardi professed, "I love ye."

"And I love ye. I will stand beside ye nae matter what, Hardi."

Hardi nodded. They stood with their arms around each other as Hardi thought aloud. "Ye're right that I need to find ma guard and ask him what he kens. Laird Menzies is here, too. He may ken what the Macphersons have been doing near our borders. Once I find out what I can from them, I will decide whether I should inform the king. If I canna do all of that this eve, then I will still ride out in the morn. I dinna want to leave ye here, Blair, but neither will I take ye when ye arenae ma wife. And I will nae ride ye into battle."

Blair nodded. There was nothing she could say other than agree with Hardi. Their romance was hardly the most pressing matter, and she knew he was right that she shouldn't leave court with him while they were unwed. Or at least not until a betrothal was set. Blair accompanied Hardi to the barracks, where he asked for his guard. The man exited the barracks with just his plaid slung around his waist and heel of bread hanging out of his mouth. He choked when he saw Blair and hurried to bow. Blair covered her mouth and looked away so the man wouldn't see her laugh. When she felt composed and the man no longer coughed, she looked back at him and offered the kindest smile she could, hoping it would ease his discomfort.

"Bran, Lady Blair and I are in need of information. Do ye ken what Faolán included in the missive?" Hardi asked.

The guard looked between the couple and shook his head. "Nay. He said it was urgent clan business that couldnae wait and that I was to ride like the Devil was poking a pole up ma arse." The man's eyes widened as he looked at Blair. "I beg yer pardon, ma lady."

"I imagine that would be most uncomfortable. I dinna blame ye for hurrying," Blair grinned, and the man relaxed.

"What aboot the raids?" Hardi interjected.

"Raids?" Bran's forehead furrowed. "Ye mean how many heads of sheep we pilfered from the Macphersons?" The man grinned from ear to ear. "We took at least fifty from the bastards."

"Ye raided the Macphersons?" Blair demanded as she leaned forward. When she realized what she'd done, she stepped back. Hardi's arm shot around her waist and pulled her back beside him.

Bran looked between the two until Hardi growled, "Answer Lady Blair."

"Aye. The council said we should raid while the weather's been good," Bran explained.

Blair glanced up at Hardi, and he nodded.

"How far into their territory did ye have to ride to do that? I've ridden through Macpherson land every time I come and go from court. Ye have to ride pretty far from yer border into their territory to get to their pastureland."

"Aye, from the keep, it's a day's ride to the border and another day's ride to where we found the first flock."

"First?" Hardi snarled. "How bluidy many flocks did ye take?"

"Two," Bran beamed.

"*Shite*," Hardi's hands fisted, forcing himself not to take his ire out on the messenger.

"Faolán ordered this?" Blair asked. When Bran nodded, she continued. "So there wasna a raid by the Mackintoshes or the Macphersons?"

"Nay." Bran shook his head, confusion clear on his face.

"And there are nay members of their clans camping on yer land?" Blair pressed.

"Nay. Drostan doubled the patrols once we made it back with the flocks. We dinna want them retrieving the sheep. Half of them are ours anyway."

"Ours?" Hardi's face showed his confusion.

"Aye. When ye and David went to the Macquaries the last time, there was a raid where the Macphersons stole several sheep and a few cows."

"Did David learn of this?" Hardi wondered.

"I dinna think so. The battle with the Mackintoshes came too soon after. I dinna think there was time. And since it seems ye didna ken, I doubt he did."

Blair and Hardi exchanged a look before Hardi dismissed his warrior. Blair and Hardi returned to the gardens and found a bench near where they'd stood earlier.

"I dinna understand why Faolán would lie and nae think that ye would ask. Hardi, I dinna think Bran is lying. He seemed too surprised at times to be spinning falsehoods."

"I've kenned Bran since we were weans. He isnae a liar, and I believe he supports me. I think Faolán truly didna tell him what the missive contained. And it wouldnae surprise me if Faolán told the men it was ma order that sent them on the raid. I should have asked Bran that, but I didna think of it."

"Ye can ask him later. There was plenty of other news to work through. I didna think of it either," Blair assured him. "What next?"

"I find the Menzies. He arrived after I did, so he may be aware of the raid. Clan Menzies minds their own business and doesnae get involved with the feuds around them. But that doesnae mean they dinna ken

153

what's happening." Hardi looked toward the castle. "I'll find him before the evening meal and see what I can learn."

Blair nodded as she followed Hardi's gaze to the castle. As though Hardi knew what she thought, he wrapped his arm around her shoulders. When Blair rested her head on his shoulder, he tilted his over hers. His other hand took both her in his. His thumb ran along her ring finger on her left hand.

"I amnae going anywhere," Blair promised.

"I still dinna want to leave without ye. But even though Faolán lied, I'm nae convinced it's safe to bring ye to Tor. If Faolán wants to oust me as laird, I dinna ken how far he will go. I willna risk yer life."

Blair sighed, but nodded. "Even if this didna happen, I ken ye need to return home anyway. Ye canna linger here much longer. The moon ye were willing to spend is over, and ye've been away too long. I dinna think Mama and Da will dawdle with their permission. I think it's a matter of how long it takes the messengers to travel that far north." Blair entwined her fingers with Hardi's. "It gives me a chance to decide what to teach ye when next I see ye."

"I ken what I want to teach ye, lass. And it's nae aught ye can learn in a scriptorium. I'd really hoped to return home with ye on ma arm. Or better yet in ma arms on ma horse."

Blair laughed. "Buannaiche willna care for that. He is sure to let ye and Uaill ken that he believes ma place is on his back."

Hardi chuckled. "I'm jealous of a bluidy horse."

"We shall sort this all out, *mo chridhe*," Blair smiled. Hardi kissed her temple before they returned to the castle.

TWENTY

Hardi was certain steam radiated from his ears as he listened to Laird Cathal Menzies laugh at him after Hardi asked whether the fellow laird was aware of the situation with the Macphersons and Mackintoshes.

"Aye, I heard," Cathal chortled. "Faolán barely got his arse out in time, from what I hear. He's too old to be playing a young mon's game."

Hardi ground his teeth. Bran neglected to mention that Faolán rode out with them. He fought to keep his face impassive, and he knew Blair had her courtly mien in place. It was the one that he knew meant the wheels were turning in her mind, but she would give nothing away.

"It does surprise me that he can sit a horse that long. His gout tends to flare when he's out in the damp," Hardi noted.

"It surprised me to hear he rode to the border, but he'd rather send someone else to their death than he would his own. Macphersons chased them to the border, but yer men were out of sight before they got there. A Macpherson band ran into one of ma patrols as they swept the border to see if yer men lingered. That's how I learned of it."

"I admit I wouldnae mind listening in when the Macpherson tells the Mackintoshes aboot how the Camerons pulled the wool over their eyes." Hardi's pun elicited another chuckle from Cathal. He nodded several times before taking a long sip from his mug.

"Och, I wouldnae worry aboot them too much. They're still licking their wounds from the last time they encountered ye. I mean they didna suffer the defeat and lose all their men like ye did, but they arenae in the mood to fight ye again."

Hardi clenched his fists and bit back his angry retort as Cathal blandly mentioned the battle where he lost the last of his cousins and nearly lost his own life. Blair wasn't so willing to ignore the slight.

"Clan Cameron is lucky that Laird Cameron was the one to survive, or they would have lost the last of the laird's family that day," Blair hissed. Cathal blinked several times before looking contrite.

"That was rude of me, lad," Cathal clapped a massive paw on Hardi's shoulder. Had his tone not confirmed his words, Hardi wouldn't have stood for being called "lad." "For what it's worth, I think ye should breed yerself a passel of yer own lads and get an heir sharpish. She looks like she could bear yer braw sons."

Hardi narrowed his eyes at Cathal, fighting to keep his temper in check. "'*She*' is Lady Blair, and I willna have ye speak of her as though she's little more than a brood mare."

"Come now, Hardwin. Ye're being awfully sensitive. Perhaps all that time I hear ye've been spending with yer little lass has softened ye." Cathal chuckled once again, amused by his own inuendo. "I thought ye'd be harder than that."

"Menzies," Hardi warned. Cathal sobered when

he realized Hardi hadn't found any humor in his comments.

"Aye, well. There isnae anyone camped on yer land unless they are passing through. Faolán is a deceptive bastard, and I'd still get yerself married to someone sooner rather than later and get her with child. Pray it's a lad and useful unlike ma gaggle of daughters." Cathal turned away from Hardi and Blair before waving over his guards. Blair and Hardi moved toward the side of the Great Hall where they could talk without an audience.

"Nae one word in the missive was true. Except mayhap the part aboot making the decisions for the clan," Hardi said.

"The way he finished the missive tells us everything. He didna call himself yer loyal servant. He said he was a servant to the clan. He doesnae back ye, and he will make excuses under the guise of protecting the clan to oust ye," Blair replied.

Before they could say more, a young page interrupted to inform them the king expected an audience with them in his antechamber. Blair cast Hardi a glance that told him this was not good news. They followed the page until they reached the small chamber attached to the Great Hall. Often used to meet with esteemed guests or a place for the king and queen to be alone, it was also a place where the king could let loose his temper with few to witness it.

"Och, hell. I didna ask Blair to join you, Laird Cameron." King Robert's greeting made their stomachs drop to their feet. Blair didn't miss the lack of honorific before her name, and it indicated how irritated the king was. "You're both here now. Come to the table."

Hardi placed Blair's hand on his arm as they approached. King Robert cocked an eyebrow before releasing an annoyed sigh.

"Everyone knows you're courting. I bluidy well said you could. You don't need to remind me. Apparently, your kissing in the gardens reminded everyone. Och, aye. I heard aboot that." When the couple were within arm's length, the king thrust a piece of parchment at Hardi. "Read this."

Hardi glanced down at the document but knew he wouldn't be able to pick out more than a few words that he recognized, and he suspected they wouldn't be words he understood.

"May I see, too?" Blair asked quietly. When Hardi turned the vellum toward her, she trailed her finger over it and murmured what she read. She made it seem as if she were reading to herself, but Hardi was relieved she'd intervened. She'd only read half of the missive when King Robert harrumphed.

"Still canna read it on your own, Cameron?" King Robert asked. His voice was calmer and unaccusatory, but Blair shifted to put herself in front of Hardi. Both men looked down at her, the king grinning and Hardi surprised when they realized she wasn't aware of what she'd done. It was only when she had to look back over her shoulder that she noticed she'd turned her shoulders to be a barrier in front of Hardi.

"I've made great strides with Lady Blair's tutoring, but nae, I still canna read and understand all of this," Hardi admitted.

King Robert drummed his fingers on the table as he considered his next course of action. When he stood upright and crossed his arms, Blair and Hardi feared what would come next. The king looked back and forth between them until he finally nodded. "You know the Macphersons brought the raid Faolán led to my attention. They are threatening to lay siege if you don't return the sheep." King Robert held up a staying hand. "I know half the flock was yours to begin with. But are a bunch of ewes worth what the Macphersons are demanding? Your clan can't afford to pay recompense right now, and you most certainly won't survive a siege."

"I'll give them back the bluidy sheep. I dinna care aboot those. I didna even ken they'd been stolen. That's ma real concern now. Nay one thought fit to tell me aboot them, and then Faolán thought to act in ma stead. He could've gotten every mon killed, and now I have this mess to sort out. Macpherson will never believe I didna have aught to do with this. It doesnae matter that I didna. I'm the laird." Hardi fumed.

"Laird Cameron, I don't know what Faolán is up to, but I suspect it's no good. Until he can be removed from the clan council, you would do well to find someone who can read and who you can trust," King Robert advised.

"Nae possible, Yer Majesty. The only other mon who can read is Drostan. He willna side with me over his brother. I canna refuse to sign documents, and I canna trust them to read what's really written." Hardi wanted to pull his hair out. Blair watched him as her own frustration grew. She wanted to comfort Hardi, but even if they didn't have the king as an audience, she wasn't sure what to offer. She glanced down at the table and noticed a map of the Highlands poking out from beneath several scattered pieces of parchment. She stepped forward and pushed the vellum aside until she could see the map. She turned to look back at Hardi.

"Is Inverlochy Castle really that close to Tor Castle?" Blair asked.

"Aye. Less than an hour's ride," Hardi answered. He came to stand beside Blair as she looked up at King Robert.

"Let me go there. I can meet Hardi halfway each

day, and he can bring aught he needs reading or have me write what he needs." Blair looked over at Hardi. "I'm certain ye can buy yerself time to meet me before ye make any decisions based on documents ye receive."

"Nay," both men spoke at the same time. Hardi bowed to the king, but King Robert shook his head. "She'll be your wife."

"Blair, I'm nae sending ye unaccompanied to stay in a keep that hasnae been properly occupied since before the wars. It's on ma land, but ma clan hasnae seen to its upkeep. The MacDonalds have had the run of it for years now. I willna send ye there with only two guards. Even if I sent ye will all of ma guards, I wouldnae want ye to be there."

"Ye dinna trust yer allies?" Blair shot Hardi a skeptical glance.

"Nae with ye alone and unwed. I canna imagine Laird MacDonald will be too excited to have the woman I intend to marry living in a keep he'd like to claim for himself."

"Laird Cameron, would you be more amenable if I sent a contingent of my own men with Lady Blair? You don't have the men to spare, but I see reason in what Lady Blair proposes."

Hardi shook his head. "Laird Sutherland wouldnae approve of his unwed daughter in a keep where neither he nor I can assure her safety. Do ye expect me to ride up and drop her at the gate, wishing her well? I dinna ken who else is living there. I havenae visited there in months. I dinna ken if the building itself is clean and safe for anyone, let alone Blair. I havenae had time to tour ma land since I became laird. I dinna ken aught aboot where ye're asking me to leave Blair. That doesnae sit right with me."

"Then take her home with you," King Robert suggested.

"And if Faolán is planning to remove me as laird, how can I protect Blair then? Even if we could marry and Blair came as ma wife, that would make her a target, too. I'm nae risking Blair's life," Hardi argued.

"Do either of ye ken that I'm still standing here?" Blair spoke up. "Hardi, I understand yer concerns. I ken ye're trying to do what's best for me. But ye're a laird, and what's best for me isnae what's best for yer clan. What is best is for ye and yer clan is for ye to remain laird. To do that, ye need help. I'll send for Lach. While we wait for him, I'll stay at Inverlochy with King Robert's guards. Once Lach arrives, I'll either return here or go to Dunrobin."

"It'll take at least three sennights before Lachlan would arrive. I can hold onto ma clan that long. Blair, stay here. Please."

"Doesnae ma opinion count for aught? I thought ye said we were partners. The first time that's put to the test, ye make all the decision by yerself." Blair tried to keep the hurt from her voice. She wouldn't allow her emotions to show if she was to prove to either man standing beside her that she wasn't a useless, simpering woman. She issued an ultimatum. "Hardi, take me and ken I'm settled safely at Inverlochy. Or ken that I'm going on ma own. Either way, I will be there when ye need me." Blair turned away and was prepared to leave when Hardi's arm shot out in front of her. Unable to stop her forward movement, his arm came around her belly as he pulled her back against him.

"I'm nae trying to make ye feel useless or unwanted. I ken I need yer help, and I want it. I didna say ye would never be able to go to Inverlochy. What I said was that I canna ensure it's safe for ye at this point. And I told the truth that yer father wouldnae agree to ye going there unmarried. Allow me a chance to ride out ahead of ye. If I'm certain it's safe for ye, then I will either come for ye or send for ye. Blair, if we arrive and ye canna stay there, then what? I take ye to Tor? People will question if ye're ma mistress because we arenae married. I'm nae destroying yer reputation. I just need a little time."

"Ye dinna have a little time, Hardi," Blair reminded him. "Inverlochy is three day's ride from Foulis. If I canna remain at Inverlochy or join ye at Tor, I'll go to Cairren and Padraig. Regardless of what we decide, I'll write to Lach and ask him to meet ye at Tor."

Hardi saw the merit in what Blair suggested, so he nodded. When she wrapped her arms around him, he inhaled her lemongrass scent. He realized that the scent was as soothing as the feel of her against him. Lemongrass would always make him think of Blair, and the thought of her was enough to ease any tension.

"I'm nae trying to make decisions for ye, Blair. I'm trying to make decisions with yer wellbeing in mind," Hardi whispered. "I want ye with me always, but I would never forgive maself if I rushed to act, and ye came to harm."

"I understand. It didna feel that way, but I ken now that ye've explained." Blair turned her face up for the kiss Hardi offered, neither caring that King Robert watched or that he cleared this throat twice before they broke apart.

They'll be handfasted before the end of her first week at Inverlochy, the king mused to himself. *I don't know what's in the air in Caithness and Sutherland, but the Sinclairs and Sutherlands are a different breed altogether when they fall in love. I blame Liam and Hamish. Neither of them could wait three sennights for banns to be read once they and their brides decided to wed. Their weans are no better.*

"I will send a score of men to accompany you to Inverlochy. Half will remain with Lady Blair, and the other half will go on to Tor Castle with you, Laird Cameron. Until you know where you stand, at least you'll have ten men to guard you. They'll follow your direction, but they answer to me. Leave in the morn."

Blair and Hardi said their thanks and showed their respect before hurrying out of the antechamber. The meal had already begun, and Blair winced, knowing the king wouldn't be pleased to arrive late. Eating proper food at a real table was the one thing he enjoyed most about not being on campaign. He wasn't forgiving when he was unable to partake in a full meal. Hardi guided Blair to where they noticed the Camerons and Sutherlands sat together. They informed the men that they would all depart at sunrise. Once they'd finished eating, none of them were long for their beds.

TWENTY-ONE

Before the sun was awake, Blair stood in the bailey surrounded by the king's men, Camerons, her Sutherland guards, and her maid. She attempted to rub the sleep from her eyes discreetly and stifle a yawn. Neither she nor her maid was awake as early as she intended, so she was grateful that her maid finished packing the few things she needed the night before. Maeve accompanied her for decorum's sake, both women knowing Blair could take care of her own toilette and wardrobe. It would have been impossible for Blair to maintain her reputation if she traveled with twenty-eight men and not had a chaperone.

Hardi approached as Blair covered her mouth over a yawn she couldn't swallow. Hardi's loving gaze warmed Blair against the brisk morning air. When he stood before her, he pulled her Sutherland plaid tighter around her. He welcomed the image in his mind of Blair wearing his Cameron plaid one day soon. Standing among the horses, Hardi dared to rub his hands up and down Blair's arms. Glancing around over Blair's head and the horses' backs, confident no one was watching, he pulled her into his embrace. Blair sighed as her body absorbed the heat

Hardi's body radiated. She didn't understand how he could be so much warmer than her when he only wore a leine with a swath of plaid over his chest and shoulders. She could only assume it was the bulky muscles Highland men carried that kept them from freezing. Her father and brother were the same. That or they refused to acknowledge any discomfort, but Blair discarded that explanation as she grew hot standing close to Hardi.

"I ken it's vera early, lass. I wish we didna have to draw ye away from ye bed, but it is best if we can ride a few extra hours today. I dinna want to hurry to Inverlochy because it means leaving ye, but I must return to Tor." Hardi explained.

"I ken. Hardi, it isnae that early," Blair reassured even though they both knew it was a falsehood. They couldn't even see the gates from where they stood in the predawn light. Hardi kissed Blair's forehead before leading her toward Uaill.

"Ride with me for a few hours, and ye can sleep," Hardi offered as he lifted her into the air. An angry whinny and snort followed by stomped hooves filled the air. Blair laughed as Hardi set her feet on the ground.

"I warned ye. Buannaiche doesnae like to share," Blair giggled. She eased away from Hardi, but he grasped her hand, pulling her back toward him.

"And neither do I. Blair, it's still dark. I can hold ye in ma arms and touch ye in ways I canna do in the light," Hardi whispered. At Blair's sharp inhale, he knew she'd decided. Calling out to one of her guards to attach Buannaiche's reins to his saddle, she squeezed Hardi's hand. Another angry whinny rent the air as Blair landed in the saddle, but a sharp word from her, and the horse remained quiet. Hardi was soon behind her, draping a spare Cameron plaid over Blair's lap. She unfolded it enough to pull it up over her shoulders. Ever practical, she knew they would ride into the wind. Hardi's heat from behind her and the extra layers of wool would make the early morning hours more comfortable, but it also offered the couple privacy.

Despite being the laird, Hardi had already arranged to ride in the center of the party while Blair rode with him. Blair's maid rode a mare who refused to get near Uaill after he nipped at her rump in the bailey. Hardi silently promised his steed extra apples and carrots. They hadn't passed through the Stirling Castle gate before Hardi's hand cupped Blair's breast. She shifted, her backside rubbing against Hardi's groin. He bit back a groan, his already aroused length begging for Blair's attention. Beneath the extra layers, Blair eased Hardi's plaid up his thigh until she touched bare skin. Her fingertips grazed the inside of his thigh. Hardi's muscles flexed as they instinctively pressed around her hips.

"I may have conceived of the most excruciating but arousing torture," Hardi's voice rumbled in Blair's ear. He kneaded her breast before sliding his hand over her belly and cupping her mons. He slipped his hand beneath Blair until his thumb pressed against her nub. Despite the fabric between them, the friction made Blair's heart race. Her fingers dug into Hardi's thighs as her arousal grew. Hardi didn't relent, and Blair rocked her hips with every forward motion of the horse's gait. It was only a matter of minutes before Hardi felt Blair's body go rigid before sinking back against his. "*Mo ghaol*, remember that feeling when I canna be near ye. Ken that I want naught more than to be with ye, bringing ye such pleasure ever night."

"Soon," Blair gasped as her hand gripped Hardi's hand, keeping it in place when he tried to withdraw it. "Let me feel ye there a little longer."

"I canna deny ye aught," Hardi whispered against her ear. He gathered the yards of material until he could ease his hand beneath Blair's skirts. He brushed his fingers over her inner thigh until he reached the apex. His cock twitched as he felt the moisture coating Blair's nether lips. "Ye are as wet for me as I am hard for ye."

Blair's rapid breathing was the only outward sign that she was eager for Hardi to continue his ministrations. But her dripping entrance told the story as well. His forefinger rubbed her pearl as his next two fingers eased inside her. She tilted her hips, making it easier for Hardi's fingers to slide in and out of her sheath. His thumb once more torturing her pearl.

"I would tell ye all the things I wish to do to ye once ye are ma wife, but I dinna want to shock ye. I dinna ken if I should ever wish ma lady-wife to do some of the things I crave," Hardi admitted.

"Do ye mean me taking ye into ma mouth?" Blair whispered. "Ye already ken I know that's one way a woman can pleasure a mon. Are ye worried that even though I ken of it, I willna agree to it? Let me assure ye, *mo chridhe*, I amnae scared or opposed to aught we can do together. Just teach me."

Hardi groaned as his cock throbbed. Blair's words made his pulse jump. "That's one thing I would enjoy vera much." Hardi cleared his throat and glanced about him, ensuring no one was too intent upon their conversation. "Did ye ken that a mon and a woman can enjoy such pleasure at the same time?"

Blair was silent for a moment as a lurid image of her backside in Hardi's face filled her mind, her mouth going dry and a longing she'd never felt to have something in her mouth made her shiver. "Aye. I can picture that. I am picturing that. Hardi, I ken more than I should. Nae from experience and nae from what Maude shared. I've heard far more than any maiden should, but," Blair swallowed. "I once stumbled upon a couple who werenae at all discreet. They kenned I saw them, but they didna stop, and I couldnae look away."

"What did ye see, Blair?" Hardi's voice encouraged her. It surprised her that he sounded calm and reassuring rather than impatient.

"I saw the woman had her gown loosened, so her breasts hung over the top. The mon had her pressed against the wall, but his hands were—were pinching her nipples." Blair closed her eyes, not to remember the erotic scene but embarrassed to admit she'd watched.

"Blair, ye dinna have to fear telling me aught. Ever. And if it's something private like this, that ye are curious aboot, I willna judge ye for it."

Blair nodded before continuing. "He had her gown pushed over her shoulder while he thrust into her from behind. The sounds they made—they were both enjoying it. I didna ken that people could couple that way. I thought only animals—"

"Is it something that ye want to try?" Hardi forced his voice to remain calm while he prayed she said yes. He knew Blair was a passionate woman, but he'd wondered if she would only agree to making love in a bed in the most traditional position. Her curiosity and courage to share with him her desires had him wanting to pull her off the horse and find a private place to ravish her.

"Aye." Her voice was barely louder than a breath.

"We can do aught ye want. If ye dinna enjoy it, we willna do it again. If ye do, then we can do it as often as ye want."

"Is it something ye enjoy?" Blair wondered.

"Blair," Hardi warned.

"Ye made it sound as if I could ask ye aught."

169

"Ye can, but do ye really want to hear of ma past? Blair, I dinna want to hurt ye, and to be honest, I dinna really want to remember aught before ye."

"That's sweet, Hardi, and it makes me feel good to hear it. But I want to ken what ye like. I dinna want it to just be aboot me. I dinna want ye to avoid something ye enjoy because ye dinna think a lady should do it." Blair paused, realizing that Hardi may have coupled with ladies and not just village women or wenches. "That ye dinna think ye should ask someone as inexperienced as me," she clarified.

"Blair, is part of the reason ye're saying this because ye fear turning me away will make me find someone who will do what I want?"

Blair nodded. "But that's only a wee part of it. I believe ye when ye say ye'll be faithful. I trust ye completely, Hardi. Yet, I dinna think it's unreasonable for a virgin to worry aboot being enough for her husband. I just want to give ye the same pleasure ye do me. I want to offer that to ye. I dinna ken if that makes sense."

"It does. All of it. I can understand how a maiden worries aboot keeping her husband's interest. And unfortunately, some dinna. But I pledge to ye that nay matter what happens between us, I willna ever disgrace us both by being unfaithful. I'd rather be abstinent than humiliate ye." Hardi's hand had slipped up to Blair's belly as they spoke. His fingers squeezed her waist in reassurance. "As for offering me the same pleasure. I understand ye because I believe we are of a like mind. Ye're offering because ye're giving me a part of ye. The part that ye want only me to have. I feel the same way. I want ye to enjoy making love because of how I can make yer body feel. But I also want to do it because it's a part of me, part of ma soul, that I will only give to ye."

Blair tucked her chin and nodded. She felt raw

admitting what she had, and it also overwhelmed her that Hardi understood what she muddled saying. Hardi drew her leg over the horse's withers until he cradled Blair in his arms. She burrowed into his chest, kissing him where a tiny patch of skin showed behind the laces of his leine.

"Hardi?"

"Aye, lass." Hardi glanced down at Blair's up-turned face.

"I love ye."

"I love ye, ma bonnie lass." He brushed an all-too-quick kiss against her lips. "Sleep now, Blair. I will hold ye." Blair's eyes drifted closed. Hardi felt as drained from their unexpected conversation as Blair. It was far too early in the morning for the physical turmoil of dallying on horseback, and he hadn't believed he could articulate his feelings as well as he did. He had given Blair a piece of his soul, and he knew he held the most precious gift, a piece of hers. He prayed he'd be a worthy husband and a laird she was proud of. The weight of his own expectations pressed down on him, making him weary.

TWENTY-TWO

Blair slept until the sun rose, and the light forced her eyes open. She remained in Hardi's lap until they stopped at midday to rest the horses and eat. Before their meal, Hardi recited all the verbs he knew how to conjugate in the past and present tense, naming the past participles that Blair hammered into him. They were both pleased with his memorization, and Hardi was relieved that not only did he remember them, he could pronounce them along with understanding each of their meanings and uses.

After a meal of bannocks and dried beef, the party mounted and carried on. Blair opted to ride Buannaiche. The horse nodded his head and nickered as Blair rubbed his neck before climbing onto his back. Hardi was certain the horse pranced with his owner once again in the saddle. Throughout the afternoon, Hardi recited his sums and multiplication tables until his throat grew dry and his voice hoarse. When they made camp for the night, Hardi's head ached, but Blair's blinding smile of praise and pride made him glad he'd kept trying.

The following four days continued much as the first. They started out before dawn and rode until twilight. Blair was stiff from sleeping on the ground but found rising in the morning much easier. She rode with Hardi, enjoying his touch until the sun was bright enough to make discretion difficult. Buannaiche was only well behaved when Blair was nearby, so the other horses and riders welcomed her return to her steed. After the first morning, Blair opted to ride in a modified sidesaddle position with Hardi. It allowed them both the freedom to snake their hands beneath folds of material. Hardi feared he would fall from his horse the first time Blair's bare hand touched his cock. She'd leaned against his chest with her eyes closed as if she dozed, but all the while, she stroked him until she felt something coat her hand and Hardi sighed. Then he flushed bright red. Blair was certain she could see his blush even in the dim light. He'd cleared his throat several times before reaching between them to wipe Blair's hand with his plaid.

After her initial introduction to pleasuring a man, Blair's confidence increased as Hardi's questing hand became more insistent the more Blair aroused him. Unable to kiss or show any public displays of affection, the couple settled for what they could enjoy beneath the blanket Hardi spread over Blair each morning. Their illicit touches along with their inability to act upon their desire heightened their need for one another. Both Hardi and Blair breathed easier when Inverlochy Castle came into sight. Despite arriving midmorning, Hardi promised not to depart for Tor until the following morning. He refused to leave until he was convinced Blair would have proper accommodations and would be safe amidst the MacDonalds they discovered living there.

Blair swept her gaze around the Great Hall and wanted to tuck tail before racing back to Stirling. She'd grossly underestimated what it meant to walk into a keep with few women and a clan she knew little about. It relieved her to see the chieftain was married, and his wife wasn't much older than Blair. The chieftain was old enough to be both women's grandfather, but Blair observed that he acted kindly toward his expecting wife. The keep's structure hadn't been well-maintained since King Robert's ascension to the throne forced the Comyns to relinquish it; however, it was clean. Blair turned her head to whisper over her shoulder to Hardi.

"It's on yer land, but the MacDonalds have taken over. Who's responsible for its upkeep? And why did yer uncle allow them to live here?" Blair asked.

"As far as I ken, the agreement was the MacDonalds would be guardians of the castle in return for maintaining it. It's nae falling down around our ears, but I'm nae pleased with its condition. I suspect the MacDonald will ask for funds I dinna have, but I canna send them packing. I need his warriors to help protect Cameron territory from the Clan Chattan Confederation. With the Mackintoshes, Macphersons, and Davidsons banding together with the Chattans to create a unified clan, I need every able-bodied mon to fight." Hardi slipped Blair's arm around his. "Let's meet our hosts."

"Laird Cameron," a deep bass boomed as the couple approached. "We didn't expect the honor of your company."

The chieftain's accent, or rather lack of a burr, took Blair aback. She hadn't expected to hear the bear of a man speak as though he belonged at court. Blair shifted her gaze to the woman sitting beside him. She squinted as a memory tried to force its way forward. Before she and Hardi stopped, she recalled why the woman looked familiar. She'd once been a lady-in-waiting, but she'd left court within a fortnight of Blair and Maude's arrival. Blair struggled to recall her name and came up blank. She wondered if the chieftain adopted the speech pattern to match his Lowland wife's expectations. She also wondered how a chieftain married a former lady-in-waiting.

"MacDonald, I apologize for nae sending more warning than an advance rider, but our journey here was unexpected, and our plans were hurried." Hardi's voice had an air of command despite their humility. "I would introduce ye to ma betrothed, Lady Blair Sutherland."

Blair forced herself to maintain her neutral expression despite the shock of Hardi's introduction. She dipped into a shallow curtsy, offering deference to her host even though in theory, she outranked him. Hardi's authority was clear to everyone in the Great Hall, and servants scurried to set extra places at the table for Blair and Hardi. Neither spoke until they took their seats.

"Lady Blair will be a guest at Inverlochy for the foreseeable future. Ye are to treat Lady Blair with the respect due ma future wife and the daughter of the Earl of Sutherland." Blair often forgot that her father's accurate title was Laird Hamish Sutherland, Earl of Sutherland. However, her father's position registered with her host. "Lady Blair, I introduce ye to Chieftain Artair MacDonald and Lady Robena MacDonald."

"Thank you for your hospitality, and I, too, apologize for the brief notice." Blair sensed adopting her courtly tone would earn her more respect than her father's title as she looked at the other couple. She'd almost apologized for inconveniencing them, but then recalled that she was soon to be the wife of the MacDonalds' overlord at Inverlochy. At least she prayed she was. She wondered where her parents' missives would end up if they were already en route to Stirling. Blair turned a warm smile toward the pregnant woman. "Lady Robena, I believe we met at court when I was newly arrived."

"I remember, Lady Blair. It is a pleasure to see you once more and to have you visit our home." Lady Robena's soft voice felt at odds with her choice of words, as though she was asserting her authority over Blair. It felt as if Robena was reminding Blair that Inverlochy belonged to the MacDonalds, rather than the Camerons allowing them residence. Keeping her courtly expression in place, she locked eyes with Lady Robena. She wore a similar mien as Blair, both understanding the challenge laid forth when no one else appeared to notice. Blair refused to look away. If she was to be Hardi's wife, she would outrank both Chieftain Artair and Lady Robena. At present, they were on near-equal footing, both daughters of lairds. Lady Robena blushed and offered the subtlest of nods, deferring to Blair.

Hardi observed the silent interplay between the women, not fully understanding what passed between them, but acutely aware that Robena challenged Blair, who did not back down. He noticed the slight dip of Robena's chin, acknowledging Blair's elevated position. It was only moments later that the women leaned toward one another and chattered like old friends. It relieved him to see women could resolve their battles with stares rather than fists like most men. Hardi arranged for Blair's stay and explained ten of the king's guards would remain as Blair's personal detail.

"Faolán still a boil on a witch's arse?" Artair's voice boomed. Hardi would have preferred they not share their conversation with everyone under the same roof. He nodded before taking a sip of ale. He sensed Blair's attention split between her conversation and the one Hardi was having.

"Ma cousin once removed has made decisions

that dinna align with the ones I would have made," Hardi hedged. He'd known Artair for years, but had no dealings with him until now. The dynamic of their relationship had shifted, but Hardi wasn't convinced Artair saw him as more than a guardsman.

"I take it that it wasn't your idea to lead the raid on the Macphersons," Arthur noted. "I didn't think so, but Faolán swore you'd given him permission to act in your stead, and that he only acted in alignment with your wishes."

Hardi wondered why Artair jumped directly to discussing the raid rather than engaging with small talk, and he wondered why the chieftain was so apt to speak against Faolán, a man he'd known for decades.

"You've seen Faolán recently," Hardi stated rather than asked.

"Aye, he and his men stopped here for the night on his return. It grew too late for them to continue," Artair explained.

His men. Those are ma bluidy men. Artair is fishing. He's baiting me with information aboot Faolán, but he sides with ma cousin. Hardi fumed but forced himself to remain calm. He would learn nothing more from Artair if he played his hand too soon. He also feared backing Artair into a corner that would make the man come out swinging. He wouldn't jeopardize Blair's safety, since he would leave her in Artair's care in less than a day.

"I appreciate ye accommodating ma clan twice in so little time," Hardi toasted as he raised his mug.

"My home is your home, after all." Artair raised his own mug, a smirk on his face. Shifting his gaze to Blair before looking back at Hardi, his voice held a smug note. "Faolán expected you back at Tor Castle sooner. He was certain you would have preferred to lead the raid. But I can see what delayed you."

"An issue with the taxes delayed me," Hardi

spoke the half-truth. He wondered what Artair knew of that situation.

"Faolán explained he stole the sheep to sell them. Once he realized you hadn't calculated the taxes accurately, he knew you would return asking for more money." Artair narrowed his eyes a sliver, but Hardi noticed.

"The delay was an audience with the king. I resolved the taxes," Hardi's nonchalant answer made Artair frown. It was clear to Hardi that the man expected to hear a tale of woe, perhaps even curses against Faolán.

"It will please Faolán to know that. I ken he was anxious aboot you going to court and not being able to read."

And there it was. Artair had grown impatient trying to goad Hardi into admitting his own shortcomings, so he abandoned his subtlety and went straight to the point. Hardi's peripheral vision caught how Blair's hand gripped the arm of the chair so tightly that her knuckles were white. He was certain she was listening to the conversation and struggling to remain uninvolved. But Lady Robena's attention shifted to the men at Artair's proclamation. Blair straightened; her chin held high. Hardi admired her regal grace and realized he'd fallen in love with a woman who would be the silent force behind his clan's survival. Her whisky hued eyes flashed a warning at the chieftain, but the man took no notice.

"It was of little consequence," Hardi kept his calm, sipping his ale as though the battle he'd fought to learn even a modicum of Latin hadn't happened.

"Someone must have assisted you," Artair pressed.

"Aye. Lady Blair." Hardi lowered his mug to the table as Artair burst into laughter, holding his hand to his side as his shoulders jiggled up and down.

Lady Robena turned a horrified gaze from her husband to their guests back to her husband.

"A woman? You turned to a woman to read to you? Are you sure she wasn't just reciting lullabies her mother taught her?"

"Chieftain MacDonald, do you ken who my mother is?" Blair asked softly. Before Artair could answer, she continued. "She was the daughter of the Earl of Ross and is the wife of the Earl of Sutherland."

Artair's laughter ceased immediately. He bubbled an apology, but Blair raised her hand. Artair fell silent. Blair raised an eyebrow, her imperiousness a ruse, but one she'd used often at court.

"Perhaps because I'm only a woman, I cannot understand why my mother wouldn't have taught me to read." Blair turned her palm up, offering Artair the opportunity to explain. The man gaped at her, his mouth opening and closing like a floundering fish. "I assumed you knew my father, but perhaps not as well as I thought. If you did, you would know my father expected my sister Maude and I to be raised to be chatelaines to a laird-husband. I understand that is a unique position from which most women are destined, but it is one that I am comfortable with."

"I meant no offense, my lady," Artair stammered. "It just surprised me that Laird Cameron couldn't find a more apt tutor."

"And what skills would such a tutor possess, Chieftain?" Blair kept her tone casual.

"I'm sure you are well versed in reading inventories and writing weekly menus, but a mon must be able to read contracts and understand clan business. It's a mite more complicated than ledgers filled with tick marks for hams and beef." Artair's condescending voice grated on Blair's nerves, but she kept her expression placid. She placed her hand on Hardi's leg under the tablecloth. He ceased bouncing it and wrapped Blair's hand in his.

"Such a shame my years of Latin will go to waste if all I'm to read are ledgers and menus once I marry," Blair mused.

"You read Latin?" Robena whispered her question. Blair suspected Robena could only read Scots, at best. Even if she did, Blair guessed Robena didn't parade her knowledge before her husband. Blair had no such reservations.

"And Scots, Gaelic, and French. I write them too. Sometimes a lady just needs to write to her Mama," Blair smiled angelically.

"I suppose a lady of your standing would prefer these pursuits. A chatelaine who isn't an earl's daughter must complete the more mundane tasks," Artair attempted to take back control of the conversation.

"Prefer? I loathed having to sit for my Latin lessons. It meant I wasn't climbing trees with Laird Cameron and his brother. I would beg Laird Cameron to tell me stories of his time in the lists while I embroidered and made candles. My mother made me count everything in French and Gaelic when we took inventory. I'm certain it took twice as long, but even earls' daughters must finish their mundane tasks." Blair shrugged as she leaned back and smiled at Hardi with a look of adoration that she didn't have to pretend.

"Lady Blair was of significant help to me, and we enjoyed rekindling our friendship." Hardi lifted Blair's hand from the arm of the chair where she'd placed it when she leaned back. He brought her knuckles to his lips, desire sparking in his gaze as he kissed the creamy skin. "All teachers should be as kind and patient as ma betrothed." Hardi lowered their joined hands to rest on the tabletop where anyone with a view of the dais could see.

"Laird Cameron, you have a strange way aboot you. I suppose Lady Blair's knowledge was useful, but you're fortunate you won't need it once you are at Tor Castle. Once you wed, Lady Blair will assume her position as Lady Cameron and not have time to read to you."

Hardi ground his teeth at Artair's patronizing words and tone. He would make his thoughts clear once and for all about Blair's position in his life. "Faolán and Drostan may be ma family, but I choose Lady Blair to be ma wife. The Lord expects a mon to leave his father and mother and hold fast to his wife. The Lord never said I needed to cleave to ma father's cousins. Lady Blair's place is at ma side as we lead the Camerons together. One day ma son shall sit to the other side of me. That doesnae leave room for anyone else."

Artair remained quiet, nodding his head as though he'd agreed with Hardi all along. Robena signaled the servants to bring out the midday meal. Blair and Robena picked up their conversation. Hardi turned to his senior guardsman while Artair spoke to an older clan member. Both leaders studiously ignored one another.

TWENTY-THREE

Hardi stood outside Blair's chamber door in just his plaid and leine, both Sutherland guards glaring at him. He knew the men didn't approve of the two times he and Blair slipped away into the woods, and he was certain they'd deduced what went on beneath the blanket, but they said nothing. Their reproachful gazes spoke loudly enough.

"Blair, it's me," Hardi whispered as he tapped on her door. He heard movement before the door opened a crack. Blair glanced over Hardi's shoulder at her guards. She offered a sympathetic smile that ended with a look of warning. It amazed Hardi how Blair's expressions could convey so much more than words. He slipped into her chamber, and she reached past him to lock the door. Hardi cupped Blair's face as their mouths fused together. It was the first proper kiss they'd shared in days. Unable to do more than drop a peck on the cheek while they traveled, they hungered for the taste of one another. "Where's yer maid?"

"She retired for the evening. I wasna in the mood for her nattering. I'll listen to the servants' gossip tomorrow. I wasna sure if ye would come, but either way, I couldnae manage her buzzing aboot," Blair waved her hand in the air.

"I thought yer men might bar me from yer door, but they just gave me dirty looks," Hardi grinned.

"They've kenned me since I was a wee lass. They are rather protective," Blair explained.

"Blair, they both used to knock me on ma arse when I still hadnae learned to swing a sword. They arenae keen on seeing wee Hardwin lusting after their laird's daughter," Hardi chuckled.

"I dinna think they are so fond of watching their laird's wee daughter lusting after the braw Laird Cameron," Blair corrected. Blair went onto her toes as she wrapped her arms around Hardi's neck, her brown eyes locked with his hazel. "Will ye kiss me again?"

Rather than answer with words, Hardi grasped Blair's backside and lifted her off the ground. Her legs came around his waist as they clung to one another. Hardi walked to the foot of the bed before taking a seat. His hands inched along her thighs until her chemise hid their ascent. He grazed his hands over her hips and bottom before caressing her ribs then cupping her breasts. It was the first time Hardi could touch the full length of Blair's body without clothes hampering his exploration. He kissed her neck as her head fell back. Blair's hands roamed over Hardi's back and chest, but frustration led her to tug on his leine. She gazed into Hardi's eyes as she unpinned the length of plaid from his shoulder. She handed him the brooch he dropped into his sporran that now rested against his back. She pulled his leine free of his belt and lifted it over his head.

Blair was mesmerized. She'd seen plenty of men train in the lists without their shirts on in summer, but she'd never been close enough to touch, to notice, the tiny white scars that marred his shoulders and chest. She leaned forward to look down his back. Her fingertips traced over them as her breasts pressed against Hardi's chest. He tugged the ribbon of her chemise until one side came loose. Blair sat back, allowing the fabric to fall from her shoulder, one breast exposed. Hardi groaned as his hand massaged the flesh, enjoying the weight in his hand. He lowered his head as he brought her breast to his mouth. He suckled like a bairn, but just as he promised, Blair was aware he was all man. His other hand gripped her bottom in a punishing hold, Blair's moans encouraging him each time his hand tightened. He widened the space between his thighs, keeping Blair suspended. His hand traveled down the crease that separated the cheeks of her buttocks until his fingers dipped within her sheath.

"Do ye ken why ye get so wet?" Hardi asked between kisses.

"So ma body can take yers into me one day." Blair nipped at Hardi's earlobe. "And because ma body wants to do just that." She rocked her hips against his cock that stood at attention beneath his plaid. The feel of his fingers within her along with the friction against her pubis made Blair lightheaded. She clung to Hardi as she opened her mouth to his questing tongue. Hardi pulled the ribbon loose over her other shoulder, leaving both of her breasts bare. Hardi rolled her nipple until it puckered before grazing his teeth over it. Blair's hips thrust forward in response to the stimulus. She ground herself against him until she moaned with her release.

Once again looking into one another's eyes, something passed between them that neither could name. Hunger consumed them as Blair panted. She pulled her chemise over her head, leaving nothing hidden. Hardi gorged his eyes on the trim figure and soft belly. It had pleased him to discover Blair wasn't as slim as she appeared. The first time he ran his hand over her satiny skin that covered her belly, he'd nearly spilled himself. He would have desired Blair no matter what she looked like, but he preferred that she wasn't bony. Blair noticed what held Hardi's attention, and her hands covered his. A different longing passed between them.

"I've never thought aboot having a family, having ma own bairns, like I have since seeing ye again," Hardi confessed.

"The idea of joining ma body with a mon never appealed until ye came back into ma life. I hope one day that we can build a family together," Blair confessed.

"Aye. One day. Blair, I ken ye realize we canna make love yet. But ken that it's honor that keeps me from ye. It has naught to do with nae desiring ye," Hardi explained.

"I understand." Blair frowned for a moment as her hands rested on his shoulders. "I want to make love to ye, and I want to bear yer bairns, but I also dinna want to be in the position that Lady Mac-Millan was. I dinna think ye'll die before we wed, but neither of us can ken for sure. Nae with how things stand for yer clan. I would cherish having a bairn as a way to remember ye, to have a piece of ye with me, but I dinna ever want that bairn forced to deny ye're his or her da."

"I wouldnae put ye in the position either, *mo ghaol*." Hardi kissed her tenderly.

"But I ken that I dinna want to attend a feast after our wedding. I want to leave the kirk and go to our chamber," Blair grinned.

"And dinna fear a bedding ceremony. Nay one will watch us as we make love for the first time."

Blair laughed. "Ma da wouldnae allow it anyway. I'd be a widow if ye tried to insist."

"That does sound aboot right," Hardi grinned. They sat together in silence for a long moment before their mouths sought one another again. The kiss combusted as need swept over them in yet another crashing wave. Blair raised up onto her knees, bringing her breasts to Hardi's face. Her mons brushed his chest as he grasped her bottom. The object of his desire was close yet still too far away. He stood and turned them before lowering her to the mattress.

Blair propped herself on her elbows as Hardi kneeled on the floor at the end of the bed. There was no preamble as he slid his hand beneath her bottom and lifted her sheath to his mouth. He was ravenous for the first taste, and his tongue thrust into her entrance. His masculine groan made Blair quiver. He lapped at her folds as his fingers bit into her waist and hips. His teeth skimmed her nub before tugging, then sucking. Blair fisted the sheets and struggled not to scream. The sensations were more intense than she ever guessed.

Hardi thrust two fingers into Blair's entrance, feeling the silky walls tightening around his digits. Blair watched him as he worked her core. He couldn't take his eyes off her flushed cheeks, her mussed hair, and passion-filled eyes. He reached beneath his plaid, grasping his cock as he stroked. He nearly toppled backwards when Blair jerked upright.

"That's mine. Dinna do that," Blair snarled as she pointed to where she could make out Hardi's hand wrapped around his rod. No longer interested in the sensations Hardi introduced to her to with his tongue, she refused to be cheated out of an opportunity to bring him to release after he'd already made her climax once. She scooted off the end of the bed before sinking onto his lap. Her tone softened, she whispered. "I—I want to see."

Hardi swallowed and nodded, knowing he treaded in dangerous waters. Blair's look of rapture was nearly too much temptation, but when her hand wrapped around him as she watched, he struggled to catch his breath. He wanted the pleasure to last, but he was racing toward the finish far too fast. When Blair settled on his thighs, he felt her dew against his skin. His hands went around her waist as he prepared to lift her onto his shaft. It was only at the last moment that he realized what he was about to do.

"Ye're too close, Blair. I want ye too much," Hardi croaked.

"I ken, but God how I ache to feel ye. Hardi, I —" Blair broke off unable to describe how badly she craved joining them as one.

"Stroke me. I'm almost there." As though his words signaled his body, his cock pulsed as his seed spilled over Blair's hand. He had a moment of panic that she would be disgusted. He'd always wiped her hand clean before she pulled it out from under his plaid. She raised her hand to her mouth, the tip of her tongue tentative before sweeping the flattened breadth over the viscous liquid that coated it. Hardi surged upward, Blair's waist in his hands. He tossed her onto the bed before prowling toward her. Rather than bring his body over hers, he returned his attention to her entrance and the feast he hadn't finished. It was only moments later that Blair turned her head into the pillow to smother her scream.

Hardi eased beside Blair, scooping her into his arms as they both panted. Hardi's hand caressed her shoulder, arm, and back until he reached her bottom. His gentle touch running up and down her body calmed Blair as she caught her breath. Their gentle kisses were affectionate as Blair's hand rested over his heart.

188

"*Mo chridhe*," Blair whispered as she felt the steady thud of his heartbeat beneath her hand.

"I love ye." They spoke at the same time.

"Can ye stay?" Blair asked timidly.

"Aye. Two of ma men will relieve yers in a couple of hours. They ken to knock if I dinna appear before the servants begin stirring. I want to sleep with ye in ma arms, Blair."

"I want that, too."

"I will send Bran with a message to ye as soon as I ken when I can meet ye. He will be our go-between, and he already kens." Hardi lifted up onto his elbow. "Blair, until I'm sure of what's really happening, dinna trust anyone but yer guards and Bran. Unless ye receive a missive in ma handwriting—ye'll ken it's mine from the horrible writing—dinna believe anyone but Bran is bringing ye the truth."

"That makes me feel a little better. I wish we didna have to be apart, but just remember, I will come as soon ye ask."

"Ma hope is that within a sennight, I can arrange things so I can meet ye either in the morn or afternoon without too many people taking note," Hardi explained, but Blair shook her head.

"If ye can leave the keep every day to see me, then ye should consider using that time to tour yer land. See me if ye need me, but dinna take time away from yer duties for me."

"Ye're a better woman than I deserve," Hardi pulled Blair closer. "I wish I never had to put aught before ye, but I canna thank ye enough for understanding. Nae only understanding but supporting me."

"Hardi, I plan for us to have a vera long life together. One where we are together until all yer hair and teeth fall out," Blair giggled as Hardi tickled her. "This is but a wee moment in time. I will do all I can to help ye, but ye must put yer clan first. That's another lesson Mama and Da taught me. I saw how it pained them to do so at times, but they are a better couple and better leaders for it."

"I will do ma best to never take ye for granted, *fear glic.*"

"I still dinna think I'm a wise one, but I am devoted to ye and that means yer clan. I hope soon they will be ma clan too." Blair traced the scars on Hardi's chest until they both grew too tired to keep their eyes open.

TWENTY-FOUR

T he cords in Blair's neck strained as she struggled to keep from crying as Hardi rode away from Inverlochy. They'd slept in one another's arms, waking twice to share intimacies that were over far too fast now that Blair was unsure of when she would next see Hardi. They'd said their goodbyes in private before he slipped from her chamber as the first servants began to move about the lower level of the keep. Blair waved one last time as Hardi turned back to look at her for a fourth time. His stoic appearance belied his conflicted emotions, and Blair didn't envy him his position.

"Ma lady," Donald whispered. "Laird Cameron will return before ye ken it. I've kenned the mon since he arrived when he was ten summers. We all believed ye two would marry if ye'd just been the same age. It doesnae surprise either of us," the guard jutted his chin at his partner, "that ye wish to marry now. He'll be back soon enough."

"Thank ye," Blair whispered. She inhaled a deep breath, trying to cleanse the sadness from her heart. She gathered her courage and entered the keep. She'd avoided conversing with Artair at the evening meal, leaving Hardi and the chieftain to discuss the

MacDonalds ongoing use of Inverlochy. Blair heard Artair bring up the Laird Donald's daughter and the alliance the laird offered the Camerons, but Hardi was swift and decisive in his refusal to consider it. Blair also heard the warning that Artair was to respect Blair's position as his betrothed. As she made her way to the dais to break her fast, she noticed Robena rubbing her swollen belly.

Blair learned the night before that while Robena carried the chieftain's babe, their relationship was generally more paternal. Blair wondered if that was why the man was so incredibly patronizing. She tried to convince herself that it was age, rather than gender, that made him condescending.

"Good morn, Lady Robena," Blair greeted as she took the seat beside Robena. "Is there aught I can help you with today?" Blair hoped that by offering her help, it would make her indefinite residence less burdensome.

"Do you not have books to pour over or poems to read?" Artair laughed as he lumbered up the stairs. It was clear the man suffered from gout. Blair understood the healing arts that a chatelaine was expected to possess, but she'd never taken an interest like Maude or Cairren. At that moment, she'd never been more grateful for lacking empathy as she hoped his inflammation pained him.

"I didn't plan to while away my days in leisure whilst being here, so I'm afraid I brought no books with me," Blair explained before turning back to Robena. "What can I do to help?"

"Lady Robena is quite capable of tending to this keep without your assistance," Artair spoke once again before Robena could answer.

Blair cast the man a withering glare. "I don't doubt that. The food was excellent at both meals I've partaken, and my chamber is spotless and comfortable. That doesn't mean I can't offer assistance to a woman clearly approaching her confinement. It's the least I can do."

"I wouldn't mind company while I work in the orchard," Robena hurried to speak.

"Work in the orchard?" Blair looked at Robena, fearing the answer to her next question. "Are you still climbing ladders to pick the fruit?"

"Depends on whether there are others who can be spared to help," Robena explained quietly.

"Spared to help? Harvesting the fruit is one of the most important late spring tasks. And you shouldn't be balancing on a ladder." It horrified Blair to know that Robena was risking injury to herself and her babe because not enough people were helping. Blair clenched her jaw to keep from snapping at Artair, who muttered something about meddlesome women coddling the weak. When the meal ended, Blair walked to the table where the Sutherland and king's guards sat. She glanced back at Robena who shifted, trying to find a comfortable position in which to sit.

"I don't like asking this, but I will," Blair kept her Scots accent in place while speaking to the king's guard. Her experience at court taught her that while many of the king's warriors were Highlanders, only a Scots accent made them move with a sense of haste. "I need you all to come with me to the orchard this morning. Lady Robena has little help to harvest the fruit, and her husband sees no problem with his expectant wife climbing ladders."

Twelve faces looked as one toward the dais. Scowls and looks of disgust made Blair breathe easier, knowing the men wouldn't grumble about the work. She agreed to meet the men in the orchard, hoping that it would be less obvious that she'd recruited the helpers that Artair believed were unnecessary. She carried the stack of baskets as she and Robena made their way into the copse of fruit trees.

"What are they doing here?" Robena gasped as she noticed the group of men leaning against the wall that separated the orchard from the bailey.

"They will be working." Blair signaled the men to gather the baskets, and they set to work without instruction. Blair carried a basket while Robena picked fruit within easy reach.

"Artair won't be happy when he learns of this, Lady Blair," Robena warned.

"It's Blair, and I don't give a fig whether he's happy or not if you're safe."

"Thank you," Robena whispered. "He's not a bad mon or a bad husband. He's just insensitive. He doesn't realize what he says can be hurtful or insulting. It's not done with malice."

"I can tell," Blair nodded. "I ken we both have thick skins after serving at court. But that doesn't mean his insensitivity should put you and your bairn at risk."

The group of guards and the two ladies worked through most of the morning, gathering more fruit than Robena could have done in a sennight. One of the king's guards helped Robena to the ground where they all sat in the shade, each munching on an apple and passing around a waterskin.

"What the devil is going on?" Artair bellowed as he wove his way through the trees. Artair noticed his wife's red face and sweaty brow, but it didn't seem to affect him since he hadn't asked how she fared. Four guards had acted the moment they noticed how overheated the pregnant woman was; she was the first to drink from the waterskin. "Lady Blair, a word."

Blair rose and dusted off her skirts. She suspected there would be quite a few words. She clasped her hands in front of her and offered a serene smile.

"You may not understand the importance of men training, but I'm certain the king does. His men should not be picking fruit like a peasant when they should be in the lists training." Artair's voice rose with each word.

"I wasn't aware you married a peasant," Blair said blandly.

"I what?" Artair demanded.

"If you believe it's peasants who should pick fruit, and you expect your wife to do that job, you must have married a peasant. Otherwise, why would she be left to do the work of field hands?" Blair asked innocently.

"You know very well that I married a lady," Artair huffed.

Blair leaned forward and hissed, "Then treat her like one." Blair made to step around the angered chieftain, but he reached out to stop her. Twelve men rose to their feet in what appeared to be one swift choreographed move. Hands reached for swords, but Blair shook her head. She looked back at Artair before walking around his hand. "I believe my men are already well trained."

Left standing alone, Artair stormed back toward the keep. Blair watched him, ruing her sharp tongue. She feared making Robena's life miserable, and she hadn't intended on antagonizing her host within a day of her arrival. She frowned at Robena as she offered her apologies. Robena smiled and thanked Blair for arranging the help. She admitted she never would have finished the harvest before the fruit spoiled and fell from the trees. She thanked the men for their help before the men carried the baskets to storerooms and the ladies retired to the cooler air within the keep.

TWENTY-FIVE

Hardi had always looked forward to riding through the gates at Tor Castle, returning home to the people he knew and the land he loved. But as he entered the bailey, he was torn between regret and suspicion. He hadn't thought of anything but Blair during the brief ride to Tor. He worried about whether he made the right decision entrusting Artair with her protection. He feared bringing her to Tor when he hadn't been home in over a month, and so much had happened while he was away. He worried that she would regret agreeing to marry him if he lost his position as laird. And he feared Hamish and Amelia would refuse his suit.

The bells clanged above his head announcing the laird's return. He'd waved to families in the village as they left their homes to cheer his arrival. As he entered the bailey, men and women stopped in the middle of their tasks to gather around him. He noticed that Faolán and Drostan were conspicuously absent from the group of older men who made up the clan council. He wondered if the brothers were away from the keep or purposely insulting him by not making an appearance. He even considered whether they were hiding. He'd passed the enlarged flock of sheep as they approached the keep, and he'd gripped the reins so tightly that Uaill sidestepped and shook his head.

"Laird Cameron, ye've returned," Mordag, the housekeeper cum chatelaine greeted him. She'd run the keep for as long as Hardi could remember. She'd terrified him as a child, but he'd relied on her heavily while his uncle grew sicker and then in the early days of his lairdship. She offered sage advice and couldn't stand Faolán, which raised Hardi's opinion of her.

"Aye, Mordag. It is good to be home. I have missed being here," Hardi grinned.

"We wouldnae ken from how long ye were gone." Faolán's voice reached Hardi from behind, and the hair on Hardi's neck stood on end. If he'd been a dog, his hackles would have been standing straight up.

"Aye, well, I'm sure ye ken why the taxes werenae as simple as they should have been," Hardi's piercing gaze made Faolán flinch. Hardi handed the reins to a stable boy and moved toward the keep. "The council will meet me in ma solar. Now."

Hardi didn't wait to see how anyone reacted to his abrupt order. He kept his tone even, but his purposeful stride led many to scurry out of his way. He nodded to those who welcomed him, but he did not stop until he was seated behind his enormous desk. As the council filtered in, the men took seats around the table in the center of the chamber, but there was no doubting Hardi sat in the position of authority. Before his journey to court, he'd sat at the table amongst his advisors, hoping that an egalitarian approach would ease his transition. He was too angry to care much about how the council received his newly acquired confidence. He pictured what Blair would say and do if she were him. He watched each man, observing their expression, mannerisms, and with whom they shared a glance. He considered how Blair would assess what he noticed. He knew she would warn him to trust no one.

"We owe the king one hundred and three pounds, nine shillings," Hardi announced. He held up his hand to silence the raucous response. "The king has allowed me time to return here and organize our finances. We are expected to pay that in coin. That is *only* the outstanding geld and tax on the cattle. That doesnae include what we shall have to pay in kind for the grain and whisky."

"That is outrageous," Drostan declared.

"Is it, Drostan?" Hardi pulled the king's missive from his sporran. He opened it and smoothed it on the desk before glancing at Drostan and Faolán. He read aloud the parts that hadn't been read to him. He'd practiced over and over until he was able to recite it from memory, but he made it appear as though he read it from the parchment in front of him. "Drostan, ye were aware of this since ye were the first to read the missive. Faolán, can ye explain why neither of ye informed us of the entire contents of the king's missive? Why ye didna tell me or the council the accurate amounts?"

Drostan stammered and Faolán glared at Hardi. He refolded the document and returned it to his sporran. He looked at each member of the council, noticing the levels of shock, disgust, and mockery. He waited until the men quietened, refusing to speak over them or to try to make them listen to him. "I can only imagine one of two things: Faolán, and Drostan by his side, have lied aboot their ability to read, or they wished me thrown in debtors' prison."

"Hardwin, that is ridiculous," Faolán spoke to him as though he were a child.

"Until I determine whether ye should be thrown into a cell or the oubliette, ye will refer to me at Laird

Cameron," Hardi corrected "Ye may have aimed to humiliate me, but ye nearly bankrupted our clan and made fools of us all. I was exceptionally lucky to be granted an audience with the king in private. Word hasnae spread that we couldnae pay our taxes on time. Nae because we dinna have the resources, but because more fool was I to trust two men who have been advising the clan since before I was born."

"I'd like to ken which it was," Paul, a man only a few years older than Hardi, spoke up. "Was the goal to embarrass our laird and even have him imprisoned? Or have we all been fooled for years by two men who dinna have any business making decisions in any laird's stead?"

Hardi sat back as the bickering among the men began. He remembered the suggestions Blair offered him when they discussed how he should proceed with his first council meeting. She'd advised him to stir the pot enough for it to boil over and then watch how the men reacted to one another. She instructed him to remain quiet and allow the meeting to move in whichever direction the men carried it and to listen rather than participate. He hadn't believed her, fearing the meeting would spiral out of control. She grinned and said that was half the point.

As Hardi listened to the men before him, he quickly noticed the factions that broke apart. There were those who silently backed Faolán and Drostan, those who invoked his uncle's name and the shame cast upon their clan, and those who were ready to plan for how they should proceed. The smallest group was the last, and that caused Hardi concern. The number of levelheaded and even-tempered men was far smaller than the hotheads who insulted one another.

"Enough," Hardi's voice remained calm, but the clipped tone broke through the arguing voices.

"Drostan and Faolán, neither of ye have denied either suspicion—"

"Why should we?" Faolán demanded.

"I wouldnae interrupt me again, Faolán, unless ye care to dine off of rats for the next sennight," Hardi warned. "Since neither of ye denied ma speculation, and neither of ye have explained yer behavior, ye are both removed from the council effectively immediately."

"Ye canna do that!" Drostan rose from his seat and pounded on the table.

"I can. Just as the council can vote a laird in or out, the laird can remove any members he feels doesnae work with the clan's best interest in mind. Ye were the only two who could read after ma uncle died. Ye were trusted, and ye broke that trust. Nae only mine, nae only this council's, but the entire clan's trust. Men who canna be trusted canna be members of the council."

"Were?" Faolán sneered. "Memorizing what someone tells ye isnae reading. How do the others ken ye arenae the one telling falsehoods?"

"Because Laird Cameron never attempted to be laird, but accepted a position thrust upon him," Paul broke in. "He hasnae been whinging on aboot how unfair the succession was. He stood before the king and bore the brunt of our failure as a council to advise a young laird, our failure to protect our clan's finances." Paul stood and leaned over the table on his knuckles. "To ma eye, we should all be on our knees thanking the good Lord and Laird Cameron that we still have land to call our own."

Hardi held up his hand, and the men fell silent. "Before I forget, there is also the matter of recompense owed to the Macphersons. I received the most troubling news from ye," Hardi nodded to each of the men. "That the Macphersons and Mackintoshes raided our villages, razing our fields, and killing our people only to make camp on our land. Can ye imagine ma surprise when I had another audience with the king where I intended to voice ma concerns only to learn that the Macphersons were already demanding a return of the sheep this clan stole?" Hardi's hand slammed on the desk.

Hardi rose from his seat and crossed his arms. "Faolán, ye endangered the lives of our men leading them on an unsanctioned raid, claiming ye acted in ma stead. If there is a mon in this chamber who believes I would agree to—nay, order—a raid on the Macphersons so soon after our battle with the Mackintoshes, then ye dinna ken me at all, and ye're just as daft at these two." Hardi jerked his chin in Faolán and Drostan's direction.

"Those were our sheep," Faolán argued.

"I dinna give a bluidy damn if they were sheep God handed down to us from on high. Ye risked our men's lives and weakened our position in the king's eyes. We're bluidy lucky King Robert didna strip us of the land he awarded our clan after the Wars or demand we pay a fine to the Macphersons. He'll be satisfied with us returning the livestock. And willna that be an enjoyable meeting. 'Good day, Laird Macpherson. Nay, I didna ken ma clan council is made up of bumbling eejits who want to get us all killed. Nay, I didna ken ma council care so little for our clan that they would act of their own accord with a complete disregard for the consequences. And nay, I didna fucking ken that I'm the biggest eejit for trusting any of them.'" Hardi slammed his hand onto the table again.

Hardi looked around the table at the stunned faces. None had seen him lose his temper since becoming laird. He'd always been even tempered, but he was known for his unforgiving and unrelenting drive in battle. The clan council was witnessing that determination away from the battlefield, and more than one face registered shock.

Hardi understood that this shock was caused by the realization that he wouldn't be as easily manipulated as many imagined. He studied the men who said the least, but seemed to favor Faolán and Drostan. They were the men who caused Hardi the most concern. The brothers' outward defiance was easier for Hardi to address. It was the men who gave nothing away that made Hardi the most suspicious.

"Faolán and Drostan, ye will gather the required sacks of grain and barrels of whisky and deliver them to the king. He is aware of what we owe, so King Robert will ken if aught is amiss. Be prepared to leave in the morn. I will return to Stirling at a later date with the coins. Paul, ye will gather a score of men to accompany ye to the Macphersons to return the sheep. Ye will depart in two days. Good day," Hardi sat back in his chair and pulled a sheaf of parchment toward him. He took a quill from the top drawer of the desk and dipped it into the ink. When no one moved but rather stared at him, he grinned, but it only made his expression more menacing. "I filled ma days learning to read and write while I waited to learn if I would rot in debtors' prison or have ma head cleaved from ma shoulders."

Hardi studiously ignored the men as they filed out of the chamber. Before they arrived at Tor, Hardi asked Bran and two of the king's men to stand as his personal guards once he sequestered himself with the council. He didn't trust any of them not to attempt to kill him. He knew he'd made the right choice not to bring Blair to his home until he sorted out the clan's inner politics, but he wished she was within the keep offering her advice. He even wished she'd been beside him in the solar to witness his first true meeting as the leader of Clan Cameron. He hoped she would be proud of him.

Hardi waved Bran over and kept his voice low not trusting the walls not to have ears. "Ride back to Inverlochy. Inform Lady Blair that we arrived safely and that she offers sound advice. Ask her to meet me tomorrow at dawn at the standing stone. If she says aye, find her guards—her Sutherland guards—and tell them where we will meet. Return to me before the evening meal."

"Aye, ma laird," Bran nodded and hurried from the chamber. Hardi leaned back as he looked at the table where the angry men had sat only minutes ago. He put the quill away and put the stopper back in the ink. He would take the writing utensils with him when he met Blair the next morning. They'd been merely props for him, but they would be tools for Blair. He quit the chamber soon after, his stomach demanding a meal.

TWENTY-SIX

Hardi stood beside the ancient Pict standing stone with the soft pink and purple rays of early morning sun at his back. He heard the pounding hooves before Blair and her guards came into sight. He watched as her hair flew behind her with each lunging step her galloping horse took. Her fluid movements reminded him of their first ride together after he arrived at Stirling. He grinned as he accepted that Winner was an apt name for her horse as the gelding led the rest of the party by a head. When they reined in, Hardi helped Blair from the saddle and pulled her into his arms. It had been a day since he'd last seen her, but that was the longest they'd been apart in over a month. He swore to himself that once he had Hamish's approval and their betrothal was official, nothing would keep him from kissing her, audience or not.

"Thank ye for meeting me, lass," Hardi murmured as he inhaled lemongrass.

"I told ye I would come as soon as ye asked. How did things go when ye arrived?" Blair asked.

"Just as ye suspected. I took yer advice to offer just enough information to let them squabble, and I watched. There were those who said little but nodded when Faolán and Drostan spoke. Those who swore and cursed, demanding answers to why I'd been misinformed. And the smallest group were those who proposed solutions for how to move forward."

"Are you watching Faolán's comrades the closest?" Blair wondered.

"Aye. While I spoke to Paul, a councilman close in age to me, during the evening meal, I could tell he was also straining to hear Faolán and Drostan's conversations with the men who sided with them. Faolán purposely kept their conversation light, discussing the lists and training."

"What aboot the taxes? What did they have to say aboot the amounts still owed?"

"That's what gave me the chance to gauge their reactions. I'm sending Drostan and Faolán to court with the grain and whisky. I want them away from the keep to see how people behave without Faolán there to usurp ma authority or plot behind ma back. Paul will return the sheep to the Macphersons. I trust him nae to embroil us in another battle and to be honest with both the Macpherson and me. I would take the sheep maself, but the infighting among the council makes me hesitant to ride out."

"Do ye need me to write a missive to Laird Macpherson?"

"Aye. I brought parchment, ink, and a quill for ye," Hardi offered.

"I brought ma own, thinking ye might need a scribe," Blair grinned. She looked around for a flat surface and spotted a boulder not far from the standing stone. She had no intention of touching the ancient marker, unwilling to test whether it possessed the magic of lore.

"How repentant should I sound?" Hardi asked.

"Ye canna be weak and submissive, but ye must

206

acknowledge yer clan's wrongdoing. Is there aught ye can offer besides returning the livestock? Some peace offering? Whisky, mayhap?"

"I could, though I'd rather nae send it kenning it will go to waste. They willna drink it, fearing we're trying to poison them," Hardi explained.

"Can ye spare a heifer and calf?" Blair wondered.

"Aye. I dinna want to give those away either, but they are more likely to be well-received. It would be easier if ye just wrote the missive for me," Hardi mused. "But I canna palm ma duty off on ye. I must learn how to be a laird. I'm damned lucky to have such a bright and bonnie teacher."

"Ye can thank me on our wedding night," Blair winked.

"I have much to be thankful for that night," Hardi waggled his eyebrows in response.

They turned their focus to the missive as they chose the wording together. When they finished, Blair handed the drying parchment to Hardi and asked him to read it back to her.

Laird Macpherson,

It is with respectful regret that I address this missive to you. I have learned that while away from Tor Castle, a member of my family thought to act in my place and led a raid on your herd. While he intended to reclaim our previously pilfered sheep, I did not grant him my permission to cross our border. My representative, Paul Cameron, returns the disputed livestock on my behalf, and the Camerons offer you a cow and a calf to broker peace.

It is my sincere hope that this matter is resolved and will not lead to further animosity. Neither of our clans will benefit from further fighting. We will keep to our land just as you will keep to yours, neither crossing our border. If you can abide by this arrangement, we can maintain the peace and allow our clans to prosper.

Your neighbor,
Laird Hardwin Cameron

"Are you sure I shouldnae add something like 'yer humble neighbor'?" Hardi wondered.

"Nay. The bluidy bastard stole yer sheep first," Blair reminded him. "There isnae any reason to humble yerself to him. He should accept the return of property that isnae entirely his when he could go with naught. I understand ye are suggesting it as a tactic to appease him, but returning the sheep is enough. Hardi, he will already claim ye are weak for doing this despite insisting King Robert intervene and order this vera thing. Ye dinna need him crowing aboot ye sounding subservient. It will only make his people encourage him to raid ye again. Ye are one of the most ancient clans in Scotland. Dinna bow to anyone."

"Part of me wants to bait him into crossing the border, so we have a justified reason to retaliate. If we canna have our sheep, then we can—" Hardi trailed off as he realized Blair might not agree with his need to placate his clan with vengeance.

"Then we can take some Macpherson lives," Blair finished for him. "I ken ye dinna equate a mon's life with that of a sheep. I ken this is because of what yer clan expects. Ma da has been in the same position with our clan demanding the laird take action against even the smallest slight. But Hardi, they outnumber ye. Ye can kill as many Macphersons as ye want, as ye can, but they will only come back with Clan Chattan at their sides. Ye are one clan against many. Dinna cut off yer nose to spite yer face."

"Ye are a voice of reason, *mo leannan,*" Hardi conceded.

"I dinna ken how much of a sweetheart I am calling Laird Macpherson a bluidy bastard, but I enjoy hearing it." The corner of Blair's mouth twitched into a smile. The ink dried, Blair folded the parchment. She looked around, but when she didn't find a candle among the writing supplies Hardi brought, she returned with one and a piece of flint. "Ye must seal it with yer mark."

Hardi nodded as he struck the flint Blair offered and lit the candle. She warmed the wax before pouring a dab where the parchment's folded sides met. Hardi pressed his signet ring into the wax, an armored arm holding the hilt of a sword appearing. *Mo rìgh mo dhùthaich*, "My King and My Country," encircled the crest.

"Did ye break yer fast?" Hardi asked, and Blair shook her head. "Come. I brought a repast for us. It isnae aught like what ye packed at Stirling, but it will keep the wolf from the door." Hardi nodded to one of the king's guards, who unfastened a sack from a saddle while Hardi pulled a plaid from his saddle. Once they settled on the blanket, Hardi laid out a wheel of cheese, a loaf of bread, apples, a wineskin, and cold chicken.

"This is a veritable feast." Blair looked around and realized the men were sharing food while they gave the couple privacy. She didn't miss the men who encircled them on guard. Hardi cut the cheese into chunks while Blair broke the loaf in half. Hardi teased Blair with the first piece of cheese, offering it then pulling it just beyond her mouth's reach. When he finally relented, Blair was quick to lick Hardi's finger. With the second piece of cheese, she sucked his finger into his mouth, her eyes locked with his.

"Blair," Hardi croaked. They finished their meal while telling one another about the previous day after they'd parted. Blair recounted the scene Artair made in the orchard and how she felt bad for Robena. Blair had decided to make her assistance more discreet, as she still feared Robena might bear the brunt of Artair's ire. While the sun hadn't been up for long, by the time they were ready to leave the clearing, they'd already spent a couple of hours together. Blair stepped into the haven of Hardi's arms as she laid her head against his chest. She wrapped her arms around his waist as his encircled her back. He dropped several kisses on her crown before pulling back. "I'm leaving later this morn to tour the land within a day's ride from Tor. I amnae comfortable being further away from the keep. I willna be able to see ye tomorrow."

"Ye need to do this, and I understand," Blair reassured.

"I wish ye were accompanying me. I wish I was introducing ye as ma wife, or at least as ma betrothed," Hardi sighed.

"Speaking of betrothals, what do ye think will happen to the missives ma parents have surely sent?" Blair questioned.

"If we are lucky, a messenger will bring them from court. But more likely, we will have to wait until Lachlan arrives with news."

"The most recent missive should arrive at Dunrobin tomorrow, assuming the rider had nay trouble. It'll be at least a sennight before Lachlan can arrive."

"Blair, regardless of whether yer parents grant me permission to marry ye, once Lachlan arrives, he can serve as yer guardian and chaperone. If it's safe to bring ye to Tor, I will."

"I'd like that. I canna think of a reason why Mama and Da would say nay. They ken ye, and they promised all three of us that we can marry who we choose. Maude already did, and I think Lachlan will soon. I dinna ken why I would be any different."

"Because ma clan is in the midst of a bitter feud and isnae on the winning side," Hardi offered.

Blair nodded but remained quiet. She would discuss at a later time why his allies, the MacMillans and Donalds, hadn't come to his aid with men to fight the Camerons' rivals. They stole a brief kiss before they mounted and went their separate ways.

TWENTY-SEVEN

Hardi returned to the keep as Faolán and Drostan prepared to leave. He couldn't wait to see the back of their heads, but he made certain to lift every sack of grain and barrel of whisky as he counted them. He knew the men—Faolán, Drostan, and the guards accompanying them—grew annoyed as they waited for him, but he didn't trust his kinsmen. He had no reservations about making it clear that Faolán and Drostan broke his trust. Once he was satisfied that all that they owed the crown was on the wagon, he stepped back as the party rode out of the bailey.

"Ye arenae making any friends," Paul muttered beside him.

"I dinna think there are any friends left for me to make here," Hardi answered.

"Just be careful. Dinna turn yer back to anyone in the lists, and dinna leave the walls without guards," Paul warned.

"What do ye ken?" Hardi demanded.

"Naught. It's just a feeling I have," Paul explained. "The clan is on edge, still grieving the losses against the Mackintoshes, and Faolán appeared to lead the clan well while ye were at court. I dinna believe it for a minute, but he made a show of it, slyly asking why ye hadnae returned, why ye preferred the lavishness of court to being among the clan. He implied that being laird had gone to yer head. People believe him because he's more experienced than ye. Never mind that it was only two moons ago that they swore fealty to ye and cheered ye as our new laird."

Hardi listened to Paul, not doubting what he heard, but wondering why Paul shared it with him. Hardi wanted to trust Paul, and he knew he needed at least one council member on his side, but he suspected everyone. He questioned the wisdom of riding out that day to tour his land. He needed to see those who lived in the outlying villages, but it would be the ones who lived in and around Tor who decided whether Hardi remained in power.

"Any news from our other villages? Those inland and along the borders?" Hardi inquired.

"Nay. All's been quiet except for Faolán's raid," Paul answered as they made their way to the lists.

"What did the council think aboot the contents of his missive to me?" Hardi asked casually as he accepted a blunted sword from the armorer.

"We didna ken he'd sent one until Bran's brother mentioned he'd left for Stirling. Drostan made it sound as though they felt it was our duty to send ye an update since ye'd been away so long. What kept ye?" Paul's piercing blue eyes drilled into Hardi's hazel ones.

"Sorting out the taxes meant waiting for an audience with the king. I also had the chance to learn to read and write. In the long run, it seems like those are skills that will benefit the clan, even if it kept me away longer than I planned."

"And ye dinna think Faolán or Drostan could teach ye?" Paul pressed.

Hardi straightened. Now it was his turn to bore

into Paul's eyes. "They didna tell the truth aboot any of the missives. Why would they teach me to read and write if that means they canna keep lying without me calling them out?"

"And Father Graham couldnae teach ye?" Paul wouldn't relent.

"The mon is nearly deaf and blind," Hardi snorted. "He recites the Mass from memory. He absolves everyone with the sign of the cross because he canna hear their confessions. How would he teach me?"

"So who taught ye?"

"A Sutherland." Hardi thought he sounded casual to his own ear. He attempted to move away from Paul, as though seeking an opening for a partner. But Paul followed him until, inevitably, they partnered with one another. Paul's persistence only made Hardi warier. He decided at that moment that he would remain at Tor and postpone riding out. He needed more time to learn what happened while he was away, and he needed to see Blair again. He realized he should have asked her to do more than write one missive.

"Laird Sutherland took the time to remain at court to teach ye?"

"It wasna the laird." Hardi swung his sword, connecting with Paul's as the latter blocked the attack. They went back and forth several times before Paul asked his next question.

"So was it Lachlan?"

"I spent time with him," Hardi hedged.

"But he wasna the one to teach ye. Lady Maude married and lives on Lewis. So that leaves Lady Blair or a Sutherland delegate. I didna ken Laird Sutherland teaches his warriors to read and write." Hardi didn't miss the smugness in Paul's voice despite the feigned innocence. Hardi saw no point in continuing

215

to be evasive. If Blair was to take her place soon as Lady Cameron, there was no point in hiding that he'd spent time with her.

"Lady Blair was an excellent teacher." Hardi blocked a strike before lunging forward. Paul barely moved out of the way in time to avoid a slicing sweep to his ribs.

"Ye let a woman tell ye what to do?" Paul stopped sparring to laugh. "Did she order ye to count her ribbons and slippers? Did she demand ye say yer letters backwards and forwards?"

Hardi took advantage of Paul's distraction and swept his sword behind the man's knees, knocking them out from under him. Once Paul kneeled on the ground, Hardi rested the edge of the sword's blade against Paul's neck.

"She was a gracious teacher. And while I listened to and followed a woman's directions, I didna let the thought of one distract me," Hardi glowered and backed away, seizing the chance to move on to a new opponent. Paul's taunting didn't surprise him. He knew he would hear a great deal more once others learned Blair tutored him. He just hoped no one was rude to her when she arrived.

Hardi spent the rest of the morning and after the midday meal sparring with his men. For a little while, he could set aside being laird and return to being a warrior, one whose most pressing concern was not having his head severed from his body. He bore in mind Paul's warning not to turn his back on anyone, but some of his tension eased from the hours he spent training. As much as he'd admitted to Paul about his time away, Hardi felt he'd learned just as much. When he left the lists, he felt better than he had since watching Blair ride toward Inverlochy.

TWENTY-EIGHT

B lair was surprised but happy to see Bran enter the Great Hall the next morning. She hadn't expected to see the messenger for several days. She stepped away from the dais to greet the man, but she knew people watched her. She kept her voice low but was unprepared for Bran to hand her a folded parchment. She glanced at the seal, but there was no marking.

"Laird Cameron wishes me to inform ye that he didna leave Tor Castle yesterday to tour his land. He decided it isnae the right time to be away from the keep or the clan. He bade me deliver this message and the one in yer hand," Bran informed her.

"Does Laird Cameron expect a response?" Blair asked.

"He said ye need only say aye or nay once ye read the missive," Bran explained.

Blair broke the seal, her chest tight as she feared what she would find. She remembered Hardi's warning not to believe anyone but Bran, and she hadn't expected Hardi to send a missive so soon. She unfolded the vellum and struggled to keep the smile from showing that fought to spread across her face.

Blair,

I miss you. Meet me dusk by stone.

Yors,

H

Blair's heart melted at the fractured grammar and poor spelling. It meant more to her than the finest poetry. She understood the effort it had taken Hardi to write even the brief message. She looked up at Bran and nodded. She noticed his relief when he saw her smile.

"Aye."

Bran dipped his head and turned on his heel so quickly that his plaid swished around his legs. Blair folded the parchment and slipped it into her sleeve before turning back to the dais. She found Artair and Robena watching her. She cast them a smile before walking to the laird's table.

"He wore a Cameron plaid, so he wasn't delivering a letter from your mama," Artair smirked. Blair didn't answer, since he hadn't asked a question. When his comment garnered no answer, Artair tried again. "You must have taught Hardwin an impressive amount if he's sending missives in his own hand. Faolán and Drostan aren't there to help."

Once more, Blair didn't respond. But she forced her face to remain impassive when Artair mentioned Faolán and Drostan. She hadn't shared that the brothers left Tor Castle. Blair's eyes scanned the diners below the dais. She was confident neither of her guards or any of King Robert's men shared the information with anyone. She and Hardi had been quiet while they discussed his clan business. None of the men who accompanied her the previous morning could have heard. *So who is feeding Artair information aboot Hardi?* Blair couldn't answer her own question, but she would make sure Hardi knew there was a spy in his midst.

It was Blair's turn to wait by the standing stone. The sun had already sunk below the horizon, and she wondered if Hardi would make it to their rendezvous. She knew her guards thought they should return before anyone missed them at the evening meal, but Blair would wait until nightfall before abandoning hope that Hardi would arrive. Blair wrapped her arms around her waist when she spotted Hardi cresting the hill before racing toward her. He leaped from the saddle before Uaill stopped. Hardi opened his arms, and Blair rushed into them.

In the darkening early night sky, they knew it would be difficult for the other men to see them once they stepped behind the standing stone. It measured at least three feet taller than Hardi, who stood well over six feet. Their mouths sought one another as their hands roamed over one another's bodies. They pressed kisses along each other's jaws and cheeks before once again exploring the cavernous recesses of their mouths. Breathless, they stood with their foreheads together.

"Hardi, Artair kens Drostan and Faolán left Tor," Blair blurted. Hardi straightened, but it was hard for Blair to make out his expression. "Do ye ken how he might have learned this? I dinna believe any of the men with me would tell."

"I dinna believe that either." Hardi considered the council members first. While Paul and his entourage would pass by Inverlochy on their way to the Macphersons, he wouldn't leave until the following morning. Paul had trained with him again that morning and then gone to check the herd, which grazed in a pasture on the opposite side of the village from Inverlochy's direction. He contemplated which of the other councilmen were most likely to have a

219

reason to inform MacDonald. When no one stood out, he considered other members of his clan, wondering whether a member of a patrol might have shared the information in passing with a MacDonald, who then told Artair. Hardi couldn't be certain, but it didn't please him to learn the news.

"Hardi?" Blair's voice made him realize he'd been quieter longer than he realized.

"I will visit ye tomorrow at Inverlochy," Hardi decided. "I want Artair to remember how close I am and that I havenae abandoned ye."

"If Artair kens aboot yer cousins leaving, do ye think someone in yer clan kens aboot me?" Hardi heard the nervousness in Blair's voice. He was certain the worry was for him and not for herself.

"It's probable, but nay one has said or hinted at aught to me," Hardi reassured. "I'm sorry that I was late, but a guard injured another in a fight today. It delayed me as I had to check on the injured mon and dole out a punishment to the aggressor. It's far darker than I'd expected."

"I ken. I dinna like ye riding in the dark, Hardi," Blair whittled.

"I was aboot to say the same."

"Because I'm a woman?" Blair cocked her head to the side and tapped her toe.

Hardi grasped her beneath her bottom and lifted her off the ground. Blair squeaked as her hands rested on his shoulders now that they were at eye level. "Because I love ye to distraction, Blair Sutherland." He squeezed her backside before kissing her soundly.

"But in all seriousness, please be careful, Hardi," Blair whispered as Hardi put her back on her feet.

"I suspect ye shall be just like the stories I've heard aboot the women yer Sinclair cousins married. Tenacious protectors of their husbands."

220

"Aye, and dinna forget Mairghread. We're vera much alike. When none of ye lads would teach me and Maude how to fight, Mairghread did." Blair made a fist and playfully drove it into Hardi's stomach, but with just enough force for him to understand she wasn't kidding.

"And I think I shall enjoy rewarding ma most loyal guard," Hardi murmured against Blair's neck. The heat from his breath made her nipples pucker. He kissed along her neck before nipping her earlobe.

"If ye keep doing that, it'll be the middle of the night before we leave," Blair choked out around a soft moan.

"I'm tempted to accompany ye back to Inverlochy, so I might sneak into yer chamber again. It's only ma desire for keeping our meetings a secret that reminds me nae to be impetuous. I dinna want Artair or whoever is spying to ken that we meet."

"Then I will see ye in the morn," Blair said. They kissed once more, keeping it brief lest they get carried away. Hardi waited to mount Uaill until after Blair was out of sight.

TWENTY-NINE

B lair forced herself to act surprised when Hardi arrived the following morning just after the clan members finished breaking their fast. Artair glanced between Hardi and Blair, mollified that Blair hadn't expected Hardi's arrival. Lady Robena offered Hardi food despite the meal ending. He politely declined, explaining he'd already eaten. Hardi struggled to keep his eyes off Blair as he thought about what would satisfy a distinct hunger. From the tinge of pink in her cheeks, Hardi was certain Blair's mind drifted in the same direction as hers.

"Chieftain MacDonald, I ask for the use of yer solar this morning. I am overdue for ma next lesson."

"You and Lady Blair can't be alone," Artair huffed, then a slyness that set Hardi on edge slid into the man's eyes.

"That's why Lady Blair's maid shall accompany us," Hardi explained. Hardi's earnest expression made Artair's smugness fizzle. Blair pushed away from the table, snagging an apple as she went. She tossed it into the air as she walked past Artair. It wasn't long before Hardi, Blair, and Maeve were ensconced in the chieftain's solar. Maeve discreetly took a seat in a chair across the chamber from the couple who sat at the far end of the table. Hardi pulled a stack of missives from his sporran. All were open despite being addressed to him. He was certain Faolán had justified reading them by arguing that Hardi's return was overdue and they might be urgent. Blair scanned their contents, sorting them into piles. One pile made her lip curl in disgust.

"What's wrong with those?" Hardi asked when he noticed her expression.

"They're all marriage inquiries," Blair grumbled.

"I can answer those." When Blair cast him a suspicious glance, he chuckled. "I believe I can write 'nay thank ye'."

Blair pursed her lips and shot him an annoyed look before smiling and shaking her head. Hardi ignored Maeve, who studiously ignored them. He cupped Blair's face and kissed her. She grasped his upper arms to steady her as she leaned forward. Hardi was ready to ease Blair onto his lap when he recalled that they weren't alone, even if Maeve pretended to be invisible.

"In fact, since those are the simplest to write, can we do them first?" Hardi asked. Blare nodded as Hardi pulled a sheaf of blank, folded vellum from his sporran. "I wasna kidding aboot writing nay thank ye, but I would appreciate yer help to ensure I write it correctly."

"Ye'll have to write more than just that."

"How aboot 'nay thank ye. I dinna want yer daughter because I have someone better'?" Hardi suggested with a grin.

"Incorrigible," Blair muttered. "How aboot 'I must decline yer offer. I am already in negotiations for a betrothal'?"

"Vera well. But I still like ma version better."

"I'm sure ye do. Do ye want me to write the missives or write out the wording and ye copy it in yer own hand?"

Hardi sat back in his chair as he considered Blair's question. He was unsure of what to choose. He opted for Blair's advice instead. "What do ye think? Would it be better for ye to write it in yer clear penmanship or should I respond by ma own hand even if ma writing still isnae vera neat?"

"Either would be acceptable. Many lairds have scribes, usually monks, so ye wouldnae be the only one to send missives written by someone else. But if ye'd like to try, then I think ye should. I'll write it, and ye can practice beneath until ye feel more comfortable. Then ye can write yer official responses."

"That'll take all day," Hardi grumbled.

"Then we'd best get started." Blair pulled a fresh piece of parchment in front of her and dipped the quill into the ink before writing the two sentences. Just as they'd done in the scriptorium as Hardi learned to write, he took the quill from Blair and traced the words several times before attempting to write them below Blair's original version. Hardi was pleased that he found it easier than he had in the past. It took them only an hour to respond to the pile of betrothal inquiries once they began.

Blair pulled the next pile toward them. The marriage requests had made her miffed, but the next pile concerned her more. "Hardi, these are complaints from the surrounding clans that yer patrols are crossing yer borders and encroaching on other territories. None claim that aught has gone awry, but the lairds arenae happy. They date back to four moons ago. Yer uncle was still laird then. Do ye ken if he settled any of these, or have all these clans been stewing over being ignored?"

"Which one's which?" Hardi rubbed his forehead.

"This one is the MacDonnells of Keppoch while this one is from the MacDonnells of Glengarry." Blair held up a missive in each hand before putting them down and picking up two more. She held her left hand up first. "This one is from the Macleans, and this one is from the Hendersons. Hardi, if yer men are passing into Henderson territory, then it canna be an accident. Dinna they have to cross Loch Levin? Doesnae that put ye close to the Campbells?" Blair felt warm as her heart picked up pace. The Campbells were one of King Robert's favored clans. If the Camerons were harassing the Campbells, Blair feared the worst for Hardi. Her connections would do nothing to spare him.

"*Sard,*" Hardi swore under his breath. He didn't understand much French, but he knew the important words for cursing. He ran his hands through his short hair, making it stand on end. It tempted Blair to reach out and smooth it, but she remembered how annoyed she was to see Artair pat Robena's head. She didn't think it was a wise choice. "I need to meet with ma senior guardsmen. Faolán is officially ma second, and Drostan is captain of the guard. It's time they both retired, but until then, I need to speak with men I trust. Men I've fought beside, whose lives I have saved and who have saved mine. I need to placate these lairds without sounding like I'm making excuses for nae kenning. Uncle Farlane mentioned some disagreements between the MacDonnells and us over the exact location of our borders with both septs, but he never told me our patrols crossed the established borders. I have nay idea aboot the Hendersons. What's the date to that?"

Blair glanced back at the parchment. "A week after ye arrived at court."

"Faolán waited until I was too far to turn back or to hear of his meddling." Hardi drummed his fingers on the table as he considered his responses. He glanced at Blair and knew she had her opinion of how he should respond, but he also knew she wouldn't offer it unless asked. She would encourage him to reason through the situation on his own. Hardi looked at the wooden table before him as he continued to tap his fingers. It was as though the rhythmic tapping encouraged his brain to move faster. "I canna give away a heifer and calf to every clan we anger. I also canna concede land to either MacDonnell sept. That was the land King Robert gifted the clan after the Wars."

Hardi sighed as he continued to ruminate on how to resolve the complaints he knew were just. He wished the issues were reversed, and it was another laird who had to apologize to him. He considered what he would expect if it were his land upon which other clans trespassed.

"I will grant the MacDonnells grazing privileges on the land near the disputed borders. Their cattle and sheep may eat in ma meadows, but they canna build structures of any kind. Nae even a shepherd's hut." Hardi glanced at Blair, who kept her face blank, but he knew her well enough to see the approval in her eyes. He continued his finger tapping as he considered the Hendersons and Campbells. As best he knew, none of his patrols crossed into Campbell territory, and it was essential he kept it that way. There would be no appeasing King Robert if they strayed that far. He imagined what he would want from the Hendersons if he'd been wronged.

"The Hendersons are a sept of the MacDonalds," Hardi mused. "I would cede the MacDonalds Inverlochy if it werenae in the center of ma land and so close to Tor. Mayhap, I should direct ma dealings to Laird MacDonald and let him pacify the Hendersons once I've made amends with him. Fortifying the wall around this heap would benefit me and the MacDonalds living here. Artair would be beholden to me nae only for having a castle to boast aboot, but he would have added security. I wouldnae have to worry aboot the castle being overrun should someone attack. The MacDonalds wouldnae have to pay for that part of the castle's upkeep. But I will do it in exchange for the MacDonalds paying for improvements to the keep. The wall far exceeds a few men and horses trampling the Hendersons' grass." Hardi nodded but frowned. "I must give more thought to the Macleans, but they are the least likely to cause a fuss."

Hardi once again looked down at Blair, who nodded her head. She reached out her hand, palm up, and Hardi took it. His larger hand dwarfed hers, but he was always aware of his greater size and strength. Blair lifted his hand to her lips, kissing the back of it. "I'm so vera proud of ye, Hardi. Those are solutions I'm sure ma da would devise. I wish I could suggest ye wait until Lachlan arrives to ask him, but I dinna ken how much longer ye can put these off, and we dinna ken for sure Lach will come."

"I dinna need Lachlan's approval if I have yers. Blair, ye are just as astute as yer brother and ye da. The only difference among the three of ye is yer da's got more experience. I ken ye could have told me what to do, and whatever ye conceived would've been a wise path to take. But I appreciate ye believing in me and letting me work this out for maself."

"I kenned ye would. I thought of the pastureland, but I didna think of the Hendersons being part of the MacDonalds. Using the wall are a bargaining tool didna come to me."

"What would ye have done for the Hendersons?" Hardi asked.

"I thought to offer the Hendersons unimpeded fishing rights to the eastern half of Loch Leven. That would keep yer access to Loch Linhe but let the Hendersons believe they had more than ye."

"That isnae a bad idea."

"Nay, but it forces ye to give something up; whereas, yer solution gains ye something. It may cost ye coin to fix the wall, but it adds to the security to one of yer keeps and really makes the MacDonalds indebted to ye. As yer allies, they will have to provide ye with aid if ye ask. And I believe that time will come soon with the Macphersons and Mackintoshes. Keeping a branch of them here is convenient and will make it impossible for Laird MacDonald to deny ye."

"I just need to be sure Artair isnae the duplicitous dung heap I suspect he is."

"Well, aye. That is rather important," Blair grinned.

"Ye really dinna like him, do ye?" Hardi tucked hair behind Blair's ears. "I hope Lachlan comes and soon. I'm regretting ye staying here."

"I dinna care for him, but he hasnae done aught wrong. He's an arse for sure, but I dinna feel unwelcome. I just think I annoy him." Blair shrugged.

"Ye dinna feel uncomfortable being here?" Hardi pressed.

"Nay. He annoys me as much as I annoy him. But I dinna fear for ma safety, and I dinna think he realizes when he's rude. I dinna think he believes he is." Blair shrugged again. She arranged more sheets of parchment before them, and this time they agreed she would write the missives because they were longer and more complex. It took another half an hour before she was through and pleased with the wording. She set aside the semi-dried vellum and looked at Hardi.

She kept her tone soft as she broached the next unavoidable topic. "Do ye want to deal with this last stack now? They're condolences for losing yer uncle and cousins. Or we can do it another time."

Blair wished she hadn't brought up Hardi's loss, but he had already glanced at the stack several times. She placed her hand over the pile, as though covering them would keep Hardi from reading them. She knew most were too complicated for him to understand without her aid, but she wanted to hide the freshest cause of his pain. She hadn't seen the raw anguish enter Hardi's eyes in weeks, but she'd studiously avoided bringing up recent family events. His face took on a haunted look as he stared at the floor. She wished she could take away the pain and heal the wound she reopened.

Blair glanced at Maeve, who continued to sew with her head bent over her work. She rose from her chair, nudging Hardi's legs to face away from her maid. She eased onto his lap, wrapping her arm around his shoulder. Her other hand gently pressed his head against her chest. Slowly, Hardi's arm around came around her waist, and she felt him shudder. She kissed the top of his head over and over as she stroked his arm and shoulder. He turned his face into her chest as his shoulders heaved. His sobs were silent, but Blair felt each one. She held him tighter, stroking back his hair as she kissed his forehead. They sat in silence even after Hardi's tears subsided, and he wiped away the last of the moisture.

"I love ye, Blair. I dinna want to wait to marry ye," Hardi's voice was hoarse as he whispered.

"What are ye saying, Hardi? We canna post the banns until ye and Da sign the contracts."

"I dinna give a damn what's in yer dowry. I'll pay ma last penny for the bride price. And if ye da says nay, I will marry ye anyway. Someone else, anyone else, can be the fucking laird before I give ye up. I want to handfast, Blair."

Blair cupped Hardi's face as she smiled at him. She pressed a soft kiss to his lips before pulling away. She wouldn't let them get distracted. "I'll handfast with ye this vera moment, but that doesnae change how things stand with yer clan. Are ye ready to add a wife to yer problems?"

"Ye arenae a problem," Hardi protested.

"Ye may nae think so, but yer clan doesnae ken ye arenae going through with the Macquarie or Donald lasses. At the least Faolán and Drostan have read the other betrothal requests, and who kens what they've told the others. We dinna even ken if they've sent off responses that dinna match yers. Hardi, I bring the Sutherland name, and I dinna doubt for a moment that whether we wed or nae, ma da will back ye. But that doesnae solve the inner politics that are crumbling in yer clan. Introducing a wife nae one expects, who will suddenly take over the running of yer keep, willna lessen yer troubles."

"It'll lessen Mordag's," Hardi muttered. At Blair's narrowed eyes, Hardi realized he'd spoken aloud. "Mordag is ma housekeeper. She's served as chatelaine since ma aunt died. She hates it. Complains she wasna trained to be chatelaine. She was the first one to say I needed to marry. She'll welcome ye with open arms, a hot bath, and a feast."

Blair considered their options, and she could tell Hardi was doing the same. She glanced back at the unanswered missives. "*Mo chridhe*, I'll tell ye who's written to ye. If there are any ye want to answer personally, I'll take dictation. Otherwise, let me handle these. And we can leave them until later. I think fresh air would do us both some good after being in here for hours."

"I agree. Ma head aches, and I could do with a

231

change of scenery," Hardi nodded. He wanted to ask Blair whether she wanted the handfast she agreed to, but he decided not to push the issue.

"I'd like to go to the orchard," Blair explained as she gathered the missives Hardi brought while he sealed the last ones. "We will need ma guards and mayhap Bran."

Hardi glanced at her, confused. He didn't think they needed guards or chaperones while outside and within the bailey walls.

"As witnesses. We should have at least one person from each of our clans witness our handfast. Then nay one can dispute it took place," Blair explained.

Hardi dropped the stack of missives he'd collected and pulled Blair in for a searing kiss. Hardi didn't care that Maeve gasped more than once. He only cared about the woman clinging to him, returning his kiss. When they separated, both were beaming until reality crashed down on Hardi's shoulders.

"Blair, I canna offer ye a proper wedding night. I canna guarantee I can slip into yer chamber, and I dinna ken if we can slip off somewhere. I definitely dinna want yer first time to be in a storeroom or against a tree."

"I rather like what we get up to against trees," Blair waggled her eyebrows. Hardi pulled her back against him as he leaned toward her ear.

"I'm aboot to truly scandalize yer maid by tossing up yer skirts and laying ye back on this table," Hardi growled against her neck before nipping at the muscle on the top of her shoulder.

"Hardi, I dinna care where our first time is. A storeroom, against a tree, on a table, under a table, in the stable's hayloft. I just want our first time."

Hardi shook his head. "Nay. I will do whatever I must to come to yer chamber, but it willna be to sleep." Hardi winked and grinned. "Ye'll just have to be patient. It willna be straight from the kirk to our chamber, and it willna be straight from the orchard to the hayloft." Hardi kissed Blair again. "I shall remember that last one. I rather like the idea."

"As long as the hay isnae too prickly," Blair giggled. They hurried to gather what they'd both dropped along with their writing supplies before dismissing Maeve and going in search of their clansmen.

THIRTY

Once Blair, Hardi, both Sutherland guards, and Bran made their way to the orchard, Hardi and Blair stood facing one another under the orchard canopy. Blair handed Hardi the ribbon she pulled loose from her hair, and together they tied it around the wrists of their joined hands. Hardi draped over their hands the length of plaid he'd unfastened from his shoulder.

"Blair, I would be certain we understand one another before we begin," Hardi kept his voice low, so their three witnesses couldn't listen. "This is a handfast, but I consider it a binding marriage. I willna consider a repudiation in a year and a day. If ye arenae sure ye want this, if ye arenae sure ye can go through with this without yer parents' blessing, then tell me now. I willna hold it against ye, and we can wait for yer father's decision."

"If the next word out of yer mouth arenae the beginning of our marriage vows, I shall pull yer hair and tug on yer ear like when we were children and ye annoyed me," Blair warned. She grinned as Hardi relaxed. "I love ye. If ye think to repudiate this, then ye had best run all the way to England. Otherwise, I will find ye and drag ye back. I'd drag ye back even if ye hid under Longshanks's bed."

"I love ye, Blair Sutherland." Hardi returned her smile. Blair blinked several times as she realized that would be the last time anyone would call her a Sutherland. "Blair?"

"Aye." Blair looked into Hardi's eyes and thought she would melt. The love and concern she glimpsed assured her she was making the right choice. "I was just thinking I willna be Blair Sutherland in a few minutes. As surreal as that is, I canna help the excitement of becoming Blair Cameron."

"Blair, ye'll always be a Sutherland. Yer name willna change that, but I confess I'm impatient for ye to carry ma name. I want ye to be a Cameron because it means ye're ma wife."

"And I want to become a Cameron because it means ye're ma husband. I love ye, Hardwin." They gazed at one another. Neither could remember the last time Blair used Hardi's given name. It made the moment even more sacred.

"Blair Ceana Sutherland, ma love, ye are the one person with whom I can share all that I am. I promise to trust ye and to be honest with ye. I promise to listen to ye, respect ye, and support ye. I promise to do all of this through whatever life brings us: riches or poverty, health or illness, through good times and bad, until the end of ma days." Hardi's thumb rubbed over the bare finger that would soon wear his ring.

"Hardwin Fionn Cameron, ma love, ye are the one person with whom I can share all that I am. I promise to laugh and play with ye and grow and bend with ye. I promise to cherish every day we have together. I promise to do all of this through whatever life brings us: riches or poverty, health or illness, through good times and bad, until the end of ma days."

Together they pledged, "We are now but one body and one blood. Let us from this day forth be united with one destiny."

Hardi and Blair stood together for a long moment, gazing into one another's eyes. The emotion that passed between them more powerful than the words they exchanged. Hardi cupped Blair's cheek, and she covered his hand with hers as they sealed their pledge with a kiss so filled with tenderness that tears smarted behind Blair's eyes. When they pulled apart, Hardi did nothing to hide the moisture in his eyes.

"Blair Cameron, I will love you through this life and the next," Hardi whispered.

Blair opened her mouth to speak, but the lump in her throat kept any sound from passing through. She nodded as she mouthed, "I love ye now and forever." They brought their bound hands to their chests, Hardi's resting over Blair's heart as hers rested over his. They both looked down, appreciating the symbolism of their vows and the future they would create together. Unable to resist, they shared another kiss before the bells for the midday meal interrupted.

With great reluctance, they untied their hands and Hardi returned the plaid to its place over his shoulder. They'd forgotten anyone but them existed in the world until they faced their witnesses. Blair accepted Donald's and Tomas's embraces, remembering how both men had once teased her as they swung her in the air as a child. Hardi shook forearms with Bran and thanked him for his well wishes. It was with a heavy heart that all five left their smiles and good cheer at the door of the keep, entering as though nothing out of the norm had happened during their visit to the Inverlochy orchard.

When the couple claimed their seats beside one another at the evening meal, they both breathed a sigh of relief. Beneath the tablecloth, Hardi drew Blair's skirt high over her thigh until his hand rested on her knee, then slid higher. Blair studiously pretended to ignore Hardi's teasing, but when he drew his hand away, hers pressed it back down, this time higher. She glanced at him from the corner of her eye before slipping her hand beneath his plaid to rest on his thigh, her fingernails grazing his skin. She felt the shiver that ran through his body.

"Blair, I will tease yer body for every moment ye tease mine," Hardi said under his breath. Blair skimmed her fingers higher. "I will bring ye to the edge then deny ye over and over until ye can do naught but beg."

Blair looked directly at Hardi. "And I shall have ma chance to suck on ye."

Hardi growled as his fingers bit into the flesh on her thigh. "Ye may act like a saint, but ye are pure temptation."

Blair swallowed as she peered past Hardi to their hosts before looking back at him. "I shall excuse maself early, claiming a headache. I dinna even care if Artair gloats that I overtaxed maself. Make yer own excuses."

Blair sat back as servants placed dishes on the table and filled chalices to near overflowing. Neither Hardi nor Blair drank more than a few sips. Blair pretended to catch herself before rubbing her head. She shifted in her seat several times, her discomfort real, her arousal making her entire body thrum with need. She remained quiet throughout the meal, offering only simple answers to Robena's questions and only nodding to the wives of the senior guardsmen seated at the table. Before the last course, Blair excused herself, claiming an unrelenting ache. She didn't say where, only giving the impression that it was her head when she put her fingers to her temple. Hardi understood it was an ache of an entirely different nature. Hardi endured the last course before claiming he would leave early in the morning and would retire for a full night's sleep. However, he intended to get barely an hour.

THIRTY-ONE

Hardi nodded to Bran and another Cameron guard who'd followed Blair to her chamber and stood guard outside. He knocked once before slipping inside. Blair sat at the table that held her ribbons and fragrant oil. She put down her comb as Hardi came into view through her looking glass. She turned in her seat, her robe sliding open over her leg, revealing bare skin. She didn't wait to rise and draw open her dressing gown and let it fall to the floor. She ambled toward Hardi, but his long stride brought them together. Despite her seductive welcome, there was little finesse in their kiss. Hardi's fingers bit into the flesh of Blair's buttocks as she moaned into his mouth. Her hand slipped between them as she cupped his rod.

The raw need in Hardi's eyes matched Blair's. Their courtship hadn't been long, but memories of their adolescent attraction along with their ease with one another hadn't left either in doubt. But no matter how brief the time had been, it was an excruciating duration when it came to repressed need. Hardi unpinned his plaid as Blair unfastened his belt. Once Hardi stood naked before Blair, her mouth went slack as her eyes roamed over the chiseled muscles of his chest, abdomen, and thighs. She stepped around him, awed by the hewn plains of his backside. She didn't resist the temptation to spread her hands over his tight buttocks. Her hands glided up his back as she pressed her body against his, kissing his shoulder blade.

"*Mo theampall*." My temptation, Hardi murmured as he reached back to guide Blair to stand before him. He lifted her off the ground, and her legs came around his waist. "I want what I shouldnae from ma maiden bride."

"Tell me," Blair whispered before kissing him. "I want to hear it."

Hardi wondered if he should confess, fearing his crass thought might ruin the moment. Blair rocked her hips, brushing her mons against his straining rod. The top of his cock searched for her entrance, and when it found its coveted place, it demanded Hardi thrust.

"Tell me, Hardi," Blair pressed as Hardi laid her on the bed. "Ye willna shock me. I want to hear ye desire me. I ken ye do because I can feel it. I dinna understand why I need the words, but when ye tell me what ye want, I canna help but get more excited."

"I ken I should make love to ye, but I want to fuck ye. Hard." Hardi admitted. He looked away, ashamed he'd spoken so bluntly to a woman he treasured, who would never treat like a common tavern wench. Blair gripped his chin between her thumb and fingers, pulling him back to meet her gaze.

"Then show me."

"Ye dinna ken what ye're saying," Hardi argued. "I dinna ever want to hurt ye, but yer first time may be painful. I wouldnae add to it by being rough."

"*Mo ghaol*, I ken the pain isnae on purpose. But I

242

confess, I dinna ken if I can go slowly. Hardi, ye were brave enough to say what I want. I couldnae bring maself to ask. I didna—" Blair trailed off as Hardi climbed onto the bed beside her.

"Ye didna want to sound like a whore when ye should be innocent of kenning how a mon and woman come together," Hardi supplied for her. "Blair, I ken ye're a virgin. Ye would have told me if ye werenae. I've felt yer barrier when I've touched ye. And despite the passion we share, yer kisses and touch are still innocent. I dinna think less of ye."

"And I dinna think less of ye," Blair ran her hands over his chest and back as he brought his body to hover of his. She watched his muscles strain and bunch as he held himself up on his hands. His abdomen rippled with every breath, and the tip of his cock laid atop the thatch of dark curls on her mound. Blair's voice dropped to a whisper. "By God, Hardi, every inch of ye is perfect. I want to touch every part of ye. And I have never felt so possessive of anyone or anything before in ma life. I could kill any woman who thinks to touch what is mine and nay even blink."

Blair dropped her legs wide as her hand wrapped around Hardi's shaft. His hand covered hers, and they guided him into her entrance. He eased the tip into her channel, sucking in whistling breaths as he tried to move slowly. He wanted her to have time to grow accustomed to the invasion, her untried sheath stretching to accommodate him.

"Hardi?" Blair purred. Hardi met her gaze. "Do ye need me as much I need ye?"

"Ye ken that I do," he panted.

"Then now," Blair hissed as she raised her hips. Hardi thrust into her, breaking through her barrier, making her his wife in truth. Blair's neck strained as she pressed against the pillow, the moment painful, but she welcomed it. Hardi was now undisputedly her husband. Hardi watched as Blair relaxed before pulling his head down for a kiss. Before their lips met, she whispered. "Fuck me."

Both abandoned any restraint. The bed groaned, the legs of its frame scratching the floor in rhythm to each of Hardi's thrusts. Blair's unrelenting hold on his backside she raised her hips to every thrust spurred him on. Supporting himself on one hand, his other squeezed her breast. He brushed his finger over her nipple until it hardened. He pinched as tightly as he dared.

"Blair, I'm scared I'm hurting ye. If nae now, then when we are done." Hardi slowed his thrusts and lowered himself onto his forearms. His surges pressed his sword into her sheath just as deeply as when he raced toward completion, but his movement was slower. Their kiss remained passionate, but tenderness replaced wildness. Hardi slid his palms under her shoulders as Blair's knees bracketed his hips. They settled into a rocking motion until Blair's body went taut, and she fought not to cry out. The sudden vice-like grip around his cock pushed Hardi over the edge, spilling into her. He was certain he'd never sired a bastard, but he hadn't always been as cautious as he should have. As he took in Blair's flushed face and heaving chest, for the first time in his life, he hoped his seed took root. If not this time, then soon. He cared not if it was a boy or a girl. He simply longed to create a family with his wife.

Aware that his arms shook, he worried he would crush Blair when they gave out. Hardi tucked hair behind Blair's ear before pressing a soft kiss to her lip. He moved to roll off her, but she clung to him.

"Please, nae yet," Blair pleaded, but she closed her eyes, not wanting Hardi to witness a different kind of neediness.

"I dinna want to move, but I fear ma weight is too much," Hardi explained.

"It's nae. I want to hold ye," Blair murmured.

"I want that more than aught." Hardi settled against Blair, careful not to press his entire weight onto her. But when she grunted her dissatisfaction, he tested her frame. It not only surprised him how Blair's body bore his weight but how she welcomed it as he nuzzled her neck. They pressed light kisses along one another's shoulders until their heartbeats slowed. To both of their disappointment, Hardi's sword slipped from her sheath, but he didn't pull away. They held one another until Blair's eyes drifted close on long blinks. Hardi rolled onto his back, bringing Blair with him. His fingers skimmed her back as she dozed off. He soon followed, but as he intended, they spent only an hour sleeping that night. Their unsated need rousing them repeatedly.

THIRTY-TWO

Blair rose from the bed, her body sore. Her eye caught sight of the red stain that marked the end of her maidenhood. Hardi came around to her side of the bed and slipped his arms around her.

"How do ye feel, *mo leannan*?" Concern laced Hardi's voice, and Blair refused to admit the truth, unwilling to cause Hardi a moment of guilt or worry.

"Like a well-satisfied wife," Blair grinned. She pulled away and turned back to the bed. She pulled at the corner of the sheet at the head of the bed until it came loose. She leaned over the bed and continued to tug until the other side allowed her to gather it.

"I can dispose of that," Hardi offered.

"Dinna ye dare," Blair warned as she looked back over her shoulder. "Whether people ken this will be old or they believe it's fresh, they will expect proof once ye announce ye have a wife." Blair folded the sheet into a tight bundle and placed it at the bottom of the small chest she'd brought with her. They walked to the stand with the jug and ewer, Hardi insisting upon helping Blair with her morning ablutions. His gentleness as he cleansed between her thighs made her eyes water. Neither of them was certain when next they would see one another. They dressed in silence, but before they left Blair's chamber, Hardi led Blair to the chair before the fire. He sat down and eased her into his lap, careful not to touch her in any way that might cause discomfort.

"Before yesterday in the solar, I hadnae cried since Dougal died, and then I didna let anyone see me," Hardi confessed. "Leaving ye behind makes me want to sob as I did yesterday."

"I'm trying to be brave and nae turn into a bairn, but I'm struggling," Blair admitted.

"If ye need aught, send one of yer guards or one of the king's. I will come nay matter what," Hardi pledged.

"I make the same offer. Ask, and I will come with haste. Hardi, it scares me that ye're going back, and we still dinna ken what's happening."

"I will send Bran with updates when I can. I promise."

Blair nodded as she leaned her head against Hardi's chest. She wished they could stay together, behind their locked door, and forget the rest of the world existed. But the sun was already over the horizon, and they could hear movement outside the chamber. Neither doubted that their night spent together was no secret. Without a ring on her finger, Hardi worried about how the MacDonalds would treat Blair. They'd come to an agreement between couplings that Blair would wear one of her own rings but on her left ring finger. She'd brought a few pieces of jewelry with her but had worn none since arriving at Inverlochy. Hardi had slipped it onto her finger, and they'd recited their handfast vows again. As they held hands before the fire, Hardi twisted the ring, the feel reassuring to them both. When they could no longer put off Hardi's departure, Blair joined him in the bailey. They'd said their goodbyes privately in

248

Blair's chamber. A swift kiss was all they shared before Hardi swung into the saddle and spurred his horse. Just as he had the first time he left Blair at Inverlochy, Hardi turned back four times before Blair was out of sight. She waved until he disappeared.

The next three days felt like an eternity to Blair. Despite the ring on her finger, her welcome at Inverlochy had run out. Between what people heard firsthand and what developed through gossip, looks of disdain from women and leers from men followed her everywhere. She refused to cower or hide. She wasn't ashamed of what she and Hardi did. If people chose not to believe the ring on her finger signified their handfast, Blair wasn't interested in convincing them. While Tomas and Donald trailed more closely, she went about the keep and bailey as she had before her wedding night. She helped Robena, who she sensed now wanted to turn Blair away but couldn't afford to refuse help given her ever-expanding belly. The one person who made life truly miserable was Artair.

"Lady Blair, I'm certain there is a copy of *Tristan and Isolde* in my library. Mayhap you would prefer that to toiling alongside a mere chieftain's wife. After all, you are the daughter of an earl," Artair announced at the morning meal shortly after Hardi left Inverlochy. Blair rued mentioning her lineage, but she'd been annoyed her first day. Now, those veiled insults were a drop in the bucket compared to Artair's blunt comments. She wasn't interested in reading the chivalric romance.

"I planned to go riding this morn, but I thank you for your offer, Chieftain," Blair explained.

"I'm not sure that riding this morning is best for

your constitution," Artair responded. Blair refused to be embarrassed and willed her cheeks not to blush. She kept her attention on her porridge. "You see, a woman's body is more fragile. Such vigorous activity too often will surely weaken your already weaker body. I wouldn't want Laird Cameron to return to find his—lady—ill."

Blair could imagine a wealth of words Artair would have preferred to calling her a lady. She would never give him the satisfaction of knowing that she was sore from making love almost all night, but she was desperate to be away from the keep, even if only for a few hours.

"Your council will be kept in mind." *Nay, it willna. I'll ignore it, ye oaf.*

"Suit yourself. But know there will be no hot water for a bath," Artair warned. "Lady Robena is having the ovens cleaned today," Artair warned.

Blair slid her gaze to Robena, who looked surprised at Artair's announcement but soon recovered, shooting Blair a sympathetic look. Blair looked down at her half-finished bowl of porridge and decided she'd had enough. Discussing her intimate life with Artair, even in a roundabout way, was ruining her mood. Hardi's departure already saddened her. She excused herself and found her guards before spending most of the day away from the keep.

Blair's second and third days were not much better. Artair continued his condescending comments, which made Blair bite her tongue so many times she was certain it would be shorter in a week's time. *At what point do I put an end to this, even if it causes a scene? I dinna want to read poetry aboot forlorn lovers because I must feel the same way. I dinna want to rest every afternoon to keep from overtaxing maself as the weather warms. I'm nae a bairn nor his expectant wife. I dinna need to be sent to bed. Nae, I dinna need ye to explain to me that Hardi will surely nae want*

a wife with hands like a fieldworker. If ye offered Robena ade-
quate help, I wouldnae be involved. I dinna understand why he
expects her to do so much with so little help. If any lady-wife
must have hands like a servant, it must be Robena.

Artair's unceasing advice forced Blair's wan-
dering mind back to the present during the third
evening's meal. She picked at her overcooked,
charred duck. It was the first time anything came out
of the Inverlochy kitchens that wasn't of superior
quality. She looked at Artair as he began his newest
explanation of why she should understand a man's
world.

"Lady Blair, moping won't bring Laird Cameron
back any sooner. He has important business that he
conducts as laird. He mustn't be distracted, because
leading his clan is a heavy responsibility. He will visit
you when he can make time to leave the more
pressing matters until later. You'll understand once
you're married longer. You're still young."

Blair couldn't decide which part of Artair's su-
percilious comment irked her the most. However, it
was the first time he'd acknowledged that they were
married. The lesson in how to be a wife, specifically
one married to a laird, made her want to drive her
fist into his priggish visage. She opened her mouth to
thank him for his insights when the door to the keep
opened. Blair gripped the armrests of her chair to
keep from running into Hardi's arms. When his eyebrows lifted as if to ask why she wasn't greeting him,
her restraint withered. She rose and glided from the
dais. She fought the urge to run, but her pace increased to what she was certain was a trot when he
opened his arms to her. Neither considered their audience as Hardi lowered his mouth to hers. The kiss
was brief, but held all the intensity it normally did.

In the near-silent Great Hall, Hardi's voice carried to those sitting closest to them. "I've missed ye,

wife." Those within earshot repeated his comment, and it spread among the diners. Four words gave their relationship more credibility than the ring Blair wore. They stood with their arms around one another as Hardi leaned forward to whisper to Blair. "The only evening meal I want is ye. How close to the end are ye?"

"Nay more food is being brought out. I will share ma trencher with ye," Blair kept her voice low. "But stay away from the duck. I dinna ken what happened, but it was on the spit too long." Hardi took Blair's arm even though he wanted to hold her hand, and they made their way to the dais. Hardi assisted Blair with her seat before taking his. She added more food to Hardi's side of the trencher and remained quiet while he ate.

"You are learning to be a wife, Lady Cameron," Artair commented. Blair noted it was the first time the chieftain acknowledged her by her proper title. She'd chosen not to fight that battle and continued to respond to Lady Blair rather than insist upon being addressed as Lady Cameron. She was aware it was for Hardi's sake, not hers. "I feared you would bombard Laird Cameron with questions. No mon wants to hear yammering the moment he sits down."

Hardi straightened to glare over Blair and Robena's heads. He narrowed his eyes as he laid down his eating knife. "While I appreciate my wife's attentiveness, I was about to ask her why she wasna speaking. I look forward to the sound of her voice, and would like to hear how she's spent her time while we were apart. I'd be insulted if she didna have questions for me."

Hardi returned his attention to their trencher, but before he took another bite, he asked from the corner of his mouth, "Is he always that insufferable?"

"Aye," Blair didn't hesitate. She wouldn't lie to

Hardi, and she saw no reason to downplay Artair's obnoxiousness. "He seems to have an endless supply of advice."

Hardi looked down at his food and suddenly was no longer as hungry as he had been when he rode into the bailey. He put out his hand for Blair's and rose. He disregarded Artair's calls for them to share a dram or two of whisky while they discussed topics that would surely bore their wives. He ignored Artair's indignant snort. He led Blair to the stairs and didn't look back.

THIRTY-THREE

Once inside their chamber, Hardi and Blair tore at each other's clothes. Closer to a wall than the bed, Hardi pressed Blair back against the hard surface, raising her leg over his hip, his cock pressing against her seam.

"Wet for me already, *mo ghaol*?"

"As wet as ye are hard," Blair grinned. "Is this one of those times ye want to fuck rather than make love?"

"It is." Hardi thrust into her. The only sound became their moans as Hardi surged into her over and over. Their difference in height soon had Hardi lifting Blair and carrying her to the edge of the table where her comb and ribbons lay. They scattered to the floor as Blair sat on the edge, but when the table began an ominous creak, Hardi walked them to the bed. He came down over her as they clawed at one another, and Blair met each thrust with her own.

"Hardi," Blair moaned. "Dinna hold back." With Blair's encouragement, Hardi lost control. He fisted her hair as he moved with an urgency and roughness he never imagined.

"Blair, what're ye doing to me?"

"I want to feel how much ye desire me. I want all of it."

"Ye want me to fuck ye harder than any woman before. Ye want me to desire ye more," Hardi growled, his words punctuated by thrusts. "Ye dinna need to worry, Blair. I have never needed aught more than I do ye. If ye want me to give ye all that I can while I fuck ye, I willna turn ye down. If me losing control is what ye need to know ye possess every part of me, then I'll gladly give it to ye." Hardi pinned Blair's arms above her head as he continued to grasp a handful of her hair.

"Take me and do whatever ye want. Just dinna stop," Blair moaned. Her body now trapped beneath Hardi's, she wanted to give herself over to him, wanted him to know she was his. In the next breath, the pleasure the friction of their bodies created broke free. The wave of ecstasy bowed her body off the bed as she tightened her core. The need to hold Hardi within her was something out of her control. Hardi's hand released her wrists to move to her hip. His fingers bit into her backside as he spilled. The jets of his seed seemed endless as his cock throbbed within her.

Hardi's spent body lay atop Blair's as they panted, their minds trying to make sense of what they'd shared while their bodies attempted to recover. Without thought, Blair's fingers roamed over Hardi's back, stroking the taut muscles. Hardi pressed soft kisses against her neck as his hips continued to rock within her, the movement small and gentle. A nagging sense of regret and self-doubt crept into Blair's mind as they lay together, Hardi continuing to bask in the moment until Blair grew uneasy, and he sensed it.

"What's the matter?" Hardi asked as he continued the tender kisses. When Blair didn't answer, he pushed up onto his forearms. She stared into his eyes as though she searched for something, but he understood she was searching within herself. "Blair, what's wrong?"

Blair's brow furrowed. Her emotions were still too charged, and she feared she would cry, only making things worse. "I dinna ken why I become so possessive when we make love." Blair closed her eyes to dam the tears she felt threatening. "I canna help it. Even when it's wild like this, ma mind insists that it's lovemaking."

Hardi cupped Blair's head as he kissed her. It was hungry and demanding. Blair sighed as she gave into it, welcoming Hardi's forcefulness. When Hardi pulled back, Blair was unsure of the meaning in his eyes. The uncertainty made her chest pinch. "Blair, as much as ye want me to show ye how I desire ye, I want the same. I need the reassurance too. Ye arenae a possessive woman by nature. Ye dinna try to control me or demand aught from me. If ye're possessive of me when we're making love, I feel loved. I feel like ye willna give me up or turn away from me. I want to give ye all of me, and I want to ken ye'll accept it and that ye'll protect it."

Blair cupped Hardi's cheek and strained to reach his mouth with hers. The kiss was brief and tender before she settled back against the pillow. "How are ye able to express what passes between us so well? How do ye understand me and what I need so well? I'm the woman. I'm the one who should speak of feelings, and yet there isnae a brawer mon than ye, but ye can explain the deepest emotions I have."

"Because I recognize them. They're what I feel too."

"But ye have the words to describe it. I canna seem to sort out ma own feelings enough within ma head, let alone explain them to ye."

"Did ye assume that because ye're more educated than me that ye would reason it out when I couldnae? That ye should be able to speak of something so deep better than I could?" Hardi felt his temper and pride flair, but it didn't compare to the ice that entered Blair's eyes.

"Hardwin, dinna ye make this aboot who's smarter or who's more learned. It's aboot me being a woman, and ye being a mon. I feel like I should be able to speak ma feelings, but I canna. I just dinna ken how. I'm embarrassed that ye can, and I come up with naught. It's ridiculous, and I ken that, but it makes me feel lacking. If aught, it shows ye're the more intelligent of the two of us. Dinna ever, ever doubt ma respect for ye because ye learned to read and write after me. I dinna think there is aught that will ever make me angrier and more defensive. One emotion I do understand is that I'm fiercely protective of ye even if the threat is yer own self-doubt."

"I'd say ye understand me well, *mo chridhe*. I suppose it makes me unusual to talk aboot feelings, but as long as ye dinna think I'm weak for it, then I'm happy we understand one another," Hardi admitted.

"I swear by all the saints and archangels, I love ye more than I ever thought a mind and heart could."

"I love ye." Their kiss soon became passionate, and Hardi's body responded with urgency. "I need ye again, Blair."

Blair moaned as she raised her hips. "I havenae had nearly enough." There was no frenzy this time. They kissed as Blair cupped Hardi's cheek and tunneled her fingers into his hair. The drawn out, slow movements enhanced the exquisite pleasure. This time, tenderness and devotion replaced their insatiable hunger. Each slow glide of their bodies spoke to how neither wanted their intimacy to end. When their climaxes swept over them, it was a wave that lapped at every inch of their cores rather than crashing over them.

"Hardi, mayhap the word for what we did earlier is fucking because of its intensity, but I meant what I said," Blair gazed into Hardi's eyes, needing to share her thoughts while they joined their bodies. "It's love-making to me, and it means as much to me as what we're doing now. I love ye in more than one way, and the distinct ways we make love is the best that I ken how to explain it. I may never have the words like ye do, but how I move with ye, how I sense what ye want, that's how I can express maself, *mo ghaol*."

"I am at a loss for words, *leannan*. What ye said is perfect, and ye take ma breath away. I canna explain how much I love ye, but I do."

They drifted off to sleep in one another's arms and awoke the next morning in the same position. Their soft smiles and knowing look said they wished they never had to leave their bed. But both knew the day would begin and spending it in bed may have been what they wanted, but it wasn't what they could do.

THIRTY-FOUR

B lair and Hardi avoided breaking their fast by gathering a loaf of bread and half of a wheel of cheese before leaving through the postern gate. There was a loch a brief walk from the keep, so they made their way there and sat beneath the shade of the trees along the bank. Hardi pulled a missive from his sporran, hesitating for a moment before handing it to Blair. He'd opened it the day before but hadn't understood enough of it. It was the excuse he needed to justify to himself leaving Tor Castle to see Blair. He'd fought himself, barely maintaining the willpower to remain at the keep rather than rush to see Blair. But not understanding the missive meant he no longer had to battle his longing.

"Bran intercepted this yesterday. He was on the way to let ye ken I wanted to visit but duty prevented it. He rode out and caught up to one of ma men returning from Inverlochy. Bran told him that he'd come out to check on a clan member who lives away from the village and was on his way back anyway. Bran offered to take the missive, so the mon could have a drink at the tavern in the village. I tried to read it since I thought it would make more sense in Scots, but I dinna understand it all."

Hardi handed the parchment to Blair. She glanced at it, but when she saw no salutation, she turned it over to see if the sender addressed it to anyone.

"Do ye ken who it's for?" Blair asked.

"Nay. Bran asked who he should give it to, expecting Alan to say me, but the mon shrugged. Bran told me Alan only kenned he was to bring it to Tor. When he asked who it was from, Alan said he didna ken that either. He picks up missives from behind a stone in the western wall."

"Someone's hiding and passing messages. If this mon, Alan, came from here, then someone expected the message at Tor and may have been expecting a messenger to carry a response here. Or mayhap this is the response. I didna hear aught yesterday aboot a Cameron rider approaching, and I didna see anyone. I never knew anyone from yer clan was here. Who do ye think would pick Alan to be a messenger? Is there a reason?" Blair's mind swirled with questions.

"Alan is the grandson, son, and nephew of men on the council. He's been a messenger for years. I'm sure nay one thought twice aboot him leaving or being gone. If anyone noticed, they probably assumed he was on an errand for me."

Blair nodded as she looked down at the missive. She read aloud, her stomach churning more with each word.

Your last message was very reassuring. We are making progress, and we will have what we want in a matter of sennights. That Hardwin doesn't see what is beneath his nose proves he's incompetent to be laird. He's pathetic.

The fool says he married the lass. Mayhap they handfasted, but I think he said whatever would get him under her skirts. They hump throughout the night. He's like a rutting stallion, and his mare has no shame. But that suits us. While he's distracted by tupping his bride, he won't notice the coins missing from his coffers. I don't fear him knowing how many go missing. He may be able to count the coins in front of him, but he can't add them together. With nay one keeping the ledgers properly, you should be able to explain away the losses as expenses for the keep. Our fletcher hasn't questioned the order of the fresh arrows, so he isn't asking where they went.

They are counting on the arrows as part of the payment to oust the pretender. I pray your assurance that he has no command over the warriors is true. Make sure most still see him as their equal, not a man who can issue orders. We have two moons before they are ready to strike. This gives you that amount of time to finish the tunnel. You've promised six sennights. If you fail, so does our plan. You have accomplished an impressive amount with only five men digging. When the time comes, he will surrender because he's weak, but he will claim it's to protect his people. Once the pretender is dead, there is naught keeping you from claiming your position.

Blair and Hardi stared at one another, both speechless once Blair finished reading. Blair grabbed Hardi's hand as her heart raced. "They're going to kill ye. This isnae just aboot ousting ye. If they need to kill ye to succeed, then ye are a greater threat than they admit, which only puts ye in more danger."

"But who are they? Nae just the ones exchanging missives. But who are the 'they' that's preparing to strike? Is it the Macphersons, the Mackintoshes, the Davidsons, the Grants, the entire Chattan Confederation? I dinna ken which direction to look other than east."

"The Grants? I thought yer clan resolved yer fight with them." Blair shook her head in confusion.

"It was. But if everyone from the east is moving toward us, then the Grants may join in."

Blair shook her head. "I dinna think so. Edward and Fingal willna meddle where they arenae needed. Ma da kens Edward well, and I've met him several times. He's austere, but he is reasonable. Fingal can be a hothead from what Cairstine used to say, but he always has a strategy. There's naught for them to gain. They're more likely to come to yer aid if it'll keep the peace and keeps any clan in the Chattan Confederation off their land."

"Mayhap. Someone here has also shared that we married. I havenae heard any whispers that people ken at Tor, but it canna be long before they do. They'll wonder why ye're here and nae by ma side."

"That doesnae worry me as much as a tunnel. Is it coming from Tor, or does it start here? Do they intend to connect the keeps, or will it come out somewhere?" Blair reread parts of the missive, since it was too much to take in at one time.

"They're right that I can count the coins in front of me, but I still have a hard time doing the sums," Hardi admitted, frustrated with his own lack of knowledge. "And nay one has kept the ledgers since ma aunt died. I have nay idea what should or shouldnae be there. I dinna even ken things like how much food we should store for winter. Or how much food the keep goes through in a sennight, a moon, a year. I dinna ken any of that. Ma uncle never mentioned aught aboot that."

"Can ye bring me the ledgers? The household accounts along with the clan's?" Blair asked. "I can sort through that. Is the clan's coin kept somewhere that many people ken? Ye need to move it sharpish."

"Only members of the council are supposed to ken where it's kept, but that doesnae mean that's the case. Obviously."

"Even though we dinna ken who's exchanging missives, we ken someone in yer clan can read other than Faolán and Drostan. They're both away, and yet someone sent a missive to Tor, and it sounds like one was sent here after yer cousins left."

"Faolán's wife died several years ago giving birth

264

to a stillborn daughter. He doesnae have any legitimate children, but he has several illegitimate ones in the village. If he became laird, he has nay legitimate heirs. Drostan never married and has been more careful than Faolán."

"Who is after ye in line? Is it Faolán and then Drostan?" Blair had never thought to ask. She supposed because teaching Hardi to read and write was more pressing, and then once they planned to marry, she assumed she'd bear his heir.

"I dinna ken, to be honest. That's why I wondered why Faolán was so eager. He would have nay legacy to pass on unless he insisted one of his bastards inherit. If the clan was desperate enough, they would agree. That's why the clan council has urged me to take a wife. Kenning I've married should put them at ease, but if someone—more than someone—seeks to kill me, then I dinna want to bring ye to Tor. If it isnae safe for me, then ye are even more at risk. I canna ensure yer safety if I'm dead."

"Will ye let me write to ma da? If Lachlan were coming, he would have arrived at Tor by now. Nay messenger has come from court to deliver ma parents' missives. Hardi, I think we should ask Da's advice. It sounds like we have a few sennights before they intend to make a move. If the tunnel runs into Tor, then it's a direct attack. They'll invade from the inside. If it leads from Inverlochy, it'll be a surprise siege. Whoever it is will move warriors without being seen. Either way, we have enough time for me to send and receive a message from Da."

"Aye. I'll send Bran with it. The weather has been good, so he should be there in five days' time."

"He can be back in a fortnight. That isnae that long. In the meantime, bring the ledgers, and we must continue yer lessons. But we need to do it in Scots. Either the people corresponding canna read or write Latin, or they dinna see the need since they mean these to be private."

"Will learning Scots be easier?" Hardi's head hurt at the thought of trying to learn to read and write yet another language.

"It should be. Ye already speak it." Blair grinned as she leaned to whisper. "With the most seductive burr I have ever heard."

"Seductive is it?" Hardi switched from Gaelic to Scots. He watched as Blair's chest rose with a deep inhale, and her lips parted. "Come here, wife."

Hardi pulled back his plaid to show his fully aroused length. Blair gathered her skirts but waited for Hardi to guide her, unsure of what to do. Blair gasped at the feel of her sheath slipping down his sword. The new position made her moan as Hardi's hands held her hips beneath her skirts. He showed her how to rock against him and slide up and down his cock.

"They got one thing right. I feel like a stallion, and ye're the only one who can tame me. I shall insist we go for a ride every day." Hardi thrust into Blair as she held his shoulders to keep her balance. He pulled her kirtle down over her shoulder, and she lifted her breast free, offering it to Hardi's open mouth. If it weren't imperative that they finish quickly, it would have embarrassed Hardi at how soon he climaxed. He'd held out to ensure Blair enjoyed their new position, but he hadn't lasted but two more thrusts before he clamped her hips in place as he filled her channel.

"Are ye returning to Tor now?" Blair wondered.

Hardi's forehead furrowed. "Do ye think I will couple with ye and then ride away? Ye're ma wife, nay a leman or a wench."

"What?" Blair couldn't follow his train of thought. "Oh! That isnae what I thought. I figured that now ye kenned what the missive said, ye would need to return to Tor, so nay one wonders where ye went. I didna think ye used me." Blair smiled softly into Hardi's concerned face.

Hardi relaxed as he brushed back a strand of hair attached to Blair's eyelashes. "I dinna decide aught without ye now, Blair. What do ye think we should do?"

Blair kept her hands on Hardi's shoulders and sat back, adjusting her position as she considered his question. "I would pretend that ye dinna ken any of this. Go aboot yer business as ye have been. We'll send the missive to Da and see if he responds. I have to tell him that we handfasted."

"I want to do that part. In ma own words and ma own hand, even if it isnae perfect," Hardi interrupted.

"Bring me the ledgers when ye can. And if ye canna bring me the money to count, find somewhere else to hide it. Dinna tell anyone. Try to avoid discussing finances with the council if ye can."

"I'll be back this eve once it's dark. Can we begin ma lessons after ye review the ledgers? I'm impatient to learn. Even more than I was before."

"Will ye come through the main doors of the keep? Willna that make people suspicious aboot why ye keep coming here? If ye want to bed me that often, people will want to ken why ye dinna take me to Tor. They willna think it's because ye are trying to keep me safe. They'll say ye have a reason for hiding me."

"I'll come over the southern wall and up the tree outside yer chamber."

"Ye'll never fit! Yer shoulders will get stuck," Blair giggled.

"Then I will find a way to get to yer chamber. Dinna suggest meeting me somewhere. I dinna want ye traipsing around the keep at night. And dinna say

ye'll bring yer guards. That wouldnae be inconspic-
uous at all."

"Do ye have a plain hunting plaid? The red will
stick out if anyone spies it in torchlight."

"I have one of ma father's. It's old and faded.
The colors are muted, so they will look almost like
the blues in the MacDonald pattern. If I canna make
it to yer chamber, I will find Donald or Tomas to get
ye. I will have them stand separate watches tonight. I
willna say I suspect aught specific, just that I dinna
want their routines to be too predictable."

"Then ye should go now. Ye need to make yer
day look as normal as possible." Blair dropped a swift
kiss on his lips. "Ye ken I would spend every minute
of the day with ye, but ye canna come here during
the day anymore. Yer clan will ask questions, and
ye'll draw too much attention, and people will want
ye to explain why ye ride out if nae on patrol."

"And willna people talk here if I suddenly appear
to have abandoned ye? Part of whoever's plan this is,
is counting on me being distracted with ye."

"Then we find a happy middle. Ye visit every
night that ye can, but only visit during the day a few
times a sennight. Change up the days just like ye
want ma guards to switch up theirs."

"Can ye be laird, and I'll just be on yer arm and
look bonnie?" Hardi teased. "If I didna want ye so
much as ma wife, I would say ye should have been
born a mon. But that makes it sound as though being
a woman isnae of the same value. So bluidy
irritating."

"*Mo chridhe*, ye are a mon ahead of yer times."
Blair gave him a smacking kiss before shifting to
climb off Hardi's lap. "Now go. I love ye."

"I love ye, *mo ghaol*." Hardi tipped Blair's chin up,
and this kiss was languid and unrushed.

268

THIRTY-FIVE

Hardi and Blair developed a routine over the next fortnight. Hardi brought the ledgers to Blair the night he returned after they formulated their loose plan. She tried to hide her dismay at how barely anything had been recorded for more than a year. Hardi explained that his housekeeper Mordag could only make tick marks under columns, but the older woman wasn't sure whether she placed them in the correct columns since she couldn't understand the words written on each page. Blair bit back her tongue that at least she could have kept the tallies in columns and rows rather than randomly scribbled. She used pieces of her own parchment to replicate the information, but with accurate counts in an orderly script. She warned Hardi that she couldn't know for sure whether each tally represented only one item or that the tallies were on the correct pages.

Blair did nothing to soften the blow that there was far too little food being stored for winter. Hardi tugged at his hair as he explained that he'd raised the same concerns, but the council assured him that they spent as much as they dared and that the crops would yield enough in the fall to overcome what looked like a shortfall. Blair coaxed him out of self-recrimination when she reminded him that he'd been laird for barely two months and that he couldn't blame himself for the lies and deceit.

That same night, Hardi struggled but wrote a missive to Hamish and Amelia explaining he and Blair handfasted, apologizing for not waiting to hear their response. He explained as much as he dared in a missive about why Blair remained at Inverlochy and what concerned him at Tor Castle. He made his request for advice clear. Blair offered no suggestions, only answering his questions about spelling and the use of certain words. When Hardi finished, Blair's beaming face expressed her pride, and she dragged him to the bed where she made certain he understood how proud she was.

It took Hardi three days before he could bring Blair the clan's money. The council discussed the clan's finances just as Hardi prepared to take them to Blair. He was impatient to hide the funds from the very men who promised him that the clan was in good standing. From what he'd been able to count, the clan was in a suitable position financially, and they could pay the outstanding taxes. But he was uncertain whether they would remain comfortable afterward. He pointed out his concerns, but the council assured him that the clan had survived worse. Hardi shared with Blair that he didn't want the Camerons to just survive. He didn't want to worry about having enough resources.

Blair had opened the sacks Hardi brought, quickly adding the coinage before her. But she insisted Hardi count it himself and that he recorded the amounts of each denomination along with the total amounts. She considered it part of his ongoing lessons. She thought back to what her mother said a clan should keep in reserve and how much a chatelaine could expect to spend in preparation and during winter. Blair also pushed aside the amount allotted for the taxes. Once the couple saw what remained, neither spoke for several minutes. There was far too little left for reserve.

When they finished counting, they discussed where he would hide the money. "I want ye to ken in case aught happens to me. I dinna trust anyone else, and I dinna want to write it down in case someone discovers it."

"Where will ye put it?" Blair asked as they sat crossed legged, facing one another on the bed.

"I have a locked chest that was ma parents' that I will use. Nay one else will have a key. Uncle Farlane said there was a hollowed brick in the laird's chamber where he stored missives. I found it, but there wasna aught there. Either he gave me all that he stored there, or someone else found it. It gave me the idea to hollow out a brick in the lady's chamber. I dinna think anyone will figure that out. The chamber has been empty for a year, and when ye come to Tor, ye can make it into a second lady's solar, but ye willna occupy it."

"Willna I?" Blair smirked.

"Nay, ye willna." Hardi snagged Blair and rolled her onto her back. He spent the rest of the night showing her what they couldn't do if they had separate chambers.

After an initial rush to examine the Camerons' financial situation, they settled into sitting before Blair's fire and discussing the day's events at Inverlochy and Tor. Blair admitted that since they'd handfasted, her relationship with Robena grew strained. Blair didn't understand why her handfast concerned Robena, or why anything that transpired between a couple in private could shock the former lady-in-waiting. Hardi suggested that Robena was envious that Blair married a man she wanted, a man close to her age. Blair supposed Hardi was right, but she regretted the distance that grew between her and her only friend.

Hardi's lessons in Scots progressed far faster than Latin. Already fluent in speaking Scots, reading and writing came more naturally to him. Blair regretted not beginning Hardi's tutelage with Scots instead of Latin, not only for the practical standpoint but for the self-confidence it built.

Hardi had disagreed. "I need more time to learn Latin, so starting it first made more sense. And Scots feels much easier than Latin, but only because ye already taught me well. I ken how to put the sounds together to read and write them." He'd ended any regret Blair had by showing her how appreciative he was. Once Hardi's lessons were through each night, they seized what little time they had left to make love. As the days grew long during the northern summer, it made the hours between sunset and sunrise few. Hardi didn't correct his clan when they assumed he spent his nights away touring outlying areas of their land. He would return shortly after sunrise, fall into bed for two hours, and then repeat his day. He visited Blair during the day three times during the first week and only twice during the second. Both savored the nights when they didn't have to wait until dark for them to be together.

―――――――――――

"Shouldnae Bran be back by now?" Blair asked Hardi as they lay together in bed. "It's been a fortnight, and it should have taken him eleven or twelve days round trip. I dinna think he would dillydally there. The weather has been fair most days."

"I've been thinking aboot that for the last couple

of days," Hardi admitted, his thumbnail gliding up and down Blair's arm as she laid on her side against his chest. "I'm concerned something has happened. He kenned the importance of the missive and yer da's response. But I dinna ken if he became ill, his horse went lame, someone attacked him. There is plenty that could have gone wrong, and I regret nae sending someone with him. Even if it angered yer da, mayhap I should have sent one of yer guards with him."

"Did ye remind him that if aught went wrong that he should get to the Munros if he can?"

"Aye. I explained to him that ye and Lady Munro were friends at court and that he should explain his mission. I even told him to share the missive with Cairren and Padraig if there was nay other way."

"Did ye tell him that the Earl of Ross is ma uncle? Did ye tell him he could stop at Balnagown if need be?"

"Ye ken that I did, *mo chridhe*. Dinna fash until there is a reason to. We'll give it a couple more days, and if he doesnae appear, I'll send Paul out to look for him."

"How will ye explain to Paul why Bran was headed to Dunrobin?" Blair wondered.

"He discovered I was sneaking away each night and assumed I had a leman. I denied it, but nay matter how many times I argued his theory, he refused to believe me. I didna want him keeping that assumption and then have ye arrive. I dinna want any rumors going aboot that I'm keeping a woman who isnae ma wife."

"Does anyone else ken?" Blair rolled onto her belly to look at Hardi.

"I havenae told anyone, but I imagine it'll get around. I dinna think Paul will gossip, but if he noticed ma absences, then others have too. Even if they dinna ken of ye, they will think what he did. Nae only do I nae want people spreading made up stories that'll humiliate ye when ye arrive, I dinna want any woman claiming that the rumors are aboot her. I dinna need a woman claiming I favor her, or that I love her, or God forbid, she carries ma bairn."

Blair's eyes widened, never having thought of the outcomes Hardi mentioned. Her sense of unease grew with every breath. She sat up; the sheet pulled around her chest and tucked under her chin. Hardi followed her, the sheet pooling at his waist. Even in her distress, she noticed how the muscles rippled along his belly. He eased her against his shoulder, and she wrapped her arm around him.

"Hearing those possible rumors sours ma stomach. It hurts to think anyone would make up such lies, but I heard far worse at court. Tristan Mackay's former mistress was horrible to Mairghread, and Callum didna learn aught from it. His own mistress tried to run off his bride after he severed ties. We're lucky naught happened to Siùsan." Blair turned her face toward his chest. "And it makes me feel so possessive and competitive and jealous. I dinna want to feel this way. It's ugly. But I canna help feeling like I would tear apart any woman who tried to lay claim to ye. I have never felt compelled to violence before, but those possibilities drive me there."

Blair felt the deep rumble of laughter in Hardi's chest and looked up. She didn't appreciate the humor on his face. He dropped a quick, hard kiss before grinning at her. "Nae only would ye make an excellent laird with yer intelligence and wisdom, ye'd make a fierce warrior. I can see ye standing in the village beating the hilt of yer sword against yer targe, challenging any woman who dared to come out and take ye on."

Blair swallowed as she retreated, and Hardi's

laughter ended. She pulled her lips in until she was confident she could speak without crying. "Ye're making fun of me. Ye think I'm foolish. I kenned I shouldnae said aught."

Hardi pulled the sheet loose and lifted Blair so that her legs draped over his, and she faced him. He took her hands and rubbed his thumbs over the backs of them. "I didna mean to hurt yer feelings, Blair. I jested, but I didna mean to make fun of ye. Ye tell me all the time how proud of me ye are. Mayhap I dinna tell ye often enough that I feel that way aboot ye too. I admire yer tenacity and yer courage. Ye havenae given up on me once when I've been ready to quit the schooling over and over. And I told ye before, ye dinna try to control me, and ye dinna ever manipulate me. Ye arenae that kind of possessive. That ye arenae willing to share me, and that ye'd fight for us, makes me feel good. It makes me ken ye love me and want our marriage as much as I do."

"But it's ugly. I sound like a harridan," Blair argued.

"Do ye think I would react any differently if I saw a mon flirt with ye, if a mon claimed to be yer lover, the father of our bairns? Blair, just because it hasnae happened and we havenae talked aboot it, dinna think I willna defend what is mine. I dinna ken if other wives feel as ye do, but I'm glad that ye do."

Blair nodded, then a slight smile broke through. "I canna even lift a sword or a targe, much less beat one against the other. I'll stick to dirks."

"That's ma lass. I dinna understand why a mon being a raging bull when it comes to his woman makes him a wonderful husband and a braw mon, but when a woman wants to assert her right to have a faithful husband, she's seen as a shrew."

"Because the world is made for men," Blair explained.

"Ma world consists of ye." Hardi kissed her, his tongue sweeping inside her mouth as Blair inched closer. Breathless, they pulled apart. "I told ye, I will defend ye, and I willna tolerate any mon thinking ye are available. But I willna do it because ye are ma possession, because ye belong only to me. I will do it to keep ye safe and because I value yer honor."

"Bluidy hell," Blair grumbled. "I wish I could say the same. I mean, I suppose I feel that way, too. But I am a raging—what is the female equivalent of a bull anyway—and I feel like ye belong to me. I'd keep ye safe and protect yer honor, but I also just dinna want to share. How is it ye're the reasonable one in this relationship?"

"Someone has to be," Hardi laughed as he laid back and brought Blair with him. As she sank onto his cock, Hardi groaned. "I'm yers, take me." They both grinned as Hardi spoke the words most would expect a woman to say, but there was no doubt for the rest of the night that Hardi was a man. One who loved and admired his wife. He followed her lead as she took control of their lovemaking, and he gladly did as he was told.

THIRTY-SIX

"Lady Cameron," Artair spoke across Robena as they broke their fast. "You'll want to go for a ride with your guards or mayhap take up my offer of reading *Tristan and Isolde* or work on your embroidery today. Laird Cameron and I will meet with my laird. He's a very busy mon, so Laird Cameron doesn't have time to waste."

"Artair—" Hardi began, but Blair placed her hand on his forearm.

"The Lord of the Isles is coming to Inverlochy?" Blair asked innocently.

"He is my only laird," Artair quipped.

"I suppose he travels alone. There'd be no reason for his council to meet inland. Pity, though. My brother-by-marriage, Kieran, is one of what the Lord of the Isles calls his four greatest lairds, since he is the MacLeod of Lewis. It would have been nice to see Kieran. I've wondered why Laird MacDonald doesn't have another title besides Lord of the Isles. After all, he is the overlord for *your* clan here in Lochaber."

"Since your brother-by-marriage won't be here, you'll surely want to occupy yourself elsewhere."

"Surely," Blair demurred. She turned to Hardi,

and he saw the mirth in her eyes, but he didn't understand why. Glancing back at Artair to ensure his conversation with his senior guardsman distracted him, Blair leaned closer. "I've met John of Islay more than once. At least that's what he called himself before becoming Lord of the Isles. He attempted to court me until he realized that ma dowry wouldnae bring him any land that's of use to him. It's too far north from Lochaber and the Hebrides. He has his eye on Amie Mac Ruairi, but she's still too young. He wants to marry her because her brother is Raghnall Mac Ruaidhrí, and her family controls several of the Hebridean islands. Anyway, he'll recognize me when he sees me. I can stay out of sight if ye wish, or ye can let Artair see I'm connected yet again to someone whose power and position impress him."

"He courted ye?" Hardi had a moment where the possessiveness Blair admitted to threatened to take hold.

"Attempted to. He didna care aboot me. He just thought I would come with a dowry that would be of use to him. It doesnae, so he didna pursue it."

"And did ye wish he had?" Hardi attempted to sound nonchalant.

"Good heavens, nay. He's a pompous arse who would marry his land and his title if he could. He's dangerously ambitious, Hardi. If he isnae yer friend, he's yer enemy. Ye and Clan Donald are allies, and ye have MacDonalds living in yer keep, but dinna forget that he thinks of himself first. He doesnae see any ties back to Clan Donald and doesnae care aboot history before the MacDonalds became their own clan. He only sees where he wants to go. Dinna count on him as an ally just because he shares ancestors with the Donalds. And dinna think ye can rely on him because ye're letting a branch of his clan serve as guardians to yer keep."

"I thought the MacMillans were annoying with their branches and what they want to be called. But the Donalds, MacDonalds, and MacDonnells are a pain in the arse. They all came from the Donalds who kens how far back."

"True. Cameron and Sutherland are much easier. We are who we are, and who we've always been. Have ye met him?"

"Nay. I've seen him but only because I was ma uncle's guard during various meetings. I dinna actually ken him," Hardi admitted.

"Give it five minutes. Ye'll wish ye still didna."

Bells tolling ended their conversation and marked the arrival of John of Islay, Lord of the Isles. Hardi and Blair led the way from the dais to the bailey as the senior-ranking couple, with Artair and Robena following a few steps behind them. Blair recognized John of Islay immediately and remembered how arrogant the man was.

"Lady Blair Sutherland, what a surprise," John gushed as he stepped forward to take Blair's hand, bowing over it. "I—"

"I'm Lady Cameron," Blair's voice wasn't loud when she interrupted, but it held the authority of a laird's wife, and Hardi wanted to grin.

"I beg your pardon," John blinked. "You're who?"

"I am Lady Cameron, and I would like to introduce you to my husband, Laird Hardwin Cameron."

John MacDonald assessed Hardi as though he attempted to determine on sight whether Hardi was friend or foe. He thrust out his arm to Hardi, who grasped his forearm in a firm shake. John grinned as they released each other's arms. "I take it you're glad that I didn't have use for your dowry, Lady Cameron."

279

"Very glad. Laird Cameron and I are well suited," Blair explained.

"Well suited," John snorted. "At court, everyone raves aboot how besotted you are with one another. They say you ran off with him despite the king repeatedly saying it was he who sent you with Laird Cameron."

"You were recently at court, my laird?" Blair asked. She knew Hardi wanted to learn if John knew anything about his cousins, who were late returning from Stirling.

"Aye. It seems Laird Cameron's cousins found themselves a spot of trouble." John looked at Hardi, then Blair. "You haven't heard. It seems they claimed highwaymen robbed them along the way. They arrived short a few barrels of whisky and several bags of grain. King Robert's voice could be heard from outside the Privy Council chamber. No one could make out everything he said, but fortunately, I was in the chamber."

Hardi's heart sank. He could only imagine the lies Faolán and Drostan spewed to save themselves. He suspected that if he rode south and crossed Loch Leven and then entered Glencoe, he would find the missing goods. Hardi suspected the brothers either stored them to sell later, or they'd already conducted the transaction and pocketed the coin. Hardi turned his attention back to John as he continued the story.

"King Robert already has a ruddy complexion, but he was scarlet by the time he finished with them. He threatened to castrate them for failing to give you the correct information about the taxes. Then he threatened to chain them in a cell because he likes you and can't stand them. Then he suggested having them drawn and quartered for stealing from the crown. Perhaps he will do all three. He left the chamber swearing that Lady

Cameron marrying you and living at Tor was the only thing keeping him from seizing all your lands. I think they shit their plaids." John clapped Hardi on the back as he stepped between Hardi and Blair, taking Blair's arm. She hung back, and John looked down at her.

"I don't want to be in the way when you greet Chieftain and Lady MacDonald. I'll stand with Laird Cameron," Blair's tone sounded hospitable, but her frigid gaze made John shake his head as he let go of Blair's arm. He looked over his shoulder at Hardi.

"You are well suited. I think she loves you nearly as much as you love her," John chuckled.

"Just as much," Blair snapped, and John laughed harder as he turned his attention to Artair and Robena. His face fell, and it was clear he was less enthusiastic to greet Artair than to greet the Camerons. He was polite to the MacDonalds, but the warmth he'd shown Hardi and Blair was lacking. The two couples and the Lord of the Isles entered the Great Hall, and Robena signaled servants to bring out a repast for their guest.

"I haven't much time to spend here, so let us conduct our business. Cameron, I wasn't aware you would be here, but please join us. Lady Cameron, too."

"But she—" Artair spluttered.

"She's brighter than the three of us put together," John quipped as he walked toward the solar. "I suspect Laird Cameron appreciates that."

"I do," Hardi spoke up as he took Blair's hand in his. John had called them a love match, even if not in so many words. Hardi saw little point in hiding that they were.

"But women—" Artair tried again.

"Cease your blathering, MacDonald. I'd like to hear her opinion. If her dowry hadn't included land practically on Orkney, I would have married her for her mind."

"How generous," Blair smirked. John turned to Blair, then glanced at Hardi.

"It seems I imagined your eagerness to accept my courtship." John took the seat at the head of the table. Hardi sat to John's right, and Blair sat to his right. Artair grimaced as he took a seat to John's left but two down from where the lord sat. Blair didn't doubt that had John not sworn his fealty to Robert the Bruce, he would have called himself the King of the Isles. "Laird Cameron, I would have you address me as John. May I call you Hardwin?"

"Aye. Thank ye," Hardi nodded.

"I don't dare call you aught but Lady Cameron, Lady Cameron." Blair cocked an eyebrow at John's jest. She sat quietly, but wished the men would move forward and abandon the pleasantries for business. With no tittering and blushing forthcoming from Blair, John turned his attention to Artair.

"You are fortunate Laird Cameron honors his uncle's arrangement with you. Are you up to date on the rents?" John demanded. His shift in tone surprised Artair, but neither Hardi nor Blair blinked.

"I am, my laird," Artair assured.

"And the improvements to the keep? You are to serve as guardian of this keep. You don't look to have guarded it from falling down around our ears. I gave you funds to repair the keep and the wall. It appears you have accomplished naught. Did you assume Laird Cameron wouldn't be aware?" John persisted.

Hardi still held Blair's hand. He squeezed it, but didn't look in her direction before releasing it. He leaned forward, resting his forearms on the table. "I wasna aware of such an agreement. I offered to fortify the wall if Artair made repairs to the keep. I did so in good faith to show yer branch is still welcome here."

"You did it so he would be beholden to you and reminded of whose keep this really is," John corrected. "I don't blame you. However, if you fortify the wall, it means Artair pockets coin I set aside for him. That displeases me. Artair will use the funds given him to repair your keep and your wall. He will remain beholden to you because he continues to have a keep to call his own. A keep you might find yourself in need of at any time."

Artair shifted nervously in his seat, uncomfortable that the attention was on him, but not in the manner he wanted. He looked back and forth between John and Hardi before glaring at Blair, as if she'd caused the situation. Hardi continued to look at John but directed his comment to Artair.

"Continue glaring at Lady Cameron and making yer usual patronizing comments, Artair, and ye will find yerself living in a croft somewhere near Sleat. Ma uncle found ye easily enough. I'm certain I can find another MacDonald eager to take yer place as chieftain."

"Are you being an arse to Lady Cameron?" John's tone lowered as he looked at Artair.

"He doesn't mean to be, my lord," Blair interjected. "I don't think he realizes it. I'm certain he gives his advice with the best intentions." Blair tilted her head and looked sideways at Artair. He didn't know where to look, but his resignation told Blair he understood that now the person he was most indebted to was her.

The conversation carried on as Hardi and John discussed the rents and taxes owed to Hardi from what the MacDonalds grew on Cameron land. Hardi wondered why no one mentioned that the MacDonalds owed him banalities for the grain. He glanced at

Blair and realized she hadn't thought of them either. Since the MacDonalds were overdue, Hardi agreed to accept the fee without penalty but negotiated updated terms. When Artair mentioned his livestock, Blair leaned over to whisper to Hardi.

"Negotiate a pannage. It's a fee for his grazing rights outside the village," Blair murmured. Hardi's calm demeanor as he haggled with John impressed her. She offered her most serene smile when John glared at her after Hardi broached the subject of the pannage. Neither Blair nor Hardi had deduced who sent the anonymous missive, so Hardi seized the opportunity to gauge Artair's possible culpability.

"I might be willing to lesson these fees if ye promise me three score of yer warriors, Artair," Hardi suggested.

"Three score? Are ye bluidy drunk?" Artair snapped, his burr creeping into his words. "I will have barely any warriors to defend maself."

"Are ye expecting an attack?" Hardi responded.

"Nay," Artair spluttered. He tried to rebound by arguing, "We ken the Macphersons are breathing down yer neck aboot the sheep incident. And ye want the wall fortified. It must concern ye that they will attack here, too."

"Nae particularly. I thought to make it easier on yer coffers, but if ye believe ye need yer warriors more than ye need to afford the wool ye buy from us, then keep them." Hardi raised his hand in a dismissive motion. He suspected Artair didn't want to lend his warriors because it would diminish his numbers to attack Tor.

"The men can leave with ye when ye ride out," Artair conceded. He suddenly looked every year of his age, deflated and defeated. Blair couldn't decide if he looked so resigned because he disliked losing the negotiations or if Hardi's request altered plans for an attack on Tor. "But the repairs will take longer without the men here to work."

"Mayhap I'll loan them back to ye," Hardi grinned.

"Now that you've resolved that," John turned the conversation back to him. "Artair, you may leave. I have matters to discuss with a laird." Artair huffed but lumbered out of his chair before leaving his solar. Hardi and Blair remained silent, giving John the opportunity to play the first card.

THIRTY-SEVEN

"**T**he eejit is my mother's second cousin's son. If it had been anyone but my mother asking for him to be made chieftain, I would have laughed in their face. He's useless. All bluster, nay bollocks," John chortled as he shook his head. "Now that he's left, I'd like to discuss a topic I'd hoped to bring up sooner. But you were at court when last I was here, and then I was at court after you left. Anyway, I intended to offer a betrothal between you and my sister." John swept his gaze over Blair before shooting Hardi a knowing grin. "But that is no longer an option. I would propose a betrothal between any second son I have and first daughter Lady Cameron bears you."

John's proposition surprised Hardi so much he couldn't think of anything to say, so he was grateful when Blair sat forward. She laughed in John's face. As John's grin withered, Hardi feared the man would lash out at Blair. She rested her forearms on the table and leaned forward much like Hardi had done earlier when he spoke to Artair.

"You want to secure more land in Lochaber, and you've run out of ways to do it. You'd have us agree to wed two unborn, not even conceived, children to gain a dowry you don't even know what it'll consist of. You are either the most patient mon I ken, or the most desperate. I lean toward the latter. You aren't even married. And you think more highly of yourself than I do. Any daughter I have can do better than a second son," Blair turned her nose up.

"You married a man seventh in line to inherit. He wasn't even the first nephew of the previous laird. He was a second son in the second line," John blustered.

Blair laughed again. "We would have never suited. You most certainly don't understand me. Any daughter of ours can do better than a second son because she will choose for herself rather than being told she's only worth a spare."

"Choose? Bah," John snorted, then realized his error when Blair's family tree flashed through his mind.

"I see you're regretting mocking me. You know the Sutherlands and Sinclairs marry for love, and even the Rosses do it from time to time. There isn't anyone in the Highlands who doesn't know my mother and father chose one another. My father and grandfather were ready to kill one another over their clans' feud until Mama insisted she would marry Da. So, Lord of the Isles, are you mocking me, the Earl of Sutherland, the Earl of Sinclair, or the Earl of Ross? Or is it all of us?" Blair's eyebrow rose, and she turned her most imperious glare on John. Hardi shifted, his arousal proving uncomfortable as his sporran pressed against it. The only consolation to the pain was that it hid his rampant cockstand.

"Bluidy hell, mon," John turned to Hardi. "Call off your she-wolf."

Hardi sat back and shook his head. "If ye canna swim, dinna jump into the sea."

"Can you not control your wife?" John glowered.

Hardi eased forward so slowly that it built the sense of intimidation, and it amazed Blair to see one of the most arrogant men she knew look like he was ready to pish himself. "Ma wife is more intelligent and quick-witted than any mon I ken. Just because she makes yer bollocks shrivel doesnae mean she needs controlling. She's ma wife, nae some animal. Perhaps if men werenae so intimidated by her, they wouldnae hide behind me. I ken I'm a large mon, but I canna shield everyone daft enough to have a go at ma wife."

"You won't have many friends if your wife doesn't curb her tongue," John snarled.

"Ye mean ye willna be ma friend. If that's the case, then ye dinna need to leave yer clan at *ma* keep. Ye can find another clan to let ye into Lochaber. But considering ye dinna care for yer distant cousins, the MacDonnells of Glengarry and the MacDonnells of Keppoch, they arenae an option. Mayhap the Macleans will give ye a slice of their land. But that willna do ye much good since the Camerons are still the largest clan in the region." Hardi steepled his fingers. "Besides, I rather like ma wife's friends better. The Sinclairs, the Mackays, the Rosses, the MacLeods of Lewis and Assynt, the Grants, the Gordons, the Munros, and dinna forget her own family, the Sutherlands. And I believe she has vera influential godparents. Ye visited their home just a sennight ago."

John huffed as he tried to conjure some rejoinder, but nothing came to him, so he settled for glaring. Blair remained silent, but John opted to goad her when he couldn't think of anything to say to Hardi.

"Suddenly quiet, Blair? Mayhap your husband has better control of you than I thought."

"I am Lady Cameron. I never gave you permission to address me by my given name. I saw no reason to say aught more. You dug yourself into a deep enough grave, and Laird Cameron didn't appear to need help to fling the dirt over you. But since you don't know when to cease, let me be abundantly clear. You may rule the Hebrides—except for the mighty MacLeods of Lewis—my family-by-marriage —and the MacLeods of Skye. But my family is connected to every powerful clan in the Highlands by blood, by marriage, or by alliance. You hold sway in Lochaber because they allow it. Who do you think any Highland laird will choose? One of their own or a mon from a tiny island?"

John MacDonald, Lord of the Isles, looked at the newlyweds and shook his head. "Heaven help anyone who truly is foolish enough to cross you two. Their heads will be on pikes with their entrails decorating your gates."

They quit the solar and moved to the Great Hall, where the midday meal was about to begin. John left immediately following the meal. Hardi led Blair up to the battlements to watch the MacDonald entourage ride away. The vantage point allowed them to see for miles in every direction. If John turned toward Tor or toward the Camerons' enemies, he rode far out of his way to do so.

"Blair, it's time for ye to come home," Hardi said as they stood, arm in arm.

THIRTY-EIGHT

After Blair and Hardi quit the battlements, they returned to Blair's chamber. She lifted her few kirtles from the pegs on the wall and folded them along with her chemises before placing them in her small chest. She finished packing in less than ten minutes. When she finished, the couple sat on the foot of the bed.

"Are ye sure this is the right time, Hardi?" Blair asked.

"John of Islay will blather aboot us being wed to anyone who'll listen. Now that it isnae a secret, I dinna want word getting back to ma clan that I'm hiding ye. We already talked aboot why that willna do us any good. I trust Artair less than I did before. I dinna think he's the mastermind behind this plot, but I'm unconvinced he isnae a part of it. He didna want to give me his warriors, which makes me wonder what his role is. He's right that it'll take longer without so many men as laborers, but the wall didna bother him before today. Besides, he kens lending me warriors is part of the terms of his guardianship. That's one thing ma uncle did explain."

"How will ye account for where I've been and why I didna arrive with ye from court?"

"With the truth. Ye went to Inverlochy because it wasna appropriate for ye to stay at Tor before we wed. We chose to handfast instead."

"And ye think nay one will question that?" Blair countered.

"Let them," Hardi shrugged. "A handfast is as good as a marriage in the Highlands. They dinna have a choice."

"And if yer council wants ye to repudiate me in favor of the Macquarie or Donald lasses?"

"Then they will find themselves within an inch of their lives if they push too hard. Ye're ma wife, Blair. I am their laird. If they canna accept that, then they can vote me out. Otherwise, they will do as I command. And the first command is to acknowledge ye as ma wife. Permanently." Hardi's tone brooked no disagreement, and Blair wasn't looking to start one. She slid her hand into Hardi's and leaned her head against his shoulder.

"Is there aught else I should ken before I arrive?" Blair wondered.

"Do ye mean, do I have a leman waiting for me to return to her side? Are there women in the village that think I'll be bedding them again? Nay, there arenae."

Blair sat up and looked at Hardi. "I wasna thinking of that until now. I meant are there problems with the servants? Will yer cook and housekeeper welcome me or challenge me? Do I need to worry that yer clan will be angry at me because we wed? That's what I was thinking aboot. But now I'd like more of an answer to what ye said."

"I didna want ye to worry that there would be any uncomfortable scenes. After what ye told me aboot Mairghread, Siùsan, and Cairren's experiences, I wanted to reassure ye. I was a veritable monk for months before I went to court. The last

292

thing I was thinking aboot was bedding women. First, it was losing ma family and recovering from the last battle. Then it was trying to learn how to be laird. I havenae been with anyone in close to a year, Blair. Mayhap I should have told ye that before."

Blair shook her head. "Ye dinna owe me an explanation of what ye did before ye started courting me. Neither of us kenned we would meet again. And either way, ye're a mon who had a life to live before me."

"Thank ye for understanding." Hardi took hold of both of Blair's hands, kissing her knuckles. He gazed into the whisky-brown eyes he looked forward to staring into for a lifetime. "I should have also told ye that ye pulled me out of the bleakest time in ma life. Ma grief was eating me alive, but ye gave me purpose both as a student and as a suitor. The pain of losing ma family may never go away completely, but ye make each day worth waking up to."

Blair wrapped her hand around his neck and kissed the side closer to her. She kissed along his jaw until he dipped his head to bring their mouths together. Hardi wrapped his arms around Blair as their kiss continued, languid and tender. When they sat back, Blair saw the moisture in Hardi's eyes, but the hollowness that had been there weeks ago no longer haunted him. She saw hope instead. "I love ye, Hardwin."

"Och, Blair, I love ye." They kissed again before Hardi carried her chest belowstairs. They said their farewells, and Blair noticed Robena had returned to her warmer nature. Blair wasn't sure if it was because the woman regretted Blair was leaving or if she was eager to have her gone. Artair said little more than goodbye to Blair, keeping any pearls of wisdom to himself. Blair and Hardi waited in the bailey as their guards gathered their belongings with little notice, then they rode out together.

Blair swept her eyes over the bailey of her new home. She wondered if they rang the bells every time Hardi returned, even after a brief time away, or if it was because she accompanied him. Watching the Camerons gather near their horses distracted Blair, so she was unprepared for Hardi to reach up for her. She braced her hands on his shoulders as he slid her down the length of his body.

"It will be an early night, lass," Hardi whispered before kissing her jaw just beneath her ear. He took her hand in his, surprising her as they walked toward the keep's steps. When they stood at the top, he turned toward the gathered clan members. "I present to ye ma wife, Lady Blair Cameron. Before we married, she was Lady Blair Sutherland. Many of ye will remember that Dougal and I spent six years fostering under Laird Sutherland, ma father-by-marriage. I've kenned ma wife since we were little more than weans. It was with great fortune that we met again while I was at court. As a new laird with matters still unsettled with our neighbors, I admit I was hesitant to bring Lady Cameron to Tor, so she has been staying at Inverlochy. Now that I am confident of her safety here, I am glad to have ma wife finally beside me. If ye've wondered where I've been slipping off to, now ye ken."

Hardi and Blair looked out at the crowd of stunned faces, who gawked at them as if they'd sprouted extra heads and wings. But the initial shock wore off, and the clan cheered to their happiness and to her arrival. Blair realized the Camerons were eager to have a lady of the clan, so she didn't doubt her welcome would be warm. Hardi released her hand and wrapped his arm around her waist, drawing her body against his side. The position was endearing, but it was also unequivocally clear that Hardi cared for the woman he married.

"So there is nay misunderstanding, I speak this before ye all. Lady Cameron is ma equal and ma partner in everything. Ye will afford her the respect nae only due her position but as the woman I love. Her word is final. Dinna come to me if ye dinna like it. If I am away, Lady Cameron leads in ma stead. I look to ma wife for council and guidance, and she will be a part of any decisions that affect this clan. Ye will soon realize that I amnae the only lucky one. She is the lady of the clan that we need, that we deserve, and that we want." Hardi smiled down at Blair and pressed a soft, brief kiss to her lips. The affection and tenderness were clear to all who watched. Before leading her inside, he whispered. "I only had the strength to say all of that because ye are with me. That's more than I've said at one time since I became laird. I love ye and welcome ye home, Blair."

"I love ye, Hardi. I am proud to be by yer side. Now show me ma new home, please." Blair grinned.

They entered the keep, finding an older woman with deep wrinkles lining her face. She was thin as a rail but carried an air of authority. She wore a smile, but Blair understood she was being assessed. Blair stepped away from Hardi and went to stand before the woman. She dipped a shallow curtsy in respect for the older woman.

"Are ye Mordag?" Blair asked. The woman blinked several times, surprised to hear Blair's brogue.

"Aye, ma lady. I am." Mordag answered, wary of the young woman before her.

"Laird Cameron has praised ye many times for

taking on the duties of chatelaine. I've been here but a moment, but I can already see ye do a fine job. None of the candles have dried wax, the fireplaces are clean, the rushes are fresh, the tables shine. Will ye help me settle in as chatelaine, please?" Blair spoke the truth, but she also understood the woman had probably been the housekeeper at Tor Castle since before Hardi's parents were born. She might not want to have the duties of a chatelaine, but undoubtedly Morag had a way of running the keep. Blair wasn't interested in changing what worked.

"I would be honored, ma lady," Mordag smiled. "Ye have the look of yer mother. She visited here many years ago."

"I did, too, Mordag. It was when Dougal and Hardi began their fostering. Ma parents, brother, sister, and I came to meet them." Blair leaned forward and whispered. "Mama was afraid Dougal and Hardi would be frightened leaving home. She didna want them to make the journey with just guards. She wanted them to ken we welcomed them."

"Nay one has called Laird Cameron 'Hardi' since he was a lad. It warms ma heart that ye do, ma lady." Mordag chuckled when Blair looked aghast. She hadn't realized she'd spoken of the laird so informally. "Ye love him. He needs that after all he's endured. I welcome ye for that alone, ma lady."

"Thank ye," Blair said as she straightened. "That means a great deal to me. And I do love Laird Cameron vera much."

"We will serve the evening meal in an hour, would ye care for a bath, ma lady?" Mordag offered.

Blair nearly clapped at the suggestion She'd bathed regularly at Inverlochy, but once she handfasted with Hardi—and everyone knew they'd consummated their marriage--the servants treated her as an inconvenience. More than once the water arrived tepid. Blair sensed Mordag wouldn't stand for such.

"I will show ye our chamber, *mo chridhe*," Hardi murmured as he stepped behind her and wrapped his arms around Blair's waist. "Dismiss yer maid. One of the servants can show her to her own quarters. If they didna expect us to appear for the evening meal, I'd request that Mordag send up a tray."

"Mayhap tomorrow eve," Blair whispered. She turned in Hardi's arms. "I willna hide how I feel for ye, but neither will I flaunt it. I need yer people to take me seriously and respect me because I ken what I'm doing, nay because their laird likes to play with his bride."

"But the laird does like to play with his bride," Hardi rumbled against her ear. "I can think of many places I'd like to play."

"That wasna what I meant!" Blair gasped.

"I kenned what ye meant. And if we dinna get to our chamber soon, the entire clan will ken what I meant."

"Hardi," Blair hissed.

"Blair," Hardi mimicked.

"I'm serious. I need them to ken that I am more than just a pretty bauble ye brought back from court because ye desire me."

"Blair, it will take this clan all of five minutes this eve to realize that. Ye are the bonniest woman I ken, but ye have a look aboot ye that tells how intelligent and serious ye are. Nay one will be fool enough to underestimate ye."

Blair didn't argue, but she was unconvinced. She'd seen the group of older men gathered to the side of the keep's steps, and she noticed them as they gathered by the fireplace in the Great Hall. It didn't take a leap to know they were on the clan's council, and none looked as though they took her seriously. Their looks weren't inappropriate. But they looked at her more like a child they would humor.

She set aside her worry when Hardi showed her their chamber. There was an enormous tub set before the fire. She glanced at Hardi and knew it must have been one of the few things he requested when he became laird. He was a tall man with broad shoulders and long legs. He wouldn't have fit in a normal tub. As she glanced back at the tub as servants poured steaming water into it, Hardi reassured her there was room enough for two if they sat close together. They were nearly late to the evening meal.

THIRTY-NINE

"Lady Cameron, our laird mentioned meeting ye at court. What caused that coincidence?" A man who introduced himself as Niall asked as the evening meal began.

"I served Her Majesty as a lady-in-waiting for three years, so Stirling Castle has been ma home these past years. Ma brother and I were returning from a ride when we discovered Laird Cameron in the bailey. We spent a couple of days together before ma brother had to return to Dunrobin," Blair answered. She wouldn't offer any more information than they asked. She felt uneasy around the clan council, but she was uncertain whether it was fear and animosity borne of her desire to protect Hardi or if it was genuine dislike.

"That must have been a grand adventure," Paul commented. Blair remembered Hardi mentioning him as one of the few men Hardi considered trusting. When she wasn't forthcoming, he posed it as a question. "Did ye think it was a grand adventure?"

"Rarely. It was exciting when ma sister, Lady MacLeod of Lewis, and I first arrived, but being at court means constant noise, constant changing one's wardrobe, and constant crowds of people. I missed the open land and fresh air of Sutherland. Being on Cameron territory suits me much better. And I dinna have to hide ma burr."

"Ye didna enjoy being a lady-in-waiting," Paul responded. To Blair's ears it sounded more like an accusation than an observation.

"It was more enjoyable when ma sister was still there, and it was vera enjoyable when Lachlan visited," Blair hedged.

"I'm certain once ye found Laird Cameron many things at court became more enjoyable," Niall chimed in.

"Niall—" Hardi warned. He hadn't missed the double entendre, and neither had Blair. She bumped his ankle with her foot under the table.

"It was most pleasant to reminisce aboot how Laird Cameron used to put toads in ma boots, and how I left a garter snake in his chest. It died before it did its job. We recalled how fond ma father is of Laird Cameron. He still speaks vera highly of the Cameron." Blair found it tedious having to use her husband's title every time she spoke of him, especially when he sat beside her. "It was vera enjoyable to have a childhood friend visiting at court."

"It doesnae appear as though ye are still childhood friends, ma lady," Osgar noted. He appeared very close in age to Hardi.

"How could we?" Blair asked innocently. "We're nae children anymore. Just as well or we couldnae have married." Blair locked eyes with Osgar, refusing to look away until he did. She swept her eyes around the table, challenging any who were tempted to embarrass her.

"Ye must have been vera busy going from one feast to another." Niall picked up the challenge and pressed on.

"Nae really. We follow the same liturgical calendar as ye do. We had as many feasts as any clan. The queen isnae one for extravagance and wasting time when one can better spend it in prayer. She's a vera devout woman and expects her ladies to possess a pristine reputation."

"I am certain the king looked upon ye favorably," Paul suggested before taking a bite of beef.

Blair was no fool. She understood the insinuation. At that moment, she decided she would reveal her well-guarded secret in hopes it might deter the schemers from their plot or draw out the treasonous members of the clan. "I'd say most favorably. He used to sneak me honeyed treats when I was a wean. That didna please ma mother the time ma brother, sister, and I ran around the keep when we were supposed to be napping. I remember nay long after Laird Cameron came to foster, the king and queen visited Dunrobin. The queen gave me a handkerchief she'd embroidered just before the English captured her and put her under house arrest. It's the finest gift ma godmother ever gave me. Permission to marry Laird Cameron is the most precious gift ma godfather gave me."

Blair wanted to laugh at the dumbfounded faces that stared at her. She heard Hardi clear his throat as he tried to keep from laughing. He took a swig from their shared chalice before turning to look at his council members.

"Lady Cameron has a tall family tree with many branches. Some of the most powerful men in Scotland sit upon them." He took another sip from the chalice before turning to Blair. "Would ye care for any more of the veal?"

Blair's lips twitched at Hardi's nonchalance. She shook her head and forced out the words, "Nay thank ye."

"I would think yer wedding would be quite a

fancy affair if there are so many important people in yer family," Paul mused. Blair wanted to slap him. For a man who supposedly supported Hardi, he was becoming obnoxious with his questioning.

Blair shrugged one shoulder. "I dinna need to see everyone's face to ken they're related to me or allied with ma clan. The king granted us his permission to marry and doing so meant I could accompany ma husband north."

"But ye went to Inverlochy first," Osgar pointed out.

"Aye," Hardi intervened. "I have been laird all of three moons. There are unsettled matters with our neighbors. I'd been away, and as we ken, decisions were made that I didna agree to. I believe it was ma duty as her husband to ensure it was safe to bring Lady Cameron to Tor Castle."

The doors of the keep swung wide, cutting off the conversation at the dais. Hardi gripped the arms of his chair to keep from hurling chalices and plates at the newly arrived men. Faolán and Drostan made their way to the dais, but both men stopped short when they noticed Blair seated beside Hardi. She smiled serenely at them but feigned disinterest, as though she wasn't aware they were members of Hardi's family and the clan council.

"Aboot bluidy time ye returned." Hardi's hazel eyes bore into the men as they remained in front of the laird's table. "Did ye resolve the matter of the missing grain and whisky?"

"What?" Niall spluttered. "What missing grain and whisky?"

"Since ye were welcoming ma wife and getting to ken one another, I didna have the chance to mention the informative visit I had with John of Islay this morn," Hardi explained. He sounded bored as he glanced at his council members before turning his attention back to his cousins. "The Lord of the Isles mentioned the king's displeasure at our payment being short several sacks and barrels. And yet, I counted each one before ye left the bailey. Apparently, ye had a spot of poor luck coming across highwaymen such as ye did. We're lucky ye escaped with only a few missing goods." Hardi lifted the chalice to his mouth but paused as if to add the afterthought, "And yer lives."

"It was a near miss," the man Blair guessed was Drostan agreed.

Hardi waved a servant forward and spoke softly to her before reaching out his hand to Blair. They stood and moved away from their chairs. Hardi didn't look back at the men at the table when he gave his order. "The council meets now. Faolán, Drostan, food will be brought to you."

Hardi led Blair to the solar he wished them to share. He'd quietly asked Mordag to have a chair placed to the right of his behind his desk. He was pleased to see she'd fulfilled his request. He guided Blair into the seat as they'd discussed during their bath. The couple registered the looks of shock and disgust when they noticed where Blair sat.

"I thought this was a council meeting nae a sewing circle," Faolán spat. "Can ye nae send yer mistress off until we're done?"

Blair listened to several deep throat clearings and noticed a few men's eyes widen. She even saw one or two heads shake as all the men shot Faolán a warning look.

"What? He's finally started tupping a wench after pretending his cock fell off. Now he wants her within reach. Women arenae allowed in council meetings. If they were, I'd have a whore on ma lap too." Faolán spoke, somehow missing all the warnings his fellow council members sent him.

303

Hardi withdrew his dirk and placed it horizontally on the desk before him. He placed his hands by the tip and the hilt as he narrowed his eyes. "I'm trying to decide if cutting out yer tongue is worth dirtying ma blade. Mayhap I'll have ye use yer own to do it."

"Ye canna be serious?" Faolán sneered. "Ye can dress her up in fancy clothes, but we all ken we dinna bring whores to the council meetings."

Before anyone knew what was happening, Hardi whipped his *sgian dubh* from his belt and launched the short, razor-sharp knife at Faolán, embedding it in his arm. "I dinna care for how ye're speaking aboot ma wife. Count that as yer last warning, Faolán. I have already removed ye and Drostan from the council, so yer word on how these meetings are run is worth less than yer horse's shite. Ye will apologize to Lady Cameron for the offensive things ye said, ye will greet her properly, and then ye will sit yer fucking arse down and speak only when spoken to." Hardi's voice remained even and calm throughout. It was that calmness that made the men seated around the table squirm. They could have laughed and discounted Hardi's demands if he'd lost his temper. But his cool resolve made the council realize the young laird they assumed they could control had grown more confident. Many shifted their gazes to Blair, who remained indifferent and unruffled, and they understood where Hardi's newfound confidence came from.

"I will do nay such thing. Lady Cameron, ma arse. The king would have told me if ye'd married against the council's wishes," Faolán persisted.

"Mayhap the king values ye as much as he does a carbuncle on a sow's tit. He had nay trouble mentioning it to the Lord of the Isles. Mayhap it slipped King Robert's mind because he was too busy chewing ye a new arse for lying to me, stealing from our tax payment, and trying to deceive him." Hardi grinned as Faolán continued to press his hand over his wound, red soaking the sleeve. "John of Islay is an auld acquaintance of ma wife. We had an interesting conversation this morn."

Hardi reached over and took Blair's hand, entwining his fingers with hers. He cocked an eyebrow at Faolán and waited. Faolán's defiance grew the longer Hardi waited. Hardi shook his head and looked to Blair. "Lady Cameron, what is yer recommendation?"

Blair's stomach knotted. She hadn't prepared to be the one casting the verdict. It wasn't part of what they discussed. She understood Hardi was proving what he'd said on the keep's steps. She was his equal and his partner. He would make no decisions without her. But she wasn't convinced her first night was the best time to pass judgment on a man who'd been on the council longer than she'd been alive.

"Faolán, will ye do as the laird instructed? Will ye apologize for yer inappropriate comments? Will ye greet me how I deserve as both Laird Cameron's wife and the daughter of the Earl of Sutherland?"

"A fancy title and a lavish gown doesnae make ye any less than a whore. Ye ran off with Hardwin before ye wed. He's been tossing yer skirts for more than a fortnight at Inverlochy. The whole bluidy keep kens how ye like to be fucked," Faolán seethed.

"It is Laird Cameron to ye," Blair corrected. "It's unfortunate that ye speak without listening. Ye dinna listen to chances given ye to stay alive, and ye dinna listen to yerself as ye prove ye're a liar."

Blair waited for what she said to register with Faolán. She remained silent, expecting Faolán to respond, to deny what she said. When he did nothing but scowl, Blair sighed.

"If ye ken so much, then ye didna come straight here from Stirling. But ye kenned before ye left court that I was with Laird Cameron. The Lord of the Isles shared with us how yer meeting went. We ken King Robert told ye our marriage keeps him from seizing Cameron lands. If ye kenned that I was at Inverlochy, then ye kenned we handfasted. If ye ken what we do behind closed doors, then ye ken we consummated our marriage. That makes me Lady Cameron. Ye dinna have to like it, ye dinna have to agree with it, ye dinna even have to accept it. But ye also dinna have to live." Blair paused as her words sank in. "Laird Cameron made it clear to the clan when we arrived today, that the expectation for the Camerons is the same as for any clan. The clan is to treat their lady with the same respect as her husband. Any slight to Lady Cameron is a slight to Laird Cameron. That means ye have called Laird Cameron a whore."

Blair casually looked down at her hand joined with Hardi's then at the members of the council before shifting her gaze back to Faolán. "Since ye are nay longer a member of the council, ye canna be ma laird-husband's second. That makes ye little more than a villager. Such behavior—and I'm including the thievery and lying to yer laird—entitles ye to the lash, banishment, or death."

Blair pursed her lips as though she was deep in thought. "Ye and Drostan are the last of Laird Cameron's family. Until I bear the laird a child, I will nae have the last of yer bloodline on ma conscious. Besides, once ye are dead, ye canna live with regret to eat at ye. I will nae suggest yer death. I dinna care for the lash because with time the wounds fade and often so does the memory of why a mon received the punishment. It's nae a permanent deterrent. While nay clan is to accept a banished mon, somehow most of the banished become another clan's burden. I willna cast ye off to be someone else's problem. Laird Cameron suggested cutting out yer tongue, but that still leaves ye with yer freedom."

Blair released Hardi's hand and stood. She walked around the desk to stand before Faolán but kept a safe distance. "I dinna give a damn whether ye like me, respect me, or acknowledge me as yer lady. I dinna care because ye are nae worth a minute of ma time. But ye sent yer laird to stand before the king, kenning he would be humiliated and possibly imprisoned. Ye either stole from yer clan the sacks and barrels, or ye are an inept warrior who doesnae deserve to be anyone's second if a handful of highwaymen robbed ye. How many were there? Three? Five? Ten? Ye outnumbered them, or at least should have had an even fight. I dinna believe for a minute yer lies. By insulting me and putting yer selfishness ahead of all else, ye have wronged the laird. That I dinna overlook. That I dinna forgive. If the laird finds ma judgement reasonable, I sentence ye to life in the dungeon." Blair peered around Faolán to the horrified faces. "To be clear, if Laird Cameron accepts this punishment and sentences Faolán to the dungeon, I will request the oubliette to anyone who thinks to free him or contest the decree. I may be smaller than each of ye, but I promise ye, ma will doesnae bend."

Blair took a step back before turning and walking back to her chair. She sat down and accepted Hardi's outstretched hand. She forced her pounding heart to slow as she inhaled deeply. She fought to keep her face neutral, not revealing her fear while confronting Faolán. She concentrated on putting back in place her courtly mien that revealed none of her real thoughts or feelings. Hardi looked at the council, many of whom didn't know where to look. He wasn't sure if Faolán's actions still stunned them or if it was Blair's pronouncement. Either way, the chamber was silent.

"Ye have heard Lady Cameron's suggestion. Faolán will keep his life and all his body parts. I willna force him from the clan. His body will bear nay scars—besides the one on his arm that will remind him of me—but he will live out his days alone but for any friends he makes with the rodents. I will ensure Faolán is well fed, has adequate clean water, has clean bedding, blankets, and clothes. Beyond that, he can rot. If ye canna accept ma judgment, speak now."

Hardi expected a barrage of dissent, but the chamber remained quiet. Faolán spun around to glare at his peers. Blair and Hardi glanced at each other. When they'd discussed Faolán and Drostan's return, they hadn't planned for Blair to pass down judgement, but they'd hoped Faolán's punishment would spur him or Drostan to reveal the conspirators. They hoped Faolán would refuse to shoulder the entire blame. But his arguments had nothing to do with plotting treason against the laird.

"I have trained beside ye, lived alongside ye, served this council with ye, and now ye'd let a wee bitch send me to the dungeon. Are ye all buggering her? Are ye all hoping to? Did he offer to share?"

"Faolán," Niall warned. "The laird has passed his judgment. Ye should thank Lady Cameron for nae sentencing ye to death. Ye ken that if it were up to the laird, ye'd be dead already. Faolán, ye brought this upon yerself. Ye lied to us, just as ye did the laird. We believed ye when ye swore it was best for the clan to raid the Macphersons. Ye swore we had what we needed for the taxes. Ye swore we had enough funds for the winter. Ye swore, ye swore, ye swore. And we were fools to believe ye."

"I have kenned ye since we were weans," Malcolm, a member who'd been silent until now, stood. "I want to believe it's ineptitude and nae selfishness that's led ye to the decisions ye've made. But the way ye are acting toward Lady Cameron makes me nae care. If I were the laird, and ye spoke such vile things to ma Martha, I would kill ye. That ye're breathing is a testament to both our lady's mercy and the laird's respect for his wife. It's all that's keeping ye alive, mon. Shut up."

"Faolán," Hardi interrupted. "Speak the truth of yer brother's involvement, and mayhap I will ask ma wife for greater leniency." Hardi and Blair intended to set brother against brother if they could. Hardi waited to see if Faolán would turn on Drostan or protect him.

"Drostan did naught." Faolán opted to protect his younger brother, but Hardi had more to say.

"We all ken that's a lie. Drostan was at least complicit. He kenned what the missives said, kenned what ye were up to, and he did naught aboot it. The only quality to commend him for is that he's loyal to his family. But that shall get him a cell next to ye," Hardi announced.

"Nay. I didna give ma brother a choice. I threatened him if he exposed me," Faolán blurted.

"And ye rewarded him when he didna," Blair muttered. She pretended to speak under her breath, but she intended everyone to hear her. She would remind them that Drostan was far from the innocent party in the brothers' scheme.

"Drostan, what say ye?" Hardi asked.

"Ma brother and I may have wronged the clan since Farlane's death, but it was to show everyone that Hardwin isnae a fit leader. Faolán or I should be laird," Drostan argued.

"Or ye?" Hardi smirked. "Faolán, did ye ken yer

brother wants to take the lairdship out from under ye? He would help ye be rid of me, then he'd be rid of ye."

"Nay!" Faolán bellowed. But he spun to look at Drostan, who didn't deny the accusation. He launched himself at Drostan, and the men tumbled to the floor. Faolán landed on top of his brother, wrapping his hands around his throat. Drostan struggled, trying to buck Faolán off of him, but they were too evenly matched and knew each other's fighting style too well. However, Faolán forgot that Drostan also knew that he kept an extra dirk attached to the back of his belt beneath the folds of his plaid. Drostan withdrew it and drove it into Faolán's neck. With his last breath, Faolán snapped Drostan's neck.

The council, Hardi, and Blair stared in shock at the scene before them. Never did Hardi nor Blair imagine this outcome when they thought to pit the brothers against one another. Blair watched as blood trickled over Faolán's shoulder and onto the floor.

"I dinna ken which is Cain and which is Abel," Blair muttered.

"They're both Cain, ma lady," Paul mused.

FORTY

The earliest rays of morning sun peeked around the hide that hung over the window embrasure in Hardi and Blair's chamber. Blair and Hardi lay on their sides, facing one another. They'd slept little that night, but for the first time, it wasn't from making love. They'd spent many hours discussing their plans now that Faolán and Drostan were dead. Hardi draped his arm over Blair's waist as her hand skimmed his chest.

"What do ye think the clan will say today? Most willna ken until the morning meal." Blair asked.

"It will shock them. Some will be angry. I will have to ensure the youngest of Faolán's bastards are cared for."

"Will they blame me?" Blair whispered.

"Nay. And if people do, I will inform them that ye presented them with a chance to live. They chose to fight one another and to kill each other. It's nae well timed with yer arrival, but we will learn who stands against us if anyone on the council blames ye or encourages the clan to do so."

Blair nodded, uncertain that was how she wanted to learn who conspired against Hardi. She had much to do that day, and she'd been looking forward to it before the council meeting. Now it made her nervous to move about the keep and the bailey. During the brief ride from Inverlochy, Hardi discussed with Donald and Tomas whether they should return to Dunrobin. The men refused until they were certain Hamish knew about the handfast and agreed to Blair remaining with Hardi. They argued their duty wasn't discharged until their laird said so. Hardi accepted the men's explanation and made it clear he was pleased Blair continued to have at least two devoted guards.

"Stay by ma side today, *mo ghaol*. Nae only because of what happened last night, but because I want yer company. And I admit I could use yer moral support when I meet with the council again. I must address the actual state of the clan's finances."

"Do ye think having me present at two meetings in a row will anger some? They humored us—me—last night. But that doesnae mean they dinna share Faolán's sentiments. They just didna have a death wish and kept quiet."

"I dinna ken, but I'm certain they realized ye are the voice of reason. Ye may have an iron will, but ye kept me from murdering Faolán," Hardi said.

"It's nae murder when it's justice. Ye were within yer rights," Blair reassured.

"And ye're trying to make me feel better." Hardi ran his fingers through Blair's brunette locks. "I swear by St. Columba's bones, if he'd upset ye—if I saw even a moment where ye wavered—I would have broken his neck."

"I wanted to skewer him, right then and there. I believe I could have hefted a sword and targe after all. I was ready to beat the hilt against ma shield before running him through. I wasna exaggerated when I said I wouldnae forgive him for slighting ye," Blair frowned.

Hardi grinned. "I will accept protection from ma wee warrior lass."

"Ye still havenae told me what ye call a female bull."

Hardi chuckled, then tried to compose himself. "*Mo chridhe,* I havenae told ye because it's just a cow. I didna think ye'd appreciate being called that."

Blair grinned as she playfully pushed his shoulder. "Well then, what do ye call a gelded bull?"

"A steer."

"Then consider me like that," Blair laughed. "I'm a raging steer ready to impale anyone who threatens ye."

Hardi took Blair's hand and wrapped it around his lengthening cock. "This bull has something he'd impale ye with."

"Then I suppose I should moo-ve over," Blair jested as her hand stroked Hardi.

"Blair, I swear when this business is all over, we will lock ourselves away in this chamber for a sennight, and I will make love to ye every way we can think of," Hardi pledged as his fingers thrust into her.

"I shall hold ye to that."

Hardi's broad palm covered her breast as he massaged the mound. Blair didn't bother stifling her moan as Hardi flicked his tongue over her nipple before catching it between his teeth. Hardi had discovered tormenting Blair's nipples with licks, pinches, and bites drove her to the edge of release. He pressed her onto her back as he ministered to both sides. He marveled at how Blair's breasts were the right size to fit within his mouth. Her soft hips and belly never failed to arouse him, but her small, pert breasts made him want to devour her.

"Blair, what do ye want this morn?" Hardi whispered. "Tell me what ye want."

"Tell me what ma options are," Blair moaned.

"I make slow love to ye, I fuck ye, I suck yer pearl until ye climax, I stroke ye with ma fingers. I can take ye from on top, I can plow ma cock into ye from behind, ye can ride me. Tell me which of those ye want."

"Ye forgot some," Blair gasped as Hardi pinched her nipple to the point of pain. She pushed at his shoulders, and he rolled onto his back. "I can lick ye, I can suck ye, I can stroke ye. I can do all of those." Blair slid down the bed, cupping his bollocks in her hand. She rolled his sack as her tongue laved from stem to stern. She swirled her tongue around his tip, swiping it over the slit on the head of his cock. She teased him, taking an inch then pulling back. Taking another inch, then pulling back. Hardi's abdomen rippled, and Blair ran her fingernails over them, making his hips thrust. She drew the full length of his rod into her mouth, sucking hard.

Hardi was certain he would spill the moment the head of his cock swept the back of Blair's throat. He scooped her hair back and watched her head bob as she worked his rod. She looked up at him, and he saw the carnal need in her eyes that led him every time to be rougher than he intended.

"Ye can fuck me in a minute, husband. I amnae done enjoying this yet." Blair pressed her breasts together as she caught Hardi's length between them, her tongue flicking his tip every time it appeared as she stroked him. He grasped her nipples and twisted. He pulled just enough to bring her body toward him. She eagerly climbed over him to straddle his hips. She grasped his cock, preparing to slide onto it when Hardi rolled them over, pinning her front to the bed. His hand slid between her legs until he found her sheath. Dew coated the tops of her thighs.

"I am going to fuck ye, wife. And ye ken why? Ye make me hard as a poleaxe, and yer cunny is dripping for me." Hardi guided his cock to her entrance, then thrust into her. His weight kept her from moving much, but she lifted her hips to meet each surge. "Fuck, Blair, I'm too close already."

"So am I." A pillow muffled Blair's voice, but Hardi understood. He nipped at her ear as he continued to piston his hips into her. Blair's heaving breaths transformed into one long moan as she shattered. Hardi grasped her hands and drew them behind her back as he kneeled between her thighs. The force of his body pushed Blair's smaller one toward the head of the bed, his fingers biting in her bottom. He ground his cock into her as he flew over the precipice into pure pleasure.

They collapsed onto the bed beside one another, and Blair struggled to speak. "A sennight isnae long enough. I want ye to promise me a moon."

"Ye will never walk again if I promise ye a moon of that," Hardi chortled.

"Then ye can stick yer cock in me and carry me around like ivy climbing up a pole," Blair suggested.

"Blair, tell me true. Did I corrupt ye, or did ye always have this naughty side to ye?" Hardi wondered.

Blair rolled to face him, and he caught sight of her bright red cheeks. It wasn't exertion that made them flushed. They were red from embarrassment, as though he'd caught her doing something wrong.

"I told ye how I happened on that couple in the passageway, and I watched. And ye ken Maude told me quite a lot. What ye dinna ken is that a few months before ye left Dunrobin, I went to the loch looking for ye. It was when the puppies were born. It was dusk, and I wanted ye to come to the stables to see them before the evening meal. I found ye standing in the loch, the water just up to yer thighs."

"Ye watched me pleasure maself?" Hardi was incredulous. Then he narrowed his eyes. "Just that one time?"

Blair shook her head, her cheeks radiating heat. "I couldnae tell what ye were doing at first. I was aboot to call out for ye, but ye groaned. I thought something was wrong, so I ran toward the loch. Ye must have heard me because ye turned toward the sound, but ye didna see me. But I saw ye. All of ye. I saw ye with yer hand around yer cock, stroking it. I saw ye spill yer seed."

"And that wasna the only time?" Hardi choked. He wasn't sure if it embarrassed him or thoroughly aroused him. As his cock twitched back to life, he decided he was both.

"I tried nae to think of it, but I stumbled upon ye a second time a few days later. I wanted to bathe in the loch because it had been so warm. It was nearly dusk that day, too. Ye entered the water just as I approached. I watched everything, all of it. After that, I noticed ye often slipped down to the loch before dusk. I followed ye many times. I was fascinated, a moth to a flame."

"What did ye think aboot when ye watched me?" Hardi's voice was a ragged whisper.

"I wondered what ye thought aboot, who ye thought aboot to make ye need to stroke yerself. I wondered what it would be like to touch ye, to do it for ye." Blair's eyes darted away. But she refused to be ashamed in front of Hardi. They were married, after all. It seemed like proof they were meant for one another. Her gazed locked with his.

"And how did that make ye feel? Did it make ye wet, Blair?" Hardi slipped two fingers into Blair as he used his thumbnail to flick her pearl. "Did it give ye the empty ache ye swear ye get now when ye want me?"

"Aye," Blair whispered. Her eyes drifted closed as

316

her core tried to trap his fingers within. "I wanted ye to be thinking aboot me."

"I was," Hardi confessed. Blair's eyes snapped open. "It was like I turned around one day, and ma friend who climbed trees with me suddenly had breasts. Ma eyes seemed to always find ye when ye bent over, either seeing the tops of yer breasts or noticing how yer skirts draped over yer backside. Ye made me hard all the time, Blair. If I could have, I would have gone to the loch three or four time a day to ease ma cockstands. I dinna ken what I would have done if we were Lowlanders. Ma plaid and sporran hid how badly I wanted ye."

"Did ye ever want to kiss me?" Blair shifted closer.

"All the time. And before ye ask me why I never did, I didna want yer da to castrate me. Blair, ye were the first woman I ever wanted, and ye're the last woman I will ever want." Hardi pulled Blair's leg over his hip as he slid into her. His tongue flicked across her lips, and she opened without hesitation. They rocked together slowly. As so often happened, they coupled passionately and frantically just to follow soon after with slowness and tenderness. "Blair, if ye'd been older, I would have begged yer father to let me marry ye. But ye were too young, and I was supposed to still see ye as ma little sister. But I wanted ye. It all came rushing back when I saw ye at court.".

"It was the same for me. Any time I wondered what it would be like with a mon, doing aught with a mon, it was ye I saw. When the other ladies used to chatter aboot their secret assignations or I overhead the married women talking, I would imagine it was us doing the things I heard."

With the number of men Blair had met at court, the number Hardi was certain attempted to draw her attention, it amazed him that he'd remained on her mind. He'd assumed she'd forgotten any attraction she'd once felt for him.

"Is there aught ye imagined that we havenae done?" Hardi wondered.

"Nae exactly. But I would like it vera much if one day we could make love in the loch at Dunrobin," Blair admitted.

"I would like that, too."

Their kisses silenced them, but Hardi recalled that the first time he was with a woman was in the village at Dunrobin. He'd gone with Lachlan, Michael, and Dougal. Michael already knew he wanted to be a priest, so he stood watch for them. Hardi found a brunette wench and made her face away from him, so she didn't distract him from imagining she was Blair. Over the coming years, he imagined he was bedding Blair on more than one occasion, and he knew that was why he favored women with dark hair.

As though reading his mind, Blair continued speaking as they lay together once more spent. "I pictured ye when I heard those things. Did ye ever think of me after ye left Dunrobin?" She wasn't brave enough to ask if he thought of her while he coupled with other women. She didn't want the rejection.

"Yes. For the first few years after I left Dunrobin, I imagined any woman I bedded was ye. After I saw ye at the Highland Gatherings, I—" Hardi feared he would say too much, but he knew she didn't hold his liaisons with other women against him. "I would find a dark-haired lass and make her face away from me, so I could imagine it was ye."

"Hardi? Do ye think it upsets me to ken ye've been with other women?"

"Nay. I ken ye understand that neither of us imagined we'd be together. But I dinna like thinking aboot the women before ye. It feels wrong, and I dinna see any point to it."

"I appreciate that. But—" Blair blew out a quick breath through her nose. "it's gratifying to ken ye wanted me so much that it was me ye imagined ye were with."

FORTY-ONE

Blair stood near where Hardi sat in their solar. She'd browsed the shelves and discovered that someone in Hardi's family saved a set of primary Latin books. Blair had pulled those from the shelves and set them aside. She moved along the collections and noticed books of poetry and tales of chivalric love, much like *Tristan and Isolde*. She found several books in Greek and thought of her cousin Magnus's wife, Deirdre, who had been a scholar from a young age, translating passages and entire books from various languages. Blair picked two books in Latin that told the stories of the Romans invasion of Britannia. She thought Hardi might enjoy the battle scenes more than he would the riddles and Bible verses they'd worked on at Stirling. She found Clan Cameron history books written in Scots, so she added those to her pile.

"We shall be auld and gray by the time I read through these," Hardi jested as he rose from his chair. He came to stand behind her, his chest pressing against her back as he wrapped his arms around Blair.

"Speak for yerself. I'm never going gray. I dinna plan to look auld," Blair teased. She turned her head to look back at Hardi and winked. "And I ken what we can do to stay fit and young."

Hardi was about to whisper his own suggestions, but a rap on the door, then the sound of it being opened, made them step apart. Hardi grumbled, "Knocking isnae the same as being bade to enter. Wait next time."

"Aye, Laird," Paul grinned. Paul's questioning Blair the evening before hadn't endeared him to Hardi. When Paul attempted to resume his interview when they broke their fast, Hardi offered Blair a tour instead. They hurried to finish their porridge and grabbed heels of bread to take with them. The tour led them back to their solar, knowing the council would arrive soon. Hardi helped Blair move the stack of books out of the way of the men taking seats around the table. Paul was the first to realize Blair didn't intend to leave. "Will ye be using those books to sit on, or mayhap stand on, so ye dinna have to look up to us?"

Blair gritted her teeth before forcing a smile. "The only mon I've looked up to is ma da."

The grin slid from Paul's face as he took his seat. "I'm certain Mordag has a method of dusting the higher shelves without standing on any of those books. Besides, that's a servant's job."

"Paul, I dinna ken what ye think books are for, but ye seem to think I need them to grow a few inches. I've never stood on a book, and I amnae planning to do so." Blair cast him a puzzled look.

"I'd like to begin, so there's time for us to go to the lists this morn," Hardi spoke. Blair took her seat beside him, and the couple noticed many frowning faces.

"We kenned ye wanted Lady Cameron to meet us last eve, and it was useful having her here to deal with Faolán and Drostan. But she doesnae need to be here for every meeting. Surely, she has other duties to attend," Malcolm stated.

"Lady Cameron kens exactly what duties she has. She kens Mordag has been an excellent housekeeper all these years, but Lady Cameron is now chatelaine. As such, she's reviewed the keep's ledgers and has several items she cares to discuss." Hardi turned to Blair, who lifted the ledgers off the desk and carried them to the table. She took the seat at the head of the table left empty for Hardi.

"Ye canna be serious, Laird." Malcolm scowled.

"Why wouldnae I be? The clan's lady maintains the ledgers for the keep's accounts. She's corrected many errors and updated most of the records, but I canna explain the discrepancies. She expects ye to do so for us."

"That isnae a matter for the clan council. She should take that up with Mordag," Malcolm argued.

"It's a matter for the clan council when ye have recklessly spent the clan's money and dinna have enough to ensure the clan survives the winter," Blair spoke up. "It's a matter for the clan council when nay one kept an inventory of what's being traded and what's being kept. And it's a matter for the bluidy council because Faolán and Drostan stole from the clan and nae a damn one of ye paid enough attention to catch them or cared enough to do aught aboot it. So, gentlemen, ye will suffer ma presence until I have sufficient information to ensure this clan neither goes bankrupt nor starves." Blair felt her temper spike after listening to the men speak as though she wasn't present. It frustrated her even more that they mocked her and assumed she had nothing to contribute. She realized her family was unusual for the role women played in clan business, but that didn't mean the Cameron men shouldn't treat her with a modicum of respect.

Blair opened the first ledger and rambled off several items and amounts, turning the book to show the men as her fingers ran down the tallies. "I have written these in a manner that doesnae require Mordag or yer cook, Dolina, to read. They need only remember what the first letter of cow, sheep, grain, and whisky look like. It's the same for other household items. If they canna remember the shapes, they can remember which column is which from practice. They are to mark one tally for each item in its column whenever they take inventory. They are to strike through a tick mark whenever we use an item."

Blair held up the book near her shoulder and looked at it before looking back at the men. She pointed to the first column. "Do ye see these tick marks? They are for all the sacks of grain Laird Cameron reported ye had before Faolán and Drostan left for Stirling. Do ye see how most are crossed out? Aye? The ones that arenae crossed off are what I expect to find in the storerooms. If this is accurate, I hope nay one has an enormous appetite in this clan because it'll be a lean winter with little bread. Do ye see this column? This is the column for the number of sheep ye have. Laird Hardwin counted yer flocks before I arrived. Thanks to Faolán's muck up, ye have less than ye started with. Ye butchered several without thought to what we would need for the winter. I hope I find several hung to dry age, but from what Laird Cameron tells me, I shouldnae hold ma breath."

Blair left the book open as she laid it on the table, then pushed it toward the men. She flipped open another ledger and turned pages until she found the one she needed. She held this book up just as she had the first. She pointed to the top of the page, then moved her finger to each item she pointed out. "Each column is for the distinct coins. Doyts or pennies, shillings, merks, pounds. The recording is like the household account. Each time we count the coins, we place a tick mark in the column for the specific coin. When we take money out, we should cross off the equivalent number of marks. This way, we can glance at the ledger and ken what should be available."

Blair turned several pages over before pointing to a page covered in numbers. She pointed to the first row. "This is the amount of money the clan had before Laird Cameron went to Stirling." She moved her finger down and pointed to three figures. "The next row is the amount for the geld, then the amount for the thirlage, and the amount for the *cáin*. Further down, ye will see the original amount minus what Laird Cameron paid. Ye'll notice a balance remains. And that's because ye didna send Laird Cameron with the correct amount. This is the value of the sacks of grain and barrels of whisky Faolán and Drostan were to deliver. Here is what's left over from the taxes owed because they failed. Dinna forget we still have the geld left to pay. That's this amount right here."

Blair paused, taking in the confused and concerned expressions of the men. The only person she felt bad for in the room was Hardi. He hadn't moved from the desk, so the focus remained on Blair. She'd explained everything to him more than once, but he still struggled to understand. Part of him was relieved that the others looked just as confused, but the other part of him was furious that none of them looked to know what to do.

"This number is what I expected the clan to spend for the winter, but that was before I kenned aboot the missing grain and whisky and before I kenned about the slaughtered sheep. The amount will have to go up. Which means," she tapped the last figure on the page. "This amount goes down. And this is the amount that the clan has in reserves."

Blair slid the book down the table just like she had the other. She leaned back in her chair and steepled her fingers over her belly. She remained quiet as the men peered at the books, but she knew it meant little to most of them. However, she and Hardi were looking for anyone who appeared to understand what was in front of them. They hoped this might be a better way to ferret out the author of the missive, but nothing stood out to either of them.

"Lady Blair," Niall cast her a scornful look. "And how do ye ken all of this?"

"Do ye mean how do I ken how to keep these records? I ken because ma mother taught me to be a chatelaine. If ye mean how do I ken these numbers for the clan, I'm *Lady Cameron*."

"Ye've been Lady Cameron for a day," Niall pressed.

"Ye've kenned I'm Lady Cameron for a day. But I have been Lady Cameron for more than a fortnight."

"Ye are being evasive," Osgar accused.

"Bluidy insufferable, isnae it? Mayhap ye realize how Laird Cameron feels when ye dinna answer his questions. Mayhap ye can imagine ma frustration when I looked at the original records. The lack of timely entries is the same as being evasive. It hides the truth. Once again, either ye dinna care enough aboot this clan to help lead and ensure its welfare, or ye arenae knowledgeable enough to do it." Blair raised her hand to keep them from speaking. "If ye dinna care, ye dinna care. I canna do aught aboot that. But warming these chairs for years on end doesnae make ye knowledgeable. If it did, we wouldnae be in this jumble. I can fix lack of knowledge. Be willing to learn, and there is someone here willing to teach. If ye dinna want to learn, then be honorable and say so. I will deal with it, and I willna waste anyone's time."

"Why should we believe ye?" Niall demanded.

"Why would I lie?" Blair locked eyes with Niall, daring him to look away first. "If there is nay coin, there is nay coin. I canna make it magically appear like manna from God. If there is nay coin and I canna suddenly make more, then there is nay money for me to overspend. If ye can see there isnae enough coin, then ye canna blame me when we canna buy what we need. Either way, I live here now, and I dinna plan to starve."

Several of the men turned to one another and whispered, but Blair sat too far away to catch any of what they said. She waited impatiently, wanting to turn back to look at Hardi, but she wouldn't give away any of her doubts. The men as a one turned back to look at Blair. She realized that Niall was now the unofficial leader since Faolán was no longer a part of the council.

"Vera well, Lady Cameron. We accept yer offer to maintain the ledgers, both the keep's and the clan's. We thank ye for yer help. Ye have generously given us yer time. We dinna wish to keep ye from yer duties," Niall offered a patronizing smile.

"That isnae enough."

"I beg yer pardon, ma lady," Niall startled.

"Ye intend to tell me after ye've spent the clan's funds. I dinna agree with that. Ye will spend us into the grave just as ye are now. Me keeping a tally after the fact is nay better than nae keeping a tally at all. Ye will tell me what ye intend to spend funds on, and I will tell ye if ye may."

"That's outrageous," Paul slammed his fist on the table. Blair sensed Hardi's movement, but she was quick to reply.

327

"What is outrageous is that ye have spent years sitting around drinking whisky, gossiping aboot other clans, puffing yerself up like a pigeon looking for a mate, and all the while, only two people ever learned how to read and lied more often than nae. What's outrageous is that ye've gotten us into this mess. And what is absolutely outrageous is nae a bluidy one of ye has an ounce of regret or remorse in yer voice or in yer eyes. If ye dinna agree to me overseeing this clan's finances, I will stand on the battlements and tell every member of this clan how ye failed them. Think to silence me, and it willna be just ma husband after yer heads. *Dinna ever forget who I am and where I came from. I am Lady Blair Cameron.* When I married the laird, the wellbeing of this clan became ma highest priority. Whether it is a threat from outside or within, I willna let this clan perish. So ye had better decide vera bluidy quickly whether yer bollocks are big enough to listen to a woman, or if ye'd like to ruin this entire clan."

"Laird Cameron, deal with yer wife," Niall snarled.

Hardi stood up and rounded the desk. He stood behind Blair and put his hands on her shoulders. "Vera well. Ma solution to ma wife's demands is that I grant them. She is now responsible for keeping the accounts and has final say on all items. I ken ma wife will discuss matters with me, but if it's nae possible, her word is law."

"I ken we arenae off to a pleasant start," Blair said conciliatorily. "Ye're angry. I'm angry. But I want to believe we all have the clan's needs as our priority. I stand by what I've said, and I ken that rubs the wrong way. However, ye liking me has naught to do with the future this clan faces. Ye needed a sound slap in the face to make ye come to. Ye need to realize how serious the situation is. I have nay intention

328

of telling anyone outside this chamber that I decide the clan's finances. That isnae anyone's business besides ours. As far as the clan is concerned, naught needs to look different from how it always has."

Blair paused as she let her words sink in. The varying degrees of scorn and anger didn't deter her. If they believed they knew more than her, then they could prove it by being responsible. Until then, they would have to make do.

"Behind closed doors," Blair continued, "I count every grain of salt, every goose feather, every leaf of cabbage, and I keep track of every doyt and pound coming in and out of the clan. It is a tedious duty, and nae one I'm particularly excited to have. But it must be done. Like it or nae, I am the *only* person in this clan who's qualified. Ye havenae had a chatelaine in over a year, and I dinna ken if ye ever had a seneschal. Mayhap Faolán thought he was it. But I'm here, and I'm willing and able."

Blair's softer tone eased the tension in the room, but she didn't regret her earlier harshness. She expected more resistance, and she wanted the council to know they couldn't thwart her. Hardi squeezed her shoulders as the men continued to whisper amongst themselves. When they turned back to face Hardi and Blair, there was resignation on their faces. They agreed to Blair's terms, and she felt one weight lift off her shoulder. Unfortunately, there were still several remaining.

"Laird, if we may. We need to discuss the MacDonalds at Inverlochy. Ye said ye negotiated new terms, so we need to make them official." Niall turned back to Blair once more. "Thank ye again, ma lady. Good day."

Blair didn't move for a long moment, then she stood, but rather than walk to the door, she returned to her seat beside the desk. She smiled politely as the men stared at her. When they continued to direct owlish gazes at her, she grinned. "I can have a good day right here in this chair."

A man she still didn't know snorted. It broke the tension and several of the other men chortled. Paul looked at Hardi as he laughed. "Ye found yerself a bright one. Tongue sharp enough to cut leather with a bonnie smile while she does it. Vera well." Blair understood Paul imagined he was complimenting her, and she understood he'd dismissed her even though she remained in the chamber. She glanced at Hardi, who tried to hide his knowing smile as he took his seat beside her.

Hardi began. "I renegotiated several terms of our agreement with the MacDonalds. The chieftain's laird is aware of the updated arrangement since we met together. As ye surely noticed, the MacDonalds have lent us three score of their warriors. This displeased Artair, but it displeased him more to remember that he is only the guardian of Inverlochy. It is still our keep. We suffered a heavy loss during our trial by combat with the Mackintoshes."

Hardi swallowed as images of the battle flashed before him. Blair squeezed the hand she held, and he glanced at her. He saw the deep concern within her eyes, and he could tell she worried he wouldn't be able to continue. He wanted Blair to be proud of him during their first full council meeting together. He couldn't be prouder of her, and he didn't want to disappoint her after she bravely faced down the council.

"We need the extra warriors for our defenses. All is quiet for now. But the feuds arenae over. After Faolán's raid, it's inevitable that the Macphersons will retaliate. They demanded that the king intervene, but they will say they can justify another raid. Never mind they already have more of our sheep.

That is why I took advantage of our opportunity to change the terms of the MacDonalds' lease."

Hardi pulled out a sheaf of parchment, a quill, and ink, laying them out on the desk before Blair and him. He was of two minds as to whether he should attempt to write some information in his own hand or have Blair do all the writing. He noticed her slight nod of encouragement. He started with what he was sure he could manage.

"I am recording the dates of our fresh arrangement, who was present at the meeting, and where it took place," Hardi explained. He looked up to see several surprised expressions. He knew it still surprised most of the council that he could write. He had written little in front of them, but it was enough for them to believe he could. Hardi glanced once more at Blair, unsure of what to discuss next. When she leaned over to whisper to him, Malcolm cleared his throat.

"Lady Cameron, we've accepted yer terms for handling the finances, but if ye dinna understand contracts, ye should leave," Malcolm suggested. When he saw Hardi's expression change, he stumbled to add, "So ye arenae bored. Laird Cameron can explain it later. But we dinna have time for yer questions."

Blair looked at Malcolm and then at Hardi. At his exasperated expression, she burst into laughter. She shook her head and raised her palm to Hardi, offering him the chance to explain. She was fed up with trying to convince the council she was just as competent, if not more so, than they were.

"Lady Cameron was aboot to remind me that we renegotiated the banalities. Imagine ma surprise when I learned the MacDonalds owed us rents that I didna ken existed. Fortunately, she explained those to me while Laird MacDonald chewed Artair's ear off for nae paying them. She also explained there's a pannage owed to us. Imagine the missed opportunity that would have been. Or better yet, imagine ma embarrassment—yet again—that I didna ken the basics of being a landowning laird. Did it slip yer minds?" Hardi asked. "Lady Cameron has warned me nae to count on these funds in case MacDonald doesnae pay them straight away. We may nae be the only clan who canna pay their debts on time."

The men looked at her as though she were an exotic animal, and they weren't sure if she was tame. She greeted their stares with a serene smile before looking at Hardi. He'd been prepared to attempt more writing on his own, but his clansmen's rudeness to Blair frustrated him, and he feared he'd make a mess of the contract. He slid the parchment and quill to her.

"Lady Cameron, as the keeper of our finances," Osgar sneered. "Ye must ken how expensive parchment is. Mayhap ye could find some sewing to keep ye occupied rather than drawing."

"Osgar, ye're an arse," Hardi snapped. "I dinna fight ma wife's battles for her. She will run circles around all of us and willna tire. Ye insist upon belittling her and insulting her—despite me sitting here—because she has us all by the bollocks. There is only one person in this clan who can read, write, and do sums with ease. That is Lady Cameron. Who do ye think taught me?" Hardi ignored the shocked gasps and incredulous looks. He plowed on. "I'm learning, but I dinna have her skills. Neither do any of ye. So, we can keep going around in circles with yer petty comments that make ye look like sulking weans, or we can behave like adults and move on. Lady Cameron will attend all council meetings. She will be ma scribe until such time as I can do it maself. She will remain on the council after that. She is a voting member of this council, and she has the same authority as I do. If ye canna live with that, then it looks like one of Faolán's bastards will be yer next laird."

Blair watched as a man leaned forward and made it clear he was through listening to the council members insult Blair and that he had better things to do with his day than listen to his peers whine. Hardi leaned over and whispered the man's name was Mungan and that he and Hardi were close in age. He'd replaced a member on the council when he died in the same battle where Hardi lost his cousins.

"Laird, Lady, we accept all terms regarding Lady Cameron's position on this council and in this clan. We are fortunate to have Lady Cameron join our clan. And we are especially fortunate," Mungan looked around the table, "that Lady Cameron is still in this chamber and hasnae given up on us. She has the patience of a saint, even if she has the tongue of an asp. I think we'll soon realize she is exactly what this clan needs. Now, can we please cease the clishmaclaver and finish this bluidy meeting? I have things to do before I go to ma grave. At this rate, they'll never get done."

Mungan's declaration ceased the bickering and snarkiness, so the council finished codifying the contract. The men filed out of the chamber, and once the door closed behind the last member, Blair fell against Hardi's chest. She was exhausted.

"Wait here," Hardi murmured. He rushed to the door and locked it before returning to Blair. He swept her into his arms and carried her to a chair before the fire. He settled her against his chest and pressed a kiss to her forehead with a tender smile. "Sleep."

"What aboot ye?" Blair tried to stifle her yawn, but she was too comfortable in Hardi's lap. "Ye canna just sit here with naught to do, trapped beneath me."

"Ye may trap me beneath ye any time, and I willna complain. But I intend to get some shuteye too."

"Sitting up?" Blair was aghast and tried to right herself.

"Blair, I have slept sitting up far too many times to count. It isnae cold in here, it's dry, there isnae anyone trying to run me through, and I have ma bonnie wife in ma arms. I'd say this is a fine place to take a nap."

Blair blinked several times before nodding, her heart aching with sadness from Hardi's experiences and fear of when being both a laird and a warrior would force him to sleep outside again.

"Shh, *mo chridhe.* I didna tell ye that to upset ye or make ye worry. I told ye because I appreciate this time with ye. Now sleep, Blair. I need the rest too."

"I love ye, Hardi," Blair said around a yawn, and her eyes didn't open again. Hardi shifted and shut his. They slept through the midday meal and spent the afternoon reflecting on what was said and left unsaid during the council meeting. They still didn't know who plotted against Hardi, but they separated the council members into groups by what they had to gain. Hardi realized the man who topped their list was Paul.

FORTY-TWO

Blair shielded her eyes from the midafternoon sun as she and Hardi stood on the battlements. After the council meeting the previous day, Blair opted to spend the morning engaged in more womanly pursuits. She met with Dolina to set the menu for the week, then she met with Mordag to discuss the most pressing needs for the keep. Afterward, Hardi took her on a tour of the village, and she received a warm welcome from everyone. When she spotted councilmen, they offered a curt nod before skirting away from her. They didn't offend her since she wished to avoid them too.

As they stood together, Hardi pointed out various points across the landscape. He grinned as he told stories of how he, his brother, and his cousins used to race their horses across the pastureland and hunt in the woods to the west. It was the first time Hardi spoke of his family without a hollowness in his chest threatening to rip him apart. His grief felt lighter as he reminisced with Blair. When he startled Blair with a deep and lingering kiss, he explained how he felt.

"Isnae that Alan?" Blair pointed to a man approaching the portcullis. He was on foot, but he looked dusty and weary. "Did ye send him somewhere?"

"I didna," Hardi growled. He took Blair's hand and led her to the stairs. They met Alan as he passed through the gates. "Ye dinna look in good form."

Alan's head snapped in Hardi's direction. He dipped his head to acknowledge Blair, then looked back at Hardi. "The weather here is fine, but it's chucking it down at Inverlochy."

Blair's nails dug into Hardi's hand, but she remained silent. Hardi stared at Alan, unsure of what to say now that he could question him. He opted for directness. "Were ye picking up or dropping off a missive?"

"Picking up," Alan answered as he ran his hand through his damp hair.

"I hope the rain didna ruin the missive if it was in the wall for too long." Hardi's tone sounded nonchalant, but he felt anything but.

"It was there before the rain. I was supposed to go this morn, but ma wife and ma lass are poorly," Alan explained.

"Is there aught yer family needs?" Blair asked. "I'm certain Laird Cameron can deliver the missive, so ye can go home to yer kin." Blair's concern was genuine, but she also wished to take advantage of the situation. When Alan shifted nervously, Blair wondered what he was hiding.

"Lady Cameron is right. I can take the missive, so ye can check on yer wife and wean. It's nay trouble," Hardi offered.

"I dinna ken who it's for," Alan confessed. "Every eve, I check to see if someone left aught. If there is, then I ride out the next morn. If there isnae, then I dinna go."

"If ye dinna ken who the missives are for, or who

they're from, how did ye end up as the messenger?" Hardi pressed.

Alan glanced around the bailey, discomfort and dread written across his face. Blair followed his gaze as it hopped from one to another, before settling on Hardi. "Laird Cameron, ye ken I've been a messenger for years," Alan evaded.

"Then how did ye ken there's a hiding spot? And where is this spot?" Hardi persisted. Alan appeared to consider the questions, but Hardi knew he wanted to avoid answering questions. He'd behaved the same way since they were children. "Alan, ye canna keep shuffling yer feet to move backwards until ye have room to make an excuse and turn around. I was faster than ye when we were weans, and I'm faster than ye now. I will catch ye."

"Can we speak elsewhere?" Alan continued to glance around, as though he feared being watched.

"We can go to ma solar," Hardi suggested.

"Nay. Somewhere away from the keep. And nae in the bailey, either. Can we speak outside the wall?"

"Ye ken that means guards accompany us," Hardi reminded.

Alan sighed. He pulled the missive from his sporran and handed it to Hardi. "I dinna want anyone to overhear this. The hiding spot is between two books in yer solar, ma laird. Laird Farlane thought of several spots and instructed me years ago to check them daily. Depending on where I find the missive, I ken whether it is to go to Inverlochy, the Donalds, the MacMillans, or the king."

"Ye've been entering ma solar every evening and didna think I should ken," Hardi's voice was like a shard of ice. "Do I sneak into yer home every evening and go through yer belongings? What the bluidy hell, Alan? Who else kens Uncle Farlane's system? Obviously, someone does since the missives continue, and he's dead."

"Truthfully, Laird, until just now, I never considered whether ye kenned aboot it. Every council member kens, so I assumed someone told ye."

"If it's nay secret, then why are ye so shifty?" Blair asked.

"Because the missives to Inverlochy are never addressed to anyone, and I dinna ken who they're from. That tells me whoever it is doesnae want me to. If they dinna want me to ken, then they willna want me discussing it. Whoever that missive is for is expecting it. If they see I've just arrived and I'm talking to ye both, even gave ye the missive, they might be suspicious. I have a family to think aboot."

"If ye think whatever ye're doing involves someone nefarious enough to harm yer family, then why are ye still a messenger?" Blair wondered.

"Because ma father, uncle, and grandfather are on the council. I've been a messenger for years. It would seem odd if I just stopped," Alan explained.

"If ye have family on the council, dinna ye think that protects ye?" Blair persisted.

"I dinna care to find out, ma lady."

"Who are yer father, uncle, and grandfather? I dinna ken yet."

"Niall is ma grandfather, Mungan is ma uncle, and Malcolm is ma father," Alan explained.

Blair nodded. She would wait to ask Hardi who else was directly related on the council. She would recommend Hardi makes more changes to the council membership and not have so many family connections. It was too easy for factions to start. Faolán and Drostan were examples of that.

"If whoever is expecting the missive doesnae get it, they will look for me," Alan worried.

"Where is the spot for Inverlochy missives?" Blair

interjected. Once Alan explained where to look, Hardi dismissed him, then the couple went to their solar. Blair scanned the shelves until she found the place Alan described. Hardi stood beside a candle on the desk and heated the wax enough to peal open the seal. He steeled himself for whatever Blair read.

All is progressing on my end. The bows and arrows have been delivered, and I have stored the payment where no one knows to look. No one seems any the wiser about the unusual orders or where the weapons have gone. We will come out of this richer than when we began.

I welcomed your news that the tunnel is ahead of schedule. I worried a moon would be an interminable wait, but I can manage another sennight. I wish to see the tunnel's progress for myself. I confess curiosity is getting the better of me. I will be glad when we no longer must rely on inept messengers and secret missives. One missing correspondence was one too many. Make sure your man understands he's your clan's only messenger. I don't want more bodies to dispose of.

Keep me abreast of any changes or updates. If I hear naught within the week, I will assume it's time to summon our friends and make our move. What a gathering that will be.

Blair's ears rang as she finished reading. She looked up at Hardi, shocked by the entire missive, but one line stood out. "They killed Bran. That's why he hasnae returned."

Hardi pulled Blair into his embrace and buried his face in her hair as she gripped the back of his leine. Blair forced herself not to cry, remaining stoic as she felt Hardi's labored breathing. She understood the two men had been friends for years, and it was likely the first time Hardi sent a man on a mission only to learn of his death. She leaned back, her cool fingers resting like feathers against his cheek. "Dinna take on guilt isnae yers to bear. Every mon who rides out on behalf of his laird kens the risks. Ye didna do this. Ye didna cause his death, Hardi."

"I ken, but it doesnae feel that way." As Blair looked at her husband, his gaze appeared distant, as though he was somewhere far away or long ago. She didn't know how Hardi grieved, and she was unsure of whether she should give him space. She had her answer when she took a step away from him. Hardi's arm clamped around her waist as he pulled her back against his chest.

"Dinna go," Hardi whispered.

"I wouldnae dream of it," Blair whispered. She embraced Hardi as he held her, his cheek resting on the crown of her head. After several minutes passed, Blair asked, "Do ye wish to sit together? Or would ye prefer I remain here but give ye space?"

"Sit together." They made their way to the chairs by the fireplace. "I need to retrieve his body. Or at least try to."

Blair was already thinking the same thing. "I think ye should send one of ma guards with whoever rides out. We dinna ken where he might be, and we dinna ken if there are others lying in wait for messengers headed to Dunrobin. A Sutherland might deter an ambush."

"We have a week rather than a moon to prepare for an attack we dinna ken who it involves. There is someone within these bailey walls who seeks to sabotage us. It could be anyone at this point. We still dinna ken who can read and write besides ye."

"Who could have had the opportunity over the years?" Blair wondered.

"Uncle Farlane, ma father, Faolán and Drostan were all taught at the same time. Ma father was second to inherit before ma cousins were born. As the laird's son, they taught him alongside Uncle Farlane. They gave Faolán and Drostan the opportunity because the four of them were vera close as lads. Much like I was with Dougal and ma cousins. Until

Angus was born, the line of succession was Uncle Farlane, ma father, Timothy—Faolán and Drostan's father—then the two of them. Ma father didna see any reason for me or Dougal to learn because Uncle Farlane had four sons before we went to foster. Ma father never imagined Dougal or I would ever become laird. He said there was nay point in filling our heads with useless information when we should fill it with battle skills."

"But we ken all five men are dead along with other members of yer family. Who might have learned alongside of them?"

"Nay one, unless Faolán and Drostan were part of the secret, and they taught someone."

"True," Blair agreed. "I didna get the impression from Alan that he thinks any of his family are involved."

"I agree. He canna read nor write either. Since he canna understand the contents of the missives, he doesnae ken they contain secrets. He's been the clan's messenger for so long, nay one expects otherwise."

"If we take away, Niall, Malcolm, and Mungan, that leaves Paul and Osgar," Blair deduced. "Could anyone have taught either of them, even after their childhood?"

"I dinna think so. But I just dinna ken. Someone taught another someone something at some time. Bluidy frustrating." Hardi left his chair and went to the sideboard, poured himself a dram of whisky, and drank. When he turned back toward Blair, she was scowling playfully.

"Dinna be rude!" Blair laughed. Hardi refilled his mug and poured a dram for Blair. He chuckled when she downed it in one gulp. Her eyes watered, but she didn't choke.

"We have a sennight to find Bran's body, discover

who's plotting against me, and determine who's aboot to attack," Hardi surmised.

"We assume it's the entire Clan Chattan Confederation, which means the Macphersons, Mackintoshes, and Davidsons are on their way. We prepare for a siege. Send out yer best hunters to bring back everything they can: deer, rabbit, squirrel, boar. Bring to the keep any outlying villages ye imagine the enemy might attack. Tell the men to bring their pitchforks, shovels, aught that can be a weapon." Blair's mind scrambled for everything she'd learned from her parents. Few people dared attack the Sutherlands, but her parents taught all three siblings what to do in the eventuality they had to lead a clan through one. "We send a Cameron and a Sutherland out first thing in the morn. We place this missive where its recipient expects it, and then we wait to see who comes for it. Ma guess is they'll slip in here during the evening meal. It'll be too obvious if either of us is missing from the Great Hall. Mordag canna do it because she's needed to oversee the meal. I dinna ken who among yer men ye can trust, but I ken both of ma guards can be. Have them wait in the passageway in the shadows, and they can report aught they see."

Hardi walked to two bookshelves and ran his hand over the wood paneling that separated them. Blair heard a latch click, and a Murphy door sprang open. She cautiously moved to stand beside Hardi. It was a hidey-hole large enough for two adults and a child or two. Hardi told Blair to wait, and he stepped into the space. He felt around in the dark until he felt a bump in the wooden door. He slid open a tiny hatch and looked out. His height allowed him to see between the tops of the books and the shelf above. He knew Blair would need to move books apart to have an unobstructed view. He called out to Blair and asked her if she could tell where he was hiding. When she couldn't find him even though she knew behind which bookshelf he hid, Hardi wiggled his fingers through the open portal before depressing the interior latch and opening the Murphy door. They agreed they would follow their normal routine, and if they heard nothing from their guards, they would take up watch from within the hidey-hole.

FORTY-THREE

B lair and Hardi were at another dead end. Donald and Tomas reported a young boy of seven or eight summers slipped into the solar and was back out only a matter of moments later. The lad carried the missive in his hand, but neither of Blair's guards knew the clan's youngest members, so they didn't recognize him. In the dim light of the passageway, they couldn't make out any distinguishing features. The Cameron guard and Tomas set off before sunrise to search for Bran's remains. Blair and Hardi knew the men might have to travel as far as Dunrobin, which meant they would be away during whatever ominous event approached.

Hardi refused to allow Blair to join him when he explored the dungeons. He searched for any sign that it led to a tunnel. He found nothing that hinted that a secret underground passageway existed. Unable to search the dungeon, Blair searched the floors in storage buildings in the bailey along with storerooms in the kitchens and along other passageways. Blair feared her heart would stop when she entered an unused storeroom within a passageway seldom frequented. It led to a part of the keep that once stood

345

as a section of the original construction. Someone had walled off the end of the passageway, so it was impossible to enter the ancient portion of the castle. She slithered along the wall as she moved closer to the open hole in the floor. The unintelligible sound of men's voices floated toward her, and she noticed the dim yellow glow from candles. She didn't wait to learn how close the men were. She hurried away from the storage room and ran to the door leading to the dungeon. Blair collided with Hardi as she took her first step through the portal.

Blair explained what she discovered and expected Hardi to be relieved that they were making progress. He looked down at Blair with an expression she didn't recognize. His eyes were cold and hard, and Hardi looked at her as though she disgusted him. He said nothing and stepped around her. She trailed after him, repeating his name until they arrived at their solar. Hardi slammed the door shut and turned the key in the lock once Blair passed through. He grasped her arm and pushed her roughly against the door. His kiss was punishing and brutal, but Blair gave no quarter with her response.

Hardi ripped the ribbons from the back of Blair's gown and yanked it off her as she slipped her hands beneath his plaid. He gathered the front of his plaid and tucked it into his belt before pulling Blair's hands free. He pinned her hands together in one of his as he wrapped his other arm beneath her backside and lifted high enough for her to wrap her legs around his waist. He held her arms above her head as he thrust into her with a wildness neither recognized. He surged into Blair over and over as he devoured her mouth.

He walked them to the table and withdrew from Blair as she whimpered and reached out. He turned her and bent her forward over the table. He plowed into her over and over; the table creaked and shifted with each surge of his sword into her sheath. He once again captured her wrists in one of his hands, pinning them against her lower back while his other hand gathered her hair. He pushed it to the side, so nothing lay between his lips and her ear. He lifted one of her legs onto the table, and it forced her to go up on her toes, but the change in angle allowed him better access. Blair moaned with the intensity of their coupling.

"Dinna ye dare climax, Blair," Hardi growled. "I amnae anywhere near done with ye, wife. I have stood behind ye every time ye have gone head-to-head with men who would have run ye through if ye werenae a lady. I never tell ye nay. Never. The one time I do, ye had to have yer way. I didna refuse to take ye to the dungeon just so ye could go creeping around on yer own. Bluidy hell, Blair. I'm nae burying another fucking member of ma family."

Hardi choked out the last words as his body pressed Blair's against the table. He reached around her and rubbed her pearl as he continued to piston his hips. He released her wrists and wrapped his arms around her tightly, making it impossible to go anywhere if she had wanted to. He continued to pump his cock into her, tormenting her nub. He felt her core tightening around him, and she shifted with frustration. When he was certain she was on the edge of release, he pulled out and stepped back. Blair cried out as she looked back over her shoulder at Hardi, who stood panting, his cock glistening with her dew. She whimpered at the loss of Hardi's body against hers and the regret she felt as she understood his fear. She rolled over and scooted onto the table. She brought her hands and feet to the edge as she let her knees drop wide.

Hardi stroked himself as he watched Blair, his

bollocks demanding he return to her and relieve their ache. Once she laid on the table, Hardi was between her thighs in one stride. He slammed into her as she squeezed her eyes closed. Her hands clenched the edge of the table to keep from being pushed across it.

"I willna climax until ye tell me to," Blair moaned. She wanted him to know she understood. He'd never told her not to do something before, and the one time he did, she ignored his request. She wouldn't do it a second time.

"God, nay. Fuck. Damn it, Blair. I shouldnae have said that. I'm nay holding yer pleasure hostage, and I'm nae going to control ye. What the hell am I doing?"

"Hardi, I want to wait until ye give me permission," Blair insisted as she gripped his forearms. "Just dinna make me wait too long. I—oh God, Hardi. I'm so close. I—" Blair squeezed her eyes closed as she concentrated on trying not to climax. Hardi pulled her from the table and sank into the chair next to him.

"Ye're going to ride ma cock, and I'm going to watch every moment of ye shattering from ma shaft filling yer cunny." Hardi's fingers bit into Blair's bottom as he guided her hips up and down while her hands gripped the back of the chair above Hardi's shoulders.

"Tell me I can, Hardi," Blair begged. "Hardi? Hardi?" She could feel her core tightening, and she was losing her battle. "Hardwin!"

"Aye, *mo ghaol*, ye will spend for me right now, and I will follow ye."

Blair leaned forward, unable to support the weight of her torso. Hardi grasped her breast and suckled before biting her nipple. Blair succumbed to the waves of pleasure that burst through her, and she felt Hardi's cock pulse within her. She draped her weary body over Hardi as he kissed her cheek and neck, cooing to her as his hand stroked her back and bottom. When she could speak again, she cupped his face and pressed gentle kisses against his mouth.

"I'm sorry, Hardi. Ye're right. Ye never tell me nay. Ye never tell me what to do. But I'm too used to doing what I want. I feel like I have to prove maself to yer clan, but I should have kenned I never have to prove maself to ye. What ye asked was reasonable, and I didna even consider it. There is sometimes a fine line between being free and being foolhardy. I stepped over that line today. I'm sorry I—" Blair broke off. "I dinna even ken how to say it. Upset ye. Frightened ye. Worried ye. Angered ye. I dinna ken. I just dinna ever want to make ye fear losing me, and I dinna ever want to be a source of pain to ye."

"I ken, Blair. I overreacted from fear. Fear of losing ye, fear of hurting again, fear of losing maself to ma grief. But I willna ever use our coupling again to control ye. Making love to ye is never aboot having power over ye. I shouldnae have done it."

Blair bit her bottom lip as she sat up. Hardi shook his head at her sheepish mien. "Ye liked that, didna ye?"

"Aye," Blair squeaked. "Mayhap I dinna always have to be—" Blair shook her head, once more unsure of what word she wanted. "Mayhap I should enjoy ye taking charge from time to time."

"Only if ye're by ma side to tell me how," Hardi grinned and ducked away as Blair playfully swatted at him. Hardi helped Blair back into her gown before they sat at the table and discussed what Blair discovered and what to do moving forward. Hardi would investigate later that night with Donald, who remained at Tor Castle. Blair didn't ask to join him, but he explained why he wouldn't take her. He didn't want her skirts to cause her to fall or slow her down, and he worried about the uneven footing. He didn't mention the obvious—they didn't know who they might meet down there. The day dragged onto until the keep settled for the night, and it was time for Hardi to meet Donald and explore.

FORTY-FOUR

H ardi and Donald held the smallest torches Blair could make. She'd wrapped the tops in less linen than usual and doused them with less pitch. While they created less light, they would also burn out faster. The men agreed to light one torch and keep the other for when the first died. Both were trained warriors, so there was little need to speak. The only words they exchanged before entering the storeroom was a heated argument about who would lead. Donald insisted that the laird stand behind him, so he could shield Hardi from any attack. Hardi refused to send someone to risk their life if he couldn't lead the way. Donald shook his head.

"Laird, ye willna lead anyone if ye die over who goes first into a tunnel. Besides, if ye die, yer wife will kill me, anyway. I'd rather it be by an enemy's hand than hers. The enemy will be more merciful," Donald grinned.

"He's right," Blair hissed. She'd promised to return to their chamber and lock and bar their door after Hardi and Donald entered the storeroom. "Hardi, please."

Hardi held the lit torch, and he could see the fear in Blair's eyes. The first week he'd been at Dunrobin,

Lachlan dared Blair to climb the tallest tree he'd ever seen. Even as a seven year old, she wanted to prove herself. She'd scaled higher than any of the children watching imagined, but she stepped on a branch that snapped under her foot, and she slid several feet before catching herself against the trunk. Hardi would never forget the unadulterated fear he'd seen in Blair's eyes as she clung to the tree and caught her breath. She'd been able to make her way back down, but her legs gave out when her feet touched the ground. Hardi was the one who caught her. He helped her back to the keep, and it was the first time they sat together before the fire in the Great Hall. He recognized that same fear now.

"Vera well," Hardi conceded and handed the torch to Donald. Blair made to turn around, but Hardi stopped her as he kissed her deeply. "I'm coming back." Blair nodded as she turned away. Hardi recognized Blair's fear stemmed from this being a personal plot against Hardi. His wife was made of sterner stuff, and while she would worry any time he rode out to battle, he understood what made this different.

Hardi followed Donald down a ladder before they eased their way along the tunnel. Their eyes soon adjusted to the dim light, and Donald moved the torch from side to side to cast light onto the walls. They looked for any markings that the diggers might have left. Hardi kept a picture of the keep's layout in his mind. After five minutes, Hardi was certain they were beyond the barmkin and into the open field outside the eastern wall. They were walking in Inverlochy's direction. They walked at a brisk pace as the tunnel stretched on, wanting to reach as far as they could before the first torch burned out. Hardi estimated they walked for nearly half an hour before they hit what they thought was a dead end. Hardi nudged Donald's elbow up to shine light on the tunnel's ceiling. Donald glanced back at him when they noticed two logs and some brush covered a hole wide enough for a large man to pass through.

Donald handed the torch to Hardi before stretching to move the foliage aside. When they could see the stars, they froze and waited. No alarm sounded, and no faces appeared. Propping the torch against the wall, Hardi gave Donald a boost so he could pull himself through the opening. Donald scanned the surrounding area, looking for any movement or reflection off of metal. They were close to a copse of trees that would make an excellent place to hide or serve as a staging site for an attack. He peered into the treetops to search for movement, but when he was satisfied that they were alone, he looked down at Hardi and nodded. Hardi extinguished the torch and tossed both up to Donald. He would leave no evidence that anyone was in the tunnel. Donald lay on his belly and reached down to help Hardi when he jumped. Hardi gripped Donald's arms while the guard pulled, making it easier for Hardi to climb out.

"Ye dinna look so heavy, Laird," Donald whispered. Hardi only grinned as the men drew their swords. They had a long walk back to the keep, and neither wanted to be unprepared lest they encounter man or beast. Hardi recognized where they were and gestured toward the trees. He wanted to learn if there was anything nearby that could give him a clue to who built the tunnel and who planned to use it.

They were close enough to Inverlochy that the ground was still muddy from the previous day's rain. It was easy for Hardi and Donald to spot multiple sets of tracks. They noticed more than one set of hoofprints, and Hardi kneeled beside a set of smaller footprints. He gestured for Donald to look.

"These could be a woman's, but they're deeper set than I would expect. The ground is soft but not boggy. Whoever it was, they were heavier than ye would expect for such a short print," Hardi mused. Donald nodded and pointed to a set of hoofprints he found.

"This horse either carried two riders or something vera heavy. It's too deep set as well," Donald whispered. "Do ye see aught else?" Hardi shook his head, but they both continued to search the area surrounding the hole. When they came up with nothing, they moved the logs and branches back to what they believed matched what they found. It was difficult to tell from above. They jogged back to the keep, avoiding the moonlight and casting a shadow. They risked being seen from light reflecting off their metal blades, so they kept them pointed down and close to their sides. Rather than enter through the postern gate, they slipped over the wall and onto the battlements in the one area that was most poorly lit. They parted ways, and Hardi went to his chamber.

"I'm surprised at how far the tunnel stretches," Hardi explained as he stripped out of his filthy clothes. Blair hid them, intending to launder them herself after her next bath. She didn't want anyone to get wind that Hardi was covered in dirt at some point. "I recognized where it ended. We were near that grove of trees aboot halfway to Inverlochy. It was far beyond where any Cameron guard could see from the battlements. It must have taken months for them to dig, and it's long enough that hundreds of warriors could pass through. That means there could be multiple waves during the attack."

Blair chewed on her fingernail before speaking.

"Do ye think we erred bringing the men from Inverlochy? Did we just invite the enemy to supper?"

"I'm worried aboot that too. If the MacDonald's are part of this attack, the guards who came with us will only make it easier for their fellow clansmen." Hardi scrubbed his face and neck with soap before leaning over the ewer as Blair poured water onto his hair. She made quick work of lathering and scrubbing his locks. Once he was toweling dry his hair, Hardi mentioned what he and Donald found. "There were several sets of footprints, but one stood out to me. It was smaller—shorter and narrower—than a man's. It was deeply set into the mud, as though the person weighed quite a lot for such a small print. We noticed something similar with a set of hoofprints. They were deeper than the others, as though there were two riders or they brought something vera heavy to the site."

Blair dropped the bar of soap into the basin of water, making a plop and splash. "Small but heavy? Robena."

"What?" Hardi's brow furrowed.

"She wouldnae ride a horse alone with how far along she is. I saw no one else at Inverlochy who could have made prints like ye describe. She can read and write like I can, but I suspect only Scots. She's comfortable using it because she's a Lowlander."

"But she's a woman," Hardi stammered. He backed away when Blair grabbed the soap and looked ready to hurl it at him.

"Ye noticed?" Blair snapped.

"For better or worse, when I think aboot how yer mind works, I dinna think of a typical woman. If it's Robena who's masterminding this, then she as intelligent as ye. I've never gotten that impression."

"Neither did I, but it explains some expressions I caught. Once we handfasted, she changed. I thought

355

Artair pressured her to distance herself or that she didna think a handfast was enough to mean ye and I should couple." Blair stepped around the washstand to stand beside Hardi near the fire. "She didna like kenning we were coupling because it means I could be carrying yer heir."

"And if ye are, then even if I die, there is someone who could rightfully claim the lairdship. We wouldnae ken if ye carried a son until after the bairn was born." Hardi frowned. "It wasna just disgust that she kenned what we were doing. It was anger that something, or someone, stood in her way. Ye're just as much a target as I am."

"But why? If it is Robena, and that's assuming she isnae just aware of Artair's plan and joined him, what does she have to gain? Who is she linked to here?" Blair puzzled.

"It's nae Artair," Hardi reasoned. "He's a fine warrior and a good chieftain, but he isnae a strategist and planner like this. There are too many parts to this plan for him. He's straightforward in his tactics."

"Then we are back to Robena. Nae only do I wonder who she's connected to here, how is she linked to a clan wanting to attack ye?"

"What do ye ken aboot her from before she married?"

"Nae much. She left within a few sennights of ma arrival." Blair tried to recall what she'd seen three years ago. A memory scratched at the back of her mind as she attempted to recall any details. "She's the eldest daughter of Laird Napier."

Hardi shook his head in confusion. He'd never heard of the clan before.

"They're vera small, just outside of Stirling. They're surrounded by the Livingstones to the south, the Buchannans to the west, and the Grahams to the north. They dinna have any septs I ken of. I only ken who they are because they're close to Stirling." Blair twisted her mouth as she continued to think. "They're small but prosperous enough to support themselves. As a laird's daughter, she would have been suitable as another laird's bride or for an heir. But I dinna think her dowry would include much land, if any. I canna guess how much else she brought to her marriage. That's likely why she married Artair. He's chieftain of his branch, but I bet she grew up thinking she would marry a laird. She runs a keep, but she kens it's nae hers." Blair shrugged, unsure what else to offer. She felt betrayed that Robena might be part of the conspiracy, might even be the ringleader. She'd gone out of her way to help Robena, sympathizing with her condition and how Artair treated her. Now Blair wondered what happened behind closed doors and whether Robena had more power than she appeared. Blair was relieved she'd revealed nothing too private while they talked.

Hardi and Blair climbed into bed and lay on their backs as Blair's head rested against Hardi's shoulder. Her mind was still abuzz, and she could tell Hardi's was the same. The fingers to the arm beneath Blair's head caressed the satiny skin of her shoulder and upper arm. The touch was lulling her to sleep, but every time she thought she might drift off, another thought came to her.

"I want to ken where all the dirt they moved went," Hardi announced. "They must have started the tunnel where Donald and I came out. They couldnae have started in the storeroom because they could never haul away that much without being noticed. Even if they worked only at night, someone would notice the heaps. And they finished sooner than the missive indicated. There were nay signs of wagon wheels near the hoofprints. They drew away the last of the dirt before the rain. Those prints were from earlier today."

"With the possibility of so many men moving through the tunnel, do ye think they intend to reinforce it? Is that why they dinna consider it done? Or could there be another section ye didna see?"

"Naught branched off, but mayhap there is another section. But I canna think why it wouldnae connect to the one I was in."

Blair jerked upright as she finally pulled forth the memory she searched for. She squinted in the dark as she tried to recollect all the details.

"Blair?" Hardi sat up beside her, fearful of her sudden movement. His hand hovered against her back. She twisted to face Hardi.

"I remembered that Robena used to part of a group of ladies-in-waiting who were notoriously unkind to the rest of us. It was the same group who made Maude's life miserable. Until Kieran sent her away for embarrassing their clan and for the hateful things she said to Maude, his sister Madeline was the unofficial leader. I remember now that Robena wasna safe from Madeline's barbs. I canna remember the things Madeline and her friends said to Robena, but it boiled down to Robena being a poor country cousin with nay dowry to lure a mon of consequence. They taunted her for marrying only a chieftain. I dinna think being from a small clan mattered until then, but it was undoubtedly humiliating to have Madeline and the others shame her for it."

"I canna tell ye how glad I am ye arenae at court anymore. It sounds wretched," Hardi murmured.

"It could be. It was for Maude. I havenae missed it for a moment, and I'd ask to stay here when ye return to pay the geld."

"Assuming I have land to pay for and coin to pay

with," Hardi grumbled. "But what does yer memory of Robena mean?"

"I dinna ken that it means aught, but jealousy, shame, resentment. They may all motivate her. If she's aught like Madeline, and I'm guessing she is since they were friends, she will hold a grudge. If she canna take it out on her family, she will hold it against anyone who has what she wants but canna have." Blair cleared her throat before asking Hardi an uncomfortable question. "Can men—um—perform even at Artair's age? I mean at a certain point, women canna have more bairns, but can a mon sire them?"

Hardi laughed, "Are ye worried ye will grow auld and unsatisfied while I shrivel up next to ye?" Hardi pinched Blair's nipple and gave her a smacking kiss. "Some men sire bairns until their last breath as an auld mon. Others find their cock doesnae work as they age. I dinna ken aboot Artair, and I dinna want to."

"Aye, but unless there is something wrong with Robena, they married more than three years ago, and she's only now carrying their first child. I mean I ken it can take a long time even when there's naught wrong, but it makes me wonder."

"Only a chieftain's wife and nay bairn to show for it. I can see how that would anger a woman," Hardi conceded.

Blair laid back against her pillow as she wished she knew more about Robena's life at Inverlochy. "I'm going to ask Donald to fish around with the Inverlochy men and see what he can learn aboot Robena. Something isnae right." Blair and Hardi abandoned their conversation for more pleasurable pursuits before both fell sound asleep.

FORTY-FIVE

Blair looked up from the children she spoke to as two riders galloped through the portcullis. At first glance, it appeared there was a riderless horse with them, but then she saw long objects wrapped in Cameron and Sutherland plaids draped over the animal. She looked to the riders, but she already knew it was Tomas and his companion. They'd returned far sooner than she expected. She sent the children to fetch Hardi from the lists, then walked to the recently arrived guardsmen.

"Tomas..." Blair realized she still didn't know the other man's name. She was embarrassed to stand there, blinking, without a clue how to address the guard.

"Roddy, ma lady," the man offered without judgement.

"Thank ye," Blair smiled. "Ye are back before I expected. The laird is on his way."

"I'm here," Hardi's deep voice came from behind Blair. She turned to see Hardi approaching, the hem of his leine pulled up to swipe his face. A glimpse of his rippled abdomen shot a blazing streak of desire through Blair, but she reminded herself this was the least appropriate time to ogle her husband. "Tomas, Roddy, ye're back soon. And with others." Hardi spotted the bodies as soon as he saw the horses. Grief overtook him once more, and he fought to keep his voice even. But it was more than he could manage to acknowledge the men were dead.

"Aye, ma laird," Tomas frowned. "We should speak somewhere private."

Blair noticed several men watching them. She beckoned them and quietly asked that they take the bodies to the kirk. She would arrange burials later. She and Hardi led the way to their solar, and once inside, they waited for the food and drink Blair requested to arrive before beginning their conversation. They pulled chairs close together, so they could keep their voices low.

"We discovered Bran's horse less than a day's ride from here. He stood munching on a cluster of grass when we rode up," Roddy began. "I called out to him, kenning his name. He nodded his head but didn't budge. When I went to gather his reins, I noticed something had disturbed the earth near him. When I dug, I found Bran, face-up in a shallow grave. So shallow I'd only used ma hands to move the dirt." Roddy shook his head and looked away.

"Once we lifted Bran out," Tomas continued. "We notice several other mounds. We unearthed the bodies of other men. Ma lady, two of them were Sutherlands. Anders and Samuel."

Blair covered her mouth with her hands as tears welled in her eyes. Both men were younger than her and had only recently become messengers for her clan. She knew neither had much experience. She thought of their families and tears trickled from her eyes. Hardi pulled Blair's chair closer to him and wrapped his arm around her. He remembered the men as callow youths who were still carrying wooden swords when he left Dunrobin.

Roddy reached into his sporran and lifted several missives from it. He handed them to Hardi before explaining. "We found these on the men. It looks like missives coming or going to Dunrobin never made it."

Blair examined each one, some in her penmanship and some in her father's. She clutched the one she recognized had Hardi's handwriting. She held it up. "They dinna ken. They likely dinna ken I even left Stirling."

Blair opened each one, putting the ones she'd written in order. Then she read the ones from her father. The oldest acknowledged Hardi's interest in courting Blair and granted them permission. Blair's lips twitched with a smile, but it didn't last as she read the others. They asked why she hadn't written and where she was.

"They ken I'm nae at court. I think when they didna hear from me, Da must have written King Robert. Or Mama might have written to Queen Elizabeth. If they didna get a response from Stirling or dinna get a response to any of their missives sent to Inverlochy, they willna ken where I am or that we married." Blair held up a missive and closed her eyes. "Lachlan doesnae ken I asked him to come."

Hardi looked at the exhausted men before him. "Thank ye for this. I canna send a detail right now to recover the other men, but do ye ken which clans they were from?"

"Royal messengers, ma laird," Roddy explained.

"Then they likely have nay idea where I am," Blair choked out around her tears. "They must be besides themselves."

"Get more to eat, get cleaned up, and retire for

the evening," Hardi instructed Roddy and Tomas. "Ye have the next two days off watch and training." Hardi and Blair waited until they were alone before Blair sobbed. Hardi lifted her into his lap as she cried.

"I'd suggest sending a messenger to Cairren since she's closest, asking her to send word to Mama and Da. But I fear for any rider leaving here. I dinna dare try to send word to Maude." Blair wiped the tears from her face once she could speak. She sat up and looked at Hardi.

"Whoever this is kenned to watch for the royal messengers. They kenned missives were headed to Dunrobin before we left Stirling. But how?"

"Ma guards. Someone among ma guards is selling secrets," Hardi growled. He shifted Blair to her seat and went to the door. He called out to a nearby servant and ordered the guards who accompanied him to Stirling to appear before him. "One or all of them betrayed me. Either they're part of this plot or they intended to inform Faolán and Drostan, but either way our enemy intercepted the messages." Hardi felt the anger that bubbled at a simmer while Roddy and Tomas relayed their tale rising to a full boil, and his body felt on fire. He prayed he had the patience not to kill any of the men before he got his answers.

They didn't have long to wait before a knock sounded at the door. Hardi ripped it open and glared at the four men. "Strip off yer plaids and remove the dirks from yer boots. Show me yer forearms and thighs," Hardi demanded. He wouldn't allow any of them into the chamber armed while Blair was with him. He didn't trust any of them. One by one, they entered the solar in only their leines and boots. Hardi led Blair behind their desk, with only a wall at their backs. "One to each corner and the others against the side walls."

Blair listened in silence as Hardi did what he could to make it difficult for the men to swarm them should they attack. She appreciated his plan and his foresight to keep any weapons from entering the chamber with the men. Hardi drew his broadsword from the sheath slung across his back and held it loosely in his hand.

"Which one of ye?" Hardi offered no more to his demand. He was certain they'd learned of the dead bodies of the messengers, even with so little time since their arrival. They would understand what he wanted to know. No one stepped forward. "Ye had the courage to betray me, but ye dinna have the courage to admit it. I will give ye one more chance to step forward. Dead men are silent too."

"It was Dunn," a blond man stepped forward. "I have a wife and two weans to provide for. I amnae going down with this sinking ship."

"The ship has sunk," Hardi snarled. "Ye should have thought aboot that, Wylie, while ye kept the secret."

Hardi turned his attention to the man Blair learned was Dunn. He looked terrified, and Blair was certain he should be. She'd never seen the warrior side of Hardi before, and she wasn't certain she wanted to witness the outcome of his deadly stare. She saw the ferocity and fearlessness in Hardi's eyes that enabled him to survive the trial by combat battle against the Mackintoshes. He'd been the only one of the Camerons to survive, and now she understood why. She also understood just the depth of underestimation people held for her husband.

"Why?" Hardi barked. Dunn refused to speak. The silence tempted Hardi to run Dunn through, but he would get no answers from a dead man. Hardi spoke slowly, enunciating each word "Yer wife is purely Cameron, isnae she? There is nay clan for her and yer weans to turn to once I banish them."

Blair watched, but Dunn didn't blink at Hardi's threat. She wondered what went through the man's mind to test Hardi.

"Ye think the Hardwin ye kenned before we each wed, the one who went to the tavern with ye and drank alongside ye, still exists. He died the day ma uncle did. But a piece of him chipped away with the death of every mon in his family. What ye have left is the Laird Cameron ye see before ye. Dunn, dinna think I will take mercy on ye or yer family. I will kill ye where ye stand, and yer family will be in the woods before nightfall. I'd say test me and find out, but ye willna ken aught once ye're dead. Mayhap ye're wife will find a tavern to work in while yer children beg. How long do ye think it'll be before yer weans understand what their mama does to keep them fed?"

Blair swallowed her gasp. She wanted to believe Hardi was bluffing, but in her heart she knew he wasn't. Treachery within his personal guard jeopardized more than just Hardi's life. It spoke of dishonor and dissent among the men sworn to protect the innocent members of the clan. If he couldn't trust his warriors, he had no way to keep his people safe.

"It was Drostan," Dunn admitted. "Before we left, he told me he had someone from Inverlochy who would watch us and report to him what ye did and where ye went. He couldnae enter the castle, so I informed the mon of yer time spent with Lady Cameron. He must have kenned to look for missives sent to and from Lady Cameron. I didna have aught to do with Bran's death or any of the messengers. At least nae directly. I didna ken someone would kill them."

"And who was it ye reported to?" Hardi demanded.

"I dinna ken for sure, ma laird, but from the look of the mon, he's related to Artair. Ma guess is he's the chieftain's bastard."

"Lady Cameron sent missives after leaving Stirling, how were those discovered?" Hardi asked.

"When we left court, so did the mon. He was at Inverlochy and kenned aboot ma lady's letters and aboot ye meeting," Dunn explained.

"What did Drostan have over ye that made ye willing to betray yer laird?" Blair wondered.

"Naught but ma family's lives. He said that he would kill them if I didna do as he said. He told me that by asking me, I kenned of his plan. He wouldnae leave me alive to tell anyone. He warned that if the messages ceased coming or his mon at Inverlochy informed him that I didna cooperate, he'd kill ma wife and weans."

"What's the mon's name?" Blair pressed.

"I think it's Murray." Dunn replied.

"He's one of Artair's bastards," Hardi noted. He looked at each of the men in turn. Their lack of loyalty concerned him. Dunn might have been the only one trading secrets, but the other three were aware of his betrayal and did nothing to stop him or warn Hardi. "For yer dishonor, Wylie, Loman, and Garrett, I strip ye of yer title as members of the laird's personal guard. Ye will stand three months' watch, and ye will personally explain to Bran's parents and widow why he is dead. Dunn, ye have a new home. Ye shall reside in the dungeon for the indefinite future. I may release ye, or I may leave ye to rot. We shall see how the wind blows. Wylie, Loman, Garrett, leave. Dunn stays."

The men didn't need to be told twice. None

looked in Dunn's direction, and none dared meet Hardi's eye. The three men glanced in Blair's direction and dipped their heads before hurrying to the door. They were out of the chamber in a matter of seconds.

FORTY-SIX

Hardi waited until the three disgraced guards traipsed out of the solar before he raised his sword and went to stand before Dunn. He poked the tip of his sword against Dunn's belly. Finally, the man flinched.

"One sneeze, and I could drive this through yer gut," Hardi hissed as he leaned to whisper to Dunn. "Ye ken more. Speak." Hardi backed away from Dunn, but he didn't lower his sword.

"I dinna ken all the details," Dunn clarified. "But I ken there is a plot to kill ye during an attack. Drostan and Faolán were aware, but they werenae the ones who thought of it. I dinna ken who did. I dinna ken when, but I think the Macphersons and Davidsons plan to overrun the keep. Someone at Inverlochy is behind this, but I dinna have a guess who. There's a tunnel leading into the keep from Inverlochy's direction. I think the Macphersons and Davidsons intend to breach the keep's defenses from within."

"And?" Hardi pressed. Blair saw the sweat dripping along Dunn's forehead and heard the tremor in the man's voice. He understood what was at stake now that he was alone with Hardi and Blair.

"Whoever it is at Inverlochy, they didna want the Sutherlands to come for Lady Cameron. They dinna want them aiding ye. The Macphersons and Davidsons are to make camp near Inverlochy and attack at dusk two days from now."

"Why do ye think it's the Macphersons and Davidsons? What proof have ye?"

Dunn shrugged. "I ken it's clans from Clan Chattan Confederation, so they seemed most likely to me. I mean after what happened with the Mackintoshes, I figured…"

"Ye've helped dig. Who else?" Blair asked from across the room. Dunn's eyes shifted to her.

"Faolán's three oldest sons. The last thing we're to do is reinforce the walls with beams, so the tunnel can handle having ten or fifteen score men pass through."

"Three hundred men is more than the Macphersons and Davidsons combined. Who else is involved?"

"I truly dinna ken that, Laird. Mayhap the MacDonalds, since someone at Inverlochy is leading this."

"And who is it here? Who's the treacherous bastard leading ye if it wasna Drostan and Faolán? Who gives the commands now?" Hardi pressed. He watched Dunn's nostrils flair ever so slightly at the word bastard. Hardi knew it wasn't just Faolán's bastards, but he didn't know who else that could be. Faolán wasn't the only man in the clan to have conceived children on the wrong side of the blanket, but none of the men nor their children seemed reasonable suspects.

"Faolán gave a standing order that nay matter what happens to him or Drostan, the digging was to continue. That's all I ken." Dunn lowered his head. "That's far more than I ever wanted to. For what it's worth, Laird Cameron, I willna ever put anyone's safety over ma family's. That meant turning traitor, and I regret that, but I dinna regret protecting them."

"I understand the position Drostan placed ye in, and I respect yer devotion to yer family. But I canna overlook that Faolán and Drostan are both dead, and ye didna step forward once the threat was gone," Hardi explained.

"The threat isnae gone, ma laird. If I spoke out, Faolán's sons would have come for me. They will ken I told ye, and now ma family will likely die because of it." Dunn shuddered as sweat dripped from the tip of his nose.

"Bring yer wife and children to the keep," Blair stepped forward. "I will find a safe place for them, for however long they need it."

Hardi nodded but didn't take his eyes off Dunn. "Who stands against me among the men?"

Dunn's eyes widened. "None, Laird. That's why whoever is doing this is relying on other clans to attack. They ken our clan will stand with ye. Mayhap one of the clans wants Tor Castle for their own, but whoever is behind this kens the men willna fight against ye. Ye were one of us for more time than ye've been laird. We've fought beside ye; many of us are alive because ye saved our arses. We may nae have fought the Mackintoshes, but we saw what happened. We saw ye fight. We saw ye defending yer cousins, and we ken what ye endured. The men are loyal to ye, Laird." Dunn took a shuddering breath. "Ma fate is clear. But for ma family, I was loyal to ye, too."

"Ye will serve yer time in the dungeon, but nae until after this bluidy battle is over. If we lose, ye'll likely be dead, anyway. Trade sides during the fight, and I will cut out yer heart and hand it to yer youngest child. Until then, find men who can keep a secret. Where is the dirt from the tunnel?" Hardi asked.

"Nae far from here. It's to the north of the beginning of the tunnel," Dunn explained.

"I want ye to take five men with ye tonight. Ye will fill enough sacks with dirt to build two walls with it from floor to ceiling in the tunnel. When ye return ye will go into the tunnel and stack one wall, then construct a reinforced wooden wall. You will build a second dirt wall to give us three layers of defense. If anyone learns of what ye do, I will cut out yer heart and hand it to yer youngest child."

"Aye, ma laird," Dunn nodded. Hardi backed away and made room for Dunn to slip past him toward the door. As he reached for the handle, Hardi called out to him.

"And Dunn." Hardi waited for the man to look back at him. "I may still kill ye just because I can."

FORTY-SEVEN

H ardi stood just within the tunnel, watching Dunn and the other men work. He'd sent Tomas and Donald with his men to fetch the dirt. The two Sutherlands stood watch in the storeroom as Hardi monitored his men's progress. While the men went for the dirt, he and Blair discussed what they would do next. Knowledge of the impending attack could no longer remain a secret. Clan members living along the enemies' route would arrive the next day and their appearance would raise questions. Hardi and Blair needed to prepare their people for the worst.

It was the middle of the night when Tomas, Donald, and the others returned. Before they set to work in the tunnel, he ordered them to seize Faolán's children. They took the oldest sons to the dungeon where Hardi could keep them isolated and unable to warn anyone. They placed the younger children and their mothers under Blair's care.

She found storerooms for them to sleep in, giving them blankets and bedding. They left none of Faolán's offspring or their mothers free to sound an alarm or alert their encroaching foe. Blair did what she could to allay their fears, but there was little she could say. The men in the dungeon would likely die for their sins, and Blair prayed the clan would survive the assault. She explained the situation was temporary, but the men's choices caused the situation. She posted guards that Hardi sent to her.

It was still dark when Hardi sent his men with Tomas and Donald for a second trip. They were to fill the wagons with the remaining dirt, then hide them along the western wall of the keep. It abutted a forest that would protect them from view. Despite arguments against it, Hardi explained that once the enemy began entering the tunnel, he needed Tomas and Donald to take the wagons to the tunnel's entrance. When the last of the invaders dropped within, they were to dump both wagons full of dirt and seal the hole. Tomas and Donald refused to leave Blair, but Hardi explained the task was likely what would win them the battle. He didn't trust anyone as much as he did the two men devoted to keeping Blair safe. He reminded them that the wall they built would create a temporary logjam and would buy them time while the attackers tried to break through it.

With little sleep before morning came, Blair and Hardi stood before their clan as the members broke their fast, explaining what they could and preparing the clan for what was to come. They divided their tasks and went their separate ways. Hardi ordered his best hunters to capture anything they could find before midafternoon. He sent his fastest rider toward Inverlochy to discover whether anyone camped outside the castle. When he learned there was no one there, he mustered three details to alert the outlying villages, praying they would get there before their enemies passed through. It was a slim window of time if the attack was to be dusk the next day.

Blair arranged for servants to clear out storage

rooms for the villagers who would arrive that day and for the ones who lived outside the bailey walls. She, Dolina, and Mordag met to plan how to ration the food if there was a siege. She ordered men Hardi sent her to move every food store they had into the undercroft. She wouldn't risk the storerooms being raided or the storage buildings being burned with their supplies within. They were already in dire straits without losing everything.

Hardi showed Tomas and Donald the space behind the Murphy door, explaining he would send Blair there the moment it appeared their defenses wouldn't hold. When he told her that he wanted her to hide there if the tides turned against them, she insisted that she needed to protect the women and children. He warned her that he would carry her there, dump her in the hidden space, then lock her into the solar if she didn't go willingly. He'd seen the spark of defiance in her eyes and reminded her in no uncertain terms that after the amount of times they coupled, there was a good chance she might be pregnant. She covered her belly with her hands and nodded once.

By the time they fell into bed, the day had exhausted them. But they clung to one another, neither saying aloud that it might be their last night together. Despite their fatigue, they made love throughout the night, desperation warring with hope. They slept sporadically, coiled together, desperate for no space to separate them. Morning came far too soon, but they couldn't ignore the duties they each assumed on the days they became Laird and Lady Cameron. Before they left their chamber, Blair stopped Hardi with a request.

"*Mo chridhe*, if ma parents hadnae taught me what they did, I wouldnae have kenned even a sliver of what I do. I couldnae have helped prepare our keep and village for battle. If I bear us a bairn one day, could we name a lass Amelia or a lad Hamish for Mama and Da?" Blair clasped her hands together so tightly her knuckles went white.

"If ye bear me a bairn regardless of whether there's a battle, ye may name the wee one whatever ye want. I'll gladly let ye choose whatever ye want after enduring childbirth, *mo bhràmair bonnie*." Hardi called her his bonnie bride before he wrapped his arms around her and lifted her off her feet as they kissed.

───────

As dusk approached, Blair stood beside Hardi on the battlements. She'd spent the day assigning families to spaces in the storerooms and the Great Hall. She'd overseen extra food prepared for the swelling number of people depending upon the keep to feed and shelter them. She admired how Mordag efficiently distributed bedding and supplies to families who came with nothing or not enough. Hardi gathered the farmers who arrived with the pitchforks and shovels he requested. He discussed with them how best they could serve as part of the keep's defenses. He assigned his warriors to their battle stations and checked that men hung cauldrons of oil along the walls in case the attack should also come from outside the walls. His archers spent the day and the one prior helping the fletcher make as many arrows as they could. They weren't of the best quality, but they would fly straight and there were plenty of them. He looked over the southern wall to where Tomas and Donald waited with horses hitched to the wagons.

"Promise me ye will go inside the moment it's clear the enemy will breach the keep. Remain in there with the other women and children. Do what ye can to keep them calm. I have men assigned to protect all of ye, and they will barricade the doors as soon as everyone is inside. But they canna wait if people dinna hurry within."

"I ken, Hardi. Promise me ye willna be foolish. Ye dinna have aught to prove. Our clan already kens ye're the best warrior, and they ken ye're a fine laird. Ye're a hero without getting yerself killed. I ken ye worry aboot me, but I will be inside and guarded. Ye willna be. Promise me, ye'll be careful." She knew better than to ask a warrior to promise not to die.

"Blair, I willna do aught that will keep me from coming back to ye. I love ye with ma whole heart. Blair Ceana Sutherland, ma love, ye are the one person with whom I can share all that I am. I promise to trust ye and to be honest with ye. I promise to listen to ye, respect ye, and support ye. I promise to do all of this through whatever life brings us: riches or poverty, health or illness, through good times and bad, until the end of ma days." Hardi repeated the vows they'd said together only a few weeks earlier. It felt closer to a lifetime after the upheaval they experienced since they rode through the gates of Inverlochy.

"Hardwin Fionn Cameron, ma love, ye are the one person with whom I can share all that I am. I promise to laugh and play with ye and grow and bend with ye. I promise to cherish every day we have together. I promise to do all of this through whatever life brings us: riches or poverty, health or illness, through good times and bad, until the end of ma days. I love ye more than I ever imagined I could love another person. We have bairns to make and raise."

Just as they had in the orchard and later when Hardi slipped Blair's ring onto her finger, they spoke the last line together. "We are now but one body and one blood. Let us from this day forth be united with one destiny."

They kissed as the sun dipped closer to the horizon. They watched together as Hardi's scout raced toward the keep, lying nearly flat over his horse's neck. It was the signal that men entered the tunnel. Hardi whistled loudly. Tomas and Donald slapped their reins, and each wagon pulled forward. The bell to warn the remaining villagers to enter the bailey peeled.

"They willna run because it's took dark, and they willna want to be winded," Hardi explained. "We have aboot a half an hour." He waggled his eyebrows, hoping to put a smile on Blair's face. "What I could do in that time."

Blair grinned as she strained to kiss him again. "Come back to me with at least one piece, and I will give ye far more than just a half an hour."

"Naughty little imp," Hardi growled as he nipped at her neck and ear. They exchanged a tender kiss before releasing one another. "I love ye, Blair."

"I love ye, Hardi." Blair moved toward the steps, and Hardi watched her cross the bailey. At the keep's door, she turned to wave to him. She stood there for a long moment before they nodded to one another, and Blair went inside.

FORTY-EIGHT

"I t's the Mackintoshes, ma laird." Hardi's scout, Richard, explained. "But it's the Shaws and MacThomases who came with them."

"They brought their septs rather than the Macphersons? Are ye sure the Macphersons arenae moving toward us on land rather than the tunnel?" Hardi pressed.

"Nay. I rode wide of the tunnel's entrance and didna see aught in any direction but the men marching from Inverlochy."

"Were the MacDonalds with them?" It didn't surprise Hardi to hear that the other clans who were a part of the Chattan Confederation were accompanying the Mackintoshes. The Shaws and MacThomases were connected to the Mackintoshes through common ancestry. Once a traditional clan, the Chattans swelled into a community of allied clans through the Mackintoshes and their septs, the Macphersons, the MacBeans, and the MacPhains. The individual clans were not as powerful as others in the central and eastern Highlands, but they were a threat when they united.

"I didna see any of them. That's what was so odd, ma laird. They camped close to Inverlochy Castle, so the MacDonalds had to ken they were there, but there werenae any in sight."

"Ride to Inverlochy and watch what goes on there. If there is any sign of the MacDonalds coming, make haste back here. We are missing something here. I want to ken if Artair MacDonald is a part of this, or if he's willfully blind to what happens at the keep he's been commanded to protect. For us."

"Aye, ma laird." Richard darted back into the bailey, mounting a fresh horse and riding out. Hardi watched him until he disappeared. He swept his gaze in all directions, but there was no sign of anyone approaching. He had scouts posted to the north, south, and west of Tor Castle; so far, none had returned to raise the alarm.

Hardi made his way to the storeroom where the entrance within Tor now hid beneath crates filled with tools from the blacksmith, farrier, armorer, and sacks of lye. Hardi agreed with Blair's decision to hide the grain and food, but it meant he'd had to think of what he could use to weigh down the hatch. He wasn't convinced the wall built the previous night would hold forever or that the crates would keep the hatch shut permanently, but it would slow the advancing troops and make it difficult for them to leave the storeroom in a hurry. He stationed warriors in the storeroom and down both directions of the passageway.

When he was satisfied that everything was in order, he made his way back to the battlements. He glimpsed Blair as she held a hysterical little boy in the Great Hall. They nodded to one another before Hardi went back outside. He walked the battlements, impatient yet dreading what was to come. The situation was unlike any he'd faced before. If all worked to plan, then there would be no attack and no battle. They would trap the enemy below ground, leaving them to suffocate or starve. If the plan fell apart, he faced an attack from those who broke through the barriers and attacked from the inside as well as the potential for the Mackintoshes and comrades to come from outside the walls.

The minutes ticked by, and nothing happened. When he was certain that the forward warriors would soon meet the dirt and wood wall, Hardi made his way toward the storeroom. He found Blair running from the kitchens in his direction. She looked over her shoulder and called out, "Go, go, go!"

Hardi caught Blair by the arms as he watched warriors he assigned to the passageway carrying vats of what smelled like bubbling tar. In an instant, he realized Blair thought of a solution he never imagined. She would have the men seal the hatch with tar, making it virtually impossible for anyone to hack through it.

"I thought of it after I saw ye go back outside," Blair explained. "I was coming to tell ye once I kenned we had enough birch tar and could heat it fast enough. If they're too late, they can pour it down on the men as they try to climb out of the tunnel."

"Wife, ye are brilliant. Can ye be laird, and I'll be the pretty face at yer side?" Hardi gave her arms a squeeze.

"Keep yer pretty face just as it is now, and we can discuss it later," Blair grinned. "Go."

Hardi squeezed her arms once more and stepped around her. He hadn't taken more than five steps when the keep doors opened and someone called out, "Laird!"

He spun around to find Tomas and Donald running toward him. From the corner of his eye, he caught sight of Blair coming back to his side.

"It worked, ma laird," Donald beamed. "We

waited until the last man went down. By the time we pulled the wagons over the hole, there were nay men in sight. We opened the tail boards, and the dirt rained down on the hole. We heard cries but saw nay one. The dirt piled up too fast for them to shovel it out of the way or to climb. It's sealed now. They will have to fill most of the tunnel to dig their way back out."

"How many men do ye think are down there?" Blair asked.

"Easily ten score, ma lady," Tomas answered.

Blair and Hardi exchanged a glance. Neither wanted to be responsible for the death of two hundred men, but neither could they allow an army to invade Tor Castle. Hardi dismissed Tomas and Donald, then turned to Blair. "What do ye think we do now? Yer idea to tar the hatch was brilliant. Between that and the wall, they shouldn't be able to break into the storeroom any sooner than they can dig their way out."

"We need to ken whether they had anyone hiding who could signal reinforcements. Dunn said up to fifteen score. There could be a hundred men still lurking somewhere."

"I sent Richard back to scout near Inverlochy. I want to ken whether Artair is bringing up the rear or if he's turning a blind eye to what's happening beneath his nose."

"All we can do is wait. I will make sure Dolina and Mordag get food out to the men. Besides that, I dinna ken what to do with maself," Blair admitted.

"I feel the same. I will make ma rounds several more times, but until Richard returns, there is little anyone can do but wait. Why dinna ye see to the food, then get some rest?" Hardi suggested.

"I canna take maself off to bed as though naught is happening. Nae much is going on right this minute, but we are still under attack. Besides, I have too much nervous energy thrumming through me. There is nay way I can rest."

"Then join me at one of the lower tables when I return. I dinna want us sitting at the dais. It'll appear as though we are sitting on thrones watching those below us for entertainment."

"I agree. We sit among our people," Blair nodded.

"I canna tell ye how it makes me feel to hear ye claim ma clan as yers too." Hardi's smile made lines crinkle around his eyes, and deep brackets around his mouth appeared. There was a softness in his hazel eyes that belied the chaotic charge in the air.

"I'm a Cameron. This is ma clan, and this is ma home," Blair's voice was matter of fact, but she returned Hardi's smile. They stood gazing at one another for a long moment before they broke apart to complete their tasks.

The night dragged on as people found places to sleep in the Great Hall or returned to the storerooms Blair assigned them. She sat propped against Hardi as she dozed. Hardi's eyes were closed, but he listened to every sound around them. When he sensed movement coming from the kitchens, he opened his eyes a crack. The ominous form of a man carrying a sword and bucket emerged. Hardi watched the man turn toward the passageway where guards still lined the walls. Hardi eased Blair from his side, but her eyes sprang open.

"Stay here," Hardi whispered against her ear. "If ye hear a whistle, get everyone into as many storerooms as ye can, and tell them to use the tables and benches inside as barricades. Ye must get to the solar as soon as ye can. If I whistle, it's because we're aboot to be overrun."

"What's happening?"

"I dinna ken for sure, but I think I'm aboot to discover our traitor. I love ye," Hardi pressed a quick, hard kiss to Blair's forehead.

"I love ye," she whispered back. She watched Hardi cross the Great Hall, his sword drawn. He moved like a wraith--light on his feet and stealthy. She slipped through the sleeping clan members, taking a place along a wall closer to the passageway. She wouldn't venture down it, but she would make certain she could hear Hardi if he signaled. She held a dirk in each hand as she closed her eyes once more. She was alert, no longer tired. With her eyes closed, she found her sense of hearing was sharper. She sat, still as a statue, and waited.

FORTY-NINE

Hardi crept along the passageway, the shadowy figure several feet ahead of him. He watched as the man stopped before the doorway to the storeroom being guarded. Hardi watched in horror as the shadow thrust his arm forward. There was a bellow, but then all fell silent. The men on guard scrambled to their feet as Hardi charged past them. He entered the storeroom and realized immediately that there were only two guards —now dead—in the room where he'd posted five men earlier that evening. An overpowering odor hit him as he watched the man pour liquid from a bucket over the hatch. Hardi recognized the smell of lye and knew the traitor was trying to dissolve the tar. The scrape of metal against the ground confirmed Hardi's suspicion.

With tools aplenty, it wasn't hard for the mystery man to seize a chisel and hammer. Hardi launched himself at the perpetrator before the unknown man swung the hammer. They crashed to the floor. Hardi didn't try to learn who the lumbering form was. He rained down his fists on the man's temples as he thrashed underneath Hardi. He tried to buck Hardi off of him, but Hardi weighed more and was positioned to control his opponent. Hardi wrapped one hand around the man's throat, making his adversary gag, and his other hand covered the traitor's mouth and nose. When the man stopped flailing, but before he suffocated, Hardi came to his feet and dragged the unconscious man with him.

Guards took the man to Hardi's solar, and he called out to Blair. She ran to him as he reached the solar's door. They each took a torch handed to them. Blair stoked the fire while Hardi lit candles. The unconscious form lay barely moving on the table. Hardi carried his torch to where he could finally see the man's face.

"Osgar?" Hardi was incredulous. He never imagined Osgar would betray him. He glanced toward the door as Paul entered, but stumbled to a stop when he recognized Osgar's beaten face. Paul's eyes mirrored the shock Hardi was certain was evident in his own gaze. It stunned Hardi to have Osgar stretched out before him when he'd suspected Paul. After all, he was the one who warned Hardi not to trust anyone and implied that his own warriors were against him, even though Dunn assured him of the opposite. He wouldn't set aside his doubts about Paul, no matter how the man acted. Hardi spoke to the room at large. "Get me a bucket of water."

"Osgar is behind this?" Paul murmured as he came to stand near Blair and Hardi. "But why?"

"That's what I hope to find out when he comes to," Hardi spat.

Hardi poured a bucket of icy water over the unconscious man, who came to spluttering and thrashing. Hardi drove his fist into Osgar's belly, and the drenched man settled as he wheezed. As he became more aware of his surroundings, Blair watched Osgar's eyes harden as he sneered.

"Ye think tarring a hatch closed will stop two

hundred men. Ye're the fool I always kenned ye to be," Osgar smirked.

"If the tar doesnae work, then the wall I had built just within the entrance will hold them back. Nae to mention the dirt that now fills the other end. Ye sent two hundred men to their deaths," Hardi stated with cold-hearted detachment.

"What?" Osgar stammered.

"Did ye think that if I found one end of the tunnel I wouldnae find the other? Did ye think nay one would notice the dirt left behind? Thank ye for that."

"Ye fucking bastard, I will—" Osgar was interrupted by hammering at the door. "Alas, yer plan is a failure, just as ye are."

"Enter," Hardi called. Richard pushed open the door, but froze as he looked around the chamber. His eyes flitted across everyone standing before resting on Osgar. Richard didn't look surprised, and it sent a shiver down Blair's back.

"Artair is dead, and Lady Robena has had her bairn," Richard explained. He didn't take his eyes of Osgar. "And it's a lass."

"Fucking shite. What good will a daughter do me?" Osgar snarled. Every eye in the chamber had already been on Osgar, but many of those same eyes widened as they heard his words.

"Ye fathered Lady Robena's bairn?" Blair asked.

"Aye. That auld sod hasnae raised his rod in at least a score. Shriveled up like a pea. He kenned all along that someone else was fucking his wife. He thought to pass the bastard off as his own. Prayed she carried a lad. Stupid bitch didna do either of us any good."

"Why?" Hardi snapped.

Osgar turned his head with deliberate slowness, his eyes raking over Hardi before he grinned.

Everyone waited on tenterhooks, but Osgar did nothing but sneer. Blair shifted, and Osgar followed her. His expression morphed into a leer as he ogled her. He grabbed his crotch, squeezing and shaking his cock and bollocks. He stroked his hand over his wool covered cock. "And I'd planned to fuck ye once I killed yer husband. I bet I can make ye scream louder than he can. Ever taken it in the arse, princess?"

Hardi lunged toward Osgar, but Blair was faster. She still held both of her dirks and sent one sailing. It embedded in the wood between Osgar's spread legs. She stepped forward with more menace than any man in the chamber had witnessed.

"I didna miss. It's yer one warning before," she said as she raised her other dirk. "I cut off yer meat and potatoes and serve them as yer supper. Do ye ken what I will do after that? Since ye reminded me how expensive parchment is, I shall do ma drawing on yer chest. A pretty picture of a dead man with his head severed, his entrails hanging across his ribs, and his cock sticking out of his mouth. Threaten ma husband and ma people again, and I will make sure ye are awake for every bluidy minute that I torture ye."

Blair didn't take her eyes off Osgar as her hand whipped forward and yanked her blade free. She stabbed it through the cloth beside where Osgar's hand now protected, rather than fondled, his man parts. Blair leaned all the way forward and whispered. "The only fucking ye'll do is with ma blade up yer arse."

Blair stepped back to where she'd stood near a wall. The men didn't know where to look. They shifted their gazes between Osgar and Blair, shocked that the usually genteel lady spewed such vulgar venom. She didn't flinch or shrink under their scrutiny.

"She's the Earl of Sutherland's daughter. I dinna ken why ye keep assuming she's a mouse," Hardi chortled, but there was no mirth in its sound. He grabbed a fistful of Osgar's hair and jerked his head back as he drove his fist into Osgar's left eye. "Why?"

Osgar remained silent, refusing to speak. Hardi shifted to keep Paul in the corner of his eye while his focus was on Osgar. Another punch did nothing to loosen Osgar's tongue. Seeing the futility of repeatedly hitting the man, Hardi ordered a man to bring a set of blacksmith's tongs and hammer. When the tools arrived, Hardi looked at Paul. There was a resolve in Hardi's eyes that made everyone but Blair want to take a step back. Hardwin Cameron, the battle-hewn warrior who survived what no one else had, stood before them. The drive to remain alive that made him merciless on the battlefield was on display. Every person in the chamber knew Osgar was not long for this world.

FIFTY

"Take his boots off," Hardi instructed Paul. "Stockings too."

Hardi watched Paul from his peripheral vision, making it appear as if he looked at Blair. He could tell that she was doing the same thing. They watched to see if he moved unnaturally slowly or quickly. They watched for any hesitation or eagerness. Neither witnessed anything to hint that the plan involved Paul. Hardi released Osgar's hair and went to stand by the man's feet.

"Hold his ankles," Hardi told Paul. Then he looked at Osgar. "I will break yer foot if ye dinna speak. If that isnae enough, I will cut off each toe until there are none left, or ye speak. Yer choice." Hardi turned his head toward Osgar's feet, raising the hammer. "And if none of that works, I'll give ye to ma wife."

Hardi brought the hammer down on the top of Osgar's right foot. The sound of Osgar's scream and the shattering of bones filled the solar as the men watched in horror. Some were aghast that Osgar hadn't confessed, and others were stunned at Blair and Hardi's ruthlessness. Sweat broke out across Osgar's forehead, and his eyes watered, but he said

391

nothing. Hardi waited, giving him a chance to catch his breath and let his mind work through the pain. When nothing was forthcoming, he slammed the hammer into Osgar's right foot again, breaking more bones.

"Ye will never walk again at this rate," Hardi warned. "A warrior who canna walk is naught."

Osgar glared at Hardi as his body trembled and sweat dripped from his face. He continued his silence. Hardi inhaled deeply and sighed. He picked up the tongs, opening and closing them several times. He clamped the edge of the table and squeezed as hard as he could. The sound of splintering wood and Osgar's heavy breathing filled the room. When Hardi removed the tongs, a deep impression was etched in the wood. He held up the tongs as if to evaluate them before nodding as if he agreed with their strength. He fit the tongs around Osgar's smallest toe and eased into adding pressure. Osgar's knees jerked, but Paul held his ankles like a vice.

"Is there anyone who kens the plot?" Hardi asked Osgar. "It could save ye yer toes."

Osgar looked directly ahead of him, his eyes blank but resting on Paul. Hardi picked up the hammer once more and hovered it over where Paul's hands manacled Osgar's ankles. Paul flinched as he looked up at Hardi.

"Ye were to be his second, werenae ye?" Hardi guessed. Paul released Osgar's ankles and glared at Hardi, but he denied nothing. "A pity, because I intended to name ye as ma second. Now all I will name ye is dead." Hardi drew his dirk and thrust it into Paul's side before pressing downward, slicing him from the inside. He hadn't aimed for any major organs, so there was a chance Paul could heal if the wound was attended. If he didn't confess, Paul's death would be slow as he bled out. "Ye ken ye can survive this, so what say ye?"

"What is there to say?" Paul hissed as he pressed his hands against his words. "Ye'll kill me nay matter what, so why should I speak?"

Hardi's mouth turned down with a brief twitch before he explained, "Ye can tell me the truth, and face a merciful death with some honor as a warrior brother I've fought many battles alongside. Or I will let Blair decide. Ye've seen her hand down her sentences before. She is just in her decisions. But ye have also seen her mercy has limits." Hardi grinned. "If I were ye, I'd stake ma fate with me rather than her. I'm gentler."

Paul turned to look at Blair. Whatever he found in her visage made him nod. "I was to be Osgar's second. Ye figured that out. But nay one has ever figured out Drostan had a son. A legitimate son. Drostan handfasted with Faolán's wife before their fathers forced her to marry Faolán. She bore Drostan a son after she married Faolán, and they threatened to kill her and the bairn if she didna say the bairn was stillborn. It was the same day as ma aunt's two-day-old son died. They passed Osgar off to ma aunt and uncle with a promise that Drostan would provide for Osgar if they gave him a home."

Paul looked at Osgar as the man seethed. Pure hatred radiated from Osgar as he glared at the man everyone had believed was his cousin. Paul returned Osgar's stare, but it was pity that came from Paul's expression.

"Once Osgar was old enough to understand Drostan was his actual father, and they didn't fear him sharing the secret, Drostan visited their croft nightly. He taught Osgar to read and write. We were best friends growing up, even though I'm older by a few years. Drostan saw the benefit of having two men who could read and write eventually join the clan council alongside him. Faolán refused to consider educating his sons." Paul grimaced. "He shared the laird's father's view on it."

"Fucking bastard. Ye'll die regardless of whether the pretender does it or our friends," Osgar hissed before spitting at Paul. The wad of saliva fell far short and landed on Osgar's plaid. Paul shook his head and continued.

"Osgar met Lady Robena when he accompanied Laird Farlane to Inverlochy nae long after Lady Robena arrived as Artair's bride. They werenae in love with each other. They were in love with coupling with each other. The bairn she just delivered wasna the first one Osgar got her with, but it was the first one who would be born at what seemed like the perfect time."

Paul swept his gaze around the room as he paused to let people absorb the implication of his words. As stunned expressions morphed into disgust and anger, Paul turned his attention to Osgar.

"When Angus died, Osgar saw an opportunity, so he didna insist that Lady Robena rid herself of her pregnancy as he had in the past." Paul continued. "The idea that he could make his way to the lairdship took root. Nay one could have imagined David, Peter, and Seamus would fall in the same battle, but Osgar swore it was a sign that his plan was to work. He shared his idea with Drostan, and they agreed Osgar would go forward. At the same time Faolán wanted to sabotage Hardwin, aiming to become laird. Drostan and Faolán were always together except for when they went to their women. Or at least when Faolán went to his women and Drostan went to see Osgar. Drostan kept Osgar a secret until the day he died."

"That doesnae make any sense," one of the guards who dragged Osgar into the solar muttered.

"But it does," Paul corrected. "Faolán never acknowledged his illegitimate children, and everyone kenned that they are bastards. Nay one kenned that Osgar was Drostan's son, but auld Father Graham recorded his birth in the church records that name Drostan and Anne as his parents. The priest recorded their handfast the year prior, and the dates prove Osgar's legitimacy. Six sennights after Drostan's birth, there is an entry for his baptism with his full name, but they list ma aunt and uncle as his parents. With proof of his legitimacy, there was only one person standing in his way to inherit. Ye, Laird Cameron."

"He would kill Laird Cameron," Blair stepped forward, not taking her eyes off Osgar. "Then he would wait out Faolán and Drostan's lives—or mayhap kill Faolán and only wait for Drostan to pass away—then he would be laird. With none of Faolán's children able to claim the lairdship, it would be his. Faolán and Drostan didna conceive the plan, but they benefited from it, so they went along with Osgar. Same reason Paul did. Position and power."

Blair turned her head to Paul as she thought for a moment. She glanced down to where her knife still pinned Osgar's plaid to the table. She nodded as she figured out the last of the plot.

"Ye wanted Robena to bear ye a son, so yer bloodline would inherit Inverlochy. Ye would have removed the MacDonalds and reclaimed the keep for the Camerons." Blair stepped closer as she squinted, another idea coming to her. "Why did ye ally with the Mackintoshes if ye want the lairdship and all the land for yerself? The Mackintoshes were the original owners of this territory. It wasna that far back that the Camerons claimed it for themselves, arguing the

Mackintoshes abandoned it. That's what yer feud is aboot. What did ye promise them in return for their aid without seizing the land?"

"Who do ye think supposedly stole the whisky and grain?" Osgar finally spoke. "Robena and I have been paying the Mackintoshes off for months with goods stolen from Tor and Inverlochy. As Lady Blair so brilliantly pointed out, there isnae enough coin left. If I stole that, ye would have realized ma plot too soon."

"Whisky, grain, and arrows? That's enough to satisfy the Mackintoshes? Ye've been played for a fool," Hardi stated.

"How do ye ken aboot the arrows?" Osgar demanded.

"Ye arenae the only one who can intercept missives. We just dinna kill the messenger. Did ye kill Bran?"

"Nay," Osgar shook his head. "That was Robena's responsibility."

"Is Robena bedding the Mackintosh laird too? Short of giving her to him, there is naught in yer arrangement that will appease him for long," Hardi said. "He would have overrun ye within the year, and ye would have let him through the gate."

"She was supposed to bear me a son. She failed. I dinna care who beds her now. Useless sow."

"Ye're a bampot if ye think anyone but God decides whether a bairn will be a lad or a lass," Blair snapped. "Nay woman controls that. Mayhap it's yer seed that failed. Mayhap ye didna give her strong enough seed to make a son."

"Bitch," Osgar hissed, then screamed as Hardi landed the hammer's head on the top of Osgar's left foot.

"I'm fed up of hearing the way ye speak aboot ma wife. I'll leave yer death up to her, but I'll make ye suffer in the meantime," Hardi snarled. He looked around at the guards in the chamber. There were only the four who dragged Osgar into his solar. It wasn't enough if Paul tried to rebel. He went to the door and bellowed for more men. He heard booted feet racing toward him. When six more men squeezed into the solar, Hardi ordered Osgar and Paul to be locked in the dungeon, their cells on opposite ends, and their mouths gagged. He wouldn't risk them conspiring anymore.

FIFTY-ONE

Blair wiped sweat from her forehead as she watched the last of the villagers who lived away from Tor leave the keep. The past two days had been exhausting as she and the clan worked to restore normalcy to their homes. She wasn't sure how she felt about the events that left everyone in shock.

It stunned the clan to learn about Osgar, Paul, Faolán, and Drostan's betrayal. None had imagined such corruption within the clan. Hardi and Blair met with Niall, Mungan, and Malcolm several times. Word had spread of Blair's threats to Osgar, and after witnessing her resolve to protect the clan, no one underestimated Blair's willingness to punish those who threatened her people and her husband. The council agreed unanimously that no cluster of familial relationships were allowed on the council. Blair and Hardi agreed to exempt the three men from the recent rule, but going forth, the selection of members would change. All the Camerons were related through shared ancestry, but they selected only men who shared relations two or more generations back.

Blair decided arguing for women to join the council was ill timed. She would fight that battle another day. Hardi supported her suggestion when they discussed it in private, and she knew he would agree when she eventually presented the idea to the council. Until then, she continued to share equal responsibility and authority with Hardi. That shared position meant that Blair weighed in on the punishments for Osgar and Paul. It was Blair who recommended that Paul and Dunn both spend the rest of their days in the dungeon, and she put forth the idea that Osgar receive a more merciful death than her initial suggestion. Hardi decided that Osgar would be hanged before the clan, both so they could see justice done and to serve as a reminder that he and Blair would tolerate no disloyalty.

Hardi wrapped his arm around Blair's shoulder as they turned toward the keep. They hadn't reached the steps before a call came from the battlements. "Sutherlands approach!"

Blair hoisted her skirts to nearly her knees as she darted toward the gate. Hardi ran at her side. She passed through the gate as she recognized her father, mother, brother, and sister with her husband, ride at the front of what appeared to be an endless line of warriors. Blair wondered if her father ordered every man in their clan to muster and follow him. Her mother, Lady Amelia Sutherland, Countess of Sutherland, dismounted from her still-moving horse and swept her daughter into an embrace, the force of which would have knocked them over had Hardi not caught them. In a breath, Hamish engulfed the women in a hug that would have suffocated weaker women. Maude and Lachlan forced their way into the family cluster while Hardi and Kieran stood back and watched. Neither Hamish nor Lachlan appeared embarrassed by the unabashed tears that streamed down their faces.

When the five Sutherlands broke apart, Hamish set his sights on Hardi. Blair hung from her father's arm as she tried to keep Hamish from plowing his fist into Hardi's face. "He didna steal me, Da! He did naught wrong! *Da!*"

Hamish looked at the woman whose feet were off the ground, and he recalled how she and Maude used to hang from him the same way as he marched around pretending to be a giant stealing the princesses. He pulled Blair back against him as he continued to glare at Hardi. When Blair couldn't breathe, she pushed back against her father's broad chest.

"Everyone to our solar. Now," Blair ordered.

"Still just as bossy," Lachlan muttered. Blair waited for Lachlan to walk even with her before she pinched him on the back of his arm.

"I am." Blair followed Hardi and her parents into the solar she shared with Hardi. Servants had scrubbed away the blood on the floor, and there was no evidence left of Osgar's torture. While her family settled into chairs around the table, they watched as Hardi pulled back Blair's chair behind their desk and took the one next to her. "Maude, what are ye doing here?"

"It's always nice to see ye too, sister," Maude grinned. "The weans are with a maid right now. Mama was nearly strangling ye, so ye didna see me hand the bairn to Kieran." Her enormous mountain of a husband turned in his chair to show a sleeping baby in a sling across his back.

"There isnae any way Maude would leave without the weans, and she would have murdered me if I didna bring her with yer family," Kieran explained. Blair walked around the desk to peer at her youngest niece. The baby blew bubbles in her sleep, and Blair's heart melted. She brushed her finger along the baby's fingers until they opened and grasped hers. She cooed at the infant before returning to her seat.

"Och, it figures. Ye get soft and gooey around the bairn, but ye abuse me," Lachlan bemoaned with a grin. Blair held up her thumb and forefinger to make a pinching motion toward her brother. She looked at her parents and noticed they both seemed to have aged. She realized that Maude's injuries a few years earlier, and then her disappearance, had taken a toll on the Sutherlands.

"It's a lengthy story, and we can give ye more details with time," Blair began. "Lachlan kens we found Hardi just as he arrived at court. Ye also ken he didna benefit from the schooling we did. While I was teaching Hardi to read and do sums, we discovered his clan sent him with far too little to pay the taxes. We met with the king more than once, and we sent ye missives to keep ye abreast of the situation, but only a few days ago we learned only one of ma missives made it to ye."

Hardi picked up the story as he laced his fingers with Blair's. "A Cameron messenger came to tell me there'd been a raid, but I soon learned it was a ruse led by ma father's cousins, Faolán and Drostan. Either way, I had to return here. We hadnae heard back from ye aboot ma request to court Blair. King Robert granted me permission in yer stead. We went to Inverlochy, where Blair spent a fortnight. Without a betrothal agreement and things up in the air with ma council, I didna want to bring Blair here until I kenned it was safe. But I was in need of someone who could advise me and also read or write ma correspondence."

"It wasna that long after I arrived at Inverlochy

that we decided to handfast. Mama, Da, I'm sorry that we didna wait for a kirk wedding. There were many reasons to handfast immediately, but the greatest one is that we love each other. I think we always have." Blair glanced at Hardi, and they shared a private look, both remembering their early infatuation with one another. "It began as a love you might think of between siblings, but we arenae children anymore."

"Blair remained at Inverlochy even after we handfasted. I visited often, and she continued to teach me to read and write. It was a visit from the Lord of the Isles that made us realize we couldnae wait any longer to bring Blair here. There was far more afoot than we imagined. I can swear to ye that through this all, there was never a direct threat to Blair's life. Though I canna say the same for some of the men caught in Blair's sights. She frightens most of ma men," Hardi chuckled as he brought Blair's hand to his mouth, and he pressed a kiss to her knuckles. "We unearthed a plot to attack the keep and remove me. Through Blair's intelligence and some lucky coincidences, we learned of when the attack would come, and we were able to thwart it."

Hardi stopped telling the story as he looked at Blair. They hadn't decided what to do with the men in the tunnel, especially if any still survived. They didn't want to release them for fear that they would attack, but neither could countenance leaving them all to perish. Hardi shifted in his chair as he looked at Hamish. The same need to please Hamish overwhelmed him, just as it had when he was an adolescent. He wanted Hamish to be proud of him, and he feared that this was doomed when he learned that Hardi ordered two hundred men to their death.

"What came of this threat?" Hamish prodded,

but his voice lacked accusation or judgement. Blair nodded to Hardi to continue.

"We learned there was a tunnel leading from the keep toward Inverlochy. Piece by piece, we learned who intended to attack us and when. We sealed the entrance to the tunnel within the keep." Hardi swallowed. "Laird Sutherland, I used yer men for ma personal use rather than have them remain with Blair as the time drew near for the attack."

"But," Blair hurried to interrupt. "Hardi did it because Tomas and Donald were the only two men he trusts implicitly." Blair rose from her chair and walked around the desk. She glanced at Hardi and raised her eyebrows as he nodded. "Hardi only sent them on a mission because I would be safe here." Blair pressed the tiny level, and the Murphy door swung open. She stepped aside so her family could see the secret cubby behind the bookcase.

"I sent Donald and Tomas to dump the dirt we found from the tunnel into the opening at the other end. Once all the Mackintoshes, Shaws, and Mac-Thomases were inside the tunnel, we trapped them between the mountain of dirt and the wall made from dirt sacks and wood. Blair thought to pour birch tar over the hatch to seal it," Hardi explained. He shifted once more as he watched Blair return to her chair. He felt his gorge rise at the prospect of telling Hamish that they'd never released the men. He feared the older laird's reaction—his horror, his disgust, his denouncement.

"Dinna be ill, Hardwin," Hamish chuckled. "They're still down there, arenae they? Ye fear ma reaction?"

Both Hardi and Blair nodded as they once more held hands, more out of moral support than affection. They waited for Hamish to continue.

"Were ye able to send for the Donalds or the MacMillans?" Lachlan asked.

"Nay," Hardi answered. "There wasna time between when we learned of the impending attack. At first we thought we had nearly six sennights, but it wasna long before we found out we had less than a moon. Then the tunnel was ready even before that. The conspirators killed messengers who carried missives to and from ye."

"Da, Tomas and a Cameron went in search of a Cameron messenger's body and found Anders and Samuel's bodies, too."

"We kenned something happened to them both," Hamish nodded. "We just didna ken what."

"Osgar, a man who turned out to be ma second cousin, plotted with Lady Robena MacDonald, Chieftain Artair MacDonald's widow. They devised a plan that Faolán and Drostan supported. We only learned that Drostan was Osgar's son on the night set for the attack. A rather twisted and complicated family feud that I didna ken I was a part of. It boils down to Osgar wanted me out of the way and would wait for Faolán and Drostan to die, so he could become laird. Lady Robena carried Osgar's child, and they hoped to unite all the Cameron lands under their names and their child's."

"Ye said the Mackintoshes, Shaws, and MacThomases," Kieran spoke up. "Didna this mon, Osgar, nae realize they would surely kill him as soon as ye were dead. The land is what ye've been feuding aboot for years."

"He was certain that he could keep paying them off by stealing from us and the MacDonalds," Hardi explained.

"Bluidy nutter," Maude muttered.

"So now ye have how many Mackintoshes, MacThomases, and Shaws trapped in yer tunnel?"

Hamish brought the conversation back to the men trapped underground. "What will ye do with them?"

"Blair and I havenae decided," Hardi confessed. He watched as Amelia's eyes darted to Blair, pride shining from them as she dipped her head in a brief nod. He caught Maude doing the same. It reminded Hardi how blessed he was to marry a Sutherland lass.

"Ye fear they'll come out swinging. Or at least what's left of them," Hamish volunteered.

"Aye," Hardi grimaced.

"Well, I brought all but the absolute few I couldnae spare to protect Dunrobin. Kieran's done the same. We outnumber those eejits, so let's free the ones who survived. They can see that they dinna just fight the Camerons." Hamish shook his head before continuing. "The MacMillans and Donalds are good people, but they havenae done shite to stand beside ye during these feuds with the Chattans. Besides, the MacMillans are too far away to be much help. Ye ken who stands behind ye now." Hamish didn't have to name the Sutherlands, the Sinclairs, the Rosses, the Mackays and the MacLeods of Lewis. It went without saying that Hardi and the Camerons had the backing of the most powerful clans in the northern Highlands.

"Take us to the beginning of the tunnel," Kieran broke in. "We'll set up camp there, and they can have a full view of their welcome party. I would say, though, if ye really want them to live, we should walk the horses. If that many horses canter or gallop, the tunnel will likely collapse."

Blair's eyes went as wide as saucers, and Hardi sucked in a whistling breath. When everyone looked at them, Hardi spoke up. "Ye likely rode right over the tunnel on yer way here. Did ye come from the east or the west of Loch Lochy?"

"West, and we stayed west. We didna pass between Tor and Inverlochy," Amelia reassured the couple.

"Then we should go while there's still plenty of light," Blair suggested.

FIFTY-TWO

It took close to two hours for the Sutherland and MacLeods to pitch their camp and dig into the tunnel. There was an agreement that unsealing the hatch in the storeroom and breaking down the wall was more efficient, but no one wanted to let the enemy into the keep.

Men from the Cameron, Sutherland, and MacLeod clans set to working digging through the subterranean dirt mountain. Tomas and Donald scowled, but they took their turn with shovels too. When they reached the bottom, the last men digging called out to any survivors. They lowered two ladders into the hole and waited to see who emerged. Filthy and weak from two days below ground, a mixture of plaids climbed the ladders. The array of tents, cook fires, horses, and men were expected but still astounding to see. Several men were certain they heard a baby crying.

From the two hundred who entered the tunnel alive, one hundred and seventeen breathing men exited. They carried their dead with them. Blair arranged for men to distribute bread and water to the survivors. When the last man alive groaned at the sunlight, Hardi and Blair met with Hamish and

Lachlan to determine what the Camerons' demands would be. They'd all seen Laird Shaw was dead, and Laird Mackintosh appeared to be on his last leg. Only Laird MacThomas looked to have suffered mildly. He surrendered on behalf of all three clans, but it satisfied neither Hardi nor Blair. Hardi, Blair, and her family returned to the keep for the night, and Blair and Hardi met in their solar after the evening meal. Between them, they drafted a treaty of sorts to end the feud with the Mackintoshes. It didn't end their troubles with the Macphersons, but it would lessen the ongoing threat.

Blair watched in amazement as Hardi labored over writing the document after they agreed upon the terms. It took him at least three times as long as it would have taken Blair, but he did it on his own. To ensure the treaty would be recognized if ever disputed, they'd agreed to write two versions, one in Latin and one in Scots.

"I canna believe I just did that," Hardi murmured in awe as he gazed at his handwriting on the numerous sheets of parchment. He laid the quill on the desk and rose, so he could move each piece to the table to dry. He put the stopper in the inkwell before putting it and the quill into a drawer. Blair watched in silence, unsure of what Hardi intended. She squeaked when he caught her around the waist and lifted her to sit on the desk.

"I have wanted to make love to ye on this desk since ma first lesson," Hardi shared as he slipped his hands beneath Blair's gown and pushed her skirts up her thighs. "I want to strip ye bare and taste every inch of ye before I bury ma cock in yer cunny."

"Then get yer hands out from under ma skirts and get these ribbons untied," Blair grinned. She twisted to give Hardi access to the back of her gown as their arms tangled while she unpinned his plaid and loosened his belt. It was only a matter of moments before they were undressed. Blair's hands roamed over Hardi's abdomen and chest before sliding down to wrap around his rod. She kept her eyes locked with his as she stroked him with tantalizing slowness.

"I shall remember this, and ye shall rue yer teasing in just a minute," Hardi warned.

"I dinna think so," Blair scooted off the desk before kneeling before him. With little preamble, she took Hardi's shaft into her mouth, sucking before licking it. She alternated between swirling her tongue around the iron length and taking it into her mouth. Hardi's breathing rasped as he leaned over to grasp the table, certain the light-headedness Blair induced would keep him from remaining upright.

When he could endure the temptation no longer, he lifted his wife to the desk and pressed her to lie back. He kissed along her neck and collarbone before drifting to her breasts. He lavished attention on them as his fingers worked her core. Blair arched her back as she pressed her breasts together. She knew he enjoyed suckling them as much as she loved the way he tormented her nipples. Blair's moans blended with Hardi's deeper groans to create a duet of passion. Hardi withdrew his fingers as he sank to his knees, and Blair watched as he sucked her juices that coated his digits. It was her turn to experience the fine line between pleasure and torture.

Blair thought she would lose all sense of reason as Hardi's tongue plunged into her over and over before he grazed his stubble over her nub. His teeth followed only for him to suck the pearl that contained hundreds of aroused nerves that pulsed within her. She dug the fingers of one hand into his shoulder as she pinched her nipple with her other. Hardi's view of his wife writhing on their desk aroused him and

411

kept him hard as he focused all of his attention on pleasuring her.

When they both reached the point where physical need approached agony, Hardi plunged his cock into her entrance. Blair rocked her hips as Hardi thrusted. Almost immediately, Blair's body erupted with sensation as her climax burst through her. Her long moan and the tightening of her core empowered Hardi in a way that nothing else ever did. Knowing that he connected so deeply with Blair and brought her such pleasure gave him its own type of pleasure.

"I want ye so badly, *mo chridhe*," Blair panted. "I dinna ken if this will ever be enough. I want ye every minute of every day." Blair's breath hitched with each thrust as Hardi held her body against his. She'd become addicted to the emotion and physical enjoyment of their coupling.

"Good, because I intend to make love to ye until I shut ma eyes for the last time. Then I shall find ye in Heaven and continue loving ye, *mo ghaol*."

Neither could speak as their synchronized movements pushed them both over the edge. They clung together as Hardi's hips continued to rock into Blair, and little bursts of aftershock coursed through her. When Hardi feared the desk was too hard beneath Blair, he lifted her, and her legs went around his waist before he carried her to a chair before the fire. They sat together for a long time as Hardi caressed Blair's back, and her fingernails trailed along his arm and shoulder. Eventually, Blair sat back.

"I never imagined we would find ourselves together in Stirling, and I never imagined the girl who was once infatuated with ye would be blessed with the chance to love ye," Blair cupped Hardi's face. "God, how I love ye, Hardwin. We've been through more in the few months we've been together than most would endure in a month of Sundays. But I dinna ever want to be anywhere but at yer side."

"I would keep ye there always. I love ye, Blair. I would likely be dead if it werenae for yer intelligence and yer persistence in teaching me, believing in me, supporting me. And more than aught, loving me. I couldnae be laird without ye." Hardi grinned. "And I dinna just mean the part aboot being alive. I mean I didna ken how to lead ma people, and I feared they would be better without me as their laird. I've learned far more from ye than reading and writing. I feel brave enough now to be laird as long as ye're ma lady."

"Always," Blair promised before they kissed. It wasn't long before they dressed enough to make their way to their chamber. It was one of the rare nights that they slept all the way through, but their arms and legs remained entangled, no space between them.

FIFTY-THREE

"I 'm nae signing that," Laird Mackintosh refused.

"Shut up, Angus, and sign the bluidy treaty," Laird MacThomas hissed. "The day is lost. Cameron and his wife outmaneuvered us, and now Michael is dead and so are half his men along with too many of mine."

"Ye're nae the one losing what rightfully belongs to them," Angus Mackintosh snarled.

"It's been lost since before ye were born," Hardi pointed out. "If yer clan wanted Tor Castle, they never should have left. But they did. We are here now, and we arenae leaving."

"I hope yer bollocks fall off," Angus spat.

"They arenae going anywhere, just like ma clan. Sign the treaty, Angus. Ye can walk away with some dignity, and yer men can limp away with their lives," Hardi stated.

Lairds Cameron, Mackintosh, MacThomas, MacLeod, and Sutherland, along with Blair, sat in the laird's solar in Inverlochy Castle three days after they freed the men from the tunnel. It had been uncertain whether Laird Mackintosh would pull through. Blair was certain it was spite that kept the man alive. After their crushing win over the Camerons, the Mackintoshes assumed they would maintain their superiority. But their defeat at Tor Castle made it obvious which clan would ultimately prevail.

Hardi and Blair signed the treaty first, but Angus dragged his feet, prompting Liam MacThomas to speak up. It was clear Liam wanted to put as much distance between his clan and Tor Castle as he could in one day. He pulled the parchment toward him and signed before pushing it back in front of Angus. Begrudgingly, Angus signed. Hamish and Kieran then signed as witnesses. In six strokes of the quill, their decades-long feud ceased with a truce. No one in the chamber believed there wouldn't be altercations and antagonism, but everyone—Angus Mackintosh included—prayed that the violence would end.

"Ye may have beaten me, but dinna think the Macphersons are through with ye," Angus snarled as he stood.

"Let Fergus Macpherson ken that I would be happy to pay him a visit on ma way home." Hamish's comment sounded offhand, but the steely eyes told everyone that the menace was real. Within the hour, the Mackintoshes, Shaws and MacThomases walked away from Inverlochy; their dead hung over their horses' backs. Blair and Hardi knew Angus's warning was true, but it relieved them both to know the Sutherlands were now the Camerons' sworn allies.

With the would-be invaders on their way home, Hardi and Blair turned their attention to Lady Robena and Inverlochy Castle. Hardi wrote a missive to Laird Napier while Blair looked over his shoulder. The message offered an abbreviated version of the events and downplayed much of Robena's role in the plot. They'd learned upon arrival at Inverlochy that

Robena killed Artair in a heated argument about her order to allow the three Chattan clans shelter on their way to Tor Castle. She spewed venom at her beleaguered husband, confessing to her role as the true strategist behind Osgar's plan and that Osgar, not Artair, was the father of her bairn. She'd stabbed Artair in the throat before going into labor. Murray, Artair's illegitimate son, had also carried on an affair with Robena, and she wasn't certain whether Murray or Osgar sired her daughter. It wasn't even midday when Robena, accompanied by a score of Cameron men, left Inverlochy to return to her clan in disgrace. She'd sneered at Blair, no remorse or shame to be seen. Blair kept her courtly mien locked in place as Robena rode away in a wagon, her daughter in her arms.

Upon investigation, Hardi and Blair learned that none of the MacDonalds had been privy to Robena's scheme. She'd duped many of the clan members, but none intentionally assisted her. The couple offered Malcolm and Mungan the opportunity for one of them to become the guardian of Inverlochy. They would allow the MacDonalds to remain, but they would have a Cameron governing the keep. It was decided that Mungan and his family would move to Inverlochy.

"All rather anticlimactic," Blair mused as they rode back to Tor. "Dinna get me wrong. I'm glad there was nay blood shed during a battle, but after living with so much fear, it feels odd that it's suddenly over."

"That is the ultimate sign of strong leadership," Hamish stated as his horse plodded next to Blair's. Her father leaned forward to look past Blair to where Hardi rode on her right. "Ye both did an exceptional job. I am vera proud to call ye ma son-by-marriage, Hardwin."

"Thank ye—Hamish." It still felt unnatural to call his former mentor and the man he admired above all others by his first name, but he'd almost clapped like an excited child when Hamish gave him permission. "By the by," Hamish said almost casually, "the priest will post the banns this Sunday. When we arrive at Tor, ye will meet me in yer solar to discuss marrying ma daughter properly."

Blair opened her mouth, but Hamish shook his head. "Nay, ye arenae joining us. Nay, ye arenae a part of the negotiations. And nay, ye arenae going to change ma mind."

At a feminine throat clearing, Blair looked back at her mother, who shook her head. A pointed look at Hamish's back made Blair understand that Hamish felt as though he'd missed an important rite by Blair and Hardi handfasting without her parents' knowledge.

"Aye, Da," Blair demurred. Both Hardi and Hamish whipped their heads to look at Blair, both faces shocked and worried at her capitulation. "Just dinna have too much whisky and be late to the evening meal."

"Still just as bossy," Lachlan muttered.

Blair and Maude exchanged a glance before bursting into laughter. The men looked at them, but the sisters shrugged. If their guesses were right, Lachlan would have a strong-willed wife of his own.

FIFTY-FOUR

Three weeks after the Sutherlands and MacLeods arrived, Blair patted her hair once more. She shook out the kirtle she'd made during her third visit home from court. She'd always intended to wear it for her wedding, but she'd assumed she'd missed that opportunity. Amelia explained that the family thought it likely that Blair was with Hardi since the last information they had was about the couple's interest in courting. Amelia packed the clothes Blair had left behind at Dunrobin and insisted they bring them. Blair was eternally grateful that her mother had that foresight.

Hamish walked beside her as they left the keep and walked toward the kirk. She couldn't see Hardi's face yet, but his height afforded her a glimpse of his hair. Tawny locks shimmered gold in the sun as Blair approached the church. When the clans' members parted, creating a path toward the kirk's steps, Blair's breath caught at the sight of Hardi standing, waiting for her. His brilliant smile when he finally saw her was surely enough to blind everyone. They stood together as the priest bound their wrists with the same hair ribbon they'd used at their handfasting in the orchard.

"Ye are the most radiant star in all the heavens," Hardi said. He squeezed her hands as he gazed into her eyes. He would never tire of looking at the whisky-brown swirls that surrounded her pupils. The sun on her face made her eyes shine in a way that made them almost translucent. Blair's expression softened as she peered into Hardi's hazel eyes, the blue and green reminding her of the North Sea that lay beneath the cliff where Dunrobin perched. His eyes were the shade of the summer water they'd paddled in as children.

"There is nay mon brawer than ye. Ye're the mon little girls dream of growing up to marry," Blair whispered.

They exchanged their vows and moved into the church for the wedding Mass, but it all floated by in a haze for the couple. When they arrived in the Great Hall, Blair and Hardi looked at one another, then raced to the stairs. Impatient and afraid Blair would trip, Hardi lifted her into his arms as he ran up the remaining stairs. People cheered once they overcame their surprise.

"Something they promised before they even handfasted," Maude dismissed with a wave of her hand, but when she caught Kieran's eye, her face broke into a knowing grin.

The newlyweds weren't able to escape reality for a month, but they managed to sequester themselves for a week. No one dared knock on their door except to deliver food or to prepare their baths. When they finally emerged, they enjoyed three more days of the Sutherlands' and MacLeods' company before both clans departed. Blair and Hardi stood on the battlements as they watched their family ride away. She held a newly carved figurine that resembled Blair and Hardi, with the bairn Blair announced resting in Hardi's arms. Blair turned to stand within Hardi's embrace as they kissed, the rising sun as their backdrop.

"Ye shall surely be a saint one day, *mo chridhe*," Hardi whispered against her lips. "Ye have the heart and the bravery of one already."

"Mayhap one day, but there are far too many days I intend to spend with ye before anyone should think on that," Blair responded before they kissed again. When they pulled apart, Blair rested her head against Hardi's chest. She inhaled and released a deep sigh. She knew no better place than being in her husband's arms.

"Ye make me happy," they said in unison. Their laughter filled the air, and the people in the bailey looked up to find their laird and lady kissing once more.

EPILOGUE

"**H**urry," Blair hissed. "I wore the weans out on purpose so they would fall asleep early. I shall regret it when they're up before the roosters, but they always ken when I'm aboot to slip away." Hardi held her hand and led the way down the path toward the loch beside Dunrobin. They reached the spot where Blair had once upon a time watched Hardi, but they moved on until they came to a spot hidden by rocks and trees.

"I may nae be able to slow down," Hardi grinned as he helped Blair slip out of her kirtle before he discarded his clothes. They eased into the warm summer water that reflected the last of the sun's dusky rays. Hardi pulled Blair against him once she could no longer touch the bottom. She wrapped her legs around Hardi as she floated before him. Hardi pressed down on Blair's hips as his cock eased into her. They remained joined but not moving.

"Thank ye for always bringing me down here," Blair murmured. "I'd hoped we might slip down here together once in our lifetime, but ye make sure we can each time we visit."

"It makes me just as happy to be here with ye. I love our weans, and I love our life, but we dinna get much chance to be alone outside our bedchamber," Hardi confessed.

"I miss the days when we could disappear into a storeroom or our solar or the stables or the woods and make love with nay one calling out 'Mama, Da.' Mayhap we will when they are aulder. But then they'll be auld enough to understand what's happening. It horrified me when I first understood why ma mama and da disappeared some afternoons."

"Now can ye blame them?" Hardi chuckled, remembering his own traumatized experience when he learned Laird and Lady Sutherland enjoyed walks that ended with guards posted around a nearby copse of trees.

"Ye were thinking aboot ma parents, but now ye're remembering our two interludes among the trees," Blair teased.

"I am. But it was three, *mo chridhe*," Hardi corrected.

"True. I dinna ken how I could forget aboot what we did when we returned to Stirling with the rest of the geld. There was nay way to pretend we hadnae been making love when Roddy quietly pointed to the leaves in ma hair."

The couple laughed together; the movement shifting their position and awakening their arousal. They moved together as the water lapped around them until they clung together as their climaxes carried them over the precipice together. They took their time recovering, exchanging tender kisses before they left the water. Once dressed, they returned to the path and turned toward the keep.

"Do ye think we might have created another bairn just now?" Hardi wondered.

Blair grinned at him before making a dash for the postern gate. She called over her shoulder, "Too late for that."

Hardi stumbled as he registered Blair's meaning. He raced to catch up with her, capturing her around the waist. No one saw or heard from them until their children stirred before dawn, asking where they'd gone the evening before. They shrugged as they welcomed their children into their bed and pulled up the covers as their little ones chattered away. Blair and Hardi exchanged a look that spoke all the feelings words could never describe. A look only those deeply in love could understand.

Celeste Barclay, a nom de plume, lives near the Southern California coast with her husband and sons. Growing up in the Midwest, Celeste enjoyed spending as much time in and on the water as she could. Now she lives near the beach. She's an avid swimmer, a hopeful future surfer, and a former rower. When she's not writing, she's working or being a mom.

Visit Celeste's website, www.celestebarclay.com, for regular updates on works in progress, new releases, and her blog where she features posts about her experiences as an author and recommendations of her favorite reads.

Are you an author who would like to guest blog or be featured in her recommendations? Visit her website for an opportunity to share your insights and experiences.

Have you read *Their Highland Beginning, The Clan*

Sinclair Prequel? Learn how the saga begins! This **FREE** novella is available to all new subscribers to Celeste's monthly newsletter. Subscribe on her website.

www.celestebarclay.com

Join the fun and get exclusive insider giveaways, sneak peeks, and new release announcements in

Celeste Barclay's Facebook Ladies of Yore Group

THE HIGHLAND LADIES

A Spinster at the Highland Court

BOOK 1 SNEAK PEEK

Elizabeth Fraser looked around the royal chapel within
Stirling Castle. The ornate candlestick holders on the altar
glistened and reflected the light from the ones in the wall
sconces as the priest intoned the holy prayers of the
Advent season. Elizabeth kept her head bowed as though
in prayer, but her green eyes swept the congregation. She
watched the other ladies-in-waiting, many of whom were
doing the same thing. She caught the eye of Allyson
Elliott. Elizabeth raised one eyebrow as Allyson's lips
twitched. Both women had been there enough times to
accept they'd be kneeling for at least the next hour as the
Latin service carried on. Elizabeth understood the Mass
thanks to her cousin Deirdre Fraser, or rather now Deirdre
Sinclair. Elizabeth's mind flashed to the recent struggle her
cousin faced as she reunited with her husband Magnus
after a seven-year separation. Her aunt and uncle's choice
to keep Deirdre hidden from her husband simply because
they didn't think the Sinclairs were an advantageous
enough match, and the resulting scandal, still humiliated
the other Fraser clan members at court. She admired
Deirdre's husband Magnus's pledge to remain faithful
despite not knowing if he'd ever see Deirdre again.

Elizabeth suddenly snapped her attention; while everyone
else intoned the twelfth—or was it thirteenth—amen of
the Mass, the hairs on the back of her neck stood up. She
had the strongest feeling that someone was watching her.
Her eyes scanned to her right, where her parents sat
further down the pew. Her mother and father had their
heads bowed and eyes closed. While she was convinced her
mother was in devout prayer, she wondered if her father
had fallen asleep during the Mass. Again. With nothing
seeming out of the ordinary and no one visibly paying

attention to her, her eyes swung to the left. She took in the king and queen as they kneeled together at their prie-dieu. The queen's lips moved as she recited the liturgy in silence. The king was as still as a statue. Years of leading warriors showed, both in his stature and his ability to control his body into absolute stillness. Elizabeth peered past the royal couple and found herself looking into the astute hazel eyes of Edward Bruce, Lord of Badenoch and Lochaber. His gaze gave her the sense that he peered into her thoughts, as though he were assessing her. She tried to keep her face neutral as heat surged up her neck. She prayed her face didn't redden as much as her neck must have, but at a twenty-one, she still hadn't mastered how to control her blushing. Her nape burned like it was on fire. She canted her head slightly before looking up at the crucifix hanging over the altar. She closed her eyes and tried to invoke the image of the Lord that usually centered her when her mind wandered during Mass.

Elizabeth sensed Edward's gaze remained on her. She didn't understand how she was so sure that he was looking at her. She didn't have any special gifts of perception or sight, but her intuition screamed that he was still looking.

A Spy at the Highland Court **BOOK 2**

A Wallflower at the Highland Court **BOOK 3**

A Rogue at the Highland Court **BOOK 4**

A Rake at the Highland Court **BOOK 5**

An Enemy at the Highland Court **BOOK 6**

A Saint at the Highland Court **BOOK 7**

A Beauty at the Highland Court **BOOK 8**

A Sinner at the Highland Court **BOOK 9**

A Hellion at the Highland Court **BOOK 10**

An Angel at the Highland Court **BOOK 11**

A Harlot at the Highland Court **BOOK 12**

THE CLAN SINCLAIR

His Highland Lass **BOOK 1 SNEAK PEEK**

She entered the great hall like a strong spring storm in the northern most Highlands. Tristan Mackay felt like he had been blown hither and yon. As the storm settled, she left him with the sweet scents of heather and lavender wafting towards him as she approached. She was not a classic beauty, tall and willowy like the women at court. Her face and form were not what legends were made of. But she held a unique appeal unlike any he had seen before. He could not take his eyes off of her long chestnut hair that had strands of fire and burnt copper running through them. Unlike the waves or curls he was used to, her hair was unusually straight and fine. It looked like a waterfall cascading down her back. While she was not tall, neither was she short. She had a figure that was meant for a man to grasp and hold onto, whether from the front or from behind. She had an aura of confidence and charm, but not arrogance or conceit like many good looking women he had met. She did not seem to know her own appeal. He could tell that she was many things, but one thing she was not was his.

His Bonnie Highland Temptation **BOOK 2**

His Highland Prize **BOOK 3**

His Highland Pledge **BOOK 4**

His Highland Surprise **BOOK 5**

Their Highland Beginning **BOOK 6**

PIRATES OF THE ISLES

The Blond Devil of the Sea **BOOK 1 SNEAK PEEK**

Caragh lifted her torch into the air as she made her way down the precarious Cornish cliffside. She made out the hulking shape of a ship, but the dead of night made it impossible to see who was there. She and the fishermen of Bedruthan Steps weren't expecting any shipments that night. But her younger brother Eddie, who stood watch at the entrance to their hiding place, had spotted the ship and signaled up to the village watchman, who alerted Caragh.

As her boot slid along the dirt and sand, she cursed having to carry the torch and wished she could have sunlight to guide her. She knew these cliffs well, and it was for that reason it was better that she moved slowly than stop moving once and for all. Caragh feared the light from her torch would carry out to the boat. Despite her efforts to keep the flame small, the solitary light would be a beacon.

When Caragh came to the final twist in the path before the sand, she snuffed out her torch and started to run to the cave where the main source of the village's income lay in hiding. She heard movement along the trail above her head and knew the local fishermen would soon join her on the beach. These men, both young and old, were strong from days spent pulling in the full trawling nets and hoisting the larger catches onto their boats. However, these men weren't well-trained swordsmen, and the fear of pirate raids was ever-present. Caragh feared that was who the villagers would face that night.

The Dark Heart of the Sea **BOOK 2**
The Red Drifter of the Sea **BOOK3**
The Scarlet Blade of the Sea **BOOK 4**

VIKING GLORY

Leif **BOOK 1 SNEAK PEEK**

Leif looked around his chambers within his father's longhouse and breathed a sigh of relief. He noticed the large fur rugs spread throughout the chamber. His two favorites placed strategically before the fire and the bedside he preferred. He looked at his shield that hung on the wall near the door in a symbolic position but waiting at the ready. The chests that held his clothes and some of his finer acquisitions from voyages near and far sat beside his bed and along the far wall. And in the center was his most favorite possession. His oversized bed was one of the few that could accommodate his long and broad frame. He shook his head at his longing to climb under the pile of furs and on the stuffed mattress that beckoned him. He took in the chair placed before the fire where he longed to sit now with a cup of warm mead. It had been two months since he slept in his own bed, and he looked forward to nothing more than pulling the furs over his head and sleeping until he could no longer ignore his hunger. Alas, he would not be crawling into his bed again for several more hours. A feast awaited him to celebrate his and his crew's return from their latest expedition to explore the isle of Britannia. He bathed and wore fresh clothes, so he had no excuse for lingering other than a bone weariness that set in during the last storm at sea. He was eager to spend time at home no matter how much he loved sailing. Their last expedition had been profitable with several raids of monasteries that yielded jewels and both silver and gold, but he was ready for respite.

Leif left his chambers and knocked on the door next to his. He heard movement on the other side, but it was only moments before his sister, Freya, opened her door. She, too, looked tired but clean. A few pieces of jewelry she confiscated from the holy houses that allegedly swore to a life of poverty and deprivation adorned her trim frame.

"That armband suits you well. It compliments your muscles," Leif smirked and dodged a strike from one of those muscular arms.

Only a year younger than he, his sister was a well-known and feared shield maiden. Her lithe form was strong and agile making her a ferocious and competent opponent to any man. Freya's beauty was stunning, but Leif had taken every opportunity since they were children to tease her about her unusual strength even among the female warriors.

"At least one of us inherited our father's prowess. Such a shame it wasn't you."

Freya **BOOK 2**

Tyra & Bjorn **BOOK 3**

Strian **VIKING GLORY BOOK 4**

Lena & Ivar **VIKING GLORY BOOK 5**